The Breakup Mix

TK Carter

To Kristyn—
Your friendship is
invaluable to me.
I love you like the book!
Love you,
TK Carter

The Breakup Mix
TK Carter

Copyright © 2015 by TK Carter

Book Cover by Sprinkles on Top Studios
Photo Courtesy of Deposit Photos

Other Works by TK Carter

"An Afternoon with Aunt Viv"
Independence
Collapse: Book One of the Yellow Flag Series
Three Meals to Anarchy: Book Two of the Yellow Flag Series

Introduction

Chance

Alissa, Michelle, Katie, Dani, and I have been friends since before puberty hit us at different ages. Katie was the first one to get boobs; Dani got the first kiss, and I scored the highest daredevil points by letting Bobby LaVet stick his hands down my pants well before either of us knew what the point was. I was on the highest pedestal until Alissa lost her virginity our sophomore year in high school. Show-off.

My name is Chance. Yes, Chance. I got my name because my teenage parents got drunk one night during their senior year in high school, and Dad forgot the condom.

The story goes that their conversation went something like this:

"Well, what do you think?" That was my dad.

"Well we're probably okay but there's always a chance," Mom answered.

And that's how I got my name.

The joke among my aunts and uncles is that no one could say my mother never had a chance. I've heard it all in these thirty-four years on Earth. My name provides hours of entertainment and the source for one-liners pretty much everywhere I go.

But I'm getting sidetracked.

Michelle was the first one to get married. Nineteen and high-as-a-kite in love with Brandon Morehead. (And I thought Chance was a bad name.) Michelle spent her twenty-first birthday breastfeeding a colicky daughter named Del Ray, named after her father's favorite guitar. Yeah, we all thought it was stupid, too, but the name fits her. At thirty-four years old, Michelle has fourteen-year-old Del Ray, ten-year-old Martin, and eight-year-old Gibson. Brandon's taste in musical instruments improved with age, obviously. With names like these, one would assume Brandon is a musician by trade; he sells insurance. If it weren't for that blessed woman he's married to, none of us would have insurance through that fruitcake. Michelle was a stay-at-home hermit until Gibson started kindergarten. After a short psychotic breakdown, she pulled herself together and now works full-time at a daycare center just north of town. I guess some people never learn.

Next was Katie. Sweet, naïve, the-world-is-my-oyster Katie went to college on a full-ride softball scholarship and dropped out halfway through her junior year when an acting scout wooed our college star and convinced her to run away to New York. Alissa and I flew to New York three months later to collect our homeless, heartbroken starlet who had to call collect from a pay phone because the bastard stole everything she owned while she was at an audition, including her phone and wallet. If I ever find that man . . .

Thankfully, she returned to school and graduated with honors (and student loan debt since the scholarship was no longer an option) at the ripe old age of twenty-three. With a degree in business management and no working experience, she landed a job working full-time at First Nations Bank with hopes of moving up in the company when other folks moved elsewhere or retired. Nine years later she's still starry-eyed about her opportunity and listens for the knock. She met Landon her senior year in college and married him a year later on Valentine's Day. If I never see the color red again, it will be too soon.

Her daughter, Marie, was born six years ago. Get it? Katie, Landon, Marie . . . KLM. They thought they were cute naming her with the next initial in line in the alphabet. Nathan is three, and God help them if they have another child. I can only imagine what name "O" will bring. Landon is prematurely bald and teaches history at the high school just so he can coach football. No surprise that all of his star players are acing his class.

Alissa and Dani were playing "beat the other to the altar" by the time we were twenty-four. Michelle had been married for five years, Katie had gotten married that February, and these two were itching for the feel of tulle and satin. Alissa had been in several relationships that lasted two years max. Just about the time she'd start practicing *I do*, he wouldn't and took off for the hills. Alissa finally got married at twenty-five, divorced at twenty-six, remarried at twenty-eight, divorced at thirty (boy *that* was a fun year), and is on the prowl, now for lucky number three. Divorcing her second husband left her financially secure, much to the dismay of the young-but-uber-rich oil tycoon's family. However, no pre-nup, and she was golden.

She has no kids and prefers it that way. Watching Michelle lose her life in formula, Pampers, and Tylenol suppositories pretty much killed any maternal drive Alissa may have had——not that she had much after her childhood. Somehow in the midst of marriage and divorce, Alissa still managed to graduate from law school and works as a prosecuting attorney for the county. (Personally, I think the woman should become a divorce attorney, since she knows the process by heart now, but I'd never have the balls to tell *her* that.) She is currently dating another attorney in town, Mark, and six months later, she still hasn't scared him off. This one looks promising.

Dani is perfect. She's the model American woman who did it all right. She graduated valedictorian of our class, went to college on an academic scholarship, had no major mental breakdowns in college, and got married at twenty-seven years old after living on her own for four years. She works as the vice president over human resources for a large corporation in Boone County and goes to work every morning dressed to the nines with every hair in place. Barry, her husband, is a perfect three-piece match for Dani and is the executive financial officer for First Nations Bank. Even the president of the bank has to have Barry's approval before writing a check. The one thing missing in Dani's perfect world is a baby. Pills, tests, shots, specimens, turkey basters (okay, I made that one up) and four years later, no baby.

That leaves me. I am Chance Bradley—a news anchor for KJAT, journalist, and occasionally a freelance writer when the mood strikes me. My co-anchor, Jack Woodrow, is the closest thing I have to a boyfriend—we drink coffee together every morning before the cameras roll. And that's exactly how I prefer it. Some may say I'm jaded, and maybe I am. However, I'm also smart and a good student to life. When she teaches me a lesson, I learn it and don't make that mistake again.

I've never made that dreadful walk down the aisle with hundreds of people looking at me with teary eyes as I walk toward a man who wants to claim me. Never did it, don't want to. I've never worn a dress that cost more than my monthly rent; I've never starved myself for five weeks to make sure the dress will still fit; I've never spent hours obsessing over shades of pink, and I certainly haven't cried over the uncertainty of picking out the wrong cake. I've never gushed, gratefully, over the third toaster received in a row and made lame excuses about the insurance of having a backup.

I got close a few times and have the rings to prove it. Three of them, to be exact. I took a few test-drives, lived with them, and discovered domesticity is not for me. I love my third-floor apartment on the east side of town too much to consider suburbia and strollers. I have no interest in participating in the march-of-the-mini-vans in front of every school Monday through Friday. My pug, Chubs, and I are a perfect fit. If he farts in the bed, I can kick his ass off and not try to play it off as a muscle spasm.

Tonight is the night we've all been waiting for. Tonight we dine in style to celebrate the twentieth anniversary of our friendship. Alissa says she has a surprise for us. God I hope it's not a diamond.

Chapter One
Mr. Know-It-All

"Michelle, I swear to God, if you don't put down that damned phone, I'm going to throw it out the window. They will be *fine*!"

"I forgot to tell Brandon to make sure Gibson pees before bed." Michelle clicked out the fourth text in five minutes. "Send and done. There. Happy, Chance?" She offered her best go-to-hell grin and slid her phone into her purse.

"If he responds, don't check it, got it? The man has been their parent as long as you have. Relax, babe. It's only a few hours. Geez, woman, you need to get out more."

Michelle took a deep breath and smoothed her skirt. "Are you sure I look all right? With Alissa making the reservations, you never know where we'll end up."

"You look great, doll. But, I'm going to slip you a mickey if you don't calm down and put your BFF hat on."

Michelle laughed and relaxed into the passenger seat. "I have been looking forward to this for weeks. I was so worried something would come up, and I would have to miss it. But here we are!"

"Here we are, and we are going to have a blast tonight, sister."

"Do you know where we're going?"

"Nope. Alissa wouldn't tell me anything, either. We're supposed to meet her at the Clairmont Hotel at 6:30. That's as far as my marching orders went."

"Have you talked to Katie and Dani?"

"I got a text from Dani around five saying she was going to grab Katie and to remind me to bring my camera for the forty-second time."

"Did you?"

"No, I forgot it. Of course I brought it! How are things at the daycare?"

"Busy, same as usual. I'm in the three-year-old room now. If one

7

more kid bites me, I swear I'm going to smack some mouths. How about you?"

"I finally got Jack to quit biting me last week." I smiled. "No, things are great. The news has been a bit slow lately. Coming up with interesting story lines has been a bit challenging. Someone needs to create a scandal in this town. Hey speaking of scandal, has Alissa said anymore to you about her and Mark?"

Michelle said, "No, I talked to her Wednesday. She stopped by after work to drop off some stuff, but we really didn't have time to talk. I was elbow-deep in dinner prep, and she was headed to the gym."

"The gym? Ha! Really? Is she on that kick again?" Like I don't know, but Michelle doesn't know that.

"Her therapist thinks it is good stress management for her, but don't tell her I told you that."

I grinned. "So that's code for 'I'm on the prowl again.'"

"Pretty much, yeah."

"The gym. You'd think she would have learned that lesson after the Adam fiasco."

She turned in her chair. "He was a trip, wasn't he? Adam-the-Poser—always flexing, always pumping, and dumb as a box of rocks."

"Yeah and he took her for what, almost ten grand?"

"Close to it. Loser."

I pulled into the parking garage of the Clairmont Hotel at 6:23. "Seven minutes to spare! Damn, I'm good."

"Not good enough, though. They still beat you here." Michelle chuckled and pointed to Alissa's Navigator in the next row. Frantic waves and shiny teeth appeared in the windshield before three car doors flew open and out sprang Katie, Dani, and Alissa.

"See? I told you you were dressed perfectly." I nudged Michelle.

"Hello, hello, hello!" Greetings all around, hugs, chatter, and laughter, and the night hadn't even begun yet. We have all seen each other regularly, but getting the five of us in one place at one time has gotten more and more difficult. It's been at least four months, maybe longer.

We all piled into Alissa's car; Katie called shotgun first, so Dani, Michelle, and I moaned and called her a cheater. Dani and I made Michelle ride bitch in the middle.

"So what's this big surprise, Alissa?"

Alissa beamed ear-to-ear. "You'll see."

"Where are we going to eat? I hope I'm dressed okay."

"Michelle, you look great and will light up the town," Alissa said.

"Alissa, what's the scoop with beau-hunk? Yes? No? Still has potential?" I couldn't wait any longer.

"All of the above? Geez, I don't know. He's nice and fun to be around, but I don't know. He's been weird lately, so whatever."

Katie joined in. "Weird how? In a good way or bad way?"

"Well I don't really know. He's so damned moody. I stayed at his place two nights in a row last week, and he freaked out thinking I was moving in or something."

Dani spoke up. "How long did you pack for?"

"A week."

We all laughed and groaned.

"Oh Alissa! What were you thinking?" I said.

"What? I don't know; I just thought it would be fun to play house. Try it out." She smiled.

"No, no, no, no! Six months? You don't play house at six months. Have I taught you nothing?" I shook my head.

"Ease up, ladies; she made a bone-headed decision." Michelle-the-mom appeared.

"Why was it bone-headed?" Alissa looked at Michelle in the rearview mirror.

"Were you invited?" Katie asked.

Silence.

Bursts of laughter filled the Navigator causing Alissa to laugh at herself as well. "Okay, okay, so I jumped the gun. Geez. Next victim, please? Dani, what's new with you?"

"Oh no, girl. You're not pointing that smoking gun at me. I have no drama." Dani laughed.

"Katie?"

"Well, there are rumors going around the bank that Harry Langstedder is messing around with that new teller over on Brookfield Drive."

I shrugged. "That's it? That's all you have? I don't care if Harry's boning a—"

"Jesus, Chance, are you ragging? What's your deal?" Dani chuckled.

"I was teasing! And this is PMS week, so you should have known better and scheduled this outing more appropriately."

"So we need to add chocolate and chick flicks to the itinerary, is that what I'm hearing?" Dani asked.

"No time for that," Alissa said.

"Why are we hitting the highway?" Michelle fidgeted when she realized we were leaving town. "Where are we going, Alissa?"

"Chicago." Alissa glowed.

In unison we all yelled, "Chicago?" Katie and Michelle ranted and argued while Dani and I chimed in with a few hell yeahs and high fives.

"Before you all start freaking out, I've already made arrangements with your households and have a bag for each of you in the back. We're hopping the eight o'clock flight to Chicago and will get back Saturday evening at five. Chance, I called your brother and told him to check on Chubs for you, by the way."

"You rock, Lis!"

"How in the . . . how can I . . . when did you . . . ?" Michelle was beside herself.

I leaned in and whispered, "Remember the mickey I threatened you with? I still have that, ya know."

Michelle slapped my leg and snorted. "This is incredible but insanely over the top!"

Katie asked, "How did you *ever* get Landon to agree to this?"

Alissa grinned. "Simple. I gave him five hundred dollars and told him this trip was on me."

"You gave Landon five hundred dollars? What the hell, Lis?" Katie's mouth dropped open.

"Feeling like Julia Roberts yet?" Alissa grinned and winked at Katie.

"I don't even want to know what you offered Brandon." Michelle said.

"He got the same deal and a promise I would toss his name around at the court house for people looking for insurance. Oh. And you owe him a blow job."

"Ah, you know how to dangle a carrot, girlfriend."

"Indeed I do."

Dani asked, "So what did you do for Barry?"

"Not a damn thing. I told him I was taking you and that was that. Ha-ha!"

She laughed. "Well at least you didn't offer him a blow job."

"Well, I may have dropped a hint that I might consider moving one of my accounts to FNB. Heavy on the *might*."

Dani snorted. "You know how to bargain all too well!"

Alissa glanced in the rearview mirror. "I'm a lawyer; it's what I do." She flashed a perfect grin then returned her eyes to the road as she took the exit for the airport.

"We're really flying?" Katie's eyes were huge with a matching grin.

Alissa beamed. "We are, indeed. Fasten your seat belts, ladies. This is going to be one helluva night."

One thing about Alissa, the girl knew how to spend money and spared no expense when making the reservations for our twenty-four-hour hiatus. A black stretch limo awaited us at the Chicago airport complete with chilled champagne, fresh-cut strawberries, and a driver hot enough to boil water with one grin. I hoped he was part of the package and was really a stripper, but Alissa corrected me before I and my three on-flight drinks made a fool of ourselves. It was worth a shot.

The limo ride was spectacular and provided many Kodak moments including a shot of Michelle's ass and legs as the top part of her disappeared through the sunroof. Chicago got a big kick out of her serenade. Champagne always did a number on that girl.

I leaned over and whispered to Dani while the other three cackled about who was going to be puking before the night was over. "Are you all right?"

She nodded and grinned. "Yes, I'm just taking it all in." She pointed and laughed at Katie's impersonation of Landon's "O" face followed by, "Touchdown!" Nothing is sacred among us. It will be very hard not to laugh the next time we all watch Sunday football together, though.

It was nearly ten before we got to the restaurant, and by the time they served our meal, I think we could have all eaten the ass-end of a goat.

"Here you are, ladies. Complimentary wine to celebrate your twentieth anniversary?" The waiter who poured our wine looked young enough to diaper, but he was charming and devilishly cute. Michelle's cleavage was of the utmost interest to him, and as much as he tried to steal glances, I busted him every time. I winked at him, causing him to blush and scamper away.

Alissa raised her glass. "A toast!" We raised our glasses too. "To the most remarkable women God ever created, and I'm blessed to be friends with you. Here's to another twenty years. Cheers!"

"Cheers!" I looked over the raised glasses and met the misty eyes of my life's blood. Each one of us savored the moment then squished together in our half-circle booth for a picture. The host shouldn't have asked us to say "friendship" since our mouths puckered in the picture causing us to look like Sunday-morning Methodists. A quick do-over fixed the problem, but we kept the picture to laugh at who looked more like Dana Carvey as the Church Lady.

"So what do you think, ladies? Shall we find somewhere to dance?" Katie shook her shoulders and grinned.

"Oh Lord, I'm not sure I've got it in me. It's way past my bedtime!" Michelle rested her head on her hands. "I can't remember the last time I saw midnight and wasn't cleaning up vomit."

"It was about four months ago, drama queen, at my apartment." I swirled my wine in my glass.

Katie said, "Yes, but *I* was cleaning vomit."

Michelle gasped. "What? I said I was sorry!"

"You want to know what's weird? I haven't seen any of you dive-bomb for your cell phones all night. I'm really proud of you." Dani grinned and took another drink of wine.

"Chance threatened to throw mine out the window when she picked me up." Michelle told on me.

"Well damn, girl . . ."

"Personally, I don't care. Landon has the kids, I'm with my girls, and unless a catastrophe hits, I'm on base. I'm safe." A round of cheers followed Katie's announcement.

Michelle's mouth gaped. "You can't just tap out when you're a mom."

"Bullshit. I just did." She leaned over the table and belly-laughed.

"Atta girl, Katie!" Alissa toasted Katie and called for the check.

We gathered our purses and secretly tried to check our phones without the others realizing.

Dani slid out of the booth. "Come to the bathroom with me," she whispered.

I nodded and followed her through the restaurant. As soon as we entered the bathroom, she burst into tears and threw her arms around my neck.

"Honey, what's wrong?" I rubbed her back as she stifled her sobs in my hair.

"I'm barren."

"For sure? Oh God, when did you find out?"

"Yesterday. I'm barren, and because of that, Barry is leaving me. He says he wants a family more than anything, and if he can't have it with me, he's leaving." Dani's body shook with sobs.

It all made sense—how quiet she'd been, how disconnected she felt. I knew something was wrong with her the minute I'd seen her.

"Honey, why didn't you call me?" I pulled away from her and smoothed her hair.

"I didn't have time. He told me this morning he was leaving, so this weekend getaway provides him with the opportunity he needed, I guess."

She sighed and looked in the mirror. "Shit . . . stupid wine." She wiped her eyes and took a few deep breaths. "I haven't told anyone else yet, but I will in the morning. Tonight? We drink." She offered a weak smile and hugged me again. "I'm sorry I crashed and burned. I was about to lose it out there."

"Hey, no apologies. How many times have you been my lean-to in the midst of heartbreak?"

"It's what we do. I have to pee." She stumbled into the stall just in time, because in walked the other three.

"What's she doing, taking a dump?" Michelle has class when she's drunk. "What's taking you so long?"

"Oh, shop talk. Is it a pit-stop before limo time?"

"Yes!" Katie sauntered over and draped herself across my shoulders. "You look good in black. Have I ever told you that?"

"Only every time I wear black, honey." Katie laughed and half-walked, half-fell into the next stall. "Whoops! Shit, that door moves."

"It closes, too, woman. Take a hint!" Alissa held the door while Katie slipped the lock in place.

"Thanks whore!"

"No problem, slut."

The hotel was even more impressive than the limo. Not that any of us got to enjoy it that evening, because our lightweight asses passed out thirty minutes after the argument of who had to sleep with Alissa-the-cover-hog.

I woke up to the sound of someone puking in the bathroom and Alissa's groaning as she snatched the pillow out from under my head to cover her ear. "Someone close that damned door."

Katie stumbled to the bathroom, grabbed a wet washcloth, and started wiping Michelle's face. "Rough night, kiddo?"

"Rougher morning. Thanks."

Katie closed the door and slid in next to Dani. I squinted at the clock next to the bed: 7:42 a.m. I snatched my pillow back from Alissa and buried my head in it.

14

"Nice," she mumbled.

"Mine," I sassed.

Katie sighed and gave up on sleep. She kicked the covers off in a huff and asked, "Who wants coffee?"

Three hands raised and dropped. Michelle opened the door and crawled into bed next to Dani. Katie pointed a finger at her, which was met with a raised hand to say, "No thanks, I'm dying anyway."

Alissa said, "Katie, this isn't the Super 8. Call the bastards downstairs and order what you want. They bring it to you."

"Ya know, I forgot how much of a bitch you are when you're hung over." Katie kicked off her flip-flops and stomped to the phone.

Dani sat up. "Well, none of us have new tattoos, so I'd say that was a pretty successful evening in Chicago."

Alissa's laugh shook the bed even though it wasn't audible.

"Michelle, your phone just went off." Katie fished through the mound of purses dropped by the door until she located Michelle's phone. She started to toss it to her but the pillow covered her face. "Are you going to make it?"

"No. Ship my body back to Columbia and bury me in my yellow pajamas. And tell my kids not to drink. Ever."

"Hey, Katie, will you grab my purse, too, please?" Dani sat up and rubbed her eyes.

"Might as well hand them all out, honey." Alissa and I joined the ranks and sat up in bed. "You look like shit, girl." Alissa said to me as she ran her fingers through her hair.

"Back atcha." I swatted her leg.

"I meant to tell you. Ix-nay the terra-cotta jacket on TV. It's not a good color for you."

I chuckled and went into the bathroom. She was right. I looked like speed racers had practiced on my face. Sleep wrinkles, smeared eyeliner, mascara rings. Not pretty. However, then again, none of the others had seen themselves yet, and that made me smile. I fared pretty well compared to Dani-the-practicing-panda.

I'd just finished brushing my teeth and hair when the bellhop brought up our breakfast. He barely had the door closed when I said, "Geez, are there no ugly men in Chicago? Damn, did you see him?"

"Sure there are. But they are all home with the kids while their wives are gallivanting through Columbia on a girl's weekend get-away."

"Oh I'm sure people from Chicago are dying to go to central Missouri. Maybe closet Chiefs fans."

Michelle's phone chirped again causing her to groan and come alive. My next glance up saw my four best friends all checking their phones and responding to the ignored texts from the night before. Dani's face was pale.

I shot her a text. *You OK?*

She met my stare and shrugged. Her chin started to quiver. She disappeared into the bathroom as Alissa and Katie chuckled over a picture Landon had sent of the kids dressed like pirates with Katie's big hoop earrings tucked over their little ears. The clanging of their spoons against their coffee cups seemed incredibly loud——it beckoned me.

"Man, this room is huge. Very impressive, Lis." On the other side of Dani's bed was an open living room complete with a big-screen TV nestled over a stone fireplace. A sofa, love seat, and two chairs created a U-shape around the coffee table that was large enough to hold a staff meeting. I snuggled into the closest chair facing the window and curled my feet under me.

"Holy shit. What floor are we on? That's a long way down." Katie's eyes were huge as she pointed out the window. "Chance, come look at this."

I held up my hand. "Not on your life, Katie. I'm trying *not* to throw up. Thanks."

"So what's on the agenda today, maestro?" Michelle joined us and chose a seat on the couch next to Alissa.

"We have to be at the spa by ten and lunch reservations are at 12:30 I think. We have to be at the airport by three o'clock."

"Are we getting facials?" Katie beamed.

"Facials and massages all around." Alissa glowed.

"Oh, not so sure about that one, Lis." Dani rounded the corner looking skeptical. "You know I'm not a big fan of other people touching me."

Alissa laughed. "Says the girl who's been in stirrups for four years. Really, Dani, it will be fine."

I bit my lip and glanced up at Dani's pale face. Alissa had no idea how untimely her comment had been.

"What? What'd I miss?" Alissa looked at me and shrugged. "Did I say something wrong?"

"Dani, if you don't want a massage, I can . . ."

"No, Lis, it's fine." Dani sat in the chair opposite me and Katie chose the love seat. "Well, I have some bad news." Her eyes filled with tears. "The doctor told me yesterday I'm barren. We've tried it all, but the last round of tests showed no eggs."

Michelle gasped. "Oh honey, but you can adopt, right? You and Barry are so successful and—"

"Michelle . . ." I shook my head.

"Barry's leaving me." She barely got the words out before she broke down. The other three swarmed to her chair to console her. I kept my seat—I'd already had my turn. "He said he wants a family in the worst way—*his* family, not someone we have to buy. Isn't that a horrible thing to say? Like you just go to a shelf and pick."

"Dani, he's just overreacting right now. He's just as heartbroken over this as you are, but he'll come around." As usual, Katie didn't have a clue.

"No, he's moving this weekend; he told me yesterday morning."

"It sounds to me like the bastard had this in mind the whole time." Alissa stared at the carpet shaking her head. "No wonder he didn't give me any grief over the trip," she mumbled.

"Maybe I'll pee in his coffee Monday." Katie scowled and we all laughed.

Silence and what-do-we-say-now glances filled the room.

"Anyone else need a warm-up?" Michelle took Dani's cup and headed to the breakfast cart. Everyone else took their seats and let the

17

weight of the news settle over them.

Dani looked at me. "I keep thinking about the house. We bought it with the hopes of filling it with children. It's a mighty big house for a one-woman show."

I winked at her and smiled. "Dani, you're going to be fine. Life is going to suck for a while, but you're going to be fine."

"I know. But I had this vision of my life with Barry. Soccer games, dance recitals, first birthday parties, weddings, graduations, hopefully not in that order." She grinned and wiped her tears. "My beautiful painting has just been wiped clean. All I can see now is a blank canvas."

Alissa grinned. "And have we got the perfect colors for you, my dear." Unity filled the air, and a spark ignited in Dani's darkened eyes.

Chapter Two
Irreplaceable

Dani

Against the advice, and perhaps interference, of my dearest friends, I went home alone to face my new reality as a soon-to-be divorced woman. I didn't know what to expect. For all I knew, Barry's sitting at the dining room table waiting for me to come home so he could profess how wrong he'd been and beg me for forgiveness. It would be completely out of style for him to do such a thing, but childish hope won over rational thought as I eased the car into the driveway and held my breath as the garage door lifted. His car was gone, and so was my hope. I panned the garage and made mental notes of everything that was missing. This dead space was a testimony to what the house had in store.

The kitchen looked normal, only minimal damage there. The dining room was untouched, but he'd gutted the living room. He'd taken most of the furniture minus the couch and my great-grandmother's antique rocker that had been passed down to every daughter when their first child was born. Mother got anxious and gave it to me when Barry and I bought this house. The chair now seemed to be mocking me. Our entertainment center, his chair and end table, the coffee table . . . everything was gone. However, he left our wedding picture. I took it off the wall and placed it face down in the rocker. They could mock me together.

I made my way through the rest of the house. After witnessing the living room, I knew his office would be an abandoned tomb and I was right. Nothing left in there but a power strip and a potted plant. Our bedroom was unscathed except for his empty closet, but the guest bedroom was also empty. Mr. Efficiency must have hired movers to help him.

Thirty-two hundred square feet and Barry had managed to take exactly half of everything we owned. A bed for me? A bed for you. A chair for me? A chair for you. Seven years to build and one weekend to divide. And all because my body had failed us.

"I can't stay here tonight." My voice sounded hollow bouncing off the walls of the nearly empty living room. I grabbed my purse and the overnight bag Barry had so *lovingly* packed for my surprise get-away and headed for the door.

When I turned around, Alissa stood in the main entrance waving a bottle of wine. The dam broke on my held-back tears as I let her in.

I grabbed her in a huge hug. "You scared me to death, but I'm so glad you're here."

She chuckled. "Going somewhere?"

I wiped my eyes. "Actually, I was headed to your house. I can't stay here tonight."

She threw her arm around me. "Let's see the damage and then we'll head out."

"I've already been through here. It's awful."

Alissa surveyed the once meticulous house, now sporadic at best. I followed her and pointed out things she might have missed along the way. She held my hand the entire time.

When we finished the devastation tour, she turned to me and sighed. "Well, you know you can stay with me as long as you want. I wouldn't want to stay here either."

"What about Mark? Don't you have plans tonight?"

She sighed and tried to chuckle. "I got a Dear Jane email. So that bottle of wine is for both of us." She threw her arm around my neck, grabbed the bottle and my bag, and we headed out to her car.

We drove in silence for a few blocks and then she looked at me out of the corner of her eye. "I have just the thing for you. You might remember this." She turned on the radio and Beyoncé's voice, along with Alissa's, resonated in the car.

I laughed in spite of myself. "You still can't sing for shit."

"No, but I can still make you laugh. Do you remember this CD? Chance made it after her first fiasco. She burned me a copy during my second divorce and now? *Voilà.*" She handed me a red CD.

I took the disk and read the label. "The Breakup Mix? What all is on here?"

"Your new life's blood, my friend. You will grow to cherish that CD. I'm actually on my third copy, truth be known. I didn't know it was possible to wear them out."

Three bottles of wine and two chick-flicks later, I knew I was slurring my words, but I really didn't care. "You know what that bastard had the audacity to do? He left some of his *shit* lying around the house. Like he can just waltz back in whenever he wants to *my house* and get it whenever he decides. I swear he did it on purpose. I found his cuff links, his . . . oh wait!"

I tried to jump off the couch but ended up stumbling around until I got my balance. I pointed at Alissa. "Stop laughing at me." I grabbed up my purse and dumped the contents until I found the CD. I waved it at her. "She's right! She's totally right! He thinks he can just discard *me* and I'm going to be calm and professional about it. Well *fuck* him. He's going to pay me half for all that shit he took, *and* he is going to buy me out of that house. And you know what else I'm going to do?"

Alissa laughed. "I've never seen you like this. Tell me, what are you going to do?"

"I'm going to box up all his leftover shit that he didn't care to get the first time and put it out in the yard. That's what I'm going to do. I'll change the locks and make him regret the day he ever walked out on ol' Dani." Alissa didn't have time to cheer before I crumpled to the floor and cried, "Why did he have to do this to me?"

"Oh, honey." She slid to the floor beside me. "I know."

"We had it all. Money, house, careers, each other . . . no babies, though. I'm never going to be a mother, Lis. I'm never going to be a mother." My sobs rolled through my body as my grief surfaced. "Now I really am alone in this world."

She pulled my face up to meet hers. "Never." She shook me once. "Never. You got that?"

Sunday morning I woke up in Alissa's guest room with very little recollection of how I got there. I was barely over my Chicago hangover when Alissa uncorked our first bottle last night. Now it was a double whammy. I made a pot of coffee and scowled at the clock that read 7:43 a.m. Why I can't be more like Chance and Alissa and sleep until ten o'clock on the weekends, I'll never know. The weight of life changes settled heavily on my chest. Everything has changed and now I don't know what to do with myself. I don't have to go home any time soon, I have no shots to give myself, no appointments to make. My entire paint-by-number life just changed in twenty-four hours. As I'm sitting here in another woman's house, drinking another woman's coffee, I wonder how to do this in my own house—in my own life. Chance makes it look so easy—being single and no plans. All of my plans involved Barry and children. Now what?

I curled up on the couch and buried my head in the throw pillow trying to suffocate the random thoughts racing through my head. *Maybe I'll take a long trip. But who will be my emergency contact now? How long has he been planning this? What did I do to deserve this?*

Alissa lifted my legs off the couch, plopped down, and set them on top of her lap. I tried to sit up a little but the weight of grief mixed with a hangover is mighty heavy.

"You need to shave." She pulled my pajama pants over my ankles.

I sighed and waved her off. "No point in it now."

"How long have you been up?" She took a drink of her coffee.

"I don't know. What time is it?"

"Almost nine."

"Is it really? A little over an hour, then. You know how when something bad happens, you start remembering clues you missed along the way? Well, I've been replaying the last few months in my head and I can't find any. Not one. And you know Barry. He doesn't make a snap decision about anything, so he had to have been planning this. We just found out Thursday morning I have no more eggs. He was so supportive, so caring and nurturing, and he *knew* he was about to devastate me even more. I don't get it, Lis. I don't understand."

22

"So what if he was? Does it matter?"

"Yes, Lis, it does matter." I sat up.

"What I mean is, are you going to be any more hurt than you already are now if you keep going back to figure out missed warning signs? No. You won't. My point is you already know how the story ends. Rereading the shit you've already lived isn't going to write the next chapter faster or easier. The best thing I can tell you is get on with today. And we're going to start with the gym."

I stared at her blankly. "The gym."

"Yep." She slapped her thighs. "Get up. We're going to the gym."

When we walked into Reggie's Total Fitness, my jaw dropped open at all of the equipment. I just saw pain in my future. "Lis, I do not belong here. I haven't broken a sweat outside of planting flowerbeds since high school P.E. I mean, look at me. I look ridiculous." I did look ridiculous in Alissa's black spandex-tight capris, a neon pink tank top, and a sports bra that made my shoulder blades look bigger than my C cups.

Alissa waved me off. "Don't start bitching. I'm going to introduce you to your new best friend." She gave a long-distance wave to someone sweating on an elliptical. "Don't be too intimidated. Most of the people here have had at least one surgery to make them look the way they do. You've just been blessed with a good metabolism."

"Then why am I here?" I was already out of breath just trying to keep up with how fast Alissa was walking.

"Anger management, by dear Watson." She stopped in front of a service desk outside of what appeared to be a boxing ring. "Two sets of gloves, please?" She slid her membership card across the counter, the service rep scanned the cards then the gloves and handed all three back to Alissa without so much as a thank you.

"There are friendly people around here."

"Yeah, you get used to it. Here, take these." Alissa handed me both sets of gloves and maneuvered her long blond hair into a high ponytail. She flashed a perfect grin at me. "Are you ready?"

I shrugged and followed her into the boxing arena. "Shouldn't they

23

be playing 'Eye of the Tiger' right about now?"

Alissa chuckled. "I'll see what I can do about that." She stopped in front of a black and red punching bag suspended from the ceiling. "Here we are." She walked behind the bag and put both hands on it. "Meet Asshole. Asshole comes to us from some place in China and has been provided to you as an outlet for all your frustrations." She rubbed her hands up and down the punching bag. "He is much like your typical asshole in that he has no feelings and never gives a shit how upset you are when you approach him. Put your gloves on."

I stared at her wide-eyed. "You don't expect me to punch this thing, do you?"

"I absolutely expect you to punch this thing. Here. Watch." Alissa let the bag go and donned her set of gloves. She punched her hands together a few times then hauled off and punched the crap out of the bag as she yelled, "Asshole!" The bag swung backward then toward her. She punched it again. "You piece of shit!" She gave it a few more taps then looked at me grinning. "See? Oh, man does that feel good. You try."

After Alissa helped me put my gloves on, I approached the punching bag. She stood behind it with her head poking out giving me instructions on what to do. "Now. Pretend this bag has Barry's face on it."

I dropped my arms to my sides. "I would never hit Barry. This is stupid, Lis, I would never hit anyone!"

"Don't make me swing this bag at you. You are going to hit this punching bag. Now put your hands up. Good. Now, on the count of three, I want you to swing and punch this bag with all you have. Ready? One, two . . . three."

I pulled back my fist and punched the bag. It barely moved.

"Really? That's it? Jesus, Dani, I think Katie's three-year-old smacked me harder than that two weeks ago. Come on! Are you a woman or a pussy? Punch the fucking bag!"

I punched a little harder. Alissa stepped out from behind the bag and put her hands on her hips. I punched again and looked at her. She faked a yawn and investigated her fingernails through her boxing gloves.

I tried again.

"Dammit, Lis, I told you, I can't do this."

"Wrong. You've just never done this. It's not that you can't. There's a difference. Again."

I muttered, "Bitch gets me drunk then takes me to the gym hung over. Nice fucking *friend*!" I hauled off and punched the bag with everything I had and sent it sailing into Alissa, knocking her backward. "Oh my god, Lis, I'm so sorry!"

Alissa grinned. "Atta girl, now do it again." She stopped the swinging bag and held it in place.

I focused on the bag and yelled, "Asshole!" as I punched the bag as hard as I could. "You think you can just discard *me*?" Wham. The rage that had built up inside me poured through my arms and before I knew it, I was whooping the shit out of Asshole-the-punching-bag and I added a few knee kicks to the groin for good measure. Sweat poured off my forehead and dripped down my back, but I didn't care. Alissa still held Asshole, laughing, cheering, and egging me on.

"Hit him again, Dani! He has it coming! Whoa, good shot! Do it again!"

When I fatigued, I stood back from Asshole and looked at Lis. A slow grin stretched over my face. "How'd I do?"

She bent over and put her gloved hands on her knees. "Well, you looked freaking hilarious doing it, but how did it feel?"

I laughed. "It felt really good." I wiped sweat from my forehead with my arm and wiped it on my shirt. "Really good. What's next?"

An hour and a half later, we left the gym completely exhausted and more dehydrated than we were when we got there. My legs and arms were jelly—lifting a water bottle to my lips took longer than normal, felt like it weighed twenty pounds. When we pulled into Alissa's driveway, she gave me instructions to shower while she made lunch.

"Can I just crawl up the steps? I think I left my legs back in the gym."

Alissa giggled. "Come on, Dani. You did a great job. But you're definitely going to be sore tomorrow."

25

"Tomorrow? I'm already sore now!"

"Then tomorrow is going to royally suck for you." She laughed. "Come on. Inside."

"Actually, I think I want to go home now."

It startled both of us.

She looked at me with a tilted head. "Are you sure?"

I nodded my head. "Yeah, I think I want to go home. Plus, I have to work tomorrow, anyway."

Alissa slid the keys out of the ignition. "If you're sure. If it gets too tough, you know where I am."

"I would hug your right now, but I'm all nasty and sweaty."

"Yeah, save that for later. Go grab your stuff and I'll take you home.

Chapter Three
Big Girls Don't Cry

Alissa

I see Chance got to you, first. No doubt she vomited all of her I-am-single-hear-me-roar bullshit onto the page. She talks a big talk. Sometimes it's hard to tell if she's really that hardened or just a coward when it comes to love.

Each of us have something the others either want or admire. I have the body and the money, Michelle and Katie have the families, Chance has the career, and Dani has stability. Correction: Dani *had* stability until two days ago. We've had a breach in security, and I think after Dani's revelation everyone is feeling introspective.

Mark's email was pretty cut and dry. Things weren't working out, moving too fast, expectations were too high, blah blah blah. I admit, part of me was relieved he did it first——kinda relieved—a little. He was a great guy, but I knew in my heart that he wasn't the one even though I wanted him to be.

After my last several relationship indiscretions, Mark was a nice change. He had a good career, was financially stable, and he didn't give two shits that I was wealthy. He didn't offer to invest my money for me, didn't lose four inches off of his manhood when I divulged my millionaire status, and he never once asked me for a dime. We had a lot in common with our careers and interest in fitness, but outside of that, life with Mark was pretty boring. Yeah, he probably would have been my third divorce.

My therapist keeps asking me what void I'm trying to fill with men. If I knew the answer to that, I wouldn't have to pay her one-hundred and fifty dollars an hour to work through my relationship issues. To me, it's not rocket science; I want to be in love. I don't think that's too much to want out of life.

I love my girlfriends, don't get me wrong. But lately I feel like they just don't take me seriously anymore. It's not exactly heartwarming to know that they know every single romantic relationship of mine has ended. I mean, I'm a good catch! I'm smart, successful, beautiful, funny, and I have no baggage. I'm rich, I'm good at everything I do, and all I ask for in return is love. Yet, it evades me repeatedly. However, seeing Dani lose her sanity over Barry, and watching someone who looks like she should be in ballet slippers tear up a punching bag, maybe Chance has the right idea.

Though I would never admit to her she's right.

A text notification chimed, and of course I thought it was Mark. I guess it will take some time to reprogram my thoughts away from him. I'm still excited to hear from him even though he just told me in very clear 12-pica font that I'm not who he thought I was, and the life we were headed into was "too involved" for him. I guess I shouldn't have planned things so thoroughly. I just don't know how to let it go. Maybe I sent him over the edge with the let's-move-in-together suggestion. In my defense, it'd been six months, and things were going well. It was a natural progression, or so I thought. I guess some guys don't want to commit no matter how awful singlehood is for them.

The text was from Dani: *Thanks for everything. I owe you my life.*

I responded with a smiley face and left it at that. I walked through my now-empty house and considered hiring painters again. Happiness may be able to elude me in my personal life, but dammit, I can slap it across interior walls in two days flat. I added "contact my decorator" to the to-do list of the day and wandered into my bathroom, peeled off my sweaty clothes, and stepped into the shower. Sighing, I envisioned the sadness and disappointment running out of my lungs, sliding down my body, and disappearing down the drain. My therapist taught me that as well as, "Exhale venom, inhale freedom. Exhale venom, inhale freedom."

My text tone went off again, which sent me racing out of the shower toward my phone on the sink. It wasn't Mark. I slipped back into the shower and started the process all over again. Out with sadness and disappointment, in with . . . with . . . with what? It's a little early to find gratitude for another failed relationship, so I tried to envision my life as I wanted it. The sad thing was, I had no idea how I wanted it to look anymore. My chest filled with that vacant gloom I knew too well. I was alone.

I finished my shower and got ready to go. I had to keep moving. If I stopped moving, I would start thinking, and thinking never did anything for me. Most of the people I knew had Sunday afternoon rituals. I figured Michelle and Brandon would be knee-deep in kid fights and housework. Chance would probably be eating up her *alone time*, and Dani had just left, so I couldn't look like a desperate stalker-type just yet. That left Katie and her family. I called and got her voicemail but left a message anyway, hoping she would be up for a round of golf or shopping. I grabbed my keys and headed out the door.

Gotta keep moving.

Chapter Four
Just Give Me a Reason

Michelle
One Week Later

"Del Ray! What is this?" I stormed down the hallway to meet her with my horror in my hand. "Del Ray! She better come clean or I'm going to rip her legs off and glue them shut backwards."

She appeared in the hallway with big eyes and a curious expression. "What'd I do, now?" She pulled her ear buds out of her ears and tucked them into the front of her shirt.

I shoved her back into her bedroom and slammed the door as I held up my new trophies. "What are these, my sweet child?"

She had the audacity to laugh and cover her metal-filled mouth with her hand then play with her necklace. "Wow. Um. Where did you find those?"

"Keep playing around, Del Ray." I walked toward her.

"Okay, just calm down, Mom. It's no big deal. I got them from school. There was a sex ed fair, and I swiped a few condoms as a joke. Okay? Relax, Mom." She strutted past me and my dropped jaw, opened the door, and went down the hall into the kitchen. *That little lying piece of . .* .

She was eating an apple when I rounded the corner. "Oh, how appropriate. Eve, Snow White . . . all over an apple!" I threw the condoms at her face.

"Whoa, dude, really?" She bent over and picked them up. She started to put them in the pocket of her skinny jeans.

"Back the f— Give them to me. Give them to me. Now." My face cracked in fury, and I knew I had to have *that* look, the look I swore I'd never give my children. When she handed them over, I took a deep breath. "Del Ray, you are way too young to consider a sexual relationship."

"Mom, I'm not, okay? I promise. But I'll be sixteen, soon."

"Yeah, in two years! Jesus, come on!"

"One year three months—"

"I swear I thought I had at least a few years before I had to deal with this bullsh— Honey, listen . . ."

"Mom, please don't go on about you and Dad waiting for marriage. I know it's a lie."

"What? It is not!"

"Oh really? Care to take the test?"

I stuttered as she grabbed the last and final source to end all arguments in our household. It had been deemed the undisputed final answer for years amongst the children. Now it was my turn to face it.

"Magic 8 ball, Magic 8 ball . . . did Mom sleep with Dad before marriage?"

"Now listen, Del Ray—

"Ha! *It is certain. You* are a liar." Del Ray laughed and danced.

"That was a long time ago, and things are different now. I had to. Lottie-the-body was after him and—" My husband, Brandon, rounded the corner as I chased after our gloating daughter.

"What about Lottie-the-body?"

I eyed him suspiciously. "Didn't you finally win my chastity by telling me Lottie-the-body was hot for you?" An evil twinkle followed by an eyebrow twitch sold him out as he, too, bit into an apple. "You horny piece of no-go-rotten . . . I can't even tell my children I waited for marriage because ruined my virtue, pecker-head!"

Brandon laughed as he dodged my swinging arms and wrapped them behind my back. "You're mighty feisty for a Sunday."

I looked up at him with pure insanity running out of my eyes. "You lied to me about Lottie-the-body, didn't you?"

Brandon kissed me with sticky, wet, apple-glazed lips. "Maybe, but it worked. And now look at us." He released my hands from behind my back and grabbed my bottom. "Come here . . ."

I spun away from him and pulled out the condoms from my elastic waistband. "See these? Still think it's funny when high school girls have

31

sex, you big, fat douchebag?" I threw them in his already-chalking face and went to find my wine bottle.

This was not how I pictured my life turning out. At all.

When I pictured my life, all I ever wanted to be was a mother. As I tipped the nearly-empty wine bottle and drained it into my favorite wine glass from three girls' weekends ago, I dismissed the fact that it was three in the afternoon and reminded myself that my fourteen-year-old daughter had in her possession, right now, condoms.

While I'm certain some mothers would be relieved to find out that their daughters were being responsible, I couldn't let go of the fact that my little girl was considering sex. I stopped myself at "considering" and couldn't allow it to go further. In my mind, right that moment, she was still a virgin, and the only kissing she had done was the practice make-out sessions she probably had with the bathroom mirror. "I hope her lips get stuck in her braces," I muttered as I took a drink of my wine.

I sat on the edge of my bed looking at myself in the mirror wondering what happened to the last sixteen years of my life. I was such a baby when I married Brandon. I felt sick to my stomach when I realized I was only five years older than Del Ray is right now when I married her father. I took another drink of wine and studied my reflection in the mirror a little harder. I'd lost track of how many days in a row I'd worn the wrinkled Aerosmith T-shirt with the holes in the armpits and these black yoga pants. I worked on Friday, so really it had only been since Friday night. I didn't even realize I hadn't taken time to shower yesterday until I sat on the bed examining my life, and the image before me proved how right I was. I was lost. Domesticity had completely enveloped me, and all I had to show for it was stretch marks, a bad haircut, and memories of one helluva fun concert when I was eighteen.

To my friends, I'm the one who's got it all together but paid a price for the prize. I know that; it's no secret. I can see the grimaces on Chance's and Alissa's faces, specifically, when I describe yet another fun-filled weekend of laundry, housework, and sewer problems. Hell, even our trip to Chicago was weird for me, because I felt like the Goodwill kid going to the big city. And, it's true! My whole outfit came from Goodwill because Del Ray's braces are costing us a small fortune. Brandon makes a decent income, sure, and my job at the daycare helps us make ends meet, but damn I thought we'd be living higher on the hog once the kids were out of diapers and eating real food.

However, there's football cleats, baseball uniforms, band instruments, lunch money, braces, emergency room visits for my sweet-but-clumsy ten-year-old Martin, and that doesn't include anything that I would ever want to spend money on for myself.

Which, for the life of me, I can't think of one thing I've done for myself or anything I even enjoy doing outside of my family.

Brandon knocked softly on the door and stuck his head inside. "You okay, babe?"

The tears welling up in my eyes dripped down my cheeks. I wiped them with the tail of my shirt and scratched my face with the dried gravy from breakfast. "Who am I, Brandon?"

He came into the room and closed the door. He leaned against the door with one hand on the knob. "What do you mean, Chelle?"

"Look at me! I'm not even me anymore. And I don't even know who 'me' is. I went from being a kid to being your wife to being their mother."

He muttered, "Oh boy," and took a few hesitant steps toward me. "Listen, Michelle, she's probably just trying to fit in."

"This isn't about Del Ray, this is about me. I'm lost. I've been wearing these same clothes since I got home from work Friday night. I have no life outside of this fifteen-hundred square foot house and outside of our family."

"You're not supposed to, honey. This is what we do: we grow up, we have families, we work, we retire, and we're happy."

"Who's happy?" The words slapped the air.

He paused and looked at me as if I'd shape-shifted right before his eyes. "I'm happy; the kids are happy, and until this moment, I *thought* you were happy."

I sat my empty wine glass on the nightstand and threw myself onto my pillow. "I thought I was, too. What's wrong with me?" I moaned into the pillow.

Brandon sat on the bed beside me and rubbed my back. "Is this coming from the trip to Chicago? Chelle, we aren't like Alissa and Chance. Hell, we're not even like Katie and Landon. We're blue-collar, normal Americans trying to make a living and provide for our families. You think I wanted to be an insurance salesman? Remember me in high school? I wanted to rock the world with my music. I was going to be a big star someday. But those are just kid dreams."

"All I ever wanted to be was your wife and a mother," I cried.

"So see? Your dreams came true."

"While I know you mean well, this isn't helping."

Brandon sighed and moved to the edge of the bed. "Maybe you should get out of the house for the afternoon. Call one of your friends and go do whatever it is that girls do when they're having a moment."

"We don't have any money for me to do anything like that, Brandon, and you know it."

"We'll figure it out. Hell, call Alissa and ask her to take you somewhere. She's got more money than God."

I sat up and reached for a tissue. "I don't even have any hobbies."

Brandon's aggravated sigh said I'd reached the end of my rope with him. "I don't know what you're getting at, Michelle. I'm beginning to feel blamed for giving you everything you wanted."

He didn't get it. So, I did what I always do when Brandon doesn't get it. I offered a smile and reached for his hand. "I think I will call Alissa and see what she's doing today."

He smiled and patted my hand. "Go spend a few hours with your friend, and by dinnertime, you'll be right back to normal." He left the room, and I curled up on my pillow to have a good cry. When I was done, I jumped into the shower, got ready, and called Alissa.

Chapter Five
Don't Cry

Chance

I was surprised to see Katie pull up at Rocky's. Landon's a great guy, don't get me wrong, but Katie's been nervous as a cat since the day she hooked up with that dude. She doesn't get too far from him and I think she resents him for it. I was glad she texted me to tell me about Michelle, though. I was about to start pulling my eyelashes out one by one out of complete boredom. The news stories I had to choose from for the early-morning news tomorrow were exceedingly lame. A completely new set of lame.

Alissa's Navigator was already in the parking lot, meaning she and Michelle had a head start on us. I grabbed my purse and waved at Katie who was already walking my direction.

"Wow, you escaped!" I smiled at her and winked.

She grinned and shrugged. "I'm not going to stay long. Landon's watching a game tape, so I need to—"

I threw my arm around her. "You need to be here with your friends. And that's completely fine."

She curled her arm around my back. "Yes, you're right. I'm sorry."

"Don't apologize. Do you know what all this is about?"

She shook her head. "Not a clue. Dani's on her way."

"Really! Wow, that's surprising. I'm glad. It'll be good for her." I held the door open for her and she flashed her perfect orthodontic grin as she said, "Thank you, kind sir!"

"Shut up and go inside or I'll take you back to New York."

The bar was empty, which was not surprising for a pre-football-season Sunday. In a few weeks, this place will be *the* place to be for game day with televisions mounted every ten feet covering every network game on air. People who don't even like sports endure the shouts and high-fives for the awesome chicken wings and beer specials.

Alissa and Michelle sat toward the back in an oversized booth built to hold six grown men. They looked like miniature humans with their feet barely touching the floor. I stopped at the bar and ordered an amaretto sour for me and a water for Katie before heading to the table. I watched as Katie said her hellos and tried to get a bead on Michelle. She stared into space as she played with a sweetener packet.

Dani walked up behind me and whispered, "What's wrong with Michelle?"

I slid my debit card across the bar to start my tab and grabbed our drinks. "I don't know. Lis called and said Michelle was having a meltdown. That's all I got." I turned to look at Dani. "Damn, you look like you need a little hair of the dog."

Dani chuckled. "Not on your life." She looked at Michelle. "I really hope she's okay."

"Me, too."

I slid into the booth beside Michelle and faced Katie, Dani, and Alissa. "Seems like we were just doing this." I winked at Alissa and turned to Michelle. "So, what's the deal, mama-san?"

Michelle leaned against the back of the booth, looked at the ceiling and sighed. "I found condoms."

Katie sucked air between her teeth. "That son-of-a—"

Michelle snapped her head. "They're Del Ray's."

We all shouted, "*What?*"

Michelle nodded. "Exactly."

I said, "She's fourteen! How on earth—"

Michelle interrupted me. "She said she got them as a joke from some health fair at school." She looked at me through brimming tears. "I just don't know if I believe her."

I looked at the trio of wide-eyed faces across from us and gave Alissa the aren't-you-going-to-say-something look.

Lis took her turn. "Okay, let's think this through. If she's . . . active, isn't it a good thing that she's being careful?"

Michelle tilted her head and snapped, "No, Lis, nothing about this is

36

a good thing. If she's having sex"—she shuddered—"that's not a good thing."

"What did Brandon say?" Dani asked.

Michelle shook her head. "Not much. It's not just Del Ray, it's everything. I'm thirty-four years old and couldn't have more of a boring life. Three kids, a minimum-wage career, no hobbies, no life of my own outside of my family."

"Michelle, that's what we do, though," Katie said. "That's the life we have right now. We're mothers. We have a family to consider." She pointed at Alissa and me. "No offense to these two, but they don't have the lives we do. They have a certain freedom that we don't get, but it won't be like that forever. Our kids will eventually grow up, and then we'll get our turn."

Michelle wiped her eyes with a napkin. "Yeah, but you at least left and did something. You went to New York—"

Katie cut her off. "Yeah and look how that turned out. I was robbed blind and had to call these two to come rescue me."

"I haven't done anything, though. I don't even have any dumb stories to share. Nineteen years old and boom—right into life as a wife then mother."

Dani cleared her throat. "Never look at that privilege as a burden, Michelle."

Michelle's face washed with guilt. "I'm sorry, Dani. I wasn't thinking. I don't resent my family; I don't. I just . . . I just want something that's mine. I want my own gold star or some sort of accomplishment, ya know?"

Alissa squinted at her. "Okay, let's talk that one out. What do you *like* to do?"

Michelle slammed her hands on the table. "*I don't know!* That's exactly what I'm saying. I don't even know what I like to do outside of my family."

"You're supposed to put your family first, Michelle," Katie said, shaking her head. "That's completely normal."

"No, I disagree," I said.

Katie gasped. "How can you say that?"

"Well, look at her. She's a mess! How can she be a good mom or wife if she's not even taking care of herself? All of us have some outlet, so what I'm hearing is that Michelle needs to find something to do outside of her family for personal accomplishment."

Alissa found her sassy side. "Yeah, because that's exactly what she already said. Brilliant research, Chance."

"You hush up." I turned to Michelle. "Okay, at this table, we have an abundance of experience. What do you want to try?"

Alissa bounced in her seat. "Oh, I know. Why don't you join the gym and go to boxing classes with me?"

Dani groaned. "Michelle, save yourself. Don't do it." She rubbed her shoulder. "What about night classes at the community college?"

"What about a mission trip through the church?" Katie asked.

Michelle shook her head. "No, classes won't work because every kid has practice and homework." She looked at Katie. "And I haven't been to church in months, so I'd say missions are out. But maybe the exercise would help me."

"Oh, it will be so much fun. You'll love it," Alissa said.

"How much is the membership?" Michelle asked.

Alissa waved her off. "I don't know. We'll figure that part out later."

"Now back to Del Ray," Dani said.

Michelle put her head on the table. "I'm pretty sure I blew it when I flew off the handle. I don't think that girl would take me seriously if the house was on fire and I showed her the flames."

I bit my lip and dreaded the next question out of my mouth. "Want me to talk to her?"

Michelle looked at me with grateful eyes. "Would you? She loves you! Maybe she would listen to you."

I sighed inside but said, "Sure, I can do that. I'll take her to the mall and casually threaten to beat her ass if she even thinks about getting naked before she's sixteen."

"Before marriage, right Chance? Before marriage," Katie added quickly.

I nodded. "Yes, before marriage. That's what I meant."

Michelle sat back in the booth and sighed. "Okay that might work. I'll talk to Brandon about it too and see if he has any brilliant ideas." She stopped and chuckled. "I threw the condoms in his face."

"How did that go over?" Alissa laughed.

Michelle shook her head. "Not good. You see where I am, now, don't you?"

"Well, you were in shock, so I can imagine you didn't handle it the best, but all you have to do is go home and apologize," Katie said.

Michelle's face fell. "I said something that hurt him. I told him I wasn't happy."

Katie sucked air through her teeth and looked at me. I said, "He's been with you a long time, kiddo. He knows when you're losing your shit, so don't beat yourself up too much, okay, honey?"

Michelle nodded her head. "Yeah, I didn't mean anything bad toward him. But, man, my life is boring."

"I would probably keep those words for us and pick different ones for him. That's pretty painful to hear," Dani said.

"What she's trying to be delicate in saying is, girl, you gotta hide your crazy and only show it to us. He's your husband, but he's still a man and will take it personally if you come at him like that," Alissa added.

Katie shook her head. "No, that's not how marriage works. She *should* tell him what's going on so he can help her work through it."

I looked sideways at Katie and bit my tongue, but Alissa said what I was thinking: "Take your own advice, Katie! Sheesh you're the worst at burying yourself in the name of wifely duty."

Katie stiffened. "Raise your hand if you're still married to your first husband." She and Michelle raised their hands. "'Nuff said." She looked at Michelle. "Here's what you do: go home and explain to Brandon that you were freaking out over the condoms and that you didn't mean anything by your comment about you not being happy. Reassure him that he's not the problem, and that you're going to take an exercise class to get away every now and then. Poof. Problem solved."

Alissa and I exchanged disapproving glances but turned to Michelle who didn't have that panicked look on her face as she smiled at Katie. I patted her hand. "Maybe you should listen to Katie on this one. I can teach you all day long how to screw up a relationship, but I'm not the one to talk to about saving one."

"Here here," Alissa said then finished her drink in one gulp. "Let me up, ladies. I need another one."

Dani and Katie scooted out of the booth.

"I think I'm going to head home. Michelle, call me later if you need to talk, okay?" Katie asked.

Michelle nodded and patted my leg. I slid out of the booth and went to the bar to get a refill. Over my shoulder I watched Michelle give Katie a big hug. Whatever Katie said had made Michelle laugh, so that was good enough for me. I bumped shoulders with Alissa. "What's wrong?"

She leaned her face toward mine. "Katie needs to take her own advice. It just pisses me off when she rattles off all that stuff she doesn't even do herself. She keeps blowing me off for golf, and you know she's quitting the co-ed softball league, right?"

"No! She loves playing!"

She slapped her hand down on the bar and grabbed her drink. "I know, girl, but something about Landon's schedule and blah blah blah."

I waved to Katie.

She came over and held her arms out for a hug. "Love you. Let me know how it goes with Del Ray."

"Of course." I hugged her tight, but when I pulled back to look at her, she was already moving on to Alissa. I grabbed my drink and headed back to the table.

"He was meticulous as usual," Dani was saying. "The way things were divided was too perfect to be a spontaneous decision, Michelle, even for Barry. This must have been his fallback plan if we got bad news from the doctor."

"Are you going to keep the house?" Michelle asked.

Dani shrugged and shook her head. "I doubt it. That's a lot of house for one person. It's paid for, so I should sell it dirt cheap." She winked at me and gave me a half-grin. "The best way to get to Barry is through his wallet."

I smiled back and looked for Alissa at the bar. She was talking to the bartender—translation: she was sizing him up as boyfriend material. I caught her eye and nodded for her to come back to the table. She flashed him a perfect grin before heading back to the table.

"Girl, you are relentless," I mumbled when she sat.

She grinned. "Gotta keep moving forward, honey."

I chuckled and watched her offer Dani a drink who grimaced and refused.

"Been there, done that, Dani," I said. "Alissa knows how to drown a heartache."

Dani nodded. "Yeah and she took me to the gym again today. Double whammy."

"Can we drop by the gym before you take me home? I want to look it over." Michelle asked Alissa.

Alissa nodded. "Sure, we can do that. There's a huge list of classes to take at all different times. It'll be an easy commute for you, too."

"Depending on the class you take, I may join you," Dani said.

Alissa clapped her hands and looked at me. "Ha! Are you in?"

I raised my hands. "Oh, hell, no. I haven't gotten over my last post-breakup-class you talked me into."

"Oh, come on. It will be a blast. I promise."

I sighed. "Let me know what class you pick and then I'll decide."

"Oh I'm so excited!" Alissa giggled.

I rolled my eyes. "Every time you say that, I regret the preceding decision."

"You hush up." Alissa smacked my hand. "You'll thank me some day."

"Mmhmm." I looked at Michelle. "You sure you're up for this?"

"Actually, I'm getting excited about it. I could stand to lose a few pounds and maybe this will give me that nudge I need. If we're going to look at the gym, we probably need to get moving. I need to get back to the house and start dinner."

"Chance, are you going with them?" Dani asked.

"Nah, I'm not ready to leave yet. Do you want to hang out for a bit, Dani?"

"Yeah, I'm craving bar food. Would you like to eat here?"

"Sure, that sounds good. I'll go grab some menus." I slid out of the booth and hugged Michelle as she stood. "Call me if you need me. Hang in there, sister."

"I will. Thanks, Chance."

Alissa slid her drink toward me. ."Here. Drink up. This is upsetting my stomach for some reason. And tip the bartender well. He's super hot and single." She winked at me and hugged Dani.

"He probably slipped you a mickey. I'm not drinking that."

"I'm sure it's fine. I'm probably just queasy from the wine last night. Have fun, ladies." Alissa laughed and walked away.

Chapter Six

In the End

Alissa

Michelle and I left the bar and headed toward the gym. She fidgeted in the seat and texted Brandon a bazillion times in the seven-minute commute. I knew I was on borrowed time.

The owner of the gym greeted us with his bulging biceps, fake-baked skin, and glowing-white teeth.

Michelle whispered, "Whoa."

I giggled. "Hey there Reggie! How's business today?"

"Good to see you, Alissa," he said. "It was busy earlier, but it tapered off this afternoon. Who's your friend?"

"This is Michelle Morehead; Michelle, this is Reggie. He's the brains and brawn behind this establishment." I watched them give awkward greetings and dropped the bomb. "I'd like to buy Michelle a year pass to the gym with all classes included." I flipped my purse open and avoided Michelle's dropped jaw.

"Alissa, you don't . . . I can't . . . that's a lot, Lis."

I handed Reggie my debit card. "Sure I can. It's not much, and I want to help you on your journey."

Reggie handed Michelle the application and a pen. "Sounds like you have a great friend, here, Michelle. Go ahead and fill this out, and I'll get you all set up. I'll throw in unlimited tanning, too. How does that sound?"

Michelle shook her head and bit her lip as her chin quivered. "Thank you," she whispered.

I winked at Reggie. "We're going to have a few more friends joining, too, so may I have a few class schedules to give them?"

Reggie slid the schedules toward me. "The 5:30 a.m. crunch class is full, but other than that, we have room in every other class."

"Oh, thank God," Michelle said. "I don't do anything at 5:30 a.m."

Then she whispered, "I still can't believe you're doing this."

"You're going to love it. I'm excited for you. Do you have time for a tour?"

Michelle looked at her watch. "A quick one should be fine."

"Reggie, do you mind if I do the honors while you're getting her stuff set up?"

"Be my guest," he said as he took the application from Michelle. "Just keep her out of the locker room, okay, Michelle?" He winked at me and turned his attention to the computer screen in front of him.

Michelle whispered, "Tell me there's no story behind you and the men's locker room."

I laughed. "No . . . not yet, anyway, but it's on my bucket list."

Michelle elbowed me and chuckled.

"Hey, you were the one saying you wanted an adventure. You never know what kind of stuff can happen at a gym."

"Scrogging in a men's locker room is low on my list."

"At least it made the list, my dear. Okay, so here are the machines. When we come back, I'll train you on how to use the machines . . ."

"Oh, good Lord, look at those guys," she said with bugging eyes. "I bet I'm at least twenty years older than them, but damn."

"The eye candy here is good." She chuckled. "I'm not a fool."

I showed her around the gym, gave her a quick explanation of how to check in and out, how to find the locker room, and showed her the tanning room. She checked her watch several times, so I wrapped it up and headed back toward Reggie.

"Here you go, Mrs. Morehead," he said. "This is your twenty-four hour pass; just slide it on the pad outside the door, and you'll get in. During business hours, check in here and try to be about ten minutes early for classes. Do you have any questions?"

"Nope, I'm all set. Thank you." She looked at me. "Ready?"

"Yep, let's get you home. Thanks Reggie!"

I dropped her off. "You're welcome," for the fortieth time in ten minutes. I watched as she half-ran/half-skipped through the front door and imagined her gushing to Brandon about her membership. It made me grin to see her so excited.

I checked my phone and sighed that I still hadn't heard from Mark. How is it possible that we could be inseparable for six months but now not hear a peep out of him? How can he just turn it off like that? I contemplated driving by his house but it's miles out of my way. If he happened to see me, he would know I was going stalker-chick and that would be bad.

A wave of nausea hit me again, so I took a few deep breaths to ward off the anxiety trying to surface. I was losing the battle, so I turned off my car and ran toward Michelle's house. I threw open the door and stopped when I heard Brandon and Michelle arguing in the kitchen. Gibson waved from the couch before he focused on the video game in his lap.

"I need to use your bathroom," I mumbled as I ran down through the living room to the bathroom.

The sounds of my retching echoed through the house, I'm sure. I shivered in disgust and when I was sure I was through, I washed my face in the sink and leaned against the wall. A soft knock on the door forced my eyes open. "I'll be right out," I said.

"Lis? You okay?" Michelle asked.

I opened the door. "Yeah, I guess something didn't set well." I pointed toward the kitchen and whispered, "What was that all about?"

Michelle waved me off and shrugged. "Brandon . . . you know how he is. Are you sure you're okay? You look very pale."

"Yeah, I'm okay."

"Why don't you lay down for a bit? You can use my bedroom, because it's not like anyone else is going to use it." She shouted down the hallway.

"Actually, I think I will. I feel awful."

"Come on. I'll get you set up."

She straightened the covers on the unmade bed and fluffed the pillows. "Climb on in, Lis. I'm going to get you a washcloth and a glass of ice water. Be right back."

I kicked off my shoes and crawled in bed. I felt my throat tighten and chin quiver. Tears pricked at my eyes, and no amount of fight was keeping them at bay.

Michelle returned. "Okay, this will fix you up— Lis? Are you *crying*? Why are you crying?"

I buried my face in the pillow and cried harder when I smelled Brandon's aftershave on the linen. "I'm going to be alone forever."

"No, you won't, Lis."

"He just wrote me off. No texts, no phone calls, no emails, just a big fat 'sayonara sweetheart' and poof—he's gone."

"Maybe he just needs some time to think things over. Maybe he just needs some space."

I sat up and wiped my face on my shirt. "He was pretty blunt in his email, Chelle. He's done. What is *wrong* with me? I'm a catch, right?"

"Yes, you are! I'd marry you." She smiled.

"But why didn't *he* want to marry me? I have enough money for three lifetimes; I'm fun and pretty. I'm successful and yet here I am at *your* house, puking in *your* toilet, laying in *your* bed. *You're* rubbing my back and bringing me ice water. Why can't I have someone to do those things for me? Am I damned?"

"Honey, having someone in the house isn't the end-all-be-all for life. Sometimes married people are the loneliest people on the planet."

I sighed and shook my head. "He said I was smothering him. He said I'm too needy and selfish and that I'd be better off finding someone who could tolerate my need for organized adventure better than he does."

"Which is code for, 'I'm satisfied with my boring life and don't want you challenging me to do things differently.' Lis, you said he was too stuffy and serious all the time. You don't want to be with someone like that. He'd suck the life out of you. Then you'd wake up an old woman wondering when you lost the thing that made you who you are."

"Is that really what marriage is like?"

A shadow fell across Michelle's face. She slumped and shrugged. "Sometimes? It doesn't start off that way, but somewhere along the way, years just fly by like mile markers on a highway." She brushed my hair

46

from my forehead. "I can count on one hand how many times I've seen you cry."

I snuggled into the covers and laid back on the pillows. "I hate to cry almost as much as I hate to puke." I closed my eyes and tried to open them and respond to the questions she was asking, but fatigue overtook me. Even the hurtful words from Mark's email couldn't dance before my mind's eye long enough to keep me awake.

Michelle

"Lis? Lis?" She was out cold. I slipped out of the room and walked down the hall to continue the silent treatment Brandon had coming to him. Del Ray was in her room, no doubt practicing her 'come hither' look in the mirror. Little jerk. I never should have let her shave the sides of her head and dye the top purple. And her black eyeliner was thick enough to pave our driveway.

I went to the refrigerator and pulled out an empty tea pitcher. I slammed it on the counter and pulled out a pan to make some more tea that I contemplated hiding from the rest of the freaks that have no clue about proper beverage etiquette.

Martin came into the kitchen and asked, "Mama, are you okay?"

I snapped, "Yeah, why?"

"I heard something slam in here and wanted to make sure you were okay."

I looked at his sweet face and smiled. "Come here, you." I wrapped him in my arms and rested my chin on his head. "When did you get so big?"

I felt him shrug and squeeze me tighter. I smiled in spite of myself. "Are you the punk that drank all the tea?"

He shook his head. "No, but Gib was in here earlier."

Gibson yelled from the living room, "I was not! I got water."

"Ten bucks says it was your sister." I craned my head and yelled toward her room, "Maybe we should ask the Magic 8 ball about *that*!" I smoothed Martin's cowlick and kissed the top of his head. "You doing okay today, bud?"

He nodded but still held onto me. He whispered, "I heard you and Dad fighting."

I lowered my mouth to his ear and whispered back, "It's all good, Martin. Don't you worry a thing about it. Sometimes adults fight. No big deal." My heart sank when he held me tighter. Martin was always troubled when Brandon and I fought, which only managed to get me more pissed off at his father for being a raging douchebag over Alissa's gift. "Any idea what you want for dinner tonight?"

Martin shrugged. "I really don't care."

I pulled away and got eye-level with him. I weaved my head back and forth until he looked me in the eyes and grinned. "How about fried chicken? That's still your favorite, right?"

Martin grinned. "Come on, I'm not *that* picky."

I smiled and hugged him again. "Just checking. Now go do boy things until I call you for dinner."

Brandon sauntered into the kitchen and huffed. "If she can afford to spend hundreds of dollars on a stupid gym membership, then why can't she call a cab if she's too drunk to drive home?"

I wheeled around and stared him down. "She's not *drunk*, you idiot, she's sick. Again with the gym membership. God forbid someone does a random act of kindness and I actually get to enjoy it."

"Now, dammit, Michelle, it's not because she did something nice for *you*. It's because she just throws her money around like 'oh look at me, I'm an oil tycoon's ex-wife.'" He threw his hands around and sashayed through the kitchen. "It's like she just rubs it in every chance she gets."

"Did it ever occur to you that she doesn't have anyone else to share it with? And if I remember correctly, you were the one who encouraged me to call her up and ask her to take me to the bar because she 'has more money than God.'"

"Well this gym thing is only going to stress you out. You're always

48

complaining you don't have enough time in the day as it is and here you are getting ready to schedule time away from your family to go—"

"To go do something for myself, Brandon! To do something for *me*. Do I complain when you're off in the garage playing your guitars?"

"Yes! All the time!"

"Ugh, you're so full of shit." I flung open the refrigerator door and grabbed a packet of chicken. I slammed the door and magnets went flying.

"Oh, that's nice. Good job. Why don't you tear it up and have your sugar mama replace it, because I sure the hell can't."

"Is that what this is all about? You're pissed because Alissa did something for me that you can't?" I slammed the chicken on the counter and tore off the packaging.

Brandon sighed and picked up the magnets. "Maybe," he mumbled.

"Brandon, Alissa and I have been friends long before she became wealthy, and she was always the kind of person who would give her last dollar to any one of us who was struggling." I paused from cutting the chicken and pointed the knife at him. "And if you remember, she bailed us out more than once when the house was on the line after Del Ray was born. She didn't have that money then but she did it anyway."

"Yes, and we paid it back, too."

"Fine! Then pay back the gym membership! Good God, why is everything such a freaking *issue* with you?"

"I'm not paying for that membership because we didn't discuss it first, Michelle."

I slammed my fists on the counter and screamed, "Enough!"

Martin came into the kitchen with his chin quivering and yelled, "Will you two just stop? Just get a divorce already and stop screaming at each other all the time!" He ran through the kitchen and out the back door slamming the door after him.

I stared blankly at Brandon whose slumped shoulders and face registered how I was feeling. My throat tightened as tears stung my eyes. I whispered, "Is that what you want?"

Brandon rubbed the back of his neck and looked up at me. "Do

49

you?"

I shook my head and whispered, "No."

He shook his head and mumbled, "Me neither."

I leaned over the sink and washed my hands as the tears dripped from my face into the suds on my hands. "I'll go talk to him."

Brandon walked up behind me and wrapped his arms around my waist. He rested his chin on my shoulder then kissed my cheek. "I'm still mad at you."

I nodded my head and whispered, "I'm still mad at you, too. I'll tell her I can't accept the membership."

"No, don't. What's done is done. Maybe you need some time away from all this. But I would appreciate it if you don't point knives at me anymore when you're pissed."

I chuckled. "I didn't mean it like that."

"Still. My balls are still in my rib cage at the moment. One good sneeze and I'll be good as new."

I laughed, dried my hands, and turned to face him. "I really need to do something by myself so I don't get like this. It's not personal to you, honey. But there's only so much I can take and I think the workouts will help me decompress."

"We'll give it a shot and see how it goes."

I felt myself bristle but decided we'd had enough arguing today, so I let it go. "I'm going to go find Martin. Check on Gibson, will ya? Make sure he's not freaked out too. I doubt Del Ray had her earbuds out long enough to hear us."

He pulled away and walked into the living room. I heard him say, "You okay, buddy?" I heard Gibson mumble but couldn't make out what he said. I dried my hands on my pants and wiped my face on my shirt. I sighed and looked out the kitchen window for Martin. He was such a predictable child; he was sitting in the same tree he's gone to every time he's been upset since he was five.

I made sure Brandon had engaged Gibson then slipped out the back door. The boards on the porch sagged under my weight, which reminded me we still needed to get an estimate to have it replaced. After Brandon's tantrum, I figured now wasn't the time to address it. I was sure Martin couldn't take another argument any more than I could. I looked over the backyard and was overwhelmed with how ratty it looked. Faded and long-abandoned toys littered the sand box that hadn't had a refill in two years——a result of another Michelle tantrum after the repeated dumping shoes full of sand onto my freshly mopped floor.

I don't know how someone like me was ever allowed to take children home from the hospital.

The half-built clubhouse leaned under the tree Martin had climbed. We were counting on Brandon's bonus last year to finish it, but the company had a rough year and didn't hand out bonuses. We got a good start on the floor and posts, but the lumber for the roof and walls is still at the store. I told Brandon we should wait and buy it all at once, but he was certain the bonus was coming.

I swatted at a mosquito on my leg and walked to the tree. I grabbed a branch over my head and leaned forward until I could look up and see his face. He used his shoulder to wipe a tear as he gazed toward the neighbor's yard.

"Are you going to talk to me, Martin?"

"I hate it when you fight."

"I know. It's a small house, so you can hear way more than we think. But we aren't getting a divorce, Martin, and I don't want to hear you say that again, got it?"

He sniffled and nodded. "What's up with the gym thing?"

I sighed. "Alissa bought me a gym membership today, and——"

His head snapped up. "Really? Can I go, too? I wanna go with you."

"Well, I'm not sure *I'm* going to get to go, now," I chuckled. "Your dad has a good point; I don't know when I'll get to go, and I think the pass is just for me." I looked away and tried not to choke on the guilt that clawed at my throat. This must have been on Brandon's mind when he got so pissed——no one in my family would benefit from this gift but me. I remembered a conversation we had at tax time a few years ago. We discussed getting a family pass to a recreation center near our house that had something for the whole family, but we decided to pay off a bill instead. Unfortunately, we'd already talked to the kids about it, so they were extremely disappointed when we had to tell them "maybe next year" yet again.

I squeezed my eyes shut and bit my lip. I looked at Martin who was back to staring at the neighbor's yard. "What do you see over there, kiddo?"

"A trampoline. They've had it all summer but I've never seen anyone on it. Jackson has one and it's so fun to jump on, but I never see anyone in that yard playing on it."

"Maybe you could ask if you could jump on it for a while."

He shook his head. "I did already but they said no. It's for family only."

I stared at the tennis shoes on his feet and wondered how long his little toe had been sticking out of the hole in the side. "Looks like we need to get you some new shoes, huh?"

He looked down and shrugged. "Yeah, I guess."

Suddenly I felt like the most selfish person on the face of the earth. How could I justify spending more time away from my family when I've been too busy to notice my own son's torn-up shoes——the same shoes I've picked up and chucked into his room day after day. How did I not know Martin wanted a trampoline? How did I not know Del Ray was going through sex-ed in school? Where had my mind been?

I blinked back tears. "Do you want to help me cook dinner?"

His eyes lit up. "Really?"

"Sure! You can't cook the chicken, but I'll show you how to make everything else. Want to?"

He turned, grabbed a branch, and jumped out of the tree, landing a few feet in front of me. He jumped and clapped his hands. "What all are we going to have?"

I threw my arm around him and herded him toward the house. "Well, mashed potatoes are mandatory; you always have mashed potatoes with fried chicken. It's in the bible."

Martin giggled. "It is not."

"Okay, maybe not, but it's a must in this house. I'll let you pick the vegetable and bread. Deal?"

"Deal."

I stopped and turned to face him. "Martin, I'll try to do better, okay? I'll talk to your dad, and we'll both try to do better. I promise."

He grinned. "Okay, Mom."

"I love you very much. We both do. We don't want you to be unhappy."

His tiny arms came around my waist. "I love you too."

Chapter Seven
Chasing Pavements

Chance

Dani and I didn't stick around the bar much longer after the others left. She got a call from Barry saying he needed to speak with her at the house, so she took her food to-go, and I headed home.

Chubs, my sweet little pug, greeted me at the door. "There's my boy!" I dropped to my knees and gathered him in my arms. "Oh he's so cute. Oh, he's *so cute*! Do you need to go potty?" He wiggled in my arms and licked my face. "Not on the face, dude." I stood up and grabbed his leash.

One thing about living on the third floor of an apartment building, Chubs and I get a workout just walking up and down the stairs to go for a walk. I hadn't caught my breath from coming up by the time we were heading back down. But it was a gorgeous late afternoon, so I didn't mind the walk as much as I do when it's raining or sub-zero temperatures. Chubs gets snobbish about pottying outside anyway. That's miserable for both of us.

I love where I live. It's such a peaceful apartment complex with the personal touch——not like so many of the complexes in town that have that stale, gated look to them. Every building had similar floor plans but the outside of the buildings were different colors and shaped like houses. Then the landscape designers were meticulous in their designs to give each building its own identity. Very clever.

Perhaps my favorite part of the complex was the common area courtyard. The designers wanted to give this area an Italian feel and they nailed it. Every time I step out the back door, I'm transported to an Italian villa filled with climbing vines, manicured trees, stone paths, and strategically-placed black iron tables and chairs. A few wooden benches line the paths and provide a perfect area for marriage proposals if you catch the moment. I've seen three so far this year; one poor bastard's answer was laughter. That was uncomfortable even for me standing three floors up on my balcony. I can't imagine how humiliated *he* was, not to mention heartbroken. Judging by her reaction, I'm not even convinced they'd been dating at all.

Chubs and I walked to the doggie playground (I told you——this complex has everything.) and waited for two Labs to be leashed up before I opened the gate to the fenced-in area. Once they were out and the small talk was completed, I secured the gate behind me and let Chubs off the leash. Watching him scamper around and put on a show always made me grin no matter how many times I'd seen him do it before.

My eyes wandered to the beautiful square pavilion in the middle of the courtyard where Tony and I decided to part ways a little over a year ago. We were on two different paths, and neither one of us were willing to let go of our lives already in progress to pursue what we hoped would be a magical life filled with nothing normal and everything exhilarating.

Tony came to me that day with an offer he said I couldn't refuse. He wanted me to relocate to St. Louis where he lived and get a slot on the six o'clock news. Rumor had it the current co-anchor was planning to make his golf game his full-time job after thirty-nine years on the air, and the station wanted a sassy co-anchor to liven up the news. As the executive producer, Tony was sure I would land the job with the first interview.

I met Tony three years ago at a fundraising ball in St. Louis. He was breathtakingly handsome in his tuxedo, but honestly, what guy isn't? I was leaning against the bar sipping on my third amaretto sour and watching local television's finest make fools of themselves during the dance competition portion of the gala. Each station had a representative on the floor. Thank God Jack Woodrow took one for the team and represented KJAT.

Tony walked to the bar and ordered a Crown and Coke. He leaned over to read my nametag. "Chance? That's an unusual name."

"It's a long story." I chuckled.

He grabbed his drink and turned to face the dance-off. I laughed as Jack took his turn in the circle during "Wipeout". Tony asked, "You know that guy?"

"Unfortunately. He's my co-anchor."

Tony's eyes lit up. "Well, that explains it."

"What's that?" I asked.

He looked at me. "A face that beautiful has to be on television or in magazines. I was wondering which was which."

I smirked. "Do you guys get pulled into class during high school and coached on the worst pick-up lines to use at bars?"

Tony tossed his head back and laughed. "I'd love to say that was a pick-up line, but I'm here with someone. I merely spoke the truth, Miss Chance."

My smile and ego deflated, but I recovered quickly. "Okay, as long as you're being truthful, I'll thank you for the compliment."

Tony tilted his head again and looked at me longer than my comfort level could tolerate. I glanced at the dance floor then looked back at him.

"Let's play a game," he said. "You try to figure out who I'm here with and if you're right, I'll leave you alone. But if you're wrong, you have to tell me the story behind your name."

"Oh come on! There are hundreds of people here tonight."

"Fine, I'll give you three chances."

I winked at him. "You only need one Chance."

"I can absolutely believe that. Three guesses——go."

I scanned the crowd looking for a woman that would be worthy of such a handsome escort. "Do I have a time limit?"

Tony looked at his watch. "Yep, forty-five seconds left."

"What? You didn't tell me that part."

"You're losing seconds arguing, Miss Chance. Thirty-eight seconds left."

I sighed and saw a thin woman sitting at a table wearing a silver dress. She looked bored and eager to leave the event. "Her," I said as I tried not to be obvious with my gesture.

Tony followed my gaze. "Nope, but I like your taste. Go again. Twenty-two seconds."

"What about the tall brunette on the floor in the red dress?"

"No, but I've dated her before. She's a nut case. That's two, my lady. You're going to lose."

"I don't lose, Tony," I said as I looked at his nametag.

His eyes raised to mine at the mention of his name. Then he grinned. "You're about to. Ten seconds."

I pointed to an older woman sitting at the table closest to us on the outskirts of the dance floor. "That's your date."

His jaw dropped open. "Are you kidding me?"

I grinned. "I'm a reporter. I have taken mental inventory of all guests and their dates already. But thank you for playing, Mr. Tony."

He dropped his hand to his side and took a drink. "Unbelievable."

I shrugged. "You can't win them all."

He leaned toward my ear and whispered, "The game is just beginning, Chance." He pulled away and smiled before he walked toward the woman at the table.

"Holy shit," I mumbled to myself as I took a deep breath to calm the electricity racing through my body. I finished my drink and ordered another one. My hotel room was upstairs and my three-inch heels were built for drunk stumbling, so I was solid.

Later in the evening, the emcee for the event announced a special dance in honor of the late Chester Agustin who was a prominent presence in the media field and large supporter of the fundraiser. "Please welcome Mrs. Chester Agustin, also known as Lydia, and her son, Tony, to the floor, please."

I shook my head and smiled in spite of myself as I put down my drink and clapped. Tony gathered his mother in his arms, looked through the crowd until he found me and grinned——quite satisfied with himself. I smiled and nodded my head in capitulation. I watched them dance for a moment then excused myself to the ladies' room. Jack barely acknowledged me, as he was deep in conversation with another anchor.

I stopped by the bar on my way back through and there was Tony. "Are you here to gloat?"

He just grinned. "Maybe just a little. I wish I could have seen your face when they announced her name."

"Well played, Sir Tony." I laughed.

"So, I lost the game, but I won with the surprise. That makes us even right now. Shall we go for three?"

"What do you have in mind?" My words sounded thick in my head, so I'm sure they were slurred when they came out.

"Dance with me."

I nearly choked on my drink. "Come again? You want me to dance with you?"

"Yes, that will give me an opportunity to think about what our next challenge will be while killing the incredible desire I have to hold you in my arms."

I blinked hard and cleared my throat. "Wow, Sir Tony, you have quite the game."

"The only game I'm playing is the one to win the secret of your name, Miss Chance. I'm dead serious about the rest."

"I think you've had one too many and should switch to water." My heart's pounding was certainly visible in my low-cut black dress. I put my hand on my necklace to make sure it wasn't bouncing up and down with each beat.

He followed my hand to my necklace. "That's very pretty." Then his eyes met mine. "Shall we dance?"

I stood up taller and put my drink on the bar. "Yes, let's dance."

Tony placed his drink next to mine and put his hand in the small of my back. God, I love it when men do that.

We walked to the dance floor when Tony said, "I'll be right back."

I waited at the edge of the dance floor for the song to end and watched as Tony went to the deejay and whispered in his ear. The fast music faded, and the deejay said, "We're going to slow it down, folks. Grab a partner and enjoy this beautiful song by request from Tony Agustin dedicated to the lovely Chance Bradley."

I shook my head and Tony's outstretched hand invited me to the dance floor. "May I have this dance?"

I slipped my hand into his and followed him to the center of the room. Elton John's song, "Something about the Way You Look

Tonight," flooded the room and my heart did a double take as it swooned with the dedication from Tony.

"I love this song."

"It's pretty perfect." He pulled me to him and wrapped his arm around my back. "Ah, that's better."

I smiled. "I'm glad I'm wearing heels." My chin touched his shoulder, the perfect height to talk to him without killing my neck.

We danced in silence through the first chorus, and then Tony found his voice. "There's something magnetic about you, Chance."

"And you're extremely charming when you're trying to woo, but what do you do for fun?"

"I stalk women I find fascinating. I'll need your address before you leave tonight."

I laughed. "You would have quite the commute to make that happen, Sir Tony. I live in Columbia."

"See? You just told me where you live. I'll probably be back at your house before you are tomorrow."

I laughed again. "Just don't boil my dog on the stove, okay? I love that little guy."

He pulled away to look at me. My heart stopped beating, and I held my breath. "I want to see you again, Chance."

"I'm sure we can make that happen." I took my place against his body. He smelled so good and I heard the earth sigh with me. I was a goner.

As I stood in the doggie playground looking at the pavilion, I felt the weight of regret drape over me. We'd been perfect together in every way, and I blew it. I blew it.

Chubs pranced over to me and announced he was ready for his treat. I gathered up his offering in a plastic bag, tossed it into the trashcan and attached the leash to his collar. "Come on, baby, let's go in and see what Mommy has for dinner."

I walked past the pavilion and could see Tony and me sitting at the table discussing our future. I saw the pleading in his eyes as he begged me to reconsider his offer. He wanted me to move in with him, but after my three previous dry runs, I knew that was not something that was in the cards for me.

His was an all-or-nothing offer, though. No matter how much I loved him, I couldn't take the risk that it would end up like all the other failed relationships had with me finding another place to live, dividing our belongings and discovering that all we had worked for was dissolving like fog in sunlight.

They say you never really know someone until you live with them; truer words were never spoken. Unfortunately, these are undiscovered realizations until you actually bite the bullet and try. Things with Tony were so perfect, and I never wanted to lose it, but in the end I lost him anyway.

I don't talk to my friends about this because I don't want to hear it. I don't want to see Katie's hope-filled eyes encouraging me to man-up and go find him. I don't want to see Michelle's told-ya-so head swivel or hear Alissa's battle cry for action. I could talk to Dani about it, but she would be too logical and would probably support my decision to stay in Columbia. It's easier for everyone if I let them think I'm over him and too annoyed with relationships to take another chance.

In truth, I don't want another man. I want Tony. I don't want another man's hands on my body, another man's attention, another man's devotion. I just want Tony. That's what I have to live with.

Chapter Eight
You Oughta Know

Alissa

I woke up feeling horrible again Monday morning, so I called in sick to work and made an appointment with my doctor. God, I hope I didn't wait too long for that flu shot. I don't have time to be hugging toilets and sleeping the day away. When I got home from Michelle's, I went home, ate some soup, and went straight to bed.

I checked my phone and responded to a few email questions from my assistant, Cynthia, then told her I would be unavailable the rest of the day. She's a smart cookie, so I trust her to call me if she needs me.

I sent a text to my girls: *Hey, have any of you been sick and shared your funk with me? I'm dying, just so you know.*

Chance was the first to respond: *Quit fondling bartenders and you won't get cooties. ;) Feel better soon, honey.*

Katie was next: *Oh no! Are you still sick? Do you need me to bring you anything?*

Dani said: *I've been healthy, but there's an unusual flu virus going around right now. Better get it checked out.*

Michelle didn't respond, but she can't when she's with the kids at the daycare. I didn't bother to respond to the texts, not that I had time before another wave of nausea sent me running to the bathroom.

My appointment was at eleven-thirty, but by eleven, I was certain I was doomed for the hospital, so I called Chance.

"Hey, girl, how are you feeling?" she asked.

I sniffled and cleared my throat. "I can't drive. Can you come get me? My appointment is in thirty minutes."

"Sure, I'll be over in a minute."

I hung up and jumped in the shower to wash the stench of illness off my body. I was dressed with my wet hair in a ponytail when Chance came in the front door.

"Lis? I'm here."

I walked down the hallway to join her in the living room. "I'm not going to hug you even though I want to. Thanks for coming."

"I have rubber gloves and a mask for you to wear. It's nothing personal. It's for my own protection."

I chuckled. "Can we just go, please?"

In the car I reclined the seat to prevent an unfortunate mishap in Chance's nice car. She didn't talk to me, and I was grateful for it.

When we pulled into the parking lot of the doctor's office, she asked, "Want me to stick around?"

"Yeah, if you can. I might need you to take my last will and testament before I die."

She laughed and turned off the car. "You're probably just hung over but I won't tell anyone."

I scoffed. "I would never do such a thing . . . twice."

After I checked in, Chance and I sat in the waiting room. She looked sideways at me. "You really look like hell, Lis. If you're dying, can I have your bank account?"

"Which one?" I chuckled.

"Any one of your accounts would probably set me up for life. I don't want to be greedy, but I want the one with the most money in it——to mourn appropriately over your passing, of course."

I shook my head and sighed. "I should have called Katie."

"Yeah, probably, but this is way more fun for me than sitting at work. Have you heard anything out of Mark, yet?"

Her words stung like a slap; I even winced. "Nope, not a peep." Tears welled up in my eyes and I blinked hard to make them go away.

"Man, he must have really got to you. I thought he was just 'okay,' but you're taking this harder than you've been letting on."

I sniffled and reached for a tissue. "I just don't feel well. It's messing with my emotions."

"Mmhmm, you know, Lis, I can be sympathetic to heartbreak."

I laughed. "Since when?"

She shrugged. "Good point. Hey, I made that CD for you,

remember? I can be a good friend. We just need to go shoe shopping, and you'll be good as new."

The nurse stepped into the waiting room and called my name. I stood up. "Back in a flash, I hope."

"Want me to go back with you?"

"Nah, I'm just going to get told it's a virus and a flu shot. I'm wasting my time, but I'm still miserable. And probably dying."

Chance chuckled. "You're not dying. Go get better." She pulled out her cell phone and I walked toward the nurse.

After the nurse took my temperature, blood pressure, and weight she said, "Well, the good news is you don't have a fever."

I did a double take. "Really? That's surprising."

"What was the date of your last period?"

I thought for a second. "I don't know. I'd have to look at a calendar."

"Are you sexually active? Any chance you could be pregnant?"

I laughed. "No. I mean yes, but no, that's not possible."

"Do you mind if we go ahead and do a urine sample just to check?"

"Sure, but you're wasting your time. I'm not pregnant; I'm dying of a rare strand of flu."

The nurse laughed and handed me a cup. "The bathroom is around the corner. Leave the sample on the sink." I followed her toward the bathroom and watched as she dropped my chart in the holder near a door across the hall. "When you're done, have a seat in that room and the doctor will be in shortly."

I followed orders and sat in the room waiting. I sent Chance a text: *I'm still alive. Don't start spending my money yet.*

Canceling my trip to Tahiti this afternoon, now. Thanks for being selfish.

I chuckled. *I had to give a pee sample. Remind me to shake your hand when I come out.*

You're nasty. LOL

The doctor came in. "Good morning, Alissa. Not feeling so hot, huh?"

"No, and my greedy friend in the waiting room is ready to spend my money if you tell me I'm dying."

She laughed. "Well, no, you're not dying." She looked in my ears, eyes, and throat. "How long have you been sick?"

"A few days."

"Is it constant, or does it come and go? What's been going on?"

"It comes and goes. I've been throwing up everything I eat and sleeping like twelve hours a day, which is so unlike me. I have no energy."

She flipped open my chart, made a few notes, and then she looked at me. "Alissa, your urine test came back positive. You're not dying of the flu, you're pregnant."

The words slammed into my chest like a sledgehammer as the room started spinning. "Please tell me you're joking."

"No, it was very positive according to Lori. We can do a blood test to make sure, but I think it would be overkill. I take it this was not planned."

Pregnant. I'm pregnant. Oh God, no . . . "No, this was not planned. My boyfriend and I just broke up. How can this be happening? I can't be pregnant!"

"You have options if this was not planned." She stood and slipped a set of pamphlets in my hand. "I have other patients waiting for me, but stay in here as long as you need."

"Thank you," I whispered as I sat up. "I'm fine." I put my hand on my belly and tried to feel the life that had intertwined with mine two minutes earlier. "How far along am I?"

"Well, without knowing when the date of your last period was, I would have no way of guessing. We can set you up with an ultrasound to find out if you like."

I nodded. "Please. Can we do it today?"

She smiled. "I doubt it, but it will be soon. The scheduling department will call you and let you know."

She shook my hand and helped me off the table. My whole body felt numb and I didn't trust my legs to hold my body in position. I steadied

64

myself against the table then walked out of the room.

Chance glanced at me and did a double take. She stood and raced across the floor. "Lis? What'd they say? God, you look like you're going to pass out. Are you okay? Sit down. Here, sit down, Lis."

I felt my chin quiver as I looked at her and whispered, "I'm pregnant, Chance."

The blood drained from her face. "I need to sit down." She slammed into the chair next to me and we sat staring at the same awful painting of a mallard duck sitting on a piece of driftwood.

"Pregnant," she whispered.

"Yeah," I said.

"I'm not the father, you know."

I chuckled through my tears then laughed harder every time I thought about it. My eyes wandered to a toddler trying to pull up on his mother's leg and swaying back and forth before flopping to the floor. Tears flowed down my face as I said, "Get me out of here, Chance."

She stood and grabbed my arm then led me out the door to the car. "Well, at least you're not puking."

"My whole body is numb. I wouldn't feel it if a truck hit me right now."

"I'm right there with ya, sister. My house or yours?"

"Mine since we know it's not contaminated. I'm pretty sure you can't catch pregnancy."

The words fell in the car like a banging gong. Pregnancy. Baby. Nine months. Maternity clothes, stretch marks, cravings . . . my mind was spinning out of control as Chance pulled out of the parking lot.

She pointed to the pamphlets sticking out of my purse. "What are those?"

"I don't know. She said I had options and handed them to me. I just stuck them in the first place I figured wouldn't hurt."

"Glad you didn't file them in the doctor."

"I didn't have time to think about that. Turn around."

Chance giggled. "Are you hungry? Think you can eat right now?"

"I need a drink," I said.

"No-can-do, little mama. Those days are over unless you want to pickle your little private guest."

I laughed until my stomach hurt. "No, no pickling the private guest. I could go for something light——maybe a sandwich place that has soup. Do growing babies like soup?"

"Sweet, I know just the place. I don't know what growing babies eat." She laughed.

"Chance, I'm going to have a baby."

She sighed. "Good lord, that sounds so foreign coming out of your mouth."

"Do you know how babies are born? My junk will be ripped to shreds! I'll probably be able to toss my vagina over my shoulder during shopping trips after this."

Chance laughed. "Look, Michelle and Katie have both had babies, and their va-ja-jas don't hang low. You'll be fine. We have lots of time before that happens."

She pulled into the parking lot and turned off the car as she looked at me. "You okay?"

"No, I'm not okay. Chance, what the hell am I going to say to Mark? How did this happen?"

"Do you really need me to explain that to you?"

"No, Captain Obvious, I do not need you to explain *how* I got pregnant, but how did I get *pregnant*?"

"Were you using protection or contraceptives?"

"I can't even think right now. We had sex so much I don't even know when it could have happened. I have to go in for an ultrasound to see how far along I am."

"Come on, let's get something to eat."

I opened my car door and grabbed my purse. The pamphlets stuck out the side, so I flipped through them to see what jewels the little doctor had slipped me. As we walked across the parking lot, I read the titles aloud to Chance. "'What Next: Preparing for Pregnancy.' A little late for that one. No preparations just whammo—'you're pregnant.'"

"Keep that one. You'll want to read that when you're not in shock."

"'Is Abortion Right for You?'" I looked at Chance who looked at me. "It's something to consider," I whispered.

Her shoulders sagged and her head fell as she opened the door for me. "Lis, you know I've always been pro-choice, but you really need to think about that."

I shoved the pamphlets in my purse. "I can't deal with this shit right now." I wiped a few stray tears off my face and smoothed my shirt. "Let's see if we can find something the private guest won't reject."

Chance took the rest of the day off and sat on the couch with me watching movies and waiting for the other girls to get off work. I sent a *911-need my girls ASAP* text. Katie, Dani, and Michelle said they'd be at my house by five-thirty. Chance and I made a bet that Michelle would be first, followed by Dani, and then Katie would call last minute and say she couldn't make it because Landon had something else going on. Much to my surprise, Katie was fifteen minutes early, Michelle was second, and Dani brought up the tail three minutes later.

After our greetings, we all sat in my living room with their expectant eyes looking at me.

Chance was the first to break the ice. "Wow, this is a record number of times we've all been in the same room this often in I-don't-know how long."

Katie didn't fall for it. "Alissa, what did the doctor say today? Are you ill?" Her chin trembled.

I took a deep breath. "Yes, but not like I thought." My voice cracked as fresh tears rolled over my cheeks.

"Oh God, it's not cancer, is it?" Michelle asked.

I chuckled. "No, it's not cancer. I'm . . . I'm pregnant."

Three jaws dropped open, and all of the air in the room went into the lungs of my closest friends who all started speaking at once. "Holy shit! Are you serious? Jesus, Mary, and Joseph."

I buried my head in my hands. "I know! I don't know how this happened."

"What did Mark say?" Katie asked.

I shook my head. "I haven't told him, yet."

"Are you going to?" Chance asked.

I looked at her. "I don't know."

Michelle interrupted. "What do you mean you're not going to tell him? You have to tell him. He can't have a baby out there and—" She caught herself and leaned back against the couch. "You're not going to have an abortion, are you?"

I shrugged and tossed the pamphlets from the doctor on the table in front of her. "Oh, I have all kinds of 'options' according to this shit."

Michelle grabbed the pamphlets and flipped through them before she slammed them in her lap. "This shit pisses me off. They're children! Babies! And they treat them like they're disposable."

Chance looked at me. "Michelle, not now, okay?"

"If not now, when?" Katie yelled. "She has a big decision to make, and look at Dani! She'd give her right tit to be in Alissa's position right now, and I think it's pretty fucking insensitive to even discuss abortion in her presence."

Michelle's face brightened as she gasped. "Oh! Alissa! Give it to Dani!"

I looked at Dani who stared at the pillow on her lap. Her expression was blank, but her face showed the pure anguish resting in her chest. She sighed. "It's not that simple, Michelle."

"Why isn't it?" Chelle looked at me and shrugged. "Why isn't it that easy? You're going to have a baby; she wants a baby—you don't. You're as close as sisters can be without the shared uterus."

Dani looked at me. "I would never ask you to do that, Lis. This isn't like borrowing a dress or a car. This is a human life—your life for the next however-many months. I want you to do what's best for you," she whispered as she wiped tears from her face. "I need some air." She stood and went to the back porch.

Chance looked at Michelle who stared back at her. "What?"

"Michelle, sometimes you just don't think before you speak, do you?" She stood up and stormed off to talk to Dani.

Michelle looked at Katie and shrugged. "What? It's a great solution."

She looked at me. "Lis, you have an opportunity right now to give Dani the best gift ever."

"What if I can't go through with it in the end?" I cried. "What if I go through this and decide I'm going to keep it?"

Michelle sat back and sighed. "I didn't think about that. God, I'm an idiot."

Katie patted her hand. "You're not an idiot, Michelle. It's a great idea, but Alissa's right. Can you imagine handing off one of your kids when they were born?"

She threw her hand in my direction. "Yeah but it's not like she'll never see the little guy ever again. She could be as involved as she wants to be."

I stood up. "I need to go lie down. Lock up when you're done, here."

I walked down the hallway and tried to imagine a baby crawling toward me with a dirty diaper. I looked at the guest rooms and tried to envision cribs, playpens, and changing tables. The thought of twins solidified my need to lie down.

Chapter Nine
Don't Speak

Michelle

As I drove home, I wondered if I had any friends left after the biggest open-mouth-insert-foot moment in my life. Chance and Dani were still on the back porch when Katie and I slipped out the front. Sometimes I wish I could stop thoughts in my head from becoming words out of my mouth.

I walked in the front door of the house and saw Gibson, Martin, and Brandon sitting on the L-shaped sectional watching television.

Gibson sighed. "Thank God you're home. We're starving!"

I frowned and looked at Brandon. "You didn't cook supper?"

He snapped, "No, I didn't know you were going to be gone this long."

I pointed to the clock. "It is six-thirty, Brandon!" He slammed the remote on the couch cushion and stood up. Martin fidgeted in his seat and looked at me. I put my purse and keys on the floor by the door. "Don't worry about it. I'll whip something up quick-like. Go ahead and sit down." I smiled at Martin. "Hey, buddy. What are you watching?"

He smiled. "Discovery Channel."

I gave him a thumbs up and kissed Gibson on the forehead. "Hey kiddo. Put down that game and do something else for a while, okay?"

He groaned but complied. I ignored Brandon's stare and went into the kitchen to pilfer through the fridge to see what was easy and fast to make. Trying to honor my promise to Martin, I didn't slam things around and say the forty-eight hateful things running through my mind toward Brandon. But, oh, I thought them.

There weren't enough leftovers for the whole family, so I grabbed pork chops out of the freezer and threw them in the microwave to thaw. I turned on the oven and went to the cupboard to see what I could make to go with it.

Brandon came into the kitchen and asked, "What are you making?"

"Pork chops and stuffing," I said as I grabbed the box out of the cupboard.

"That'll take a while," he said.

I slammed the box on the countertop and glared at him. Martin's face came to mind, so I took a deep breath. "Nah, thirty minutes tops. Did you have a good day?"

He picked up the box of stuffing and examined the label as he shrugged. "It wasn't bad. Didn't do much really. Got to play nine holes with a potential client, so that was good."

I'm certain steam was rolling out of my ears. I turned to the beeping microwave and rotated the pork chops. "You went golfing today?"

"Yeah, I sucked as usual." He put the box down.

Martin brought some papers into the kitchen. "Mom, will you help me with my homework? I can't figure out this math problem."

I yelled to Gibson, "Gib, is your homework all done?"

"Not yet. I just need to study my spelling words."

I leveled my eyes at Brandon. "What time did you get home?"

"Around four, I think. Why?" He grabbed the tea pitcher out of the refrigerator, drained it until there was an inch left in the bottom and put it back in the fridge.

I slammed my hand against the closing refrigerator door and snatched the pitcher. I waved it in front of Brandon. "Can a family of five drink this for supper?"

"It'll probably be easy for you since you're good at math," Martin said.

"I'm in the middle of making dinner, bud. I'll help you after we eat, but right now I need to focus on this so I don't burn it." I turned to look at Brandon. "Unless, of course, you would like to contribute to your son's education and help him."

Brandon threw up his hands. "Oh no, I can't do that new math crap," he said as he walked into the living room.

"Then help Gibson with his spelling!" I yelled to his back. I heard the front door close and squinted my eyes tightly.

When I opened them, Martin was staring at me. "Are you okay, Mom?"

I turned to the sink and rinsed the tea pitcher then started a pot of water boiling. "Yep, I'm good. Tell me about your day."

He leaned against the counter. "It was okay." He picked up the box of stuffing. "This can be microwaved. Want me to fix it?"

I caught the sob in my throat and choked it down. I whispered, "Thank you, honey. That would be awesome. Just follow the directions for the microwave." I reached over his head and pulled a bowl out of the cabinet. "Use this and follow the directions."

Del Ray sauntered into the kitchen. "Hi Mom." She opened the refrigerator and asked, "Where's the tea?"

I gritted my teeth. "I'm making some more." I grabbed the pork chops out of the microwave to prep for baking.

She closed the door. "How was your day?"

"It was okay."

"What was the big emergency with Alissa?" she asked as she grabbed the tea bags out of the cupboard and started dipping three tea bags in the nearly boiling water. "Is that water in the pitcher ready for the tea?"

"Yeah don't forget the sugar or there will be a riot." I winked at her. "Thank you for helping." New tears stung at my eyes. I finished seasoning the pork chops and put them in the oven.

"So what's the deal with Alissa?" she asked again.

I shrugged. "She got some news today that was pretty shocking, so she needed her friends."

"Is she okay?" She poured the sugar in the hot tea then dumped it in the tea pitcher.

"Yeah, she's okay. It's private, so I can't talk about it, but she's fine. But thanks for asking." I grinned at her and touched the shaved side of her head. "Doesn't this itch?"

She laughed. "No, I think it feels pretty cool. The purple is fading faster than I hoped, so I'll have to do it again this weekend."

"Oh great. I can't wait to lose the bathroom for two hours again."

"Oh whatever. You should let me dye your hair too."

"I can't imagine how much your father would love that." However, the idea of pissing him off held a vast appeal to me.

Martin was done with the stuffing. "I think this is ready to go, Mom."

"Okay, put it in the microwave but don't turn it on. We'll cook it about five minutes before the pork chops are done."

"Wanna do this math homework now?"

I leaned over to see if Brandon had snuck back in, but he was probably in the garage cleaning his golf clubs. I sighed. "Sure. Do you have a pencil?" He waved one in front of my face. "Okay, have a seat at the table."

I had just finished helping Martin with his worksheet when the timer went off announcing the pork chops were ready. It was seven fifteen and an hour later than when we normally eat. Del Ray must have known I was about to lose my shit earlier, because she set the table around Martin and me and put ice in the glasses before she left the kitchen. I turned the microwave on and pulled the pork chops out of the oven.

"What else do you need, Mom?" Martin asked.

"Grab the applesauce and a spoon, and then I think we're ready. Gib, go holler at your dad and tell him dinner's ready."

"'kay," he yelled.

"Smells good, Mom," Del Ray said as she came into the kitchen.

I looked sideways at her. "What's gotten into you?"

She looked at me with a blank expression. "What do you mean?"

"This." I swirled my finger in the air. "This extremely nice, polite behavior I'm seeing tonight. What'd you do?"

She chuckled. "Nothing, I didn't do anything wrong, I promise." She looked at Martin then at me.

"Well, it's very nice. Keep it up." I winked at her and mouthed, "Thank you" when Martin turned his back.

When Martin was born, I had a hell of a time convincing Del Ray that he was my baby and not hers. She was three and half years old when he joined our family, and she was convinced I'd brought her a real-life, breathing, pooping baby doll to play with. When he cried, she took off running to get to him before I could so she could take care of him first. It was cute until it wasn't. Her maternal instincts toward him faded when he started walking and took her toys out of her room to play with them in the toilet. After that, she parented from afar until he started school, and then it started all over again. She had to escort him through the crosswalk, she had to keep an eye on him at recess, and twice she got me called into the principal's office for interfering with a teacher scolding him on the playground.

Last year she discovered she was a teenager and found that friends were more important than her nine-year-old brother, so she ditched him. That was a hard transition for the little guy, but he paid it forward and took his turn as the big kid with Gibson. Seeing her concerned about him again gave me a flicker of hope that my little girl was still inside that freakish-looking teenager sitting at the table.

We were all sitting at the table when Brandon waltzed in and went to the sink to wash his hands.

"Come on, Dad, I'm starving," Gibson said.

Brandon dried his hands. "I'm coming, I'm coming. Smells good, honey."

"Thanks," I said coldly.

"No bread?" he asked as he sat down.

I passed the pork chops to Del Ray. "You don't need bread. We have stuffing."

"I want some bread," he mumbled as he scooted his chair away from the table.

Everyone at the table groaned and put down their forks. We have a rule that no one eats until we're all sitting around the table. I looked at Gibson's face smashed against his hand as he stared at the applesauce. "Go ahead and eat, guys. It's getting cold."

The kids looked at me wide-eyed and said in unison, "Really?" Forks and knives scraped against plates in record speed.

Brandon returned to the table with a bun in his hand. He trimmed his pork chop and slapped it on the bun before he took a bite and sighed.

I stared at my husband and wondered when he turned into such a selfish prick. Watching his temples bounce up and down as he chewed annoyed me. I glanced around the table and saw my children devouring their meal. I felt my chest tighten. "Dare I ask if you guys had a snack after school?"

Martin and Gibson shook their heads, but Del Ray answered. "Nope."

"So, you guys haven't eaten anything since lunch?" I turned to Gibson. "What time do you eat lunch, buddy? Ten-fifty?"

"Yeah," he said in between bites.

I looked at Brandon who was scooping stuffing onto his fork. "That's nearly nine hours ago, Brandon."

He stopped and looked at me. "What?"

"These kids didn't have an after-school snack."

He shrugged. "They're old enough to say if they're hungry or not," he said as he went back to his meal.

I looked at Del Ray who rolled her eyes toward Martin. I followed her gaze and watched him scoot his stuffing around on his plate.

I cleared my throat. "Martin, tell me about school today."

He looked at me and shrugged. "Not much to tell. I got an A on my science test." He grinned.

"Good job! Was that the one over the planets?"

"Yep, thanks for helping me study."

"You're welcome. Gibson, after dinner we'll work on those spelling words."

"I'm too tired to study, Mom," he groaned.

"If you can play video games or watch TV, you can spell words out loud to me . . . or your dad."

Brandon chugged his tea and shook his head. "I've got to finish cleaning my clubs after dinner." He set his drink down and looked at Del Ray's dropped jaw. "What?"

She pointed her fork at me. "She worked, went to see a friend, cooked dinner *and* helped Martin with his homework . . ."

"That's enough out of you, Del Ray," Brandon said, ending the conversation.

We ate the rest of the meal in silence, but I had found an unexpected ally in Del Ray.

After dinner was over, the table had been cleared, and the kitchen cleaned (courtesy of my new teammate and myself), I sat down with Gibson and gave him a practice spelling test. He aced it, so we didn't spend much more time on it. Once showers were done and clothes laid out for the next morning, it was nine-thirty, and I was exhausted.

I walked into the bedroom, and Brandon was lying down watching TV looking as relaxed as he could be. "That was a good dinner, Chelle."

I didn't answer him. I gathered my clothes and went to the bathroom to change and brush my teeth. Gibson's clothes and puddles of water littered the bathroom floor, but he was already in bed (hopefully sleeping), so I picked them up and wiped up the water. I glanced at the sagging floor by the bathtub and wondered how much longer that floor was going to last before needing repair.

I climbed into bed and groaned at how awesome my bed felt. I stretched out then curled onto my side. Brandon and I had scrimped and scraped by on many purchases, but we went all out for a good bed. Best investment we ever made.

He rolled over and leaned against my back as he rubbed my leg. "Well, hello there."

I wished I had a Taser in my bedside table. I placed my hand over his and pushed it off my leg. "You gotta be kidding me. No way, jackass."

Brandon huffed and rolled over. He flipped channels until I rolled over, grabbed the remote, turned off the television then threw the remote into a pile of clothes in the corner. I looked at him and smiled. "Good night."

Chapter Ten
You've Got a Friend

Chance

I held my breath and watched Dani's face as Alissa made the announcement about her pregnancy. It was worse than I'd imagined; seeing someone else moan about the one thing that eludes you is torture on a good day. When the words "abortion" and "options" tossed around like high school whores landed on her, I felt myself reaching a level of anger I hadn't felt since Jeremy Newporter cheated on me in the late nineties. Then Michelle's brilliant fix . . . sometimes I really want to shake that girl until her head pops off.

I chased Dani to the back porch and wrapped her in a hug.

"Hey, you."

Dani whimpered, "How in the hell is this fair, Chance? How is this fair? She's the *last person on earth* who should have a baby. She works out for three extra hours a week if she eats a piece of cheesecake, for crying out loud. How does she get to do this?"

"I know, but it happened. Believe me when I say the guilt is eating her alive. Everything you're saying she said to me this afternoon."

She sniffled and pulled away as she shook her head. "I can't believe this is happening. I can't believe this is happening." She looked at me. "She'll get rid of it; watch. She won't carry this baby to term. And I don't know if I can get past it if she does, Chance."

"You don't know what she'll do, Dani."

"Look at this house! Can you imagine a baby trying to grow up in this immaculate place? Look out there——look at that yard. Can you envision plastic toys and sand boxes? Because I sure the hell can't."

I wiped a stray tear and cleared my throat. I rolled through all of the you'll-get-through-it speeches I've given in my life, but all of my words seemed inept for this situation. I thought about my breakup with Tony and how the last thing I wanted to hear was anyone say, "You'll meet someone new, and this will just be a memory someday." You can't exactly look at a friend and say, "There will be other babies." Thankfully, Dani just needed to talk, so I listened.

"Sometimes I wonder what I did in a different life to warrant being childless in this one. Maybe I was a horrible mother, and the universe is preventing the cycle from continuing."

My silence ended there. "Keep that shit up and I'll pretend you're Asshole-the-punching-bag. You're not being punished for anything. Don't even think like that."

She threw up her arms. "But it doesn't make sense. I did everything right, Chance. I graduated high school and college, I got married; I have lived a squeaky-clean life so why can't I have a baby? I deserve it. *She* doesn't deserve it. She's screwed up damn near everything she's touched!"

"Now, Dani, I know you're angry and extremely hurt right now, but that's Alissa you're talking about, not some cracked-out whore who's on baby number eight with six different daddies fresh out of prison." I stepped toward her. "That's our friend, and when you can peel yourself out of your own misery, think about how she feels right now. She's scared out of her mind because like you, she thinks she's unfit to be a mother too. She's sick as a dog and totally wigging that there's a human life growing in her uterus."

Dani closed her eyes and nodded. "I know you're right, but I can't get there, yet. I know it's selfish, and when the shock wears off I'll feel like a complete douchebag for my reaction, but right now, I'm . . . I . . . I just can't, Chance."

"And that's fine. Just save your crazy for me, okay? Spare her this side of you. And for the love of God, don't talk to the mother twins. I know they mean well, but Katie and Michelle can't relate to you on this. And Michelle's comment proved it."

Dani sighed. "Yeah, she didn't think that one through. I know it seems like an easy fix, but . . ."

"It's not that easy," I finished.

She nodded and whispered, "It's not that easy." She wiped her face and took a deep breath. "I think I'm going to head home."

I looked at my watch. "Yeah, I bet Chubs is about to explode right now." I paused then asked her. "You sure you're good to be alone?"

"I better get used to it." She chuckled. "I'm fine. I'm going to put the house on the market next week, so I need to fill out some paperwork from the real estate agent."

"What did Barry say about that?" I asked.

"Nothing. He came over last night to discuss the terms of the divorce. We both agreed selling the house seemed appropriate. It's paid off, so we'll each get half of the profit after closing. That will be a good down payment on something smaller." Her chin quivered.

"Ya know, I love my apartment; want me to see if there are any available in my complex?"

She shook her head. "No, but thank you. I like the feel of a house, and I want to stay on this side of town."

"Well, if you change your mind, let me know." I gave her a hug. "I'm going to go tell Alissa we're leaving and see if she needs anything."

"Tell her I love her and I'll call her tomorrow." She crossed the deck, opened the back door, and we walked into Alissa's immaculate house. Dani eyed the formal dining room and kitchen and shook her head as she wiped another tear.

I patted her on the back. "Hang in there, kiddo."

She nodded and let herself out the front door, her tall stature shrinking as she moved. I shook my head and took a deep breath, my exhale echoing in the kitchen. I grabbed a glass of ice water for Alissa then headed back to the family room where we'd all gathered earlier, but the room was empty.

I found her little body curled up in the fetal position in her king-sized bed and had to chuckle. "Do you know how many times I've come into your bedroom over the course of our friendship? Brings back memories."

Alissa waved me off. "Don't make me call the cops on you."

"I brought you some water. I've always wanted to throw it on you and see if you melted and screamed, 'what a world, what a world.' I'm so

79

tempted." I dangled the water glass in front of me.

She didn't move but the bed shook with her laughter. "Do it and I'll have Chubs stuffed."

"This looks mighty expensive."

She sat up and yelled, "Chance! Quit!"

I pointed at her. "I win. You sat up. Now, drink up, little mama." I handed her the cold water and sat on the bed.

She took a drink and looked at me. "I think we should go shopping."

"For what?"

"I don't know; who cares? Need a new car?" She winked.

I waved my hand. "Pssht, you couldn't afford my tastes."

She winked and gave me an evil grin. "Try me."

I laughed and smoothed the bedspread. "Feeling okay?"

She nodded. "Yeah, the private guest is giving me a reprieve at the moment, and I'm starving."

"Want me to cook something for you?"

"No, smells really do me in right now. Wanna go grab something?"

I bit my lip. "Actually, I really need to get home and let Chubs out. Do you want to come over and grab something on the way?"

Alissa thought about it for a moment. "Actually, yeah, I don't want to stay here. You sure you're not sick of me, yet?"

"Absolutely I am. But you can either sit next to me at home or bug the shit out of me via text, so I'd rather be able to hit you at will."

She stood up. "You wouldn't hit a pregnant woman, would you?"

"Those are my specialty. One slap to the bladder, and they're done for."

Alissa laughed as she slipped on her shoes. "I'll bring you something, too. Anything sound good?"

"Just none of that awkward-looking ethnic crap you brought last time. I'm sure my bathroom adventures offended the downstairs neighbors. It was horrible." We walked to the front door.

"Wow, really? Did you have to tell me all that?"

I shrugged and threw up my hands. "Hey, bring it on over if you want to share that experience with me."

"Noted. I'll be over shortly."

I tapped on the steering wheel and hummed off-key along with the radio. I tried to clear my mind and thought about flipping through Facebook while I sat at a red light, but I figured I'd had enough drama for one day. I saw a shiny black Mercedes go through the intersection, and my heart skipped a beat——it looked just like Tony's car. *Is he in town? Did he go by my apartment?* I grabbed my phone to see if I had any missed calls or texts, but my hands shook too much to work my phone before the light turned green.

I took a few deep breaths to calm my racing heart then focused on the bumper of the car in front of me. I chased the thoughts of Tony's car out of my mind and forced myself to think about my grocery list. I made a game out of coming up with something I needed at the grocery store that began with each letter of the alphabet a few months ago. You'd be amazed at how many bottles of wine you can slip into twenty-six letters.

Being single and successful has its advantages. I'm virtually debt-free, so I never have to worry about my cable being shut off or feel guilty for spending four-hundred dollars in a weekend on a shopping bender. I don't tell Katie and Michelle about my indiscretions, because it's been a sour subject with us in the past, so when I feel like blowing off steam, I call Alissa or Dani. I was beginning to feel the itch to do something drastic. Cutting my hair was out of the question since I'm the "face of KJAT" and I have great hair.

Why was Tony in Columbia? Was it really him? I turned up the radio to drown out the voices in my head, but every song on the radio reminded me of something we'd done together——a trip to the Arch in St. Louis, a weekend at the Lake of the Ozarks, a picnic at Shelter Gardens. Sometimes silence is my best friend.

I raced up the stairs to my door half-expecting to see a note from Tony, but there was nothing there. I sighed and threw my head back in disgust that I'd fallen for my own trick again. I entered the apartment, threw my purse and keys down, and attached Chubs' leash to his collar.

81

Back down the stairs and out to the doggie playground for his pottying pleasure.

I stood with my back to the pavilion this time.

Alissa's music entered the parking lot before her car did. She screamed the lyrics to "Mr. Know-It-All" by Kelly Clarkson and pounded the steering wheel along with the beat. I laughed, collected my dog then headed down the path to meet her.

She stood next to her car and yelled, "Man, I love that song! There's just no better song in the world." She waved Chinese take-out in my face. "Oh, so you like fried rice?" in her best broken-English impersonation.

"Long time," I answered and bowed. "Did you remember spring rolls?"

"It all sounded so good, I ordered a little bit of everything."

"Great. I'll be eating Chinese for a week."

"I just hope the private guest likes Chinese. I'm really sick of puking."

We walked up the stairs and into my apartment. I pulled a bar stool out for her and grabbed a few plates out of the cabinet.

"So, what happened on the deck with Dani?" she asked then bit into a spring roll.

I bit my lip. "This was very shocking to her, Lis."

"Yeah, be me, Dani," she mumbled.

"She'd love to be, Alissa."

She shifted on the stool. "I feel like I'm in trouble now that you've busted out my full name."

"No, not at all. But she's pretty rocked, and the abortion talk sent her over the edge. I'm sure you can understand that."

"You know, Michelle's idea isn't half bad."

I choked on my rice. "Excuse me?"

She stared at me. "I mean it. I think it's something to consider."

I said, slowly, "Alissa, you really need to think about what you're saying."

"It's the only thing that makes sense, Chance. Do you think it's a coincidence that I got knocked up around the same time one of my best friends finds out she's barren *and* her husband leaves her?" She flipped rice around on her plate and mumbled, "I don't. I think the universe is making this right with Dani."

I leaned over the counter. "Through *your* body? Come on, now. That's pretty drastic."

"Chance, I can't keep the baby. I'm not mother material."

"You just found out today that you're pregnant! Don't you think you should wait and see if the idea grows on you? What about Mark? Doesn't he have a say in it?"

"Not today he doesn't."

"Subject change, please. What do you think is up with Michelle?"

Chapter Eleven
I Will Survive

Alissa

"I don't know. What do you think is going on with Michelle?" I was determined to eat my Chinese meal without puking, but Chance's twenty-questions made me nervous. I grabbed a glass of water and leaned over the sink to make sure I wasn't going to embarrass myself in the kitchen.

Chance was talking, but I wasn't listening. I was still transitioning out of our conversation about the private guest and trying to brainstorm through the worst possible scenarios involved with the decision I was about to make.

I stared at the folded dishtowel and put some puzzle pieces together. "I've got it!"

"Shit, you scared the hell out of me. What'd you get?"

I rushed to her and grabbed her arm. "I know how we can do this."

"I'm all ears, Twinkie."

"Twinkie? Oh, 'cause I'm stuffed? You're a jackass." I laughed.

She shrugged. "Yeah, it just comes naturally to me. So what's your big idea?"

My mind raced with the sheer perfection of it all. "We go to Florida."

"What's in Florida?"

"Anonymity, my good Twatson."

"Oh now *you're* clever?" She laughed.

"Now we're even. I'll need time to work out all the details, and we'll all have to take a leave of absence from work, but . . ."

"Whoa, leave of absence? I can probably take a weeks' vacation but not a leave. Why Florida, and why now?"

"We don't have to go now, but when I start to show." I grinned at her. "Chance, this will fix it all!" I paced in the kitchen and ran the plans through my head again.

"Good lord, your head has been spinning way more than I gave you credit for. Okay, let's talk this out."

Three hours later, we had formulated a complete plan. All we had to do was get Dani on board. Rather than call her and have her ignore us, Chance and I jumped in my car and went to her house.

I had to keep moving. I had to make this plan official so there was no opportunity to back out. If there's one enduring thing about me, it's that I'm loyal to my friends and my word.

Dani opened the door and frowned. "You guys, it's like ten o'clock. What's wrong?"

I grinned. "We need to talk."

"I'm really not up for it right now, Lis," she said as she walked to the couch and plopped down. She pulled a pillow over her lap and curled her feet under her.

Chance eyed the house and muttered, "Man, he *was* meticulous with the stuff he took." She wandered into the living room and sat next to Dani. I couldn't sit down, so I half-paced/half-swayed and tried to get my words to come out just right.

Dani said, "Maybe we should talk about this later. I'm really tired and –"

I blurted out, "I want to carry your baby."

Dani's face blanched. "Shouldn't we go to dinner and a movie, first?"

I watched Chance roll off the couch laughing and looked at Dani as tears filled her eyes. "I'm serious, Dani. We all know I'm not cut out for motherhood, and you are. I could never have an abortion, and so that only leaves adoption. So, I'm asking if you will be my baby mama."

Dani's body erupted with sobs as she buried her head in the pillow. I looked at Chance who looked at me with raised eyebrows and a hopeful grin.

Dani whispered, "I'm going to be a mommy!"

I jumped up and down as I squealed, "Oh, Dani, you have saved me! I couldn't do this without you." I sat on the floor in front of her. "Now for the tricky part."

"You mean there's a door number two?"

"And three," I winked.

She sighed and wiped her face. "I don't know if I can take much more today. I . . . okay, let's hear it."

I took a deep breath. "You know I'm incredibly vain, and we need to use a lot of discretion about this—"

"Legally, you have to tell him, Lis," Dani said. "You should know that better than anyone."

I waved her off. "I already have that planned out. I'm not talking about hiding the baby from Mark. I'm talking about everyone else."

She frowned at me. "I'm not following."

"I don't want anyone to know I'm pregnant or that I've had a baby—after the fact, of course."

"Well, how do you plan to hide that?" She laughed.

"I want to go to Florida when I start showing, and I want you and Chance to go with me." I sucked in my breath and waited for her to object.

She looked at Chance who shrugged and pointed at me. "What's in Florida?" Dani asked.

I looked at Chance. "What is it *with* that question?" I looked at Dani. "Anonymity. I can just be a pregnant woman in Florida. Around here, I'll be the knocked-up single attorney and I can't have that."

Dani scowled and shook her head. "That's the most ridiculous thing I've ever heard."

"Just imagine, though! The three of us in Florida for months, sunning, shopping, napping on the coast . . . oh, it will be perfect!"

Dani looked at Chance. "Are you seriously considering this?"

Chance shook her head. "I don't know. It's extremely appealing, and I could certainly use a break from normal life."

"But what about your job? What about the station?"

"That's the tricky part. I don't know if I'll get approval to leave for however-many-months and still be able to come back when Alissa's done calving."

86

I snorted, "Oh that's nice. Real pretty, Chance."

She winked. "Aren't you glad I did that story on livestock farmers a few weeks ago?"

I rolled my eyes and said to Dani, "You know money won't be a problem. I'll rent us a house on the coast. I'll pay for everything, and you will be there with me to listen to me piss and moan about stretch marks and swollen ankles. But, you'll have to rub my feet." I winked.

"Oh, that might be a deal-breaker. I don't do feet." She laughed. "You're dangling a mighty carrot in front of me, Alissa."

"I want to do this for you. We've never done anything like this, so imagine the stories we'll have to tell."

"Yeah, but you won't be drunk in any of them," Chance pointed out.

I sat back on my heels. "Shit. That's right. Okay, so scratch off all the drinking I'd envisioned. Will you do it? Will you go with me?"

Dani sniffled and sighed. "Of course I'll do it. Are you crazy? Spending the winter in Florida with my best friends and coming home with a baby? Oh my gosh, I can't believe I just said that." She burst into tears again and looked at Chance. "Is this really happening?"

Chance looked at me and shook her head. "This is the most selfless thing I could ever imagine anyone doing. Lis, you're my new hero."

"I've always been your hero. You're just too stubborn to admit it."

Dani chuckled. "What about the other two? Are you going to ask them to come?"

"No, there's no way they can bail on their families for that long, and I'm not spending months on end with Brandon Morehead." I shivered.

"Here, here," Chance said as she toasted an imaginary wine glass.

I looked at Chance. "What about you? Are you in?"

She nodded then laughed as she threw her head back on the couch. "I can't believe I'm going to consider this. I can't commit right now, but I'll think about it. If I go, I have to take Chubs."

"That shouldn't be a problem. We can take my Navigator. It's time to stretch her legs, anyway."

Chance teased, "What, no private jet? I thought you liked to travel in style."

"Actually, I thought about that but, I can't imagine flying back with a newborn."

Dani's eyes twinkled as she whispered, "Newborn."

I grinned at her. "A baby. Your baby!"

We stayed up way too late dreaming about our trip and making plans for the fun things we would do in Florida. Since I was the bank in the equation, they agreed I could pick what city we would call home and when we would leave. That would take some research and planning, so I made the decision that I would turn in my notice at work and get busy planning for the next nine months of my life.

I laid in bed that night thinking of how in less than a week my entire life changed. The ceiling fan turned in slow circles and I imagined the five blades as five generations repeating the same patterns repeatedly. Round and round it went never creating much of breeze but using a lot of energy to stay in motion.

That was my family.

By the time I was thirteen, my mother and I had moved five times in seven years to accommodate her five boyfriends who turned into three husbands, three babies, and three divorces. I was more like Mom's friend than her daughter. After a breakup, she would say, "Gotta keep moving, baby!" She relied on me to help with the kids and housework and shared all of her joys and troubles with me when she was single, but the minute she hooked up with a man, I was the nanny and housekeeper. Raising three children at the age of thirteen left me no time to be a kid, and our constant relocation efforts gave me no opportunity to form friendships.

Our final move landed us in Columbia, Missouri, where I started high school and met the girls who would be my life's blood as an adult. They'd been chattering in the locker room getting ready for P.E., I'd overheard Michelle yelling that she didn't have socks. I'd watched her slam things around in her locker, digging through her bag for the fourth time, and Katie frantically searching through her things to help her out. Chance had been tying her shoes while Dani stood at the door announcing how much time was left before they'd have to run laps.

I'd grabbed an extra pair of clean socks out of my backpack and took them to Michelle. "Here you go. I always have extras." I'd smiled and went back to my area to shove my overstuffed backpack into the half-sized locker that was perfect for sports' uniforms but not for the bag I'd packed.

I had learned a long time before that day to be responsible for myself because there was no one else around to help me. When I had no socks for P.E. at my last school, the girls in that class made fun of me, talking about how grossed out they were that I'd worn my tennis shoes with no socks. I hadn't had a choice, but from that moment on, I carried extra everything with me——I was always prepared lest humiliation take hold, and I couldn't have that. Always be prepared, and stay moving—— my life's mottos.

Michelle had yanked on her laces and looked at me as I walked by. "Thanks. You're a life saver."

Later that day I'd been sitting at the lunch table reading the same milk carton I could recite from memory——the same milk carton served at every school I'd have ever attended, when Katie nudged my shoulder with her elbow. She'd readjusted her lunch tray and nodded toward the other three girls sitting a few tables away. "Wanna sit with us?" she'd asked.

I'd looked at the three smiling faces and grinned. "Sure."

They'd chattered like squirrels through lunch and thankfully didn't ask me questions I didn't know how to answer. The following weekend, Chance had had a sleepover, and the bond was formed. I had friends. I finally had real friends. When I was with them, I didn't have to worry about what I was going to make for supper, baths, or dirty diapers. I had a temporary reprieve from adult responsibility and learned how to belly laugh.

I loved my siblings and still do, don't get me wrong. However, my life was lived backwards. I raised my siblings as children of my own since I was old enough to carry a baby from room to room. I couldn't wait to go to college and leave it all behind. I never expected to feel as guilty or

89

miss them as much as I did. I needed to embrace the freedom I'd waited so long to have. Mom couldn't make it on her own financially, so I worked and sent the money to her until the kids grew up and left the house. I'm not sure anyone has ever paid child support for their own siblings, but leave it to me to be the first.

From that moment on, I knew there were two things I never wanted to be again——a mother and broke.

Mom sold the house in Columbia shortly after I moved out, and the cycle continued. My sisters have fallen victim to the family curse. All of them have multiple children by different men and have bounced from man to man in search of that un-gettable get. They're scattered across the U.S. and check in when the money runs out or when a new baby is born. Thank God my life turned out differently.

Chapter Twelve
Somebody That I Used to Know

Michelle

I stared at the frying hamburger meat and cursed the electric burner for not heating evenly. Half of the meat was trying to burn while the rest of it was barely cooking. Just like life—we're all on the same burner, but some of us get done a lot faster than the rest.

I caught the tear that bounced off my sweaty cheek with my shoulder and wondered how many of the same days I'd have to live over and over again while waiting to have a life. Six days in a row I've tried to get to the gym to start my workout routine, and six times something has come up and prevented me from going.

Meanwhile back at the ranch, my best friends were planning a winter in Florida to hide the illegitimate child of one of the wealthiest woman in Columbia. Nice.

I scraped the nearly burnt burger off the bottom of the skillet and replaced it with half-cooked, mediocre, probably flavorless meat that never had a chance to be a decent addition to the meal, because it was probably married at nineteen with no hopes of a bright future. It was probably a delusional little cow led to slaughter by a sweet-talking, beer-drinking musician that promised a life of band sets on green pastures with thousands of other little cows crooning and worshipping them like gods. But one wrong turn, and you're ground up burger that can't even fry properly and bound to be mixed with lasagna-flavored dry seasoning and pasta in a one-skillet meal——the daily feast of a family of five.

I checked the bread in the oven and slammed the door when no heat blasted from it.

"Brandon! I think the oven just broke!" I yelled. "And this freaking burner won't cook for crap anymore."

He rounded the corner. "You sure you turned it on?"

I wheeled around. "I'm sure I'm incompetent in a lot of ways, but I know the damn thing was on."

Brandon held up his hands. "It's a legitimate question, here. Is it on?"

"Of course it's on!" We both looked at the knob set to four-hundred degrees, and then he reached across me and flipped the other switch to "bake". The oven indicator light turned on and the oven clicked to life.

I hung my head and went back to browning the hamburger meat as he left the kitchen.

Chance had called earlier to apologize for biting my head off at Alissa's and then she told me about their big, fancy plan. As long as Alissa's not showing by Christmas, they're leaving the week after for Florida. Alissa, Chance, and Dani . . . just uprooting and checking out of life for a while to sun and shop while waiting for Alissa's——no, scratch that, *Dani's* baby to be born.

I know Alissa is the queen of dissociation, but she really has no fucking clue what she's just done. Just wait 'til that baby moves for the first time——that's when she'll look at Dani and wonder what the hell she's done. I know she had a rough upbringing and she's terrified of turning out like every other woman in her family, but dammit, this is nuts.

However, I admire her all the same for being so selfless and giving Dani the only thing she wants out of life. That's Alissa, though—the big fixer. This one is going to bite her in the ass, though,—mark my words.

I yelled, "Guys, dinner's ready," as I turned off the burner and poured the one-pot meal into a serving bowl. That's me——the one-pot-wonder. I grabbed the corn out of the microwave and hissed as I sucked on my burning fingers.

Del Ray strolled into the kitchen. "You okay?"

I nodded and waved my hand in the air. "Crap, that hurts. Will you set the table, please?"

"Way ahead of you, there, Mom," she said as she walked to the table, her arms loaded with dishes from the cupboard.

"Martin, will you get the drinks going?" I yelled.

"Mom, I'm right here," he said as he poured milk in two glasses and iced tea in the other three.

I sighed and muttered, "Why am I even here?"

Del Ray came over and kissed me on the cheek as she grabbed paper towels off the roll. "Because you love us and make good food."

I frowned. "I sure wish I knew what you want." I looked at her fading purple hair. "It's about time to do something with that, don't ya think?"

She ran her fingers through her hair. "Nah, I'm going to let it fade so I can go red next. Like bright red—fire-engine red. It's going to be awesome."

"Awesome," I repeated.

"Yes, with black tips." She grinned. "I still think you should let me do your hair."

I chuckled. "No way."

"You couldn't get enough red to cover all that gray," Brandon said through a chuckle.

I flipped him the bird when the kids weren't looking and took my place at the table.

"Where's the bread?" he asked.

I jumped up and yelled, "Shit!" The French bread wasn't quite burnt, but it was close. I cut it up anyway and ran my fingers under cold water to calm the angry burns on my fingertips.

I put the bread on the table, and Brandon mumbled, "I'd say the oven is definitely working," as he stabbed a piece of bread with his fork.

"Looks good, Mom," Martin said.

Gibson asked, "How was work?"

I flipped my pasta around on my plate. "It was fine. Work, you know. Same ol' same old. Thanks for asking, Gibson," I said as I stared at Brandon.

Del Ray caught me and shook her head as she looked at Martin. I sighed and asked, "What's the scoop with you guys?"

Everyone mumbled but no one followed up.

Once I finished the same routine I'd had for years, I crawled into

93

bed and stared at the same page of a book I'd been trying to read for two months. My eyes traced the lines while my teeth gritted and temples bulged.

Branden sighed as he walked in the bedroom and closed the door. "Man, I'm beat." He pulled off his shirt and threw it in the floor by the hamper. I closed my eyes and bit my lip.

"Tough day?" I snapped.

He scratched his head and flexed. "Look at that, babe. Thirty-four years and still hot as hell." He grinned and climbed into bed. "Whatcha reading?"

I showed him the cover of the book and he rolled his eyes. "Looks like chick lit."

I sighed and flipped it back open. "I can't read anymore."

"I could probably entertain you a bit," he winked.

I did the math in my head and figured it was close to time to give it up. If I prolonged it much longer, I'd have to deal with a fourth child in the house in the form of a pissed-off, horny thirty-five-year-old. I sighed inside and put my book on the nightstand before I curled up next to him and smiled.

Right on cue, we entered the same routine we'd had for at least three years. I spent the next twelve minutes thinking back to our first time together and how turned on I was while thanking God it was me and not Lottie-the-body satisfying him. Of course, now we know that truth. I should have known it then, but I was too naïve and in love to get it through my thick head that there was no snowball's chance in Hell that she would ever give Brandon Morehead the time of day.

I noticed the ceiling fan needed cleaning again and that the dust on my nightstand was thick enough to write one helluva grocery list. Somehow I never noticed it when I looked at my alarm clock, and now really wasn't the time to be bothered with it. I played my part——gave an Oscar-worthy performance, might I add——and waited for Brandon to fall asleep.

I lay next to my husband and tried to figure out exactly when I'd started hating my life. I bit my lip to stop the sob clenching my throat and the guilt from overtaking me. Who does this? What mother lies in bed after having sex with her husband thinking about how she hates her life? What is *wrong* with me? I signed up for this gig. It's all I ever wanted, and I'm reaping what I've sown.

I've never given two shits that my friends were successful, wealthy, or married well or had more opportunities to begin again than I had. I was too busy changing diapers, running to doctor appointments, and having babies to realize how quickly time was passing until I'd spent eleven years mothering and being a homemaker. I loved my life, then, so what's different? After Gibson started school, Brandon kept nudging me to get a job, but I had no skills outside of parenting, so working in a daycare was really my only option.

And I see the career moms pick up their kids in their cute dresses and three-inch heels and wonder how in the hell they ever made it through pregnancy. My most difficult choice when picking out work clothes involves fewest wrinkles and shirts that won't hold stains. Piss stains, puke stains, and Kool-Aid stains . . . not fancy five-dollar coffees or au jus from a mistrusted French dip business lunch.

I sighed and rolled over while nudging Brandon to roll onto his side to kill his snoring. My first thought was to smother him with a pillow.

Maybe I need to up my medication.

Chapter Thirteen
Against All Odds

Chance

I had to use extra concealer to hide the dark circles my sleepless night left under my eyes. It's just like Alissa to make a life-altering decision and drag me along for the ride. I finished getting ready for work and left the house at five-thirty to get to the station. I couldn't wait to hear Jack Woodrow's nagging about having to do the six-o'clock show on his own last night, so to ease the blow, I stopped and got us both coffee. God knows I needed the extra shot of espresso, and his personality needed a helluva lot more than that.

I walked into the newsroom and waited for the news producer to give me my marching orders. Jack and his hideous yellow tie were glaring at me from the news desk, so I waved his coffee at him until he broke down and smiled. I joined him at the desk and handed him the cup. "Sorry I had to bail on you last night."

He sipped the coffee and sighed. "You're forgiven. I just hope it was worth it. Did you watch?"

I shook my head. "No, I missed it. Family emergency."

"You don't have any family, Chance."

"I got adopted yesterday. Lucky me!"

He rolled his eyes. "Whatever. I hope it was worth it. Stuart is pissed."

I scanned the room for our boss Stuart then looked at Jack. "Maybe I'll luck out."

Behind me Stuart said, "Luck's never been on your side, Chance."

I spun in my chair. "With a name like Chance, a girl's gotta have luck, sir." I offered my best apologetic smile. "I'm really sorry I couldn't be here yesterday. I had an illness I'd rather not discuss."

Jack mumbled, "I thought you had a family emergency."

"One of my personalities was sick. Happy now? How's your coffee,

Jack? You feeling okay?" I grinned maniacally at him and made him contemplate finishing the coffee.

"Cut the shit. Chance, after the show, come in my office. I need to talk to you." He straightened his suit jacket and left the set.

I looked at Jack who grinned and sipped his coffee. "Way to go, Slick Willie, you got me in trouble." I smoothed my shirt and slipped my earpiece into place.

He took another sip of his coffee. "This tastes much better. Must be the victory in the air."

I smirked. "Could be the laxative, too."

He stared at me and shook his head. "You really need to get laid."

"You really need a face lift." I smiled as I turned my attention to the producer awaiting my cue to open the show.

After the broadcast was over, I went to the ladies room to kill time before facing Stuart and his rambling, round-the-bush reprimand for missing a live broadcast. I slipped off my jacket and pulled my hair up in a loose bun in preparation for the long day. Once these folks smell blood in the water, the piranhas start circling. If someone makes a mistake, all their current work comes under scrutiny with triple checking and rewrites. I needed to prepare for battle.

I went to my desk, grabbed my coffee and headed to Stuart's office. It reminded me more of a modern jail cell with the floor-to-ceiling glass walls and door and grey walls. Black and white framed prints were Stuart's cellmates along with his degrees and achievement awards. The only color in the whole office came from a framed picture of Stuart with his family in matching red sweaters from three Christmases ago. I had a feeling Stuart's life ran a close parallel to his office colors.

I cleared my throat and took a seat in the black leather chair in front of Stuart's desk. He continued typing as he held up one finger. "Two seconds."

I threw up my hand and took another sip of my now-cold coffee. I choked it down and stared out the window at leaves of gold and red glowing in the morning sunshine. The tree yawned and stretched in the easy breeze, and the leaves peeking through the window offered yet another example as to how something simple and average like a windowpane can separate a dull, boring life from something extraordinary. Only the curious of souls open the window and stick their head out.

I bet Stuart didn't even know there was a tree outside his window.

Stuart wheeled around and placed his hands on the desk. "What's on your mind, Chance?"

"Just imagining how I'm going to decorate this office when it's mine," I said as I winked. "You told me to come see you after the show, so here I am."

"That's right. First of all, Chance, we're a team here, and while I know you have a life outside of the office and I don't need to know all the details, each of us has an important role here and you can't just run out on the team, dammit."

I did my best deadpan face to prevent bursting into giggles. Sometimes it's so hard to take Stuart seriously when he is really a dumbass. He's great at what he does, but his interpersonal skills are lacking to say the least. "I'm sorry, Stuart. It won't happen again," was the best I could do.

He sat back in his chair. "Good. Now that that's over, let's get down to business. I need you to go to St. Louis and cover the president's visit and press conference. Get your road crew together and be ready to go live at five."

My heart stood still. "Jack's senior anchor. Don't you think he should go?"

"Look, to be blunt, Jack has a family and can't be gone for days on end with his wife's health the way it is. You're it."

I sighed and looked at the leaves peeking in the window. The sun still shone, but the leaves sagged without the wind that was taken out of all of our sails.

Tony.

I smoothed my hair. "Sure, no problem, Stuart. I'll get it done." I stood and started to leave as I asked, "How long will I be gone?"

"Plan for three days. He flies in tonight; the tour is tomorrow, dinner tomorrow night, and the press conference is the next morning. Have Celia book your room."

"I'll book my own room, but thanks," I mumbled.

"Suit yourself. And Chance? Don't have an emergency. Your life can wait this week. I need this story. I'm counting on you."

I saluted and walked past Jack to get to my desk. "Looks like you're on your own for the week."

Jack sat up and asked, "Why?"

I packed my traveling journalist bag and snapped, "Because I'm going to be in St. Louis covering the president's spur-of-the-moment visit." I shook my head and chewed on my lip to prevent an argument.

Jack slumped in his chair. "Well ain't that the shits."

"Tell me about it."

I made hotel reservations and boarding arrangements for Chubs before I left the office, but all I could think about was the insane fear mixed with excitement of seeing Tony again. With a story like this being in his back yard, there was no way he would miss an opportunity to be in the front lines.

Normal journalists would be envisioning the president pointing at them and getting a chance to ask a mind-blowing, politically slanted question to make the asked squirm. All I could picture was Tony's sexy body in a suit leaning against the wall with one hand in his pocket giving me that "come hither" look that drove me wild.

I rounded up the road crew and gave them instructions to meet me at my hotel in St. Louis no later than four o'clock. I'd learned the hard way never to carpool to such events with the road crew. I need the capability to drive around and research without the big KJAT television van advertising a brewing story or attracting the bystanders seeking five minutes of fame to make Mom and Dad back home proud.

I shot a text to my girls: *Just got word I'm in . . . wait for it . . . St Louis for the next three days for work. Unbelievable.*

Alissa responded: *Could be worse. You could be meeting with your ex-boyfriend to tell him about a baby.*

You win, I replied. One-upped again by good ol' Alissa.

I flew home and changed into my favorite jeans, a white blouse, and my black jacket. I packed half of my wardrobe to accommodate whatever the next three days would have in store——another lesson I'd learned the hard way. Racing through a dress boutique trying to find the perfect cocktail dress for an event that begins in less than an hour will make the pits sweat like crazy.

I wished Alissa and I had gone on that shopping trip we'd discussed a few weeks ago. Having a new dress to wear when I saw Tony would offer a certain satisfaction and hopefully hide the ten pounds I'd gained when I drowned my sorrows in mint chocolate chip ice cream and an uncountable amount of wine bottles.

Red. He always loved me in red. I looked at my watch and did the math in my head. "I can make it work," I said to myself as I gathered up my luggage and led Chubs to the car. After I dropped him at the doggie hotel, I hit the road and headed to the nicest dress shop in town.

I was just about to give up and go with what I had when I saw it shimmer in the corner. I excused myself from the hovering attendant trying to encourage me to go with a nice cream color to compliment my age (um, go to hell) and hair color. It was the only dress like it and exactly the size I needed. I held it up to me and saw the flames of regret licking the air around me.

Perfect.

I tried it on and admired myself in the mirror. The sleeves hit just below my shoulders while the neckline plunged in a sweetheart point just between my breasts. The dress hugged my body as if we were separated at birth and reunited on Oprah. It hit just above my knees, which showed off my fabulous legs. I chose a pair of red three-inch heels and diamond jewelry, and the best part of the whole shopping spree was it was on Stuart's dime. Many, many of them. Oh, I was definitely making him pay for this trip in multiple ways.

I took the final dress test and sat in a chair. Nothing snapped, sagged, or climbed up to my hips. Sold. I took my treasures to the car and headed toward St. Louis with a new grin and a sassy attitude. Maybe I was the one who said no, but he was the one that stayed away, and he was about to be very, very sorry.

Chapter Fourteen
Here Without You

Alissa

I went to work the next morning and lied through my teeth that my mom had fallen ill and I needed to leave immediately to go take care of her. I kind of felt guilty leaving my assistant and the other attorneys high-and-dry, but I had other things to think about. I packed up my desk, gave instructions on each case to my assistant and was out the door before eleven. I pretty much just sealed my fate that I would never work here again, but I didn't need the job and sure didn't want to take the chance of having a puking fit in the middle of court or a deposition.

Out with the bad, in with the good . . . out with the bad, in with the good . . . I took several deep breaths and pulled out of the parking lot headed for Mark's office.

I tried a few times to get in touch with him since his email breakup, but he wouldn't return my texts or emails. I guess I shouldn't be surprised since he's so black and white in his thinking. There is no grey in Mark's life——it is or it isn't. It's fact or a lie. Hot or cold. So my visit to his office should prove to be interesting. It's his place of comfort, though where he feels normal, so maybe that will make this whole thing easier.

I sat in the parking lot in front of the building where Mark works and rehearsed my speech. When I was certain I wasn't going to pass out, I got out of the car and walked with purpose toward the door. If I came in like an attorney with an appointment, I had a better chance of making it past the receptionist. However, like always, I had a back-up plan.

I approached the receptionist. "I'm here to see Mark Gideon, please."

"Do you have an appointment?" she asked.

"No, but we have an important case to discuss. I'm an attorney for the state."

"What's your name, please?" she asked as she accessed Mark's calendar.

I slipped two one-hundred dollar bills onto her keyboard. "I know where his office is. Thank you."

She stared at the money then looked at me. I winked. "I'll tell him I forced my way past you. Have a little fun tonight, okay?"

She grinned and looked over her shoulder as she nodded. I smiled back at her and walked toward Mark's office.

He was on speakerphone standing over his desk looking out the window when I slipped into his office and took a seat in front of his desk. He turned and walked toward me. "Listen, let me call you back. I have an unexpected visitor in my office." He reached across his desk and ended the call before looking at me again. "I thought I made myself pretty clear, Alissa."

I smiled. "It's good to see you, too, Mark. You might want to close the door."

He eyed me and shook his head, but he closed the door. "You have five minutes. I have an appointment——a *scheduled* appointment—who will be here any minute."

I took a deep breath and pretended he was on the witness stand. "Mark, we find ourselves in a strange predicament. It seems one of the last times we slept together resulted in the conception of a child that neither one of us wants."

He sighed and sat on the edge of his desk. He ran his hands through his hair and locked his fingers behind his head. He scratched his head and mumbled, "I need to sit down."

I chuckled. "Yeah, I had that same reaction."

He swung his chair around. "Wow, you're a real piece of work." He stared at me.

I frowned. "I'm sorry?"

"I thought you were trying *not* to be like your mother and sisters."

There was no hiding the impact his words had on me. I heard myself exhale as I leaned over my lap and put my face in my hands. *Out with the evil, in with the good . . . out with the evil, in with the good.* "That . . . was unexpected." I cleared my throat and sat up straight. "We have a few options—"

"No! There are no options, and there is no 'we'. End it. You're not locking me into this. I want no part of it or you, and I do not want to be permanently linked to your crazy ass."

His words slapped at my skin like freezing rain on the coldest day in January. "Mark, it's not like that," I whispered.

"Really? You're not here to trap me into your latest 'fantastic ever-so-awesome' life scheme?" His hands flailed around his head. If he was imitating me, he was way off.

I jumped to my feet and leaned across his desk. "I would sooner be bound to this fucking wooden desk which has way more personality and hope for a fun future than your stuffy ass. I came here to do what I had to do legally before I make the decision I'm about to make, you stupid prick. But if you want to take cheap shots, fine by me. Your point is proven. My only regret is wasting six months of my life listening to your monotone self-absorbed monologues about shit no one cares about."

"Are we finished here?" he asked as he moved toward the door.

"Totally. I'm leaving town—"

Mark cut me off, "Alissa, I don't give a shit what you're going to do or when or where. Just go!"

I grabbed my bag and marched out the door. I clenched my teeth and took a deep breath to hold my tears in place. I smiled at the receptionist as I gave her a finger wave and made it to my car as the sobs slammed against my chest. I pulled out of the parking lot and said to myself, "I don't cry. You will not cry. Do not cry. He doesn't deserve your tears. He doesn't know how to be a decent human being, and he's got a small penis."

I took a few more deep breaths. "Okay, so that's done." I felt my chin quiver as I heard him spit the words "I thought you were trying *not* to be like your mother" at me. Wow. When I had this all planned out in my head, it went very differently. I had drawn up papers for him to sign to terminate his rights immediately, but maybe this was better. He could think I had an abortion. Last he knew, Dani and Barry were trying to get pregnant, but he's too self-absorbed to put two-and-two together. Not that he would care. He would sooner shave his head and get sleeve tattoos before he ever found an ounce of paternal interest.

God, what an evil man to say those things to me. What a total waste of intelligent DNA. I pulled into my driveway, threw my keys onto the table by the door, and went to my bedroom to change clothes. Suddenly, all of my power suits and cocktail dresses seemed inappropriate in my life. I didn't have time to be upset by that ass hat. I had things to do, clothes to buy, and a new life to plan. Gotta keep moving, right?

I peeled out of my suit and stood in front of the mirror in the bathroom. I examined my abdomen and turned sideways to see if there was a hint of a baby showing. A baby. Growing in me. "Just like your mother," echoed in my head.

"I don't have time for this," I shouted. I dressed for the gym and headed out the door. Loud music and sweat would get rid of Mark's comment. Yes, that's what I need. No, what I really need is a bottle of wine or four, but as Chance said, I can't pickle the private guest.

I did a quick warm-up then hit the treadmill. I wish Mom had informed me of sports bras when I was in high school. I'd hated running in gym because the boys always stared at my bouncing breasts. When I realized I could use that to my advantage, I picked the tightest t-shirts I could find to drive them crazy. A smile tickled at my lips when I thought of Jason Hitch's bugged-out eyes. I considered going out for the track team until I remembered I hated to run, which is ironic, because that's all I ever really wanted to do from a young age. I just wanted to run and never stop.

And here I am—on a treadmill running as fast as I can and going absolutely nowhere. All of the women in my family have been on this same track with sweat pouring off them eager to get to the next big thing, and all this time, they've been on a fucking treadmill. I cranked up the volume on my iPod and pushed the buds deeper into my ears. *Out with the bad, in with the good.* No negative thoughts. Peace. In with peace.

I focused on the music in my ears and eventually pushed all thoughts out of my head. Once again, it was me, my heartbeat, and my music intertwined like a three-piece rope. Singly, we're nothing; together, we're an unbreakable force. That's me, bitches. I'm an unbreakable force. I've been through divorces that lasted longer than this pregnancy will, so I know I can do this. I can do this for Dani. I summoned the look on her face when I blurted out ever so eloquently that I wanted to be her baby mama. That's my peace; that's my mission. There's a plan and a purpose, and that's when I'm at my best. The little nugget growing in me was my love gift to Dani. Yes. It was Dani's baby; I'm surrogating. That's how I'll get through this. Perfect!

I haven't seen my family in three years——well, at Thanksgiving it will be three years. After I married Dirk and became wealthy overnight, an instant cloud of shame formed over them. We already had a major distance between us since my sisters think I abandoned them when I left for college.

Adrianna wouldn't speak to me for months, and I really didn't blame her. She became the head chick in charge when I left, so all of the responsibility fell on her to take care of Ella and Hilary. As much as I hated to leave her like that, I had to get out of there. I had dreamed of freedom ever since I realized I was imprisoned. It only took two semesters for me to quit waking up in the middle of the night to check on kids who weren't sleeping in the dorm room with me. I went through three roommates——not surprising at all.

I'm the only one that made it out. Adrianna stuck around to finish raising the other two, and by the time Hilary graduated, she was twenty-four and expecting baby number two. I was twenty-nine when Hilary graduated high school and I offered to pay her way through college if she'd get an IUD——the same deal I'd made Adrianna and Ella, and the same deal they'd both refused. I just wanted to give them a fair shot at life, but they mistook my offer as passing judgment on Mom and now I have six nieces and nephews with another on the way. Yeah, I just got the text that Hilary's pregnant again.

My therapist was extremely concerned with my perception of motherhood. She didn't get that I'm not talking about all moms——I'm talking about the moms in my family . . . the ones who romanticize having babies with the boyfriend du jour after two months of dating. Then when the men decide they're bat-shit crazy and hit the road, the women in my family are left balancing their broken hearts and offspring in the same hands.

And when the women in my family get their hearts broken, there's never enough room to hold a child.

Chapter Fifteen
Torn

Michelle

I've read enough stupid shit on Facebook to realize that if I want to see changes in my life, they must start with me. Well, today, I'm giving it a shot. I set my alarm for 5 a.m. and snuck out of the house to hit the gym. A maniacal giggle escaped my gut when I pulled out of the house at 5:15 with my gym shoes and MP3 player as my co-pilots in the passenger seat. I couldn't wait to see Brandon's face when he realized I had outwitted him yet again. Not bad for a high school C student, butthead!

The 5:30 crunch class was just beginning when I walked through the gym. The instructor asked if I wanted to join them since they had a few members on vacation this week. I grinned and jumped in line.

I was wearing one of Brandon's old football t-shirts and a pair of yoga pants that I prayed wasn't the pair that had a hole in the butt from a high nail on the picnic table and a fast dismount to tend to a screaming child last year. I was in such a hurry to escape, I never even thought about it. I was in the last row, though, so as long as we didn't turn around, no one should see my Hanes Her Way that might very well also have holes in the ass cheeks for all I know.

By the looks of the folks in this class, they never eat anything fried and run screaming from carbs. I was extremely underdressed compared to the Barbies in sports bras with firm, tan abs and matching pants, socks, and shoelaces. These people have way too much time on their hands.

To say I was winded by the time we finished warm-ups is an understatement. I was sucking wind hard and sweat ran down my butt crack. But, I held my own and only grunted loud enough for everyone to take notice four times. I felt my stomach muscles screaming for mercy, and my thigh muscles (which took me a minute to understand that those are actually called "quads" by the rest of the class) said, "Oh, hell no," when we were down in "core-conditioning position." Everyone else looked graceful as they performed the exercises with perfect choreography; I, on the other hand, looked like I was directing traffic during rush hour with the aggravated face of concentration included. I always thought I had good balance until I attended this class. I was just grateful I didn't fart.

The longest hour of my life ended at 6:30 with me dripping sweat and trying not to gasp for oxygen as the rest of the class left in a string of high-fives and "see you tomorrows." I was the last one to leave and tried not to make eye contact with the instructor as I willed my shaking legs to put one foot in front of the other. My stomach muscles were already sore, but my arms had fared well since I spend my day slinging forty-pound children around at the daycare.

"So glad you joined us today. I hope we'll see you tomorrow," the instructor said as she reached up for a high-five.

I gave her a limp-armed, half-assed attempt and met her on the downfall. "Sure, see you tomorrow," I mumbled as I headed toward the door.

Most of the ladies had left the parking lot by the time I got to my car, and I was ever so grateful they didn't hear me yell, "Shit!" as I tried to lower myself into the driver's seat. "I need to drink more water," I panted as I put on my seatbelt and threw my tennis shoes in the passenger seat.

At the house, I sat in my car and stared at the steps leading up to my front door. I never really noticed them before but this morning the door might as well have been at the top of a set of bleachers. I groaned as I rolled out of the car and stumbled toward the door. I saw Martin's light come on in his room and stood up a little straighter. The alarms must be going off all over the house, but the last thing I was going to do was appear whipped to my family. I clenched my teeth and bounded up the stairs and through the front door with a grin on my face and new sweat forming on my brow.

"Mom?" Martin asked. "Are you just getting home?"

"Hi, baby." I panted. "Yeah, I went to the gym this morning."

109

"Cool," he said and gave me a half-hug. "You're sweaty."

"Yes, I am. I'm going to jump in the shower before Del Ray takes all the hot water." I kissed him on top of the head and guided him toward the kitchen.

"I need to pee first," he said.

"Okay, be quick, though." I went into the bedroom and saw Brandon reaching to turn off his blaring alarm. He stretched and rubbed his eyes. "Michelle? Is it raining?"

"No, I went to the gym and just got home."

Brandon chuckled. "Whatever."

I peeled off my t-shirt and looked at him. "No, I really did. Since you threw such a hissy fit about me going during 'family time,' I decided to go while everyone was sleeping so I couldn't be accused of being selfish." I grabbed my clothes and headed into the bathroom. Brandon followed me.

He closed the door behind us. "I don't know what's gotten into you, but I sure hope you grow out of it soon." He pulled down his pants and started to pee.

I rolled my eyes and squeezed past him to turn on the shower. "It's a workout, Brandon; it's not like I'm going clubbing or getting tattoos." I stripped off my clothes and jumped in the shower. "Don't . . . flush," I groaned as the toilet kicked into motion. I flattened myself against the cold shower stall and waited for the water to readjust to a normal temperature.

Thus began the revolving door into the bathroom for teeth brushing and questions that reminded me why I never shower in the mornings anymore. Del Ray came in for the third time and asked, "How much longer are you going to be? I need hot water for my shower too, ya know."

I killed the water and reached around the shower curtain for my towel with tears brimming my eyes. I mumbled, "I'm done. Scoot out so I can dry off and get dressed, please." I heard the door shut and climbed out of the tub. I patted my legs as best I could since lifting them was out of the question and considered rubbing my back against the wall instead of lifting my arms.

I looked at myself in the mirror and burst into tears. I looked at least ten years older than my friends, and the sad woman looking back at me resembled nothing of who I was, while they all looked like mildly older versions of the girls I'd met when I was thirteen. Frown wrinkles stood like knights protecting a castle between my eyes, and there wasn't a laugh line to be found——just the downward turn of a woman who's spent most of her life stressed out and pissed off——a true reflection of my adult life. Maybe I should try wearing makeup again; that always helps me feel better about myself. I grabbed my hairdryer and makeup kit out of the bathroom closet and freed the bathroom for Del Ray who stood outside the door with folded arms and tapping foot.

"Bout time. I'll have to race to get ready now."

"Sorry. I thought I'd be done at the gym faster."

Her head snapped back. "You went to the gym this morning?"

I ignored her implication and went to my room to cover my misery with the free makeup I got during a Mary Kay party I'd hosted two years ago. Some of it was still unopened. I glanced at the clock. "Shit, I'm going to be late." I threw the makeup back in the case and dried my hair as fast as I could and opted for a headband to save styling time. A quick glance in the mirror revealed the same Michelle I'd been when I went to bed last night.

"Boys, are you about ready?" I yelled down the hall while heading to the kitchen to make lunches. I picked up the loaf of bread and did a double take when I saw the blue-green discoloration of molded bread. I slammed it on the counter then chucked it in the trash. "Boys, you'll have to eat at school today; the bread's gone bad."

Brandon said from the kitchen table, "It can't be bad——we just bought it."

"Well it is," I said as I prepared my travel mug of coffee. "I'm going to be late. Can you run the boys to school today? I'll drop Del Ray."

He sighed and grabbed his coffee. "Boys, get your shoes on. We gotta roll."

"You're going to the office in your pajama bottoms?"

"No, I'm supposed to have the day off, but I'm glad you decided to do something for yourself today and ruined my chance at having a lazy day at home." He slammed his coffee cup on the table and headed toward the front door.

I stared after him when the boys came into the kitchen for good-bye hugs. "Have a great day at school. I'll see you when I get home." I kissed them on the tops of their heads and yelled down the hallway, "Del Ray, we gotta roll, baby. Let's go!"

She appeared in the hallway pulling her black hoodie over her head and smoothed her hair. "I'm out of product. Guess I'll have to look like an idiot today," she mumbled.

"We'll run to the store tonight. I could use a few things myself." I grabbed my purse and coffee and waited for her to gather her backpack.

The drive to school consisted of me clock-watching and her texting——no doubt telling all her friends how her selfish mother had time to go to the gym but not to the store to buy the seventh jar of hair putty this month. We pulled up at the edge of the high school where I'm supposed to drop her off to meet her friends so they can walk the remaining half a block together and catch up on what they missed while being separated for the evening.

What I would have done to have instant communication with my girlfriends when I was a kid. I had a great childhood, don't get me wrong. I had normal parents with normal careers with normal siblings and normal schedules. I had to share a house phone with everyone in the house, had time limits per phone call, and I dared not have phone calls past nine o'clock. I spent my nights working on homework, practicing my clarinet, and telling my innermost secrets to the pages of my favorite journal. Nowadays, kids have Facebook, Instagram, email, texting, Pinterest, and God knows what else I don't even know about. But they will never know the anticipation of having a roll of film developed, never appreciate the exchange of hand-written letters from their dearest friends before first hour and the anxiety that comes from trying to read them before the teacher realizes you're not paying attention. I was nearly

112

busted once in English class while reading Alissa's most recent gush about the "cutest boy ever" on the track team. I don't even remember his name, now. I really wish we hadn't had the "bond-burning" when we graduated and all tossed our shoeboxes full of letters from each other into the senior class bonfire. It was symbolic at the moment, but now I'd love to read those letters and remember what it was like to be just a girl in love with a boy with friends I couldn't stand be away from.

And they're leaving me. Well, not all of them. Katie will still be here, but while I should be able to relate to her the most, she's the one I feel most disconnected from. We have such similar lives that I don't want to hear about kids, bills, repairs, and sleepovers; I live that life every day! I want to hear about Chance's exciting news chases, Alissa's crazy boy stories, and Dani's easy way of making my life sound like bliss. I never have anything interesting to share——I'm sure they're really excited to hear about fighting with a husband every day, replenishing wardrobes every three months to accommodate growth spurts, and researching the best "twenty-minute meals" to add a little spice to the redundant menu we've rotated weekly for years.

On the other hand, maybe they'd like to hear what it's like to work on your feet for eight hours a day, eat peanut butter and jelly three days a week, and bring home a weekly paycheck that never hits over $300 after taxes.

I shook my head and realized I was pulling into the driveway at the daycare; I didn't even remember driving across town. I reached in my purse and grabbed my phone to turn it off. Not like it really mattered as I still have a flip phone and have to click each key multiple times to type out a simple message. I don't get half of the texts the other girls send because my phone is too old to get group texts. It just looks at me all confused.

Dani texted me last night to tell me that Alissa and Dani were supposed to go today for the ultrasound to find out how far along Alissa is. After this appointment, they'll finalize the timeline, and their big, fancy trip will be all set. No doubt there will be a friend meeting called that I will most likely have to miss.

113

And how the hell does Brandon get to take a "lazy day" off from work and number one, not tell me in advance, and number two, get pissed at me because I interrupted his morning by asking him to take his own children to school? How does that work? I can't just take a day off from work and stay home to read or take a nap, so how does he get to do that?

I turned off my phone and slammed it into my purse so hard it bounced out and slid under the front seat. I glanced at my dashboard clock and shook my head. "I'll have to get it after work." I grabbed my coffee and headed into the daycare.

Chapter Sixteen
Be Without You

Chance

Leave it to Alissa to schedule her ultrasound on a morning when I have to be out of town chasing down the president of the United States while simultaneously trying to avoid and run into my ex-boyfriend——it changed every hour.

By seven o'clock, I was dressed in my three-piece black pencil skirt suit checking in to get my press tag and coordinating with the road crew on the best background angle preparing to go live as long as Jack didn't miss his cue . . . again. I only had a ninety-second spot to advertise the broadcast we'd be doing later in the day covering the president's tour of St. Louis. It sounded lame that they even wanted me to bother with this when the real story was taking place behind the scenes, and that's what I wanted to scoop. But I wiped off my irritation and smiled when the camera rolled.

I dropped my mic to my waist after the camera cut off and stuffed my notebook into my briefcase. I grabbed the press schedule of the president's visit and looked at the crew. "We're blacked out during his breakfast meeting and—" I looked up and saw Tony standing on the sidewalk about twenty feet from me. His face was contorted in disbelief. "Tony?" He took a few steps toward me then paused before taking a few more. I looked at the crew. "I'll meet you at the van." Then cleared the distance between us. "I wondered if I would see you here. You've never been one to miss a scoop."

He shook his head. "I can't believe you're here! I mean, I wondered if you'd make it up for the press dinner, but wow, you look great, Chance."

I smiled. "Back atcha. It's great to see you, Tony."

He fidgeted and chuckled. "I . . . I honestly don't know what to say right now. Wow, it's great to see you." He hugged me—oh he smelled so good. "How long are you in St. Louis?"

I waved at the van. "I'm here until this whole thing is over. I got in last night."

Tony ran his fingers through his hair. "Why didn't you call me? You should have told me you were in town."

I shrugged and lied. "It was late when we got into town."

"You're still a terrible liar, Chance. For a journalist, that's not a good thing." He winked.

I laughed. "So are you covering the whole thing?"

"No, I'm here with the anchor." He pointed toward the prettiest redhead I've ever had the pleasure of hating at first sight.

"Wow," I mumbled.

"That's Miriam O'Bannon. She took the anchor position I offered you last year." He looked back at her then looked at me and grinned. "You can stop cutting her with your eyes anytime you're ready."

I blinked and smiled at him. "She looks extremely . . . professional." I cleared my throat. "Where did you find her, at the strip club?"

"Nah, that girl didn't work out—turns out she couldn't read. It was a tough decision."

I smacked his arm and chuckled. "You're a pig."

He shrugged. "What? I'm a man and have an appreciation for a beautiful woman." His eyes locked on mine and reached into my throat, cutting off my oxygen.

I looked away and tucked my hair behind my ear. I couldn't help but stare at Miriam's elegant figure and salon-perfect hair. Every move she made seemed perfectly choreographed by years of reform school. "Jesus, is she even human?" I muttered.

Tony touched the small of my back and leaned toward my ear. "Now, Chance, don't be jealous. Green never looked good on you."

"Bullshit, green is one of my best colors. And, I'm not jealous by any means. I'm taking great satisfaction in knowing she stays hungry eighty percent of the time to keep herself so skinny."

Tony laughed and pulled away. "I better get back over there." He tilted his head and smiled. "I can't tell you how good it is to see you,

Chance."

I smiled back. "It's great to see you, too, Tony."

"Save a dance for me tonight," he said with a wink and walked away. He has the best swagger I've ever seen—confident and aware that people (read: me) are watching.

A redhead. She's a fucking redhead. He loves red in every shade, and his bombshell Barbie anchor is a redhead. I had an overwhelming desire to drench her in the worst shade of pink I could find to drown out her inconvenient beauty. I looked at the crew standing by the van and readjusted my briefcase. I was here to do a job, and I was going to make sure that bitch didn't get a better story. "Guys, we have work to do. Most of these guys are going to be following the president like a puppy to get the best shot of his tour, but I want to scoop the story behind his visit. I know there's more behind this than breakfast and a ball. Let's get busy."

I told the crew I'd meet back up with them at eleven and assigned each of them an area to work to see if they could drum up any local rumors that might give us a starting point. I drove three blocks and found the latest copy of the Post-Dispatch and a coffee shop. I looked at my watch and decided to sit inside and see if the locals were riled up. I grabbed my briefcase and took off my press badge—no need in advertising to the general public that I was out sniffing a story.

I ordered my coffee and chose a table near a group of businessmen shop-talking before work. The television above me flashed to an advertisement of Tony's station, and there was Miss Miriam staring at the camera with her perfect smile and luxurious locks spilling over her malnourished shoulders.

"Tramp," I whispered as I flipped open the newspaper and took a drink of my coffee. I scanned the headlines and found nothing other than the waning talent of written journalism and four typos in one article. One of the men at the table next to me cleared his throat and smiled at me when I made eye contact with him. He tipped his coffee cup at me and winked. Even in the lowlighting, the gold in his wedding ring glowed with caution. I smiled and returned my attention to the newspaper while hoping he spilled coffee on his groin and wiped it up with his eyelids.

Another man at the table asked, "So how's your daughter doing, Paul?"

"Still in the hospital. They're running more tests on her today."

"Any ideas? Are they leaning toward anything specific?"

"Nah, just some virus going around school. The children's wing is full, though, so I hope they figure it out quickly."

I shuffled the paper two pages back to read an article I'd skipped. *Local Children Hospitalized with Respiratory Virus*. The article indicated forty-two children in the St. Louis area had been admitted with severe respiratory problems and high fevers but no cause could be determined. *Bingo*.

I folded the paper, stuffed it in my bag, and looked up the address for the nearest hospital. As I stood, Tony walked in the door.

"You're easy to tail, Miss Bradley."

I raised my eyebrows. "I still carry mace, Tony. You must be really bored if you're tailing your ex who is simply going for a cup of coffee to kill time."

"Ah, see, I call bullshit on that. You smell something, and I know it."

I shrugged and took a drink of my coffee. "It's called caffeine. Where's Barbie?" Tony smirked and rubbed the back of his neck, but I didn't give him a chance to respond. "Wait, let me guess. She's already lining up waiting to get that perfect shot for the twelve o'clock live broadcast."

His eyebrow shot up. "And you're not?"

I huffed and started toward the door. "No, I'm certainly not going to stand around waiting to get a waving glimpse of the president."

"So you *do* smell a story." He whispered in my ear, "So do I."

My heartbeat quickened with the warmth of his breath and the validation that I was onto something big. I turned toward him and grinned. "You're off your game, old man. The big story is the president is touring the St. Louis area. Maybe you should have Barbie climb up the Arch to get the best view of his trip she can. Wouldn't that be a great

118

story? Then she could rappel using her long, red Rapunzel hair."

Tony laughed and shook his head. "You gonna tell me where you're going, or do I get the thrill of the chase again?"

God, he's sexy. Visions of us making scandalous use of a cheap hotel room crossed my mind, and if there weren't sick children counting on me to discover the cause of their illness, I would handcuff him and take him to the room myself. "I have nothing to tell you, Tony. I'm surprised you left the puppy unattended, so maybe you should go check and make sure she hasn't chipped a nail or lost an eyelash." I tilted my coffee cup toward him. "Cheers!" I opened the door and headed to my car. I stopped a few feet from my door and felt the rage brewing in my gut, slowly making its way up my neck to erupt on my face. The car in front of me was parked normally; the large media van behind me, however, was parked so close to my bumper it could be considered part of my license plate. I spun on my heels and started toward the coffee shop when I saw Tony leaned up against the building intently studying his fingernails. His satisfied grin and failure to make eye contact with me told the story that he'd bested me and knew it the whole time.

"Tony, move that piece of shit before I—"

He held his hand up. "What are you going to do, Chance, smash your beautiful little car into my hunk of shit? Come on. You'll total your car and I'll get another scratch."

"The only scratches will be my nails down your face if you don't move that van!"

"I much preferred your nails down my back, but I guess that goes without saying, my lady." He bucked off the wall and sauntered over to the back of the van. "Yeah, I think I can get out of here. Maybe."

I stormed over to where he stood and assessed the closeness of the car behind the van. "This isn't funny, Tony."

He turned. "Tell me where you're going, or better yet, just get in, and we can go together."

"Not on your life," I muttered.

"Come on. This is my town. I can get you there faster, and I think I've proven that a time or two."

119

I kept the sophomoric chuckle embedded in my chest and stared at him. "Why are you such a dick?"

He threw up his hands. "It's a gift—genetic. Get in."

"No, we'll take my car. I don't want to drive around in a press van and advertise that the media is sniffing around."

He looked at the van and nodded. "Good point."

"And, no way are you driving my car. I've seen you drive and I'd rather not throw up today, thanks." I fished my keys out of my purse and opened the car door. I tossed my bag in the back seat for good measure and sat in the driver's seat waiting for him to back up.

The second I had enough clearance, I threw the car in reverse, flipped my blinker on, and peeled out of the parking spot into the street. I opened my sunroof and flipped Tony off as I squealed tires heading east laughing maniacally the whole way.

Thanks to the traffic I cut off to make my escape, I had a half-block jump on him and was gaining distance. I took turns I didn't need to take to shake my tail and giggled through the exhilaration of being in a car chase. I felt like I was in a James Bond movie without the ridiculously expensive car.

My cell phone illuminated with the contact, "Do Not Answer," I'd been craving for over a year—just not under these circumstances. I tried not to sound like I was smiling when I answered. "This is Chance."

"Very clever, Ms. Bradley," he purred.

"Rule number one, Sir Tony: never trust a journalist."

"Rule number two, Ms. Bradley: never try to beat a pursuing journalist in his own town."

I glanced around to find him sitting at the red light to my right. My eyes locked on his as he gave me a finger wave. His voice purred in my ear, "You may go now, Ms. Bradley. Point—Tony."

I continued through the intersection. "Well done, master navigator. The story involves sick kids and a possible cover-up."

"That's a dead story, Chance. We've already looked into it. There's nothing there. It's a random strand of virus that's mutated and has to run its course."

"Maybe so, but maybe it's not."

"Look, don't go Brockovich on us. I'm telling you it's a dead end."

"The president has access to nearly every city in the world. Why is he in St. Louis?"

"He needs a PR visit—baby kissing, shaking hands with the elderly and the vets, and then back to Washington with renewed hope in his constituents."

I thought for a moment. "Still not buying it. There's a story around here." Tony was quiet on the other end, so I checked my phone to see if I still had a signal. "Tony, are you there?"

He cleared his throat. "Yeah, I'm here, Chance. I just . . . I was . . . I really missed you, Chance."

My nose burned with tears forming in my eyes and my throat constricted. I whispered, "I missed you too, Tony," and hung up before he could tell he'd gotten to me.

Chapter Seventeen
Jar of Hearts

Alissa

I looked at the time on my cell phone then looked at Dani for the twelfth time in six minutes. "What's the point of having an appointment with a doctor if the appointment is give-or-take forty minutes?" When she didn't respond, I asked, "Do you know how many germs are on that magazine you're holding?"

Dani flipped the page. "Do you know how many germs are on your cell phone?"

I studied the phone and frowned. "Really?"

She chuckled. "When was the last time you cleaned it?"

"I never thought about it."

"Okay, *that's* disgusting." She showed me a picture of a woman with a buzz cut. "I think you should cut your hair like this."

"Ugh, whatever. You first." She leaned back in her chair. I stood up and walked to the window so I could wipe my hands on my pants. Her comment about my cell phone had my skin crawling.

I stared at the lawn care workers who resembled ants on a mission. Two were standing on lawnmowers and zipped back and forth in two different sections but their synchronized motions seemed planned and purposeful. Three guys with wheelbarrows toted mulch from a truck to the flowerbeds that they'd cleaned out in preparation for fall. I wondered how many thousands of dollars this complex spent on landscaping instead of researching birth control pills that, oh, I don't know, *won't* allow unsuspecting women to get pregnant.

I sighed and walked toward Dani. She handed me a tissue with a dab of antibacterial hand sanitizer. "Here. Clean your phone so you'll calm down."

"Oh thank God." I focused on smearing the sanitizer all over the screen and case and asked, "Did you talk to your boss, yet?"

Dani shrugged. "I mentioned that I needed to take some time off for personal reasons."

"How'd that go over? Great, now the tissue is leaving little white particles all over this thing." I wiped the phone on my pants and swiped at the remnants on my pants. "Great."

Dani chuckled and set her magazine on the table before shifting in her chair to look at me. "I'll have to quit my job. They won't let me off for six months then give me maternity leave after the baby is born."

I glanced at her. "What do you think about that?"

She shrugged and looked at the same poster I'd memorized thirty minutes ago. "I think I've got no choice. I'm going to turn in my notice this afternoon."

"Really? That's so great! We can go . . ."

The door to the waiting room opened as a nurse called my name. I locked eyes with Dani. "Ready?"

Her eyes misted as she nodded and whispered, "Yes."

My legs felt like I'd deadlifted four-hundred pounds a minute earlier as I stood. "Moment of truth. Let's go see the private guest."

"The baby," Dani whispered.

The room was dimly lit with a bed and ultrasound machine nearby. The most awkward thing about the beds was how far apart the stirrups are while you're sitting half-naked waiting for the doctor to come in. If you let your legs dangle, you feel like a kindergartener waiting for the principal to scold you; if you put your feet in the stirrups, you look overly eager for the procedure. I split the difference and paced in my gown while trying not to moon Dani in the process.

"Geez, you're making me nervous with all this pacing."

"Have you ever noticed how much time people expect Americans to sit? Everywhere you go there are chairs, benches, beds, seats, and everything in between. It's no wonder obesity is so rampant. People sit too much."

"Are you channeling Michelle today? You sound a lot like her right now. I've never seen you so irritable."

"I didn't sleep much last night," I mumbled.

"Why?"

"Maybe you should ask your child. I puked a good part of the evening then had stupid dreams and woke up drenched in my own sweat bad enough to change my sheets."

"I've heard that's normal."

"And, I fart . . . a lot. Like explosive, house-shaking farts."

Dani curled over her legs and covered her mouth to stifle the laughter pouring out of her. Every time she tried to speak, she burst out laughing again.

"I guess I shouldn't tell you about my boobs itching."

The doctor walked in and looked at Dani still chuckling and wiping the tears from her eyes. "Looks like I'm late to the party. Hi, I'm Dr. Moreau. I assume you're Alissa since you're the one dressed for the ball."

"Clever," I said as I shook his hand. "This is my friend, Dani."

He raised his eyebrows. "Oh, well hello, Dani."

Dani blushed. "No, it's not like that. I'm just here for moral support."

The doctor smiled but didn't appear to be convinced. "Pleasure to meet you. Okay, Alissa, let's take a look and see how far along you are. Climb on up on the table."

Dani stood. "I'm going to come up here by your head. I don't need to see all that."

"You'll get enough of that in the delivery room." I shivered and pushed the images of childbirth out of my mind.

Dr. Moreau said, "Now, this is an internal exam; you're aware of that, right?" He picked up an instrument at least a foot long with a ball on the end of it.

I looked wide-eyed at Dani and mumbled, "Impressive."

She covered her mouth and laughed into her hand.

"Okay, here we go," he said as he inserted the instrument into my vagina. For some strange reason, the humor in the bizarre scene set before me attacked, and I started laughing. The more I saw my legs up in the air, the gown of modesty to protect me from my own junk draped across my knees yet my crotch was wide open in front of a man sticking a lube-slicked instrument in me.

"Are you going to buy me dinner after this?" I said. Dani howled, and my stomach bounced up and down on the table with my own laughter. "After seeing that thing, I'm really disappointed in my last boyfriend."

Dani had to sit down to prevent herself from falling. She gasped for air as I wiped the tears rolling out of my eyes. I tilted my head up to get a visual of the doctor who was trying to maintain his professional composure while appreciating the humor in the situation. He cleared his throat and shook his head while focusing on the monitor that was coming to life with white and black swirling images.

"Is this a Rorschach test? I'll play; I see my mother."

Dani sprang toward the bed and leaned closer. "Is that it?" she pointed to the screen.

"That," he said, "is the baby, yes. Good job." Dani's face registered complete awe as she stared at the grey image. "See that little flutter right here?" he asked. "That's the baby's heartbeat."

I stared at the screen and watched the black hole move, and there, off to the side, was the tiniest little fluttering mass. "Oh, I see it!"

Dani giggled. "Lis, that's the baby!" She wiped the tears off her face and asked the doctor, "Can you tell how far along she is?"

"Looks like about five weeks and a few days."

Five weeks . . . five weeks ago I was in a relationship ignoring the warning signs of a man who was growing more disinterested in me. The blip on the screen was my mother's grandchild. I thought to myself, *God, let this baby be a boy. Let him have a fighting chance.*

The doctor took several screen shots and measurements. I looked at the little peanut-shaped mass and tried to make out the image of a baby. "Okay, it looks like your due date is around May eighth. We'll be able to get a better idea when you're further along, but let's go with that date for now."

I looked at Dani's face and grinned. "May eighth it is! That sounds so far away."

"It'll go quicker than you think." He removed the instrument and stood. "I'll step out so you can get dressed."

I sat up and mumbled, "Don't step out on my account. You've already seen the jewels."

Dani tapped my leg and smiled at the doctor. "She didn't sleep well last night. She's a little cranky."

The doctor smiled and left the room as Dani walked to the chair and brought me my clothes. She shook her head. "You never cease to amaze me."

I grabbed my clothes and scooted off the bed as I untied my gown. "What? I thought it was funny. I didn't see a ring on his finger. Maybe he's single."

Dani chuckled. "Oh yes, that's exactly what you need—a man whose profession involves seeing other women's nether regions daily."

"I've never understood that—guys who go into the hooch business. Seems like it would be a killjoy."

Dani shook her head and whispered, "Hooch business . . . did you see that little teeny tiny heartbeat?"

I smiled. "Yes, I saw it. It was very sweet, very tiny. So where to next? Do you have to go to work after this?"

"Yeah, unfortunately. What are you going to do?"

I pulled my jacket over my shirt and slipped on my shoes. "I don't know. Everyone I know is still working. Chance is in St. Louis. I could crash the big ball tonight." I grinned and shook my shoulders.

"Never mix friendship and business—that's our rule, remember?"

I huffed. "You're no fun. Maybe I can convince Katie to take off at noon and go shopping."

"Good luck there," she mumbled.

"I haven't seen or heard much out of her, have you?"

"Not really, but that's not uncommon. You know how she is—she'll pop up sometime. Ready?"

"Yep. Wanna grab something to eat before you go to the office?"

Dani chuckled. "What's with you? You act like you are scared to death to be alone or something."

I scoffed. "I am not! I've been thinking about having the living room

126

painted again, so maybe I'll run by there and see what they say."

"Paint fumes might not bode well for the nausea," she said as she got in the car.

"Everything makes me puke right now. I don't see how paint fumes could make it any worse."

Dani turned in her seat. "Lis, are you absolutely sure about this?"

I glanced at her and bit my lip to stop my quivering chin. My words were thick as they left my mouth. "I can't be like Mom, Dani. Or my sisters."

She put her hand on mine. "But maybe you won't be! Maybe you'll be the best mother in your family."

I chuckled and wiped the tears rolling down my face. "It wouldn't take much to best the women in my family. I . . . I can't take that chance, Dani, and I really don't want to. I feel like the worst person on earth. Your face—the way you looked at the monitor when we were seeing the private guest for the first time—*that's* how it should be. That's how *I should* be, but I can't find it in me. My therapist will have a hay day with this next session, I can tell ya that. Sure, I could provide for this baby and hire the best nanny, send it to the best schools, and give it the life that no one in my family has ever had, but I've already raised three kids and look how they turned out. Nothing I did, no amount of advice, no effort I gave could break that family curse. Hell I even tried to bribe them! And now I'm the bad guy because I wanted them to have a fighting chance, and look at them."

"Are they happy, though?" she whispered as she wiped her tears.

I shrugged. "Hell, I don't know. Maybe they are. I'm the bad guy, remember? The rich bitch, as they call me."

"You're going to have to work through that guilt and not let them shame you like this, Lis."

"Well if you can figure out how to get rid of it, I'll start seeing you instead of my therapist."

Dani slipped on her seatbelt and stared out the window. I took my opportunity to get moving.

Chapter Eighteen
Grenade

Michelle

At the end of the day, my boss called me into her office. "Close the door, please."

I felt my peanut butter and jelly sandwich twist in my stomach as my shaking hand reached to close the door. I took a deep breath and sat across from her. "Is something wrong?"

She looked at me. "I was about to ask you the same thing, Michelle. I don't know what's gotten into you, but you're short-tempered and irritable with the kids these days, and that's so unlike you. I have had a few complaints from the other employees, but thankfully none from parents yet."

I put my head in my hands and willed my throat to reopen. "Ever feel like you're going insane, Cheryl?"

She chuckled. "I run a daycare. Of course I feel like I'm going insane . . . every day."

"Am I too young for a mid-life crisis?"

"I don't think age ever factors into that. I think it's something we all go through at some point." She leaned across her desk. "But you have to leave it at the door, Michelle. We all have things going on at home, and when we come in here, we have to set ourselves aside and be healthy, nurturing providers for these kids."

"Sounds like my house," I said before I could think.

She stiffened. "This is a hard job, Michelle, especially for parents. But, your behavior here lately is unacceptable and if it doesn't change, I'm going to ask you to seek employment elsewhere." She slid a piece of paper across her desk.

"What's this?"

"It's a written reprimand to go with the verbal you're getting right now. You're putting me in a very difficult position, because some of the complaints I've had on you borderline on verbal abuse, and if I'm ever investigated, I have to show that I've taken appropriate steps." She handed me a pen.

"Abuse? Are you serious, Cheryl?"

"Yeah, I know, it shocked me, too. But I've watched you this week, and unfortunately I find the complaints valid. I want you to try to find that woman that started working for me three years ago and bring her back. This . . . this angry, sullen woman sitting in front of me is very different than the woman I hired."

I groaned and took the pen. "I have no choice but to sign it. Guilty as charged, Judge!" I scribbled out my name and slammed the pen on the desk.

"Michelle," she glared at me and took the paper. "This isn't personal, but you are giving me great ammunition to make it that way. I don't want to pry into your personal life, but maybe you could benefit from medication . . ."

"I'm already *on* medication, Cheryl. I just have a shit-hole of a life and can't do a damn thing about it." I stood up and grabbed my purse. "Are we done here?" I heard the blood rushing through my ears and felt my pulse in my eyeballs. It reminded me of standing too close to the speakers at Brandon's gigs and seeing the speakers thump with the beat. Tears brimmed my eyes, and I was about one tooth-grind away from breaking my own jaw to keep them from falling.

Cheryl leaned back in her chair and stared at me. "You're suspended. One week——unpaid. Get your shit together and come back in here with your head on straight. And I highly encourage you to leave this office and not say one more word if you want to have a job to come back to in a week."

I stared at her trying to decide if I gave enough of a shit to keep this job or not. I stared at her bad haircut and long-overdue need for a wardrobe update. I saw myself in her. "That won't be necessary, Cheryl. I quit."

I glared at my coworkers as I left the building in a blur of swirling colors representing the levels of responsibility I'd just flushed down the toilet. My beautiful purple Del Ray, the serene-but-hopeful blue Martin, my stuck-in-gaming-land yellow Gibson. Mix that with the black-hole Brandon, and I'd just made a mess of our paint-by-number life.

I couldn't go home. Not now. I couldn't face my family and tell them I'd just quit my job and had no idea how we'd have groceries or pay the house payment. Dammit, I should have collected my check from Cheryl while I was there. Now I'll have to wait until payday. I reached in my purse for my cell phone then remembered I'd dropped it under the seat this morning. God, can nothing be easy for me? Does everything have to be such a fucking struggle? I take one step in the right direction and get hit by sixteen Mack trucks with no concepts of brakes or steering wheels. Just splat! Deal with it!

I just quit my job. I just got written up for borderline abusive behavior toward three year-olds and my co-workers. I could see the headlines, now: "Former Sunday School Teacher Jailed for Arguing with Toddler." Brandon is going to have a fit. I hope he enjoyed his blissful "me time" day off—pecker head. Cheryl wanted me to take a week off and be good as new. That's almost comical to think about—one week off will just rectify everything in corporate America. Stressed out? Take a day off. Tired of struggling? Take a week, but make sure you come back to work with a new shiny smile and great attitude, and oh, let's just add to your problems by withholding a week of income that will remove the food from the only room where you have a place in life—the kitchen.

I think I know why Britney Spears shaved her head. Only she didn't nearly get fired from the lowest-paying, thankless job like I did. I looked in the mirror and tried to envision myself bald. I think I could pull it off. It would save me a ton of money on hair dye to cover the grey that Brandon so eloquently pointed out the other day.

I pointed the car toward the store; if I had to go home and tell my family I'd failed them financially, then at least I could do it while I handed out the goods they needed before the money ran out. I stared at the rows of cars in front of me and how everyone in life is herded by colors and lines. If you're lucky, green is your ruling color; yellow throws caution toward you, and red just stops you in your tracks. Lines on the highway, lines at the grocery store, lines on your face, lines for a signature stating you've become unsatisfied in life and your behavior shows it, and if you ever mix the two phenomenon and fall below the red line in your checkbook, you're pretty much screwed.

I bought more than I should have at the store, but I really didn't care. Maybe I'll put the receipt on Brandon's hamburger tonight. That would be a great conversation starter at dinner. "Hey, kids! Make that deodorant last, because Mommy's officially unemployed! Eat up! Pass the ketchup."

It was nearly six before I made it home and walked into mass chaos. Del Ray was in mid-rant when she wheeled around and yelled, "Mom, geez, where were you? Why didn't you answer your phone?"

My heart pounded in my chest. "What's wrong? What happened?"

"Oh, I don't know, maybe that no one picked me up from school and the door was locked, so we couldn't get in the house after we all *walked* home?"

I glared at Brandon. "Where were you?"

He tossed the remote on the coffee table. "I had some errands to run! Where were you? We all tried to call you."

Del Ray yelled at me, "You said we were going to the store after school today, but you never showed up!"

"I *went* to the fucking store, dammit!" I slammed the bags on the coffee table. "My phone fell under the car seat this morning, and no one ever calls me anyway, so I didn't think it would fucking matter!"

"Michelle, language!" Brandon yelled.

I looked at the wide-eyed, gaping-mouthed faces of my children and hung my head in shame. I gestured to the bags. "Dig out what's yours and I'll put the rest away." I walked into the kitchen and opened the refrigerator. Brandon came up behind me and slammed the door out of my hand.

"You and I need to talk. Bedroom, now." He stormed off.

Maybe I'll get written up for this, too. Maybe I'll get put on a week's unpaid leave from my home life,, then I can come back with a new

131

attitude and fresh outlook on the same life I had when I left. Maybe that will happen. Sure. I shuffled down the hallway and closed the door to our bedroom. I crossed my arms and looked at everything but Brandon.

"What in the hell has gotten into you, Michelle?"

I walked around the bed and climbed in on my side. I clutched my pillow to my chest and buried my face in it. "I don't know," I mumbled.

He pulled the pillow away from my face and sat across from me. "Seriously, Michelle. What's going on with you? You're not even close to the same person you were even two months ago."

I stared at his face, the same face I've envisioned shredding with my fingernails, and there looking back at me was my Brandon—the man who won my heart as a young boy, who bought me flowers (cheap gas station roses, but hey, they were flowers) every week while I was pregnant with Del Ray and sang to me from stage like I was the only girl in the room even though hundreds of other girls would have gone home with him that night. He looked at me with those eyes for the first time in years, and my dam exploded. I threw my arms around his neck and let go of months of frustration and misery. I envisioned each tear as a memory of wrongdoing that I was no longer going to hold.

He held me until my memory was wiped and pulled away from me to look me in the eyes. "I just have one question for you, Michelle. Just one, and I want an honest answer, okay?"

I nodded and wiped my face with a corner of the sheet. "Okay."

He cleared his throat and took a deep breath. "Are you seeing someone else?"

Out of the fifty questions that ran through my mind, that was the last one I would have ever considered. I chuckled at first then burst into laughter. I caught a glimpse of the relief softening his features and stopped laughing. "You were serious?"

He shrugged and smoothed the pillow on his lap. "Well, yeah, I guess."

"Brandon, what on earth makes you think I'm seeing someone else?"

He twirled his finger in the air. "All of this . . . your outbursts, your

132

dissatisfaction with the life we've worked so hard to build, your new fascination with the gym . . . I don't know, I just thought maybe someone else had taken my place." He choked on the last few words, which made my heart seize.

I put my hand on his face and made him look at me. "No, Brandon, no one has taken your place. I just don't know where mine is anymore. I don't know what's wrong with me. I'm a mess. I don't know who I am!"

He sighed and looked at me. "You're Michelle Morehead; wife, mother, employee, and you're good at all of those things. You're beautiful, smart, and a little quirky, but that's one of the things I love about you."

"Well, about that employee thing . . ." I turned my head. "I lost my job today, Brandon."

He stood up. "What the hell? Are you kidding me?"

I held back the tears trying to form in case they needed to be a memory to release later. "No, I'm not kidding. I'm so sorry, Brandon."

"What happened?"

My lip trembled as I lied, "Downsizing I guess."

"At a daycare? They can't do that."

I squirmed on the bed and reached for the pillow. "I—"

"You're lying, and I know you're lying. Michelle, I've known you half your life."

"I got wrote up for my attitude, and it escalated from there," I mumbled.

Brandon sighed and threw his hands on his hips. "So this isn't just something you save for home—you're spreading your crazy all over your life, is that what I'm hearing?"

"I said I was sorry. I don't know what happened. She was all up in my shit and I lost it. She tried to suspend me for a week, but before I knew it, I was unemployed."

"Call her tomorrow and tell her you'll take your week and see if she'll let you come back. We can't afford for you to not work right now, Michelle."

"I can try to find something else."

"Like what?"

"I don't know, like maybe an office job or something at the bank. Maybe Katie can pull some strings and get me a teller job."

"You don't have any experience in any of that," he snapped.

"Maybe I could look at taking some college classes?" I felt like I should welcome Brandon into my pity pool where he was drowning in my reality.

"No, Michelle, we can't afford for you not to work, and I sure the hell can't afford to put you through college when I'm trying to plan for the kids' education first."

"I'll look tomorrow, Brandon. I'm really sorry."

"You're unbelievable, you know that? You act like your life is so freaking miserable, and you don't really have that much to worry about, Michelle. Kids, house, and dinner—boom, that's it, and—"

"'That's it?' That's it! Do you even hear yourself, Brandon? That's a lot! And I work on top of it!"

"Correction—you *did* work before you flaked out and lost your job today."

I flew off the bed and stood in front of him while remembering why I spent most of my time wanting to claw his eyes out and shove them up his ass. That look—that look of annoyance and boredom he gets when he looks at me—that's what makes me want to barrel into him like a linebacker after the boy who took his girl to prom. "When did you get so pompous?"

"Oh, big word alert; you've been reading again." He rolled his eyes and started toward the door.

I caught him before he got there and planted my body in front of the door as I stared at him with my maniacal eyes and air stuck in my throat. "Do you lie around trying to figure out what kind of asshole things you can say to make me feel worse about myself?"

"Nope, it just comes so easily. Excuse me." He moved me out of the way and opened the door. "Your kitchen awaits you. I'm tired of your pity party, and the kids are hungry."

And like that, it was over. The moment was gone, and the truth had

134

been revealed. I was insignificant.

Chapter Nineteen
These Days

Chance

I tapped my pen on my notebook and stared at the clock while hearing Tony say, "I just missed you, Chance" on repeat in my head. I shoved the notebook on the dashboard and put my head on the steering wheel. "I don't have time for this. I don't have time for this," I chanted. It was nearly eleven o'clock, and I had no story to report to my team. *"It's a dead story, Chance; we've checked into it."*

"We" . . . as in he and the redheaded slut-for-brains who probably never had an original thought a day in her life. Judging by her outfit, she has nothing better to do than study Pinterest and starve herself to death. I sighed and got out of my car to stare at the growing crowd waiting for the president to make an appearance. If I was an honest woman, I would admit that I was looking for Tony, but I'm not.

"Any luck?" I asked my cameraman, Eddie.

He crushed out his cigarette under his boot and shook his head. "Nah, there's nothing going on, Chance."

I frowned and looked back at the crowd. "This seems like a waste of a beautiful day to me. I could be home and feel equally as bored."

Eddie chuckled. "Yeah, but tonight should be a helluva party." He grinned. "I even brought my 'kill-em-dead' suit."

I clapped him on the shoulder. "There's too much stud in that body, kiddo. Go easy on the ladies tonight, okay? Don't let the big story of the night be something stupid you did."

"Aww, now, you don't give me enough credit."

I scanned the crowd again and mumbled, "I still can't believe there's no scuttle-butt about the president's visit."

"No luck at the coffee shop?"

"Oh I found something, all right, but nothing that will help me with my career." I waved off Eddie's questioning look. "Nothing, never mind.

Okay, let's figure out what we're going to say at the twelve-o'clock and help me try not to look bored for the lovely folks in Columbia."

I checked my phone and found two new texts from Dani and Alissa. Dani's version of gushing relayed the events with a smiley face. Alissa's said, *Yep. Still knocked up.*

I replied to Alissa and was about to toss my phone in the car when a text from Tony came across the screen. I tried to convince myself a year ago that I was done with him, so I changed his name in my phone to Do Not Answer. I looked toward the crowd again then slid the message open.

Still on the prowl for a story?

I smirked and replied: *I've got a few things to check on, yes. You?*

Look up.

He stood on the other side of my car grinning at me, looking like he was freshly released from the sexy farm. He cocked his head to the side and gave me "the look" that always sent the blood rushing through my body and my butterflies into a sheer panic. I considered walking toward him but was afraid my wobbly legs would make my intended sexy strut look like a newborn calf, so I played it cool and let him come to me. Which he did.

I cleared my throat and waited for my saliva glands to start working again, but my tongue was adhered to the roof of my mouth. I turned to the media van and slid the door open to retrieve a bottle of water from the cooler. My shaking hands betrayed me; Eddie smirked and grabbed the bottle from me to open it. I mouthed, *Thank you* before I turned toward Tony.

"Shouldn't you be chasing a story, Sir Tony?"

He grinned. "What makes you think I'm not?"

I laughed. "I know you well enough to know you wouldn't be caught dead in front of a media van if you were on the hunt."

He took a deep breath. "Touché. You're in front of the same van, Ms. Bradley."

Shit. "I'm getting ready to head back out. I've got to meet with someone in about an hour."

137

He looked at me sympathetically. "Chance, you're such a terrible liar. How do you even sleep at night knowing what an awful liar you are?"

I shrugged. "All right, I call. What's your hand?"

He folded his arms across his chest. "What makes you think I'm going to tell you and let you scoop me?"

"Because I can tell by that shit-eating grin on your face that you're dying to tell me, so you might as well come out with it."

He shook his head and bit his lip. "Nope. I'm not telling you." He looked at Eddie and extended his hand. "I'm Tony."

I felt my cheeks turning red as I fumbled over the words, "Oh yes, of course. Eddie, this is Tony; Tony, this is Eddie."

As they exchanged niceties, I studied Tony's face. I didn't think it was possible for men to anti-age, but the man standing before me looked younger than he did a year ago when I last saw him. His eyes twinkled as he shop-talked with Eddie and sized up the young man on my crew. I had to put my ego in check as my chest puffed up and a grin tickled my lips.

Tony whispered in my ear, "Walk with me for a minute."

I glanced at Eddie. "Are we on at noon?"

He checked the schedule. "I don't see that we're cutting live at twelve, but I'll call Stuart and see."

I nodded and walked after Tony. "Whatcha got?"

He sniffed. "There's really no story here, Chance."

I frowned. "Are you sure?"

He scratched his head. "Yes and no. Yes is what I've found, but no, I'm not convinced."

"None of this makes sense. Why would Stuart send me out here for three days if there's no story?"

Tony grinned and bit his lip. "Well, I may have kind of called Stuart and given him the idea that there was something brewing up here."

I gaped at him. "What? Why on earth would you do that?"

He leveled his eyes at me and chuckled. "Why do you think?"

I closed my eyes and took a deep breath to stop the spinning in my head. "This is a bit extreme, even for you." I panted and took a swig on my water before whispering, "Why didn't you just call me?"

He grinned. "I couldn't. See?" He showed me his phone—the last text was sent to "Do Not Call."

I snickered and showed him my phone. "You're 'Do Not Answer.'"

He laughed. "There ya go. That's why I didn't call. I . . . I should have called," he finished with a groan. "Okay, well, I'm done humiliating myself. I'll catch up with you later."

I smiled. "You should have called."

"Yes, but would you have answered?" he teased.

"Oh hell no, not the first time." I winked.

Tony laughed and shook his finger at me. "I'll see you very soon, Ms. Bradley."

"I look forward to it, Sir Tony."

What the hell just happened? I stood there watching Tony walk away and had the same urge I did a year ago to take off running after him when I watched him leave the courtyard with his shredded heart in his hands. I felt his name clawing at the back of my throat begging to be yelled and knew the feeling was mutual when he turned to look at me.

By the time I made it back to the van, I felt I'd run a marathon through wet sand uphill in a hail storm, but I'd only walked half a block. Eddie sauntered over to me and gave me another bottle of water after taking my nearly empty one. "You wanna tell me what that was all about?"

"Ever make such a gargantuan mistake in your life and have it stand before you on the beat?"

He chuckled. "I'm twenty-six, so the answer is no, but I had a few awkward moments on campus a time or two. Come on, Chance. Let's get you ready for a live broadcast. Stuart wants your pretty face on at noon."

"What the hell am I supposed to say? There's no story here, Eddie."

"We're going to be boring and welcoming to the president. Here. I've already written something up for you. You, uh, looked like you could use some help."

"Oh I could kiss your young face right now, Eddie. Thank you."

He laughed. "Please don't. I don't want to get my ass beat by that dude that's *still* staring at you. Don't look."

I trained my eyes on Eddie's face and fought every urge to find Tony's face and tell him I felt the same way. "Where?"

"Don't do it. Be cool. You'll get your chance to dazzle him tonight, but right now you keep your eyes right here on my face. Trust me on this one. It will drive him crazy."

I laughed. "Because you're a man—well almost—I'll listen."

"Oh thanks a lot. I'm trying to help you, and you insult me." He faked a dagger to the heart and stumbled backward.

"Stop it." I laughed. "Okay, let's get this shit out of the way and head back to the hotel. I see no point in staying out here frying in the sun if there's no real story to scoop."

After the broadcast, Eddie and I helped the other crew members pack up the van then headed toward the hotel. We parted ways after a quick lunch in the hotel restaurant and agreed to meet downstairs at five. That left me with four hours and eight hundred and sixty nerves to kill before I saw Tony again.

One of the worst things about staying in a hotel room by yourself is the complete lack of interesting things to do in a hotel room by yourself. There are no books, no pictures of interest, no comforts of home, and no furry critters to occupy the time. I threw myself on the bed and stared at the ceiling while trying *not* to think about Tony. I should call Alissa and ask how the appointment went, but she knows my voice all-too-well and would probably be up here in less than two hours if she wasn't already on her way. That girl doesn't know how to be still.

And right now, I get why she's like that. Sometimes the best thing one can do is stay moving to avoid all of the insanity running amuck in the old noggin. I ran a hot bath and found myself doing the exact same thing while lying in the substandard bath bubbles that I was doing in bed—trying not to think about Tony—trying not to dissect every moment with him to see if I was being a complete idiot, or worse, getting played.

I managed to kill an hour talking myself out of thinking about Tony. Only three more hours until I see him again and knock him dead in my new red dress and heels. Visions of me walking into the event pretending to be bored and accidentally running into him plagued my psyche. The way his eyes grew wide, the little dab of drool that formed at the corner of his mouth, the way he trembled with desire to wrap me in his arms and declare his love for me. I groaned and belly-flopped onto the bed while pulling the pillow over my head. When did my head turn into a B-rated movie?

A knock at the door sent me bolting straight up in bed. I gathered my robe and padded to the door. My heart and lungs were in a race to see which would kill me first—my heart slamming against my ribs was about to win. I stared through the peep hole but couldn't see anything. The black cover of Alissa's thumb moved as she said, "Open this door or I'll set off the fire alarm."

I breathed a sigh of relief mixed with disappointment as I opened the door and chuckled. "Girl, what on earth are you doing here?"

Alissa sashayed into the room and threw her purse on the floor. "I'm bored. I knew you were here probably not doing anything, so I thought I'd come hang out with you." She flashed her pearly-whites at me and looked around the room. "Not bad."

"How was your appointment?" I sat on the bed and fluffed my pillows.

She sighed and shrugged. "It was all right. Dani's face was priceless, but overall yeah, things are going good. I'm five weeks along and due in May." She turned toward me. "Okay, so I've been thinking about Florida, and I think I want to stay in Naples. It's beautiful and lots of snowbirds will be there during that time, so we'd blend in perfectly."

I laughed. "Alissa, it's not like we're famous or on magazine covers. No one is going to give a shit about us being in Naples, Florida."

"No, but I think it will be a lot more fun because so many people will be there, and there will be tons of stuff to do."

I bit my lip. "I've been thinking . . ."

"Ugh, why? You know that always backfires on you."

141

"Very funny. I really don't know how I'm going to be able to just pick up my life and relocate to Florida for six months. What about my career? I'm the 'face of the station' as they call me."

"Can't you just go on assignment or something?"

"It doesn't work that way, honey. I've got my apartment and Chubs to think about, too."

"Well I just figured you'd bring the little feller with you. As for the apartment, just pay up your rent before you leave and it will be there when you get back."

"That doesn't solve the career problem, though."

"You've wanted to freelance again—maybe you could try that."

"But I like my job, Lis. That's what I'm getting at. I've worked really hard to make co-anchor."

"Chance, *I can't do this without you!* You're my best friend and my only real family!" Alissa's lip trembled.

"Okay, okay, stop with the bug-eyed thing. I didn't say I wasn't going to go. I just said I don't know how I'm going to make this work without ruining my career, that's all."

"Who cares if you do? You work at a local television studio. It's not like you're freaking Oprah!"

"Is it still considered battery if I hit you with soft pillows?"

Alissa laughed. "I need you, Chance. We'll figure it out, but I need you in Florida for six months. That's it. The rest of your life is yours for the making, but six months is all I'm asking."

Tony's face flashed into my mind.

Alissa looked at me sideways. "What was that? What was that look?"

"What look? What?" My stupid face had betrayed me again.

"I know that look. You saw Tony, didn't you?"

"Maaaybe." I pursed my lips together.

"Okay, what happened?" she folded her legs under her and tucked her hair behind her ears. "Out with it."

I sighed. "Nothing happened, really. I saw him this morning then he found me at a coffee shop. But let me tell you about the bimbo he's got working for him now—"

"Uh uh, I need to hear more about what he said or did. You're avoiding that little tidbit of information. Don't make me remind you that I am an attorney and can make you talk."

I chuckled and shook my head. "It wasn't much, really." I filled her in on the details from earlier in the day and showed her the dress I was planning to wear that night.

"Girl, you are on the prowl with that hot action right there."

I gaped. "What? I am not! I just wanted to. . ."

"Number one, it's red—his favorite color on you. Number two—you're glowing when you talk about him. Number three—you're acting like a girl amped up before prom. Chance, it's Tony. He broke your heart."

"We broke each other's hearts. *Life* broke our hearts. But seeing him today, Lis, oh my God it was fabulous. And he said he missed me."

"Then why didn't he call?"

"He couldn't. His phone told him not to."

She laughed. "You're joking right?"

I shook my head and grinned. "You know how I programmed his name as 'Do Not Answer?' He programmed me as 'Do Not Call.'"

"Is that supposed to be romantic?"

I sat down hard on the bed. "I don't know. See? God it's good you're here, because I've been going nuts this afternoon trying to figure out what the hell is going on in my head."

"Are you sure he's not seeing the anchor slut?"

"No, I'm not sure about anything other than the dark shadow that has been hanging over me for the last year has been lifted, and there's a bright ray of sunshine planted right over my head."

"If you break out into song, I'm outta here." She giggled. "But Chance, no. No, no, no. Don't even consider it. He's an ethereal being you'll never get to have. He's the un-gettable get, and that's torture for you, I know, but dammit, listen to me. He's still Tony."

"Maybe this is what needed to happen, though."

"Maybe it is! Maybe fate brought you here—"

"Um, actually, no that was Tony. He called the station and lied to

Stuart about a possible scandal behind the president's visit."

Her mouth dropped open. "He did?" She sat back and tapped her finger on her leg. "Damn, he's good."

I laughed. "Yeah, he is. But, he didn't break his promise not to call." I sang.

"No, but he cheated because he manipulated the circumstances and got you here, anyway."

"So now you see my dilemma."

"Yup. I see your dilemma." She asked, "Is this why you're rethinking Florida?"

I frowned. "No, not in the least."

"God, you're a terrible liar." She sighed and stood up to stretch. "Just know if you bail on me over a dude, I will never forgive you and will probably kill your dog in retaliation."

"I'm not bailing on you, and Chubs is too sweet to kill. Look, right now I'm in Rome doing as the Romans do. When I get back home, I guarantee nothing will be any different than it was when I left Columbia. I'm on his turf. I'm in his territory. The true colors will shine then."

She frowned. "Do colors shine?"

I groaned. "You know what I'm saying. Quit trying to be funny."

"Oh I am totally funny. And I'm also going to hang out with you until you leave for the ball, Cinderella, so get ready, go primp, do whatever you have to do except walk around naked. That's too blech for me."

"Oh thanks a lot." I laughed.

"I don't need to see all that, okay?" she reached for the remote and turned on the TV. "Let's watch something dumb before you start getting ready."

I flipped through the things in my suitcase and asked, "So do you want to tell me why you're really here?"

Alissa surfed the channels. "Nope."

I nodded. "I can probably guess—"

She interrupted. "I saw Mark."

I stopped and studied her face as she trained her eyes on the

144

television screen. I saw flickers of the TV stars in the reflection of her eyes, but nothing could mask the pain she was choking on now. "I stand corrected. How did that go?"

She shrugged and started to speak a few times, but her voice betrayed her. I watched as she bit her lip and played with her hair—the tell-tale signs from our youth that she was on the verge of losing it. "There's nothing on this tub of crap." She threw the remote on the bed. "Think we have time to go get coffee or something?" She stood up and walked to the window. "Wow, what a shitty view."

I chuckled and plugged in my curling iron. "I hadn't gotten that far." I walked over to stand beside her and stared at what she was trying to avoid. She pointed at the traffic below. "Look at all those people trying to get somewhere but held back by all of the other people trying to get somewhere."

"That's very prolific, Lis. To me, it just looks like St. Louis traffic."

"Looks like mass chaos to me," she muttered.

"Again, I say—"

She chuckled and paced the room inspecting every average hotel item with great interest. "These rooms are so small these days."

"Well, I didn't see any reason to get an apartment-sized room when I'm only going to be here for a few days." I grabbed her arm and made her look at me. "Talk to me, Lis."

She threw her arms around my neck and buried her head in my shoulder. "He was so mean, Chance. He thinks I did this on purpose. 'I thought you were trying *not* to be like your mom and sisters.' He said he wants me to end it because he doesn't want to be tied to 'my crazy ass' the rest of his life."

He'd hit her in the two areas that could take her to her knees. I instantly hated him more than I've ever hated anyone in my life. I swallowed hard to hold back the verbal assault I was about to unleash, but she was finally talking, and she needed to get all this out.

"Chance, he was the most normal guy I've ever dated. I was even on good behavior with him, and he still thinks I'm crazy. God, will I ever shed these family ties? That's it—next time I date, I'm not telling them

145

anything about my family. I'll be like you with no family."

I chuckled. "Well, I had a family; it's not like I hatched in the wilderness. But yeah, you might have to let that one stay hidden until you know you're with your permanent beau."

"Maybe I should just stay single. Maybe I'm not meant to be in a relationship." She pulled away from me and wiped her tears. "I even started studying how normal people should act in a relationship so I could have a fighting chance next time."

"Lis, is it possible you're trying so hard to be something you're not already—like your family—that you're completely losing that which makes you awesome? I don't have any problems with you, the other girls don't have problems, but when a penis enters the equation, you start trying on your best Alissa suits to see which one fits best for that man."

"Maybe I should try hypnosis. I hear that works like a reboot of sorts. Maybe whatever is wrong with me can be fixed like that."

"Well, let's wait on that until you deliver the private guest. The last thing we need is some subliminal message planted in your head about men then find out you're pregnant with a boy."

Alissa laughed and the spell over her was broken. She circled back around. Her face and shoulders relaxed, and she no longer appeared to be like a bird in a cage. She looked over the room again. "I like the colors they chose here. Maybe I'll consider that for the living room."

"Oh, no way, dude. You need something more livelily, I think. This is too sterile for you."

"The appointment this morning was kind of neat. Dani was completely enamored with the ultrasound. I didn't have any clue what I was seeing, but she had the mom lenses, I guess. It's neat to see her baby's heartbeat, though. She totally ugly-cried. It was fabulous."

I cocked my head to the side and studied the words "her baby." Has she completely dissociated herself with this pregnancy and truly sees this as Dani's baby? I thought back to when we were in high school and how she almost had to repeat ninth grade because she missed too many days. When her sisters were sick, she'd stay home with them to make sure they were taken care of; she couldn't stand to think of them being like she was at seven years old trying to measure out liquid ibuprofen to kill her own fever. Her mom had to work—when you're a waitress, there is no time off with pay. Luckily, the principal had mercy on Alissa and let her move on to tenth grade and her mom saw the impact she was having on Alissa's education. But, by that time it was too late; Alissa had no faith in her mother and worried incessantly about her sisters every time she was away from them. It's a shame those girls grew up to despise the one person that kept them afloat before their mom got her head on straight.

Chapter Twenty
Because of You

Alissa

I remember when Mom took me to the ultrasound to see Hilary for the first time. I was eleven, I think. Adriana was six, and Ella was four. I felt like a wet blanket had been draped over me as I walked into the room. Mom's belly was already revealing her secret, and I'd seen the signs before, so I already knew what was coming, but I sure didn't want to believe it. I'd just gotten Ella out of diapers six months earlier and it was all about to start all over again.

I remember staring at the black, white, and grey blip on the screen trying to find some sort of excitement for the new life growing in Mom's belly, but all I could feel was the dread of how my life was never going to change. As I stared at Mom's face, I saw she felt the same way. Things were already bad with her latest man, so I knew it was just a matter of time before we'd be moving again. I didn't even try to find friends at school that year. Not that I had time for them, anyway.

One of the great things about Chance is she has some kind of weird connection with me where she can read my thoughts. Maybe it's my facial expressions, I don't know. But rarely do I have to tell her what I'm thinking or how I'm feeling—she just knows. And for that I'm grateful. Saying out loud what I'm feeling sounds horrible when they become words. Hitting the highway to come see her was one of the best decisions I'd made in a long time. Not that there have been many as of late.

As we stood in Chance's hotel room lost in thought, I stared at my best friend who stared right back with that same reassuring, sarcastic smile that has calmed me for over twenty years.

"Are you sure you have to go to this stupid gala tonight? I think we should make good use of our time in St. Louis and paint the town. Or I could go with you."

She ran her fingers through her hair and sighed. "You know the rule.

Yes, I have to go, and no you can't come. As much fun as that sounds, I've got a job to do, and you will have to find a way to entertain yourself. You're welcome to stay here tonight, though."

"Psssht, no thanks. I'd go mad pacing in this little room. I'll probably head over to Katie's or Michelle's when I get back into town. Maybe I can piss Brandon off again. That's always fun."

She laughed and glanced at the clock. "Well, I need to start getting ready."

I eyed her. "You're really excited about seeing Tony-the-troublesome, aren't you?"

She grinned. "It will be fun to watch him squirm. And yes, I'm excited to see him. It's been over a year, and seeing him today—I don't know- it's . . . it's hard to explain."

I put my hand up. "No explanation necessary, my dear. You can get all giddy all you want, but I'm going to be holding my breath all night."

She laughed. "Be sure to take pictures when you start turning blue."

I flopped down on the bed and gestured toward the bathroom. "Move along, Cinderella. Go get dolled up; I'll sit here and complain about the lack of interesting shows on television these days."

"You do that. I'm glad you showed up, by the way."

I shrugged and grinned as the warm fuzzies flew through my chest. "Did the rock-solid Chance need her friend?"

She threw a pillow at me. "You're such a goof."

"Hey, did you bring your laptop?"

"I'm a journalist—what do you think?" She flipped her suitcase open and pulled the laptop out of it.

"Sweet! I'm going to research houses in Florida. What do you think—a three bedroom or four?"

Chance shrugged. "Probably just three, I'd say. One for each of us, because I am not sharing a bed with you for six months, I can tell you that."

"You don't forgive easily, do you?"

"Sure I do! I just don't forget shit." She chuckled.

"Okay, so I'm thinking we leave right after Christmas and will be

149

there through the middle of May."

"Don't you think we should stay through May? If you're due at the beginning of May, I doubt you're going to want to sit in a car for hours on end, and that will be a long trip for a newborn."

"Hmmm, good point. Okay, I'll stay through Memorial Day then we will be Missouri-bound."

I had a project—a mission. I had plans to make and people to contact. Mark's vicious words eventually turned from a bouncing echo to a faded whisper before they disappeared altogether. I studied the pictures of houses and volleyed questions to Chance while she primped in the bathroom.

"I want a house right on the beach. Like no yard, just sand. What do you think?"

"That's probably going to be pretty expensive, Lis. I know money isn't a concern for you, but let's try to at least pretend you're on a budget, okay?"

"You're such a killjoy sometimes." But she was right. Most of the time, I do well at hiding my wealth, but sometimes it pokes its head out and makes its presence known when I least expect it. Last month alone, I got over ten thousand dollars in interest from one account. I never have to worry about paying bills and have no debt; hell I paid cash for my house and cars. I could probably pay off all of their houses and never miss a dime of it, but we all made a pact when I became wealthy that we would all pretend I was just the same old Lis that I've always been. Every now and then I like to spoil them for a weekend getaway, and the families of my friends have come to expect it from me about twice a year. Considering I'd love to do it every weekend, I think I'm being pretty damn good.

But if I'm going to have this baby for Dani, I need to do it under my own terms, and since nothing in my life has ever been that way, I think I deserve to be a little selfish when it comes to bringing another life into the world. Maybe I should be a little more sensitive to their concerns about tanking careers and lives put on hold, but I'm the one hosting another human, and I have the money to pay for a six months hiatus for

150

all of us. I win.

If we go away for the pregnancy, I won't associate anything at home with this baby. There won't be memories of my growing belly in my home, and I won't have to face the demons I fought when my mom and sisters left the state. That vacancy in my chest won't be there, but I imagine this will be the last time I'll visit Naples, Florida.

"Chance, I have a good idea!"

"Well, good for you, honey. Did it hurt?"

I scowled. "Shut up, ass hat. I have my new mission before I go back home. And because you decided to be a douche, I'm not going to tell you."

She walked out of the bathroom, and my stomach dropped. She was absolutely stunning. Like, as in I had tears in my eyes—that kind of stunning.

"What do you think?" she asked.

"I think you're the prettiest woman I've ever seen," I whispered.

She laughed. "Alissa, are you going to cry?"

I wiped at my eyes and sniffled. "Stupid freaking hormones."

She grinned. "Aww, that's so cute that you're crying. And that reaffirms that this dress was the right dress to buy."

I nodded. "I'd love to see the look on Tony's face when he sees you."

"I told you about the redhead, right?"

I frowned. "No, I don't think so."

She gave up the fight trying to put her own bracelet on her wrist and stuffed her arm in my face. "Here, help. Okay, so the lovely Miriam-the-anorexic is his new anchor, and she's gorgeous. Beyond beautiful, borderline fairytale action, dude. She's smoking hot."

"Yeah, but you're a freaking goddess. In rock-paper-scissors, she's like the wrinkle on the end of a knuckle compared to you."

Chance laughed and asked, "Where do you come up with this shit?"

I chuckled. "I don't know, but that was pretty funny, I admit. Maybe my private guest is a comedian. There." I patted her arm. "All set." I stood up and stretched. "You really look fantastic, Chance."

151

"Thank you, dahling. Did you find anything promising in Naples?"

"Yeah, I've got a few that look like they could work. It's hard to tell from the pictures, but I'll call a few real estate agents tomorrow and see if they can help me find a place."

"You are just planning to rent, right?" she winked at me.

"Oh hell yes. I can't afford to throw down a million dollars on a house even though the idea of living on the coast year-round sounds amazing."

"Just promise me one thing, okay? We are coming back, right?"

I laughed. "Yes, we're coming back. All of us are rooted here, and I couldn't put that much distance between us and Katie and Michelle permanently. They're squirrely, but I love them and would miss them too much."

She looked at me. "I'm really worried about Michelle. Something's not right there."

I sighed. "Yeah, I feel it, too. Wish there was a way for her to come with us."

"Oh, Brandon would never go for it, and her kids would miss her too much."

"Katie won't even consider it, even for a weekend. I already asked."

"Well, maybe when we're there for a few months, we can ask again," Chance said. "The holidays will be over by then, and winter will be in full swing up here. They'll be ready for a getaway for sure."

"I guess I should get on the road so you can get one with your huge mistake. Have fun tonight and call me when you get back. I want to hear every detail about your night."

Chance smiled and hugged me. "Thanks for coming up. I'm really glad you did. Text me when you get home."

"I will. I have a few stops to make, so it will be a while; don't mama-bear out on me."

"I'll walk down with you. I'm supposed to meet the crew at five downstairs, anyway." She grabbed her clutch and slipped her room key in the side pocket. "Let's roll."

After leaving Chance, I navigated through St. Louis and hit I-70 west—homeward bound. I failed to plan properly for the five o'clock traffic, so I flipped the radio into CD mode and let the voices of the Breakup Mix flood the car and keep me company. Kelly Clarkson and Alicia Keyes represented well and deserved the repeats in rapid succession; they were speaking to my soul.

Mark didn't have any right to say those things to me. I've done nothing but be good to him, and if he didn't like me or want to spend the rest of his life with me, that's not because I'm damaged—he's the one with the problem. Kelly Clarkson said so. I'd love to buy her a vacation home just for her brilliant voice and perfect timing. Maybe I will, just to be nice. Or maybe I'll just keep buying her music and call it even.

I got back into Columbia around eight-thirty with plenty of time to hit the mall and gather my treasures for Dani. I flew through the stores and avoided the jewelry store where they know me by name. I could hear their cash registers salivating when I breezed through and intentionally looked the other way. I should've probably called Dani and told her I was coming by, but I didn't want to hear her excuses.

I pulled in her driveway, took the price tags off the gifts, and shoved them into the gift bag I'd spent way too much time agonizing over. I was about to knock on the door when it opened and she said, "I wondered how long you were going to sit out there. Come on in."

"Hi, there. I have something for you."

"Oh, you've been shopping. You have that afterglow about you."

"Hush up, now. Geez, it's already getting cold at night. I'm not ready for this."

"Ah, but soon enough seventy-five will feel chilly to us." She had a new twinkle in her eye that I'd never seen before, and it warmed my heart to know I had something to do with that.

"I have a few things for you," I said as I handed her the gift bag.

"What on earth, Lis?" She laughed as she took the bag. "Thank you."

"Don't thank me, yet. You haven't even opened it," I followed her into the living room and took my place on the couch beside her.

She retrieved the book *What to Expect when You're Expecting* out of the

153

bag and grinned. "This is kind of bass-ackwards, isn't it?"

"Well, I figured you could still use it even though it's not technically your body. That way you'll know exactly what your baby is doing when you're apart."

Her eyes teared up as she flipped through the book and whispered, "I can't believe this is real."

"Ha! Be me right now." I winked. "But wait, there's more."

She pulled out the silver picture frame that said "Baby's First Picture" and gasped as she stared at a picture from the ultrasound today. "When did you get this?"

"This afternoon before I went to St. Louis."

"You went to St. Louis? Wow, busy girl."

"I had to do something to kill time. This not working business is already taking a toll on me. I don't have anything to do and it's driving me crazy. I figured Chance would be killing time before her big event, so I went to hang out with her for a while. Your face was priceless during the ultrasound, so I thought I'd give you something to stare at."

She wiped her face and chuckled. "It's amazing. Thank you, Lis."

I watched as she ran her finger over the black and white photo and smiled. "You're going to be such a good mother. That baby's only got six cells right now, and you couldn't look prouder."

She laughed and set the frame on the table beside her. "This is such a dream come true. And you're so selfless, Lis. You don't have to do these things, and you've already established that this is my baby in your belly. Like this is really going to happen."

"That's because it is your baby. I'm just the oven keeping the little feller cooking. I want to do this for you, Dani. I'm just glad it's all working out."

"How did it go with Mark?"

I sighed. "Not good. Not good at all, in fact. He said some pretty awful things and assumes I'm going to have an abortion, so we're going to let him think that, okay?"

She paled and whispered, "Legally, though—"

"Legally, you won't have anything to worry about. He wants nothing
154

to do with this baby or me. He made that very clear. So you don't have to worry about it. Plus, he doesn't know you and Barry have split up, so if he ever hears word that you've got a baby, he'll just assume it was yours anyway."

"Speaking of Barry, the paperwork is already filed, and it's just a matter of letting it sit for the duration of the waiting period and then the judge will sign off on it. I've decided to sell the house and buy something smaller after I pay Barry for his half. I've got two people interested and it isn't even listed yet."

"So it sounds like that's working out well."

"I'm not even going to look at buying until we get back from Florida, soooo . . ."

I squealed. "Yes, yes, yes! Oh my gosh, yes! Please stay with me. I'm going out of my mind by myself over there."

She grinned. "I was hoping you'd say that. I'm going to sell everything, so I'll only have my personal belongings when I move in. I want a fresh start with new furniture—minus the rocking chair, of course."

"We'll find a perfect place for that, I promise."

"How have you felt today?"

I thought for a second. "Ya know, I don't think I've puked once today. I'm exhausted, though. It takes a lot of energy to create another human, apparently."

Dani laughed. "I imagine so. Go home and get some rest. And thank you so much for my gifts. I've got some reading to do." She winked and rubbed the cover of *What to Expect when You're Expecting*. "A baby . . . I can't believe I'm going to have a baby."

"Study well. I'm counting on you to tell me what the hell is happening to me." I left Dani's house and could barely keep my eyes open on the drive home. By sheer will, I pulled in the driveway at my house and stumbled through my house. I didn't even bother to take off my clothes or brush my teeth, and I'm pretty sure I was asleep before I had the covers over my shoulder.

Chapter Twenty-One
Rolling in the Deep

Michelle

The house would have exploded if the tension levels had risen any higher. Del Ray was still pissed off that no one picked her up from school, Martin and Gibson were still upset because I dropped the f-bomb when I got home, and Brandon was fuming because I lost my job. And, I didn't have the energy to try to pretend things were fine. The only sounds at dinner were the scrapes of forks hitting plates and the occasional request for someone to pass a dish.

My muscles were still very sore, but I knew better than to complain or make it appear I was uncomfortable lest I become the butt of several jokes and jabs. Del Ray was perched ready to attack, and I didn't want to give her any ammunition in which to get grounded over. I just wanted to go to bed.

I looked over my family. "Guys, I want to apologize for my behavior today. I had a bad day and was wrong to take it out on you. I'm sorry."

Gibson and Martin mumbled, "It's okay, Mom," or some variation around the mouthfuls of taco salad. Del Ray rolled her eyes and shook her head then excused herself from the table to start clean-up. I glanced at Brandon who stared at me with a fresh pissed-off look on his face. I had no idea how long it would take for him to not look at me like the turd in a punch bowl. I had visions of me landing a big fancy job tomorrow and coming home to announce that I would be the breadwinner and he could kiss my fat, white ass.

Or maybe I would just tell him that anyway.

I excused myself, scraped my unfinished meal in the trash and headed to the couch to wait for Gibson so we could work on homework. I picked up the remote and started flipping channels while trying to remember the last time I sat on this couch flipping channels. I wondered how many people spent their lives sitting on couches watching other

156

people live the lives they never had the balls to pursue. Reality TV was everywhere—singing shows, daredevil shows, survival shows, you-name-it. I settled on *The Voice* and watched Gwen and Adam battle it out for a contestant with a powerhouse voice and knocking knees.

"Mom, did you hear me?" Del Ray asked.

"What baby? No, I wasn't listening. What'd you say?"

She sighed. "I asked if you had decided about me spending the night at Kara's this Friday."

"How are your grades?"

"Fine, same as always."

"Yeah, it's fine with me, then. Ask your father, though." I turned my attention back to the TV then thought about what just went down. "Actually, no, you can't go to Kara's."

Del Ray huffed. "Um, can I ask why?"

I put the remote on the table and stood up. "Yes, you can, but I'm no longer obligated to explain myself to you. I don't appreciate coming home to your smart mouth and rants of how your father and I have failed you yet again when we work our butts off to give you guys a good life. You no longer get the privilege of treating me like your hired hand. I'm your mother and you're my daughter, not my equal, you got me? If you want to go to Kara's, you're going to have to work for it." I sat down and turned the television up.

"What the crap, Mom? What's your problem?"

Martin mumbled, "You just got told, Del. Good job, Mom." He sat beside me and curled up under my arm. "What are you watching?"

"Oh, I'm just flipping channels. *The Voice* has caught my eye."

"Oh, I like this show," he said.

Del Ray stomped over to the television and stood in front of it. "Um, hello, I'm still talking to you."

"Move your ass, Del Ray. I'm not even kidding right now."

She sidestepped three feet and stood next to the television with her arms folded across her chest. "I want to know where you think I'm treating you like my hired hand."

I faked a chuckle. "Well you can start with all that action you've got

157

going on there. You're posture suggests you feel superior to me and that you're entitled to a justifiable answer. That's simply not the case. See, I can say no just for the fun of saying no, and you have to obey because that's the natural law and order of parenthood. I get to make decisions and you get to obey them."

Brandon entered the living room. "Michelle, have you lost all your marbles today? What's gotten into you? She wants to go to a friend's house Friday night. Big deal. Why are you entering a pissing contest with her over it?"

"Because when I got home, she attacked me, and I don't appreciate it."

"You didn't pick her up from school like you said you were going to. She had a right to be pissed."

"You were the one that was off today, so why didn't you get the ass chewing when you could have just as easily picked her up?"

"Because I'm not the one that told her I would be somewhere and didn't show up."

"It's no wonder these kids treat me the way they do when you give them the blueprints, Brandon."

Martin looked up at me and whispered, "Mom, I don't treat you like they do."

"No, you don't, baby. No you don't."

"Suck up," Del Ray mumbled. "So Dad, can I go to Kara's then?"

"I don't have a problem with it, but make sure you get the final nod from the newly unemployed queen on the throne!" Brandon left the house and slammed the door on his way out.

Even Del Ray's eyes revealed the shock of Brandon's disrespect. She saw the tears welling up in my eyes, and her chin quivered slightly before she stomped down the hallway and slammed the door. Martin looked at me like he was mentally wishing for us to disappear and reappear anywhere but here. "I love you, Mom."

I wrapped my middle child in my arms. "I love you, too, bud." I glanced at the table to see Gibson still shoving food around on his plate. A lone tear dripped down his cheek which he wiped on his shirt sleeve.

"Come here, Gib."

He got up and ran to me, throwing himself on my lap. "I hate all this yelling, Mom."

"Me too, sweetie, me too. So I guess I should tell you that I don't have a job anymore. That's why Daddy is so upset. He's just worried, that's all. But I'm going to go out tomorrow and try to find a new one, okay?"

I felt the boys nod and take turns sighing. Neither one of them said anything, so I just held them until they were ready to let go. I needed to go talk to Del Ray, but I figured I'd get her after the boys calmed down.

Gibson looked at me. "So does that mean you'll pick us up from school tomorrow?"

"Yep, that's what that means. I'll take you *and* pick you up. What do you think about that?"

The boys smiled and Martin asked, "Will you make us a special after-school snack like you used to?"

I smiled and sighed. "Oh, I'm sure I can whip something up."

Martin turned his attention to the woman singing on television. "She's a really good singer."

Gibson turned to watch. "What's that mean when the chairs turn around?"

I said, "It means the people in the chairs think that person is good and want them on their team."

Gibson looked at me. "If I was in the chair, I'd pick you, Mom."

The bubbling brook in me overran the banks and poured onto my face. My husband and daughter thought I was a worthless piece of shit, but my sweet sons were cuddled up on my lap telling me they wanted me on their team. I couldn't help but cry with the sweet way Gibson was trying to make me feel better. I had people on my side—people under my own roof were on my side. And, after the look on Del Ray's face before she ran down the hallway, I'd say I'm close to getting another one, too. It's one thing for a child to ass-up to their parent; it's an entirely different animal when someone else starts trash talking their mama. I'll be curious to see what Del Ray says when I talk to her.

I tried to get up, but Martin squeezed me and whispered, "Just a minute longer."

I smiled. "Okay, bud. What do you think of that guy singing?"

Martin shrugged. "I think he sounds okay, but he won't get any chairs to turn."

I looked at him then glanced at the television. "Why do you think that?"

"Because he sounds like he's trying to sound just like the man that sang the song in real life."

I nodded and waited for the song to finish. When no chairs turned around, I smiled at Martin. "Wow, you called that one."

Martin gave me a half-smile and shrugged. "I like this show."

"You know, your dad was quite the musician back in the day. Sounds like you got some of his talent."

"Dad's going to teach me to play guitar when my hands get bigger," Gibson said.

"You could probably start now with a smaller guitar."

"That's what I said, but he said I have to grow up more first."

"Well, I'll talk to your daddy about that. I think it would be great for you guys to learn to play. I bet it would be fun for Daddy, too."

Brandon came in the door. "What would be fun for Daddy?"

"Teaching the boys to play guitar," I said and held my breath while waiting for him to say something stupid.

"Gibson needs to get a little bigger. Martin could start, though." He looked at his middle child. "Do you have any interest in it?"

Martin shrugged and tried not to smile. "Sure, that's cool."

Brandon tossed his keys into the basket on the table and mumbled, "Okay, we'll work on it." He took a six-pack of beer to the refrigerator and popped the top of one before sitting in his chair and taking a drink. "What are we watching?"

"*The Voice*," I said. "Have you ever watched it?"

"Nah, these shows don't hold much interest for me since I actually know what it's like to get up and perform in front of people."

I studied his face as he stared at the television and wondered how

160

this man could be the same man that just humiliated me in front of my children and now sat casually talking to all of us like we were one big happy family.

Martin asked, "Why don't you do it, now, Dad?"

Brandon scoffed. "Because I got married and started a family, kiddo. Can't chase your dreams while other people are counting on you." He glared at me. "Right, Michelle?"

I pulled my arm away from Martin and leaned forward. "Oh, I don't know, Brandon. Sometimes people make sacrifices for people because they love them and want to do whatever it takes to make them happy."

Gibson asked, "Mom, what's your dream?"

I stared at him. "Well, I don't know; I've never really given it much thought. I always wanted to be a mom and wife to your father."

Martin asked, "But you never had something you wanted to try?"

I shook my head and felt my stomach rolling. "No, bud, I've never really had anything I was good enough at to think about chasing a different dream."

"Well, you're a great mom, so maybe your dream did come true."

Tears sprung to my eyes while fear gripped my heart. Is this really the sum total of my life? I stared at the television and watched the next nervous contestant backstage shaking her hands and taking deep breaths in preparation for two minutes that may completely change the course of her life. One shot to impress four people who would have a say over her next big decision. All it took was one person's approval, and her dream would become a reality overnight. One person to just believe in her ability enough to catapult her into the next big thing. I caught myself holding my breath as she walked on stage and waited for the music to begin. She represented me in that moment; I didn't know what my dream was, but she held it firmly in her hand as she lifted the microphone to her mouth and sang for my life.

Every person in my living room leaned forward and watched the faces of the judges as she sang behind them with all she had. Sweat formed in my palms as a cloud of disappointment flickered in her eyes; the transformation in her face left tears pricking in my eyes as she rolled into a flawless chorus that ignited the crowd's excitement, yet none of the judges had reached for their button. She caressed the moment and microphone and finished with a breathtaking note that had tears swelling in my eyes. I heard Martin whisper, "Push the button, someone."

The song ended and both my heart and hers cracked with the realization that no matter how hard you try or how good you are, sometimes you just don't get the break you deserve. I slumped back against the couch and waited to hear the weak excuses offered by the judges. "Too forced . . . tried too hard . . . keep working and next year bring more of yourself and less of the original." She held herself together until she got backstage and wept with disappointment while her supportive family consoled her.

Brandon said, "Damn, that's a shame; she was really good."

"Right," I whispered as I stood and headed to the bathroom to collect myself. It was completely ridiculous for me to hinge my personal fate on the performance of a Hollywood hopeful, but the immediate parallel wasn't lost on me.

And, I still had to go face my fourth judge—Del Ray.

I splashed my face with cold water and took a few deep breaths before knocking on her door.

"Yeah," she mumbled.

"Can I come in?"

I heard shuffling then the door opened followed by her returning to her bed. I looked around the disaster of living space my oldest child preferred over the rest of the house and decided now wasn't the time to discuss the need for cleanliness. I sat on her bed and smoothed the black comforter beside me.

"So, I guess we probably need to talk about a few things," I said.

She sniffled. "I didn't know you lost your job today."

I shrugged. "No one did. I had a really bad day." My voice cracked as my throat pinched with brewing tears. "You're going to have to give your mom some grace, kiddo. I don't know what's wrong with me, but it's important for you to know it has nothing to do with you and your brothers, or even your dad for that matter. I'm having this weird, 'what's

162

my purpose' thing going on lately, and I feel just so completely lost." I wiped the tears streaming down my face and wondered if I would regret sharing this information with my daughter. She's just enough like her father that it could be used against me at the worst time. "I'm worried that you're going to fall into this teenage misery thinking your mom is going off the deep end and it's all your fault."

"Do you really hate your life?" she whispered.

I felt the crack in my heart and was certain she heard it. "No, baby. I don't hate my life. I guess you heard my conversation with your father earlier."

She leveled her eyes at me. "My room is right across the hall from yours. I hear way more than I ever wanted to. Why do you think I always keep my music up?"

"Good to know. I'll start taking him to the garage when I want to talk to him . . . or maybe you should start sleeping in the garage." I winked.

She smiled. "You're good at way more than you think you are, Mom. You're not just a cook. Don't let him do that to you again."

My allegiance with Del Ray was strengthening, but I wondered at what cost to her father and the relationships she would form with men in the future. I closed my eyes and silently prayed that I wasn't fucking up my children during this crisis of mine.

"Thank you, baby. I'm sorry I came down so hard on you about going to your friend's house Friday. I was angry for so many reasons and took it out on you. That being said, you have no right to come at me like you do when you're pissed. Now, you get it honest, because you're so much like me it's not even funny. But you need to remember that this chaotic mess of a human sitting on your bed is a human with human feelings and an ethereal love for you."

She cocked her head to the side. "Have you ever considered writing, Mom?"

Her question caught me off guard. "Why would I consider writing? I barely got C's in every class I took in high school."

She sat up. "Seriously. Did you hear what you just said? It was

163

pretty. You come up with some funny stuff when you're talking. Maybe you should think about writing—maybe that could be your new hobby."

I laughed. "Honey, the last thing people want to hear is the ranting of a middle-aged woman with no experience outside of raising a family and working at a daycare."

She shrugged. "It might not hurt, though. You bought me a journal a few years ago, and I wrote in it all the time. I still do, actually. I could use a new one, hint hint."

I chuckled. "Well, we'll see about that. Christmas is coming up, so you better start making a list."

She sat back against the wall. "Look on the bright side. Since you lost your job, you'll have a chance to work out while we're all at school and Dad's at work."

"Are you still fourteen? These are conversations I would have with my friends."

She smirked. "I have friends too, ya know. And I think you met your friends when you were my age, so just think about what you talked about, and it's probably nearly the same."

Oh, God, I hope not. At fourteen, we were talking about boys non-stop and the ridiculous drama going on at home. I can only imagine what her friends know about our family—maybe I'm better off not knowing. I'll never forget the first time Alissa finally told us about her living situation and how we were all baffled that this larger-than-life creature had been responsible for her sisters from a very young age. The rest of us had fairly normal home lives, so it was completely foreign to us. I stared at Del Ray and wondered which, if any, of her friends were stuck in the same situation, and if Del Ray was the adult voice of reason to her friends that I was hearing right now.

I had a pang of shame for the way I'd been judging my eccentric multi-colored hair, black-and-flannel wearing teenage daughter. There was a shift in the way I saw her, and as a result of that, there was a shift in the way I saw myself.

I leaned over to hug her. "You're a good friend, Del Ray. I love you."

"I love you, too, Mom. I don't have to go to Kara's Friday. Maybe we could dye your hair instead."

I slid my headband out of my hair and ran my fingers through it. "Think so? Maybe I could go auburn. I've got the skin tone and eye color to pull it off."

She grinned. "I was thinking something more dramatic."

I laughed. "Of course you were. You're a mess. Nah, go to your friend's house, but do me a favor, okay? Don't make me out to be the complete psycho I've become."

She giggled. "You're not a psycho."

I eyed her hair. "You're much braver than me. I could never do something like that to my hair."

She shrugged. "I just don't want to look like everyone else."

"That's your daddy coming out in you. I always preferred to blend in. Come see me before you go to bed. Is all your homework done?"

She slapped the top of a book lying beside her. "I'm working on it now."

"Okay, baby. Thanks for the chat."

I wandered into my bedroom and made a mental note to spend more time with Del Ray in her bedroom. I felt more normal in those few moments than I'd felt in weeks. I felt like life had rewound and I was sitting on Katie's bed watching her trim her nails after softball practice all over again. It made me long for my friend.

I walked down the hallway and leaned over Brandon. "I'm stepping out for a minute."

"Where you going, now?"

"Nowhere—just going to step out and call Katie."

He waved. "Sure, that's cool."

"I see you're still watching *The Voice*," I teased.

He smirked. "The boys are really into it. I'm just along for the ride."

Martin said, "Oh whatever, Dad. *You* were really into it a minute ago."

I marveled at the change in the house altogether in just a short amount of time. Or was this really what life was like when I wasn't stuck in my own anger?

Chapter Twenty-Two
I Can't Make You Love Me

Chance

The prickles of excitement and nerves danced through my body as I walked into the ballroom and scanned the crowd. The best of broadcast was represented in the room, and while it would have been in my best interest to rub elbows with other journalists and news anchors, I only wanted to see Tony. My crew split for the bar and left me standing near the entrance. Eddie was concerned I was going to cock-block him, so we'd prearranged for him to walk in separately and start the scouting process. I eyed the placards and realized we had assigned seats, so I wandered through the room until I found my table near the far corner. The center of the room had been reserved for speakers and a dance floor; it appeared to be the typical media event. I slipped my napkin onto my plate to indicate I'd seen my place and greeted my peers as I made my way to the bar.

I saw him out of the corner of my eye. Correction: I saw her first—dressed to perfection in an elegant green dress that formed her body as though it shot out of the womb with her. The diamonds from her necklace dripped onto her breasts and twinkled with elation at their lucky placement. Her long, red hair flowed down her back and shimmered even in the low lighting; she oozed feminine perfection, and it gave me great delight to imagine that she's had a terrible case of diarrhea at least once in her life. She and Tony were engaged in a semi-serious conversation with another news anchor from the St. Louis area. When she touched Tony's arm and laughed, every nerve ending in my body lit up. Tony chuckled, but the smile did not reach his eyes.

He glanced my way and did a double take. He faked stumbling backward and slid his hand over his heart before he excused himself from the conversation and walked toward me. As much as I wanted to look away and fake disinterest, I couldn't take my eyes off him as he excused his way through the mingling crowd. He certainly knows how to wear a tuxedo. The air in the room charged with the magnetic attraction between us and I had no idea if I was even still breathing or not. I'm pretty sure the lack of oxygen had killed the butterflies in my stomach but I feared I would be its next victim. I wished I had stayed nearer my table to steady myself then remembered my mission tonight. I took a deep breath and took a step toward him.

"Good God, Chance Bradley, you are a vision of excellence in that red dress." He grabbed my hands and leaned in to kiss me on the cheek. He whispered, "You're stunning, as usual."

I grinned. "You too, Tony."

He pulled away from me and examined every inch of my body. "Just give me a second to memorize how you look tonight. That dress was made for you, lovely lady."

I blushed, much to my dismay, then smiled. "Oh how you go on."

"Don't play coy, Chance. You're the most beautiful woman here. The rest of them are wishing they'd stayed home now."

"Well, I'm confident there's at least one other woman here that would beg to differ with you."

He tilted his head toward Miriam. "She's a B movie extra compared to what I'm staring at right now."

I shook my head and laughed. "Do you know where you're sitting tonight?"

"I do, now. If you think I'm leaving your side for the evening, you're out of your mind. I'm not going to let one man in this room think you're available."

"Jesus, do you think it would be better if you just peed on my leg and got it over with?"

Tony chuckled. "If I thought it would work, I would have done it already. Actually, I've already asked to move next to you." He put his fingers to his lips. "Shh, don't tell. Sometimes it's fun to have pull around here."

I stared at him and wondered whatever possessed me to let this man go. He looked at me with an intensity that threatened to melt my makeup (and panties) right off my body. I took a deep breath and prayed my zipper would hold if my heart swelled much more. "Shall we get a drink or just stand here staring at each other?"

He shook his head. "Sorry, I'm entranced. After you, dear lady."

"I see some new faces around here tonight. You might have to help me with some of the names."

He slipped his hand into mine and navigated us through the crowd at the bar. The touch of his hand made my soul sigh and throat tighten with memories of how much I'd missed the gentle sweetness that embodied all that Tony is. He ordered our drinks and steered us to an area unoccupied by the rest of the gala attendees. He handed me my drink and his eyes registered the same emotions I was fighting inside.

"Here's to new beginnings, Chance Bradley."

I tapped his glass with mine and whispered, "To new beginnings."

"I'll be honest, Chance, this has been the longest year of my life."

"Do you really think this is the place to discuss this, Tony?" I asked as I dabbed my eye with my pinky to prevent a tear from escaping.

He smiled. "No, probably not. I'm just so happy you're here tonight. I can't tell you how much I've missed you."

Miriam waltzed up and purred, "You must be Chance Bradley." She extended her hand. "I'm Miriam O'Bannon, Tony's girlfriend."

I know the shock of her words were intended to rock me and it worked. I painted on my best smile and shook her hand. "I'm Chance Bradley—anchor: KJAT; it's a pleasure to meet you." I glanced at Tony. "Perhaps I misunderstood your toast." I saw Eddie standing a several feet away and faked communication with him. "Sorry, if you will excuse me, I think Eddie needs to talk to me."

Girlfriend. His girlfriend. She's his fucking girlfriend. He's got a girlfriend. He's moved on. I reached for Eddie and whispered, "Get me out of here."

Eddie took his cue to escort me to the hallway and wrapped his arm around my waist. "Almost there," he mumbled.

I made it to the bathroom, handed him my drink and asked, "Will you wait for me, please? I'll explain later, but please . . . just wait here."

He gestured toward the bathroom door. "I'll be right here. Go do

169

what you gotta do."

I slid past a few ladies primping at the mirror and broke my own rule of never using the handicap bathroom stall, but I needed to pace or throw up; I wasn't sure which it was at the moment. I knew crying was out of the question, because I'm an ugly crier, and it takes me an hour to get my face back to normal color. Plus, my makeup looked fantastic and I wasn't about to ruin a great face on the misleading behavior of someone I dumped over a year ago.

Girlfriend. Nothing made sense—none of the things he'd said, his underhanded way of getting me to St. Louis, the way his face lit up when he saw me, all of the charming things he didn't have to say . . . what was his fucking game, and why was I suddenly the unsuspecting pawn? I contemplated calling Alissa to come rescue me from this burning inferno of my crash-and-burn. By the time I'd finished pacing, the bathroom had cleared out, so I moved to the mirror and stared at the eyes that an hour earlier had glimmered with new life but now looked back at me with the same hollow way they'd looked for over a year.

I stood up straight and fluffed my hair as I clenched my teeth. Nothing in my life was different than it was twenty-four hours ago. I took a deep breath and listened to the crying woman inside of me slow to a sniffle then quiet herself. No way in hell was I about to give either of them the satisfaction of knowing they'd rocked me. I stepped out of the bathroom and saw Eddie leaning against the wall holding my drink. He raised an eyebrow at me. "You okay?"

I nodded. "Yeah, I just got some news I wasn't expecting." I took my drink from him and chugged it. "I need another one, and I'll be fine. Sorry, but you're about to be cock-blocked for the evening."

He smirked. "Let's see . . . the most beautiful woman in the room wants to hang out with me. Hmmm . . . what *will* I do?"

I nudged his arm with my elbow as we walked toward the bar. "Consider it overtime, but I'm not going to sleep with you."

"No, but your presence with me will increase my desire level by the end of the night. Every girl here will be intrigued to know what it is about me that makes you want to be with me. They'll be circling soon—

just watch."

I laughed. "You spend way too much time watching chick flicks."

He shrugged. "Hey, if you want to win the game, you have to know the rules, and my lot rent just went up millions walking with you."

"Well, thank you, but I beg to differ. No woman will approach you while I'm with you."

"Shall we make a friendly wager?" he grinned.

I cocked my head to the side and put my empty glass on the bar. "Sure, what's the bet?"

"I'm betting that at least three women will approach us while we're standing here in the next thirty minutes." Déjà vu hit as I remembered the way Tony and I started our relationship with clever banter and a friendly bet. The dagger shot into my chest causing me to flinch and sway on my feet. Eddie reached for me. "Whoa, whoa, are you sure you need another one?"

I waved him off. "I'm fine—just got dizzy for second. I've had this . . . ear thing . . . never mind. Okay, we'll stand here until they call us for dinner, and we'll see." I reached for my second drink and turned to face the crowd. *Dinner.* Tony said he was pulling strings to put him next to me at dinner. If she was joining him, I'd have to sit through one of the most uncomfortable dinners in my life. "Where have they seated you, Eddie?"

"I don't know; I didn't get that far." He frowned at me indicating I'd interrupted his process.

"Sorry, but thank you."

"No problem."

Right on cue, here came a young blonde in a dress three inches too short to be considered classy, in heels that made her ankles wobble as she walked. She ambled up to the bar and slid next to Eddie. She ordered her drink then turned to Eddie and smiled. He smiled back. "Good evening. Have we met?"

She grinned and extended her hand, "I'm Erica Elan."

"I'm Eddie Ward. It's nice to meet you."

"You too!" She glanced at me and back at him.

"Miss Erica, have you had the pleasure of meeting Chance Bradley?"

171

"I have not. It's a pleasure to meet you." She shook my hand and returned her attention to Eddie.

I smiled then chuckled as Eddie's point was proven over and over again. After number five, I ceded the win to him and went to my table as he gloated and turned to the latest victim at the bar. I was still grinning and shaking my head when I reached my table and glanced at the name plates around my table. I didn't see Tony or Miriam's names, so I took a seat and waited for the event to start.

I felt him lean over me before he whispered in my ear, "He's a little young for you, don't you think?"

I grinned through an exhale. "Sometimes it's fun to play with puppies." I glanced up at Tony. "Well played, Sir Tony."

His face fell as he sighed and pulled a chair up to face me. "Chance . . ."

I held up my hand and started to speak but Miriam appeared. "Tony, I found our table." She smiled at me. "Please excuse us. They're about to get started."

I smiled back and reached for my drink as I looked at Tony. "You better run along, now."

He stared at me with a longing that nearly drew me out of my seat. I'm certain the fire in my chest flickered in my eyes as I stared back at him and gritted my teeth. I felt my nostrils flaring as they tried to keep up with my shallow breaths.

Eddie put his hands on my shoulders and leaned over. "May I speak with you a moment, Chance?"

I leaned to look up at Eddie and smiled. "Sure," I said.

Tony and I stood at the same time. I slid past him. "Have a good evening," as I followed Eddie to the corner of the room.

Eddie turned to look at me with serious look and animated gestures. "Look, I'm trying to pretend I have this incredible thing to tell you, but you looked pinned down, so I just swooped in to see if you needed an out. Now, you act like I've told you the most amazing scoop you've ever heard."

I leaned in and grabbed his arm as though I was verifying important data. "I can't believe how awesome you are. I promise I'll tell you everything later, but can we leave?"

He leaned back, crossed his arms, and buried his chin in his hand as though he was seriously contemplating the possibility of what I'd just said. If we weren't fighting to maintain my dignity, I would have probably laughed at the absurdity of our actions. But, I knew Tony and Miriam were watching, and Eddie confirmed with a short nod when he glanced toward their table.

"What about the crew?" he asked.

I arched an eyebrow at him. "What about all of the *la-dies?*"

He chuckled. "Well, that too."

I shook my head. "Okay, scratch that. I'll stay until after dinner, but the minute the music starts, I'm going to take a cab back to the hotel. Rule number one: if you're blitzed, do not drive. Rule number two: watch the other crew members. Rule number three: don't end this evening with anything you can't wash off or will eventually have to name."

Eddie's laugh roared across the quieted room and attracted the attention of the speaker at the podium. His face turned crimson as he turned his back to the guests. "Well, *that* just happened."

I giggled and pulled on his arm. "Come on, let's get this over with. Find your table and I'll let you know when I leave. Oh, and thank you. I owe you . . . again."

"I will collect; don't you forget it."

I returned to my table and extended my greetings mixed with apologies for the outburst while taking my seat. I scanned the table and waited for the shop-talk to begin. I felt my cell phone vibrate in my clutch, so I slipped it onto my lap and glanced at the text I'd received.

Do Not Answer said: *She's not my girlfriend, Chance.*

I responded: *Does she know that?*

I let my eyes roll over the crowd and looked for the silky red mane amidst the blond up-dos and balding heads; she wasn't hard to find. Her back was to me which put Tony to her side and in my perfect line-of-sight. I moved my chair slightly in an attempt to place someone's head between us, but I was unsuccessful. I felt my clutch vibrate again; I slid it under my chair and pulled my napkin onto my lap as the servers made their way to the table.

Dinner was as boring as I expected it to be and equally disappointing as I hoped to spend the evening flirting relentlessly and trying to win the heart of the man I'd released into the wind a year ago. Instead, I was continually drawn into conversations about the latest news, camera dos and don'ts, greatest on-air faux-pas, and speculation over the upcoming presidential press conference in the morning. I managed to only catch Tony's eye four times and lost my appetite after the second time. He looked completely miserable—stuck.

I tried to muster up some sympathy for the poor fellow sitting next to the redheaded bombshell, but it all became very clear as to why I never heard from Tony. When you have a distraction like that, why would he even give me a second thought? It didn't seem to matter that conversation with her appeared to be as exciting as kicking an empty shoebox, but hey when the words are coming out of a mouth you're thinking dirty thoughts about, why does it matter what those words are?

One time, Tony and I were lying in bed sharing a box of tissues under a pile of blankets and taking turns getting the other one herbal tea. We were both so sick, but it had been two weeks since we'd seen each other, and neither one of us wanted to go one more day. He drove to Columbia to see me with a fever of 101 and the heat on full-blast. We curled up and talked for hours about anything that came to mind. We muted the television and made up dialogue for scenes while laughing until we sent ourselves into another coughing jag then made shadow puppets on the walls to mimic romantic scenes. It was one of my favorite days in my life.

If I had taken that job as the anchor on his team, it would be me sitting with him at the table. It would be us shining like a lake under a full moon, it would be us sitting together happy instead of staring at each other like the missed opportunity that we'd become.

The longer I sat there, the more I wanted to put as much distance

174

between Tony and me as possible. I stood up to begin my career's suicide and walked to Eddie's table. I interrupted his conversation. "Excuse, me. Eddie, I'm leaving. Text me when you and the crew get back to the hotel."

He nodded and gave me that Stuart-is-going-to-kill-you look, but I knew Eddie would back me on this one.

I took the long way out of the banquet hall to avoid walking near Tony's table and left through a side exit in the event Tony would try to follow me. Somehow I sincerely doubted he would be able to casually leave his dinner guest without it being obvious that he was going in search of me. Which only strengthened my argument that she was, in fact, his girlfriend, and I was simply the ex he still loved.

I took a cab back to my room and kicked off my shoes then showered to wash off the grit of the night that had settled deeper than my skin. I'd been played; I'd fallen for it like a girl getting her first "check-yes-or-no" letter only to discover it was a joke.

If I miss the press conference tomorrow, I might as well clean out my desk; Stuart will never believe he'd been duped by Tony, and I would look like the journalist that bailed on the biggest story/non-story of the year. I knew there was no excuse I could give to justify the actions I was contemplating, but Florida rang heavily in my ears. If I needed to put distance between Tony and me, this was the only way to do it. After a day like this, St. Louis and Columbia were just too close for comfort.

I sent Alissa a text: *I'm in for Florida*, deleted all the unread messages from Tony then threw myself on the bed to start the process of crying myself to sleep again.

Chapter Twenty-Three
All I Want for Christmas Is You

Alissa

Three Months Later
One Week before Christmas

I stood in the bathroom and stared at the little bulge peeking over my yoga pants. I finally quit puking about a month ago, but the cravings for weird food I don't even like at odd hours of the day and night have kept me working out at the gym like a mad woman. But, there was no denying the baby bump this morning.

I wandered into the kitchen, grabbed the orange juice out of the fridge, and set it on the counter. Dani was preparing her coffee and dressed for work like it was any normal day.

I stood sideways. "Notice anything different about me today?"

She looked at me. "You're awake before nine?"

I dropped my hands. "Very funny." I smoothed my t-shirt over my stomach. "Do you see it?"

She grinned. "Lis, you're showing!"

I sighed. "Yes, yes I am. It's like it was overnight or something."

She put her hand on my belly. "You're really showing! That's just amazing! I hadn't noticed it until you pulled your shirt tight around your stomach."

"Yeah, the 28th can't get here fast enough, now. Are you ready for your last day of employment?"

She stirred her coffee. "God, you have no idea. I'm so ready to hit the road. Is everything ready for the Christmas party tomorrow? All of the ladies still coming?"

I poured some juice. "Last I heard. Chance is in, Katie's coming, and I think Michelle's still planning on coming unless something else

176

miraculously interrupts our plans like they have."

Dani frowned. "It's not unlike her to disappear for a while, but I'm surprised she's holed up like she has."

"She said she has a surprise for us, so maybe she's really coming. I don't know; there's no telling with her."

Dani looked at her watch then leaned against the counter to sip her coffee. Having her here for the last two months has been fabulous. I worried we'd be all weird around each other after living on our own for so long, but it was pretty seamless when she moved in. Her house sold within three days of being listed on the market; it was a personal record for the real estate agent. Not that they had to do much, because the buyers were already interested prior to the listing. She made bank on it, though, so she's got a nice nest egg to start motherhood. She asked, "Did Katie ever get Michelle to meet for lunch?"

"Nope. No one has seen her since we all met here to announce the private guest's existence. Not for lack of trying. Chance has kind of done the same thing since St. Louis, though."

Dani nodded. "Yeah, but *Chance* is mentally stable."

"That she is. But I know that thing with Tony really rocked her even if she won't really admit it."

"I feel sorry for her. He did her so wrong." She turned toward the coffee pot and asked, "Do you want any of this before I clean it?"

"No, thank you. I'm supposed to be limiting my caffeine, hence the OJ this morning." I winked.

Dani grinned. "OJ's good for baby."

I laughed. "I'll be ready for the 'your baby this week' reading tonight when you get home. Have a good day at work, honey! Go bring home that bacon."

"I'll be living off your dime for the next six months, sugar mama."

"Yeah but we're going to have a lot of fun in Florida. It's going to be fabulous! The house is ready to go; all it needs is three eager thirty-somethings with nothing to do but grab some sun and fun."

"Well, have a good day. I seriously doubt I'll work all day since my replacement is already acclimated and ready to take the reins. If I can scoot out early, I will." She grabbed her purse and coffee. "Take it easy today, drink lots of water, and let me know if you feel anything."

I nodded my head. "Yes, yes, I will. Geez, you say the same thing every day. Your baby is safe with me, now go or you're going to be late."

"What are they going to do—fire me?" She winked and waved as she put on her coat and headed out to the garage.

I watched Dani's car emerge from the garage, ease out of the driveway and head down the street. I squealed with glee as I shuffled down the hallway and threw open my closet. Dani hadn't wanted to bother decorating the house for Christmas since we were leaving three days after for Florida, and she knew we'd be way too excited to take it all down before we go. She's got some weird family tradition that says all Christmas decorations must be down before the turn of the New Year or it meant bad luck for the occupants of the house, and she didn't want to take a chance. But, I couldn't stand it anymore. Our sad little excuse of a Christmas tree just wasn't cutting it for me, so I made a plan to transform our family room into a Christmas miracle while she was at work today, and I knew the other girls would love it. And, who has a Christmas party without decorations?

I pulled the gifts and wrapping paper out of my closet and tossed them on the bed then went to the guest bedroom to retrieve the boxes full of Christmas decorations I'd collected over the years. It was tradition to have our annual Christmas party at my house, and it was the one day of the year that we all embraced the magic of the holiday season. Everyone smiled a little bigger, hugged a little longer, and dripped with the joy of the season. So, naturally, I had to do it up right. No trip to Florida could dampen this event.

I bent down to move a few boxes, and I felt this little tickle in my belly. I expected a large fart to follow as that had been my latest trick for two months, but nothing happened. I leaned over to pilfer through a box and felt it again. I sat back on my heels and put my hand on my baby bump. Tears pricked my eyes as my heart started pounding. *That was the baby! I felt the baby move!* I'd felt flutters. I started to call Dani but knew she would race home to put her hand on my belly and be disappointed she couldn't feel it too, but I know what I felt—the living, growing baby that had made me sicker than I've ever been and sucked all my energy had just tickled me. The child forming in my womb that I'd tried to avoid greeted me. It was the most precious thing I've ever experienced in my life.

I said, "Well, hi back! Did you like that orange juice?" as tears spilled over my cheeks. I pulled open the first box of treasures. "This one is very special; this was the first ornament I got for my very first Christmas tree. Do you like it?" I sat it on my stomach as though the private guest could see through my skin.

I waited to see if the flutter would happen again, but nothing happened. I bent over to pull the other box out of the closet and felt the sweet little tickle I'd longed to feel again. I chuckled. "Am I squishing you, baby?"

My throat tightened; that was the first time I'd acknowledged the private guest as a baby—a real live baby was moving in me, connected to me. I was no longer alone. My heart swelled as I laughed and cried while holding my belly. I tried to grasp one thought running through my head, but they swooped through so quickly, I couldn't catch one of them long enough to hold it. Tiny fingers, tiny toes, a little tongue learning how to move—the sheer wonder and magic of it all became so real in those soft little wiggles that seemed to say, "I'm here." And, I wanted to feel it again and again.

I abandoned the boxes, jumped in the bed, and curled up as I'd been on the floor. Every time I felt the flutter, I gasped, giggled, and rubbed my belly while encouraged the baby to do it again as I wiped my face with my shirt sleeve.

I woke up and was instantly disappointed that I'd fallen asleep and wondered what I'd missed while I was sleeping. I didn't feel anything, so I wandered to the kitchen to get something to eat. I opened the pantry and asked my belly, "What sounds good for breakfast?" I glanced at the clock that revealed it was already ten-thirty. "Make it brunch." I pooched my stomach out and swayed back and forth. "Anything sound good? Yes, I agree. Cereal sounds freaking awesome right now." I grabbed the box

179

of Raisin Bran and went to the fridge to grab the milk.

When Mom was pregnant with Ella, she drank a gallon of milk a day. She craved the stuff—couldn't get enough—and sighed as she downed glass after glass. Adrianna was only two when Ella was born, so we were constantly on the run to the store to pick up more milk. Back then, I could run in the store with a five dollar bill, get two gallons of milk and come back with change. And of course, Hilary was allergic to everything; boy that was a hard lesson to figure out. Poor kid.

I sat at the table and flipped open my iPad to see what was going on in the world while mine had just changed forever. I read news stories out loud and talked to the baby about what was happening on December 19th.

"It's one week before Christmas, and everyone is super excited about the upcoming holiday. Christmas is a time of year when people look at all of the good in their lives; it's hard to explain. Some people get stressed out and spend more money than they should, but you won't ever have to worry about that. I guess that's one mistake I made in my life that will benefit all of us for the rest of our lives. I know it's taboo to talk about money to kids, but child, you're rich beyond your wildest dreams. You'll have the best of everything and will never have to worry about going hungry or being cold."

My throat caught as I remembered this horrible little house we lived in before Adrianna was born or even thought of. I barely remember anything else as I was only maybe five or six years old, but I remember how horribly cold that bedroom was. We were living with one of Mom's flings "just for the winter" because we'd lost our house. He had a two bedroom shack that wasn't built for children, much like him. The room I had was an add-on with little-to-no insulation, and he was hell-bent on making me be a big girl and sleeping in my own bed. I got in the habit of waiting for them to go to bed then slipping out to the couch to sleep in the heat. During the day, it wasn't that bad because all of the doors were open, but they made me sleep with the door closed which shut off the heat into my room. Mom laughs now at the year I spent "sleep-walking," but many of her memories are much different than mine.

I shivered and cleared my throat. "Anyway, you're going to have a much better life. In a few weeks, we're moving to Florida to have fun in the sun and wait for you to be born. Your mommy . . ."

The impact of the words slammed against my chest as reality trickled over my body. I slumped in my chair and stared at the table. Dani would be this baby's mother; she would be raising this child as her own, not me. I sniffled and wiped my eyes. "Your mommy is so excited to meet you." My voice cracked, but I finished the sentence, "And I'm going to be there the whole time. I'll keep you safe and sound. I promise."

I exhaled so loud it startled me. Time to get moving and quit thinking. Thinking never did much for me, anyway.

Five hours later, I stood in the family room admiring my handiwork and started lighting candles. Dani would be home any minute, and I couldn't wait to see the look on her face. I adjusted the package I'd wrapped and placed under the tree for her then put it back where it'd been.

The smell of the soup I'd made for dinner wafted through the house and gave it that special "it" factor this house had been missing since I bought it. My house was finally feeling and smelling like a home instead of an accomplishment. Leave it to me to find that moment of nostalgia two weeks before leaving for Florida.

I heard the garage door open and sprinted to the kitchen to wait for Dani to come in the door. I gave the soup one more stir then greeted her as she came in.

Her face lit up when she saw the living room lit with candles and Christmas everything dripping from every shelf and table. "What have you done, you busy little elf?"

I squealed. "Surprise!"

She hugged me and gasped, "Alissa, this is amazing! You did all this?"

"Yep. Me and the baby."

She did a double-take and grinned. "You said baby, not private guest."

I bit my lip. "Yes, I did. *And*, I made soup."

181

"You cooked? Wow, you really are Heidi Homemaker today." She walked through the living room and admired things she hadn't seen for a year. "I've always loved this angel."

"But wait, there's more." I grabbed her arm and led her down the hall to the family room. "Ta-da!"

Her hand flew to her chest as she breathlessly said, "Oh my gosh, this is amazing!"

"Isn't it? I just love it."

She threw her arms around my neck. "This is so perfect! Oh I can't wait for the others to see this. You've really outdone yourself this year, Lis."

I went to the Christmas tree and retrieved the gift for her. "I have something for you—it's an early present, but I don't think we should wait for it."

She took the gift from me. "I can't believe you sometimes." She shook her head and peeled off the wrapping paper. Her hand flew to her mouth as she opened the box and pulled out the tiny little stocking. She read the embroidered words, "Baby Bump's First Stocking," then laughed as she cried. "Oh Lis, it's so sweet."

"Isn't it, though? I had to have it made since no one else probably has stockings that read 'baby bump.'"

She laughed. "No, I doubt they do."

I gestured toward the fireplace. "Well, go ahead and do the honors! Hang 'er on up there."

I'd placed a stocking holder in between Dani's and my stockings that eagerly awaited the little stocking. She slid the loop over the holder and giggled. "That's just too precious."

We stared at the stocking until my stomach growled. "I hope you're hungry, because your baby is."

"It smells delicious."

We made small talk over dinner; Dani told me about her last day at work, and when I couldn't stand it anymore, I said, "Something amazing happened today."

"You mean more amazing than Santa's elves overtaking your

182

house?"

I giggled. "Yes, even more amazing than that." I set down my spoon. "I felt the baby today."

Her eyes widened as her face erupted in a grin. "You did?"

"Mmhmm. . . like a lot. These teeny-tiny little flutter-tickle things. It was the most precious thing."

She sat back in her chair. "Aww dang it, and I missed it."

"Well, I was going to call you, but I knew you wouldn't be able to feel it on the outside."

She grinned. "So it's real, then. This isn't a dream we're going to wake up from. You felt it!" She sighed as a new level of love washed over her.

"We've just got a few more things to do tonight to get ready for the party tomorrow. I'm very excited."

Dani grinned. "I know that look."

I winked. "Indeed, you do."

Chapter Twenty-Four
Wrecking Ball

Michelle

Three months and six days have passed since I lost my job at the daycare—it's one week before Christmas, and we've only got two presents apiece for the kids. I finally put up the Christmas tree last weekend but only because my children were bothered. Normally I put it up the weekend after Thanksgiving, but this year I just couldn't find that holiday spirit. Personally, I'd rather skip the damn holiday altogether and get this stupid year over with.

Del Ray, Martin, and Gibson have these huge wish lists for Christmas, and I've managed to cross a few things off thanks to a few gently-used items off a swap shop on Facebook. On a normal year, the tree would be overflowing with gift-wrapped packages that the kids would fondle over and over dying with anticipation. This year, though, that tree is a reminder of how I've failed my family and myself.

The job hunt proved to be more crippling to my self-worth than I ever imagined as no one wants to hire someone who can't type and doesn't know what an office suite package means or whatever they call it. It was slightly embarrassing when one lady laughed at me when I suggested I could file. I guess most documents are saved on computers these days. Then I found out I'd been blacklisted with the other daycare providers in town, which guaranteed I'd never work in that field again.

On the bright side, my time at the gym has really paid off. I'm down another three pounds this week making it thirty-two pounds total. I've asked my parents for money or gift cards to clothing stores since I can't wear any of my old clothes successfully anymore. Not that I need a wardrobe outside of my yoga pants and T-shirts, but it would be nice to have something decent to wear to church or the kids' school functions. I did find some cute stuff at Goodwill last week. I snuck twenty bucks from the gas budget and didn't go anywhere else that week to make up for it. I don't think Brandon noticed the missing money or the clothes, so that was a plus.

I slipped out of bed and snuck down the hallway to pee and get ready for the gym. The classes were challenging at first to say the least, but once I got the hang of it, I looked forward to going and was actually pretty good at it, and that felt awesome. Brandon still has a burr up his ass that he's out "slaving away" to provide for his family while I'm at the gym "dancing and having a good ol' time." God forbid I actually enjoy one hour of my day.

I pulled up to the gym and buried my face in my coat to fight off the bitter wind that swept across the parking lot. We still hadn't seen our first snow of the season, but the air felt like the skies could open up and dump buckets on us any minute. I sure hope Alissa, Chance, and Dani considered this when they decided to hop in a Navigator and drive halfway across the country. I'm going to have to come up with a really good reason for avoiding all of my friends for the last three months, and somehow I don't think jealousy-to-the-point-of-depression is going to be a valid excuse. Basically I couldn't go on with life as usual and pretend that all of it wasn't about to change. I couldn't stand to listen to one more conversation about the "totally awesome trip" they're about to take and the "freedom of not having to work" when I was trying to decide between buying basic toiletries and groceries or paying the electric bill.

I huffed and tried to shake the cold off my body when I entered the gym. I waved at the front desk attendant while I swiped my membership card and headed toward the classroom. Everyone was standing around waiting for the instructor to show, so I took my spot in the back and stretched. The ladies in the class fell into their lines and nervously stared at the clock.

Reggie walked in. "Looks like Gwen isn't going to make it today." Several of the ladies sighed and started toward the door when he asked, "Michelle, will you lead the class today?"

I stopped mid-stretch and looked at the other ladies to see if one of the skinny-minis bounced to the front of the room. I looked at him and pointed to my chest. "Me Michelle?"

He chuckled. "Yes, you Michelle. Will you lead the class?"

I stood up and wandered to the front of the room. "Well, I can give it a shot, I guess." The music cued up, and we started the warm-up routine.

I felt like I was standing in front of the girls in high school all over again and waited for someone to try to spike a volleyball at my head just for fun. We worked through warm-ups and headed into stretching when I realized after this, the instructions had to come from me. I don't know how to lead an exercise class, hell I haven't ever been the leader of anything. I yelled out, "Do you care if I just make something up?"

A few ladies grinned. "Just wing it today! Show us what you got, Michelle!"

I grinned. "Okay, four to the left, GO! One, two, three four; to the right, one, two, three four. . ."

Forty-five minutes later, over thirty women left the classroom gasping for air and drenched in sweat. Every muscle in my body was screaming, and I couldn't wait to get home and go back to bed. I tossed my sweat-soaked towel in the hamper by the door and headed to the coat rack.

Reggie called after me, "Hey Michelle, wait!"

I turned to look at him. "I'm sorry, Reg. I've never done anything like that before."

He stopped in front of me and grinned. "Michelle, the ladies are saying that's the best workout they've had in months. Great job up there. You really have a knack for that."

I'm pretty sure my smile wrapped around my head. "Thanks, Reggie!"

"Would you be interested in working for me? Gwen just quit on the spot this morning, and I need someone to run the classes."

"Are you serious? That would be awesome! Thanks, Reggie!"

"It's just a part-time position, and the classes are staggered throughout the day, but I could also use some help cleaning up, washing towels, that sort of thing. Are you interested?"

I chuckled. "Are you kidding? Yes, I'm interested. I would hug you

186

if I knew I wouldn't cover you in sweat!"

Reggie laughed and held up his hand. "No need for all that, now. I need to figure it all out, but how about I call you later today and give you the lowdown?"

"Sounds great! Thank you so much!"

I left the gym floating on a cloud and giggled my way back to the house. I had a job! I had a paying job at the gym doing what I already loved to do, but more than that, someone saw value in me. It didn't take long for the tears of gratitude to spill over my cheeks as I whispered, "Thank you, God," over and over. I started calculating what my possible income could be and how maybe I could get a partial paycheck before Christmas. Just maybe this Christmas wouldn't be a bust after all.

I slipped into the house and listened to see if anyone was up yet. The coast was clear, so I pulled off my coat and headed into the bedroom to gather my clothes for the day. In the shower, I thought about the possibilities of routines set to certain "get-up-and-moving" songs and even caught myself flipping through a few of the moves while soaping up my arms. I had a purpose, a reason, and permission to be good at something for the first time in my life. And for the first time in months, I was looking forward to Brandon waking up.

In the kitchen, I slipped my ear buds in my ears, cranked up some tunes, and set to the task of making a big Saturday-morning breakfast for my family. My steps were intentional, my movements choreographed, and I whispered words of encouragement to the mock class in front of me as I scrambled eggs, rolled out biscuit dough, and monitored the frying crumbled sausage. Even the coffee pot seemed to gurgle in time with my routine. I grinned with the idea of seeing my friends for the first time thirty pounds lighter and finally on a path that had a light shining at the end. I finally had something worthwhile to share with them that wasn't bragging on the accomplishments of someone else. It was mine—all mine!

I tugged at my yoga pants and wiggled my hips to bring them back to where they belonged. That only added to my feelings of elation that even my workout clothes were hanging on for dear life. Today I might even stand before a mirror naked and see the results of my hard work for myself. Maybe. We'll see.

I wheeled around and came face-to-face with Martin's sleepy eyes and sideways grin. I yelled then laughed, "Oh my gosh, child, you scared me to death." I pulled the ear buds out of my ears and wrapped him in a one-armed hug with the bowl of gravy swaying in my other hand. "Hi, bud. Sleep well?"

He scratched his head and mumbled, "Smells good in here. I love you, Mom."

I grinned. "I love you, too. Are you hungry?"

He nodded and ambled toward the bathroom. "I'll be back in a minute."

"You've got a good ten minutes before breakfast is ready. Take your time." I slipped my ear buds back in my ears and returned to the preparations. I rehearsed how I was going to tell my family about my new opportunity and chuckled with the thought that the last time I was this excited was when we found out Gibson was a boy. On any other day, I would have been deflated that eight years ago was the last time I was excited about anything, but today was a new day, and I felt like a new person.

Brandon came in the kitchen and slid his arms around my waist. I grabbed the ear bud that popped out of my ear and dive-bombed for the scrambled eggs as I giggled. "Well good morning to you, too."

"This is a nice way to wake up. Smells delicious." He kissed me on the neck. "How long has the coffee been on?"

"Just made it, so it's fresh. How'd you sleep?"

He rubbed his face. "Like a rock. I feel like I could go back to bed and sleep all day. I was having crazy dreams, though, so I'm glad I woke up." He poured a cup of coffee and shuffled to the table. "Man, you're pulling out all the stops today. Biscuits and gravy, scrambled eggs . . ." I turned to look at him and hiked my pants up again. He frowned and looked sideways at me. "Have you lost weight, Michelle?"

I gaped at him and chuckled. "Are you serious? As of today, I'm

188

down thirty-two pounds, Brandon. Is this the first time you've noticed?"

He recovered well. "Well no, I mean I could tell you looked different but wow, thirty-two pounds? That's impressive. Your pants look huge on you."

I sighed. "Yeah all of my clothes fit like this. I'm going to need some new clothes soon."

He scoffed. "I sure hope you plan to wait til after Christmas for that."

I leveled my eyes at him. "Ugh, don't remind me." I nodded toward the nearly bare Christmas tree and whispered, "We've got to do something about that, Brandon."

He sighed. "There's not much to be done, honey. One income limits stuff like Christmas."

I ignored his jab and scraped the eggs into a serving bowl. Pricks of guilt stabbed at my mood as visions of my disappointed children on Christmas morning played in my mind's eye. And it would be all my fat mouth's fault. I had a good chance of making Del Ray understand, but the boys would be devastated. Both my and Brandon's families got used to not getting Christmas gifts from us years ago, and we usually only had to bring one gift apiece for the white elephant exchange, anyway. I planned to try my hand at a Pinterest creation this week in hopes of saving those dollars for another gift apiece for the kids.

Del Ray, Martin, and Gibson followed the scent of breakfast to the table and took their places while giving mumbled greetings to their father and me. I poured orange juice for the kids and warmed up my and Brandon's coffee before taking my place at the table.

We all bowed our heads, held hands, and prayed over our meal before the free-for-all began. I looked over my family and felt my spirit chomping at the bit to tell them about my exciting news, but I waited for everyone to fill their plates and begin eating before I started with my lead-in.

"So, how did everyone sleep last night?" I asked.

All four of them nodded or gave me thumbs-up as they chewed and stared at whatever held them captivated in the center of the table. It took me back to being a kid and reading the box of Honey Nut Cheerios as I ate my cereal every morning. I looked at Brandon's bed-head and avoided watching his bouncing temples as he chewed. I still can't figure out why that bothers me so much.

I couldn't stand it anymore. I set my fork down and reached for my coffee. "Well, I have some good news." I grinned and took a drink of coffee before I continued. Four sets of stunned eyes were on me; no one was used to me making positive declarations, apparently, and I pretended that didn't sting a little.

Del Ray said, "Oh god, you're not pregnant, are you?"

I exclaimed, "Ha! No, bite your tongue."

Brandon mumbled, "No kidding. No chance of that, anyway," as he tossed an annoyed glance my way. Guess it's time to give it up again.

I took a deep breath. "So this morning, I went to the gym for class, and the teacher didn't show up. Reggie asked me to lead the class then offered me a job afterward." I beamed and bit my lip as I waited for the family to erupt in accolades.

Brandon frowned. "You got a job at the gym?"

I grinned. "I know! Isn't that so awesome? He's going to look over the schedule and let me know when the classes are scheduled and he needs . . ."

"Michelle . . ." Brandon groaned. "That's not a real job. That's not what you're supposed to be doing! You're *supposed* to be finding a job working full-time with benefits and normal hours, not dancing with people who have nothing better to do."

His words slammed against me like a sledgehammer. My coffee caught in my throat, and I had to swallow twice to move it. I blinked hard and took a deep breath. I whispered, "Well, *that* wasn't the reaction I was looking for."

Martin said, "I think it's cool, Mom. You'll be like a PE teacher for adults." He grinned.

I chuckled through tears. "Yes, I guess you could say that. Great analogy, bud."

Del Ray sat up straight. "I think it's awesome, Mom. You love your time at the gym, and it's great you'll get paid for doing what you love. Right, Dad?"

Brandon shrugged and remained silent.

Gibson chimed in, "Will you still get to take us to school and pick us up?"

"An excellent question, Gib," Brandon said as he eyed me.

I shrank back. "I don't see why not, but I'll have to wait to see what classes Reggie wants me to take over." I thought for a second then sat up straight, "Oh! And I forgot that I'll also be cleaning some and doing laundry, that sort of thing." I smiled at Brandon.

He stopped chewing. "Do you think that makes it any better? Really? This is insane, Michelle. Is it full time?"

I whispered, "I don't *know* yet, Brandon. This all just happened after class today, and I came home to make breakfast instead of sticking around to hear all the details!" I shoved my chair back and scraped my half-eaten breakfast in the trash. "I've . . . uh . . . I don't feel well. I'm going to go lay down. I'll clean up when you're all done."

Del Ray stood up. "Mom . . ."

Brandon said, "Del Ray, sit down and finish your meal."

She wheeled around and screamed, "You're killing her soul! Can't you see that? She was so excited, and you just shit all over her world."

Brandon stood up and started around the table. "Young lady, you better remember who you're talking to. Get your ass in your room and don't come out 'til I come get you." He grabbed her plate and scraped it in the trash. "You're done. Go." He slammed the plate in my arms and went back to his seat.

I stared at the gravy on my shirt and shaking hands then made the mistake of looking at my boys' faces. Bile and biscuits tickled at the back of my throat as I saw Gibson and Martin take turns wiping at rogue tears that streamed down their faces. I took the plate to the sink. "Boys, go get your shoes on." I chased Del Ray down the hallway and met her in her room. "Get your shoes on. We're leaving."

Brandon's chair scraped on the floor then I heard him stomp down the hallway. "What the hell do you mean, 'we're leaving?'"

I wheeled around. "Which part are you struggling with, oh mighty one? My children and I are leaving this house right now, Brandon. I have been humiliated, and they've cried through too many meals as it is." Gibson came out of his room wiping his face with his shoes on but untied dragging his coat and heading toward the front door. Martin caught up to him with an eager, get-out-of-dodge walk, and Del Ray squeezed between Brandon and me. I moved around Brandon and went to the bedroom to change my shirt; the bedroom door slammed behind me.

"You've really gone off the deep end, Michelle. I don't know what the hell happened to you, but you're an absolutely nut job, you know that?"

I shuffled through my stuff and found the shirt I was looking for. "Yep," I said.

"And where the hell you gonna go, anyway? You have no money and no gas."

"I'll figure something out."

He sighed and choked out, "Are you coming back?"

I looked at him and watched as his quivering chin betrayed his hurt. I wiped my face. "I don't know," as I shoved past him and started down the hall. "Get in the car, kids."

He yelled, "Michelle, don't do this to our family!" as I slammed the door.

I hurried to the car before I could consider anything he'd said or register the pain on his face. A car full of sniffles and tears peeled out of the driveway and headed down the street. I took a deep breath and tried to think of something uplifting to say to my children, but no words would suffice. It seemed appropriate to let all of our hearts break in silence.

I grabbed Del Ray's hand. "Let's get you something to eat, baby." She squeezed my hand and wiped her face with her other one and nodded. I drove across town, pulled into IHOP and killed the engine. We all got out and shuffled into the restaurant to think over what just happened.

We were seated at a booth near a drafty window and I whispered to the kids, "I don't have a whole lot of money, so go easy on the ordering, okay?"

Once our order was taken and the waitress left, I took a sip of water and stared at the blank looks on my children's faces. They all stared at the nothing in front of them and fought the tears that brimmed in their eyes. I bit my lip and wondered if this was doing more harm than good.

"Guys, let's try, just for once, to have a good, happy meal, okay? Forget about what happened at the house just now and let's just enjoy being together and try to have a normal conversation. I don't even remember the last time that happened."

Martin looked up. "I got an A on my science test yesterday."

I grinned. "Good job, bud! All that studying paid off, huh?"

He smiled and shrugged, "I guess so."

Gibson said, "I got chosen first on the kickball team at recess yesterday."

"No kidding? That's cool! It's a little cold for outside recess, isn't it?"

He shook his head. "We weren't outside. We were in the gym. I kicked one ball that went over the heads of all of them and got to second base." His grin widened as he leaned forward. "And I caught Benton Forter's ball for the first time ever. It was awesome."

Del Ray took her turn. "I made first chair in band try-outs for the spring concert." She looked at me and smiled. "We're doing a flashback to the eighties thing. You're going to totally love it."

I chuckled. "Finally they're bringing coolness to the band. Well, you guys already heard my good news."

Martin said, "Tell us about the class this morning."

I took a sip of my coffee and sighed. "It was fabulous. The regular class leader didn't show up, and Reggie asked me to lead. Now, I always stay in the back of the class because I just don't feel like I'm one of them, ya know? But I guess he noticed at some point, so he asked me to lead, and at first I was so freaking nervous! I've never done anything like that, and I didn't know really what I was doing. But once the class started, I just made it up as I went along. Several women told Reggie that was the

193

best workout they'd had in months, so he asked me to take over."

Del Ray smiled. "I'm proud of you, Mom. That's awesome."

Martin asked, "While we're on Christmas break, can I go to the gym with you?"

"I don't see why not. If you're going to do the class, though, you'll have to go to the back and stay out of the way of the ladies. They get pretty vicious when it comes to cardio." I winked at him causing him to grin.

Gibson's question cut the air. "Mom, are we going back home today?"

I stared at the coffee in front of me and thought how it took the coffee, sugar, and cream to make that brew the perfect flavor for me. The sugar needed the heat from the coffee to melt it; the coffee needed a sweet touch of creamer to dilute the bitter taste, and the creamer needed the sugar to amplify what it already had to begin with. Individually, they all had their faults, but together, they made my morning complete. The three elements in my coffee reminded me of my bitter daughter, my sweet middle child, and the softness of my baby. I was the cup, and Brandon was the saucer. Or was he the spoon. Maybe he was the handle which kept me from getting burned. Or maybe he represented the cautionary heat that taught me to blow on the coffee to keep from getting burned.

I sighed. "I honestly don't know, Gib. I didn't think that far ahead. I was pissed that Del Ray's food got trashed, I was pissed that you and your brother were crying at yet another meal, and I was pissed because your father embarrassed me in front of you."

The waitress appeared with our order and hurried off to tend to a table of eight seated nearby. Judging by the looks of them, they were suffering "the morning after the night before" and there wasn't enough coffee or grease in the building to cure their hurts.

I grabbed Del Ray's hand and reached for Gibson's across from me. He grabbed Martins, and the other two completed the circle. We bowed our heads as I prayed, "Father, thank You for the opportunity to have a nice meal with my children. Keep us safe and help us to be good people

194

today. Amen."

"Amen," they repeated and reached for their silverware.

I tried to mentally calculate how much breakfast was going to cost, but I lost track as the kids sang out their orders. Best I could tell, I was looking at about thirty bucks after tip and prayed it didn't go over that because I only had forty in my purse that was supposed to go into my gas tank.

The chitchat at the table was such a nice reprieve from the tension-filled niceties we'd all grown accustomed to. I saw a side of my kids I wasn't aware they had, and while it was fun to see their personalities emerge, the realization that came from wondering how long they'd been suppressing themselves wasn't lost on me.

The waitress came to see if we needed anything else, and I said, "No ma'am, just the check, please."

She smiled. "Actually, a couple in the restaurant that wants to stay anonymous has already paid your tab. They wanted me to tell you that God loves you, everything is going to be all right, and to have a merry Christmas."

I put my head in my hands and gritted my teeth to prevent the sobs from escaping my mouth. I nodded my head and blinked hard as I whispered, "Tell them I said thank you."

She smiled as she cleared the plates. "Y'all have a merry Christmas."

I put ten dollars on the table. "Are you guys ready?"

Del Ray said, "Way to pay it forward, Mom," as she grinned and stood up.

"It's the least I can do," I whispered as I sniffled and wiped my face. I glanced around the room to see if I could pinpoint the couple who blessed us, but everyone was focused on their food.

Gibson said loudly, "Thank you! Merry Christmas!" as he waved to whomever might be delighted by this eight-year-old's declaration. Several people lifted their glasses. "Merry Christmas!"

We left the restaurant giggling and hugging as I fought another round of sobs stuck in my throat. Just for a moment, we were happy. The kids were laughing and teasing Gibson for his outburst while he reminded them what good manners were. And I ate up every minute of it.

Chapter Twenty-Five
Always on My Mind

Chance

Christmas. The happiest time of the year for three-fourths of population, and the loneliest time for the rest of us. For the last three months, I have spent every day trying to forget what happened in St. Louis. It was a hard sell, though, especially since I was forcibly asked to step down from the anchor desk and put on some bullshit reporting/writing detail for the website.

I guess I had that coming since I disobeyed my boss, tucked-tail and left the dinner then skipped the press conference I'd been sent to cover. Eddie and the crew did a great job on the segment, but "the face of the station" blah blah blah. I'd love to tell you what Stuart said, but I didn't care enough to listen. I should have just quit but needed my health insurance long enough to get through this year's checkups. But next week? Adios, assholes. I'm Florida-bound.

Tony set me up. Thousands of questions blanketed my mind from the time I woke up until the time I went to sleep—day in and day out. The only person who could answer them tried to call me four times a day and sent multiple texts for the first few weeks after the "humiliation of Chance," but I took my phone's advice and didn't answer. And eventually he took his phone's advice and didn't call.

I didn't need his lame excuses. I didn't need to hear his voice, and he damn sure didn't deserve the privilege of returned texts. He ripped me out of my life and put me in St. Louis to rub his beautiful, sexy, successful bimbo of a girlfriend in my face. All of his "she's not my girlfriend; she was joking; it's not like that; please call me; I miss you" texts were just meant to lure me in further to make it hurt that much more when he dropped the bomb. "Hey, you're the one that didn't want me." I could see his game for miles. That he didn't give me enough credit to see it was to his detriment.

But why did he have to say all those things? Why did he look at me like he did? Why would anyone put on such a performance only to yank the rug right out from under me? Was that the plan all along?

Chubs realized I was awake and nuzzled under my arm, which was the exact reminder of why I'm still single. I could accept his affection with only the expectation that I would take care of him and love him back. No strings, no games, and simple expectations. My kind of relationship.

I walked Chubs out to the doggie area and pulled my coat tighter around my body. The wind threatened to break through my walls and expose that my insides were the same temperature as the wind chill outside.

Since St. Louis, everything has felt tilted. I've been walking through life wearing two different shoes. No amount of pep talks could reroute me back to the moment before Stuart called me into his office and said the words, "St. Louis." Colors were muted, fragrances I used to enjoy were pungent, and I hadn't listened to music in months. The void in me ran rampant in my existence, and while every night I went to bed thinking the next day would be different, every morning proved to be the same.

But not for much longer. Because in one week, I'm blowing this popsicle stand and shedding this life that has me suffocating while trading it in for sand, sunshine, and friendship. My apartment is paid up through June, my mail has been forwarded, and my car will be nestled in Alissa's garage while I'm gone. And to my knowledge, Tony has never been to Naples, so there will be nothing there to remind me of him at all.

The wind attacked and forced me to turn against it placing me staring at the lonely pavilion in the middle of the courtyard. It seemed to share my sorrow as it slumped with no hint of happiness around it. It read my thoughts like last year's love letters from an opportunity lost and seemed to shudder when it got to the part where I let my fear of commitment make a permanent decision that would alter my life. I closed my eyes to keep from seeing it sigh.

I called Chubs, attached his leash, and hurried into the warmth of the building. At least my body felt relief even if the heat didn't reach my soul.

My phone was ringing when I entered the apartment; I knew it wasn't Tony, because I'd changed his ring tone to the "Imperial Death March" to keep my heart from leaping every time the damn thing went off. It was Katie probably wanting to know what time we had to be at Alissa's to make sure it still fit in Landon's "busy" schedule.

"Hello, lady bug," I answered.

"Chance, have you heard from Michelle?" she breathed.

My heart skipped a beat. "No, why?"

"Brandon just called me and said she took off with the kids a few hours ago and hasn't come home yet. He's trying to find her."

"I guess Sherlock Holmes tried her cell phone?"

She sighed. "I mean she left left . . . as in she's left him, I guess."

My knees buckled as I fell onto the couch. "Are you shitting me?"

She sniffled. "I know, right? She's not answering my calls, either, which means she's probably figured out that Brandon's trying to find her. Can you try to get a hold of her?"

I thought about it for a second. "I'm not really sure her leaving is a bad thing, Katie."

She cut me off. "She's got his *kids*, Chance. It's not just about her."

"Whoa, whoa, they're her kids, too. Did he tell you what happened?"

"Not much just that she's been hard to live with the last few months and she went off the deep end this morning and left."

I mumbled, "Yeah, well I'm sure there's way more to that story than he's letting on."

"Chance, stop with the judgment for a second and realize that we all know that Michelle hasn't been herself for a while. She could really be in trouble and she's got her kids with her."

I snarled. "Maybe *you* should remember for a second that Brandon is a complete douchebag who likes to take his jabs at our *friend*. Michelle's unstable at times but she'll never put those kids in harm's way."

"Ugh, whatever. I'll try Alissa and Dani. If you hear from Michelle, please call me." She hung up and I threw my phone on the couch to pout.

Where does she get off calling me all frantic making demands and taking Brandon's side? We haven't even heard from Michelle yet! I grabbed my phone and dialed Michelle's number. "No, this doesn't look obvious at all," I mumbled.

Michelle answered on the third ring, "Guess news travels fast, huh?"

I chuckled. "Just trying to make sure you're not holed up in a culvert somewhere with your three homeless children, kiddo. Katie just called."

She sighed. "Yeah, she and Brandon have been blowing up my phone. I haven't heard from her in months, so I figured he called her." She muffled the phone and said something to her kids I couldn't make out then returned to the phone. "Okay, they're going to go look at toys, so I have a few minutes."

"Where are you?"

"We're at Walmart." Her voice cracked when she said, "I couldn't take it anymore, Chance. He's such an absolute douche."

"Well, yeah! He always has been. What set you off, kid?"

"Everything. The way he chews his food, seeing the boys cry at breakfast, shoving a dirty plate at me, how completely disrespectful he is . . ."

"Whoa, whoa, whoa, what? Tell me what happened."

"I can't get into it right now; I'm in Walmart a week before Christmas, so you can imagine how packed this place is. I'll tell you all about it tonight at Alissa's party."

"Okay, but meanwhile what are you going to do? Where are you going to go?" She hesitated longer than I liked, so I continued. "I have nothing going on today, Michelle. Bring the kids over. They can play with Chubs and watch TV while we catch up. I just brewed a pot of coffee."

She giggled. "You know how to tease me."

"Will you come?"

She sniffled. "Yeah, we'll be over shortly."

Twenty minutes later, they filtered through my door looking like they had just emerged from a homeless shelter. I could tell the boys had no interest in being drug from place to place, but they'd just have to deal

200

for a while. I hugged Del Ray and remembered I'd forgotten to have that chat Michelle had asked me to have with her about sex at a young age. I grimaced with the thought and thanked my lucky stars I'd forgotten. I was uncomfortable just thinking about it.

I turned over the remote to the boys and set Del Ray up on my iPad then took Michelle into the dining room to have a chat. She warmed her hands on the coffee mug in front of her. "It's bitter cold out there today."

I nodded. "I'm pretty sure Chubs's piss was frozen before it hit the ground this morning."

She chuckled. "That's an awesome visual." She cleared her throat and glanced over her shoulder at the kids in living room. She shook her head. "I don't know why I'm being all secretive. It's not like they weren't there to see the whole thing."

I looked at her then noticed the drastic change in her appearance. "Good Lord, Michelle, stand up!"

She frowned. "What's wrong?"

"Look at you! How much weight have you lost? Geez, you look fantastic!"

She giggled, stood up, and held up her three-sizes-too-big sweatshirt. "I'm down thirty-two pounds as of this week." She turned around in a circle and threw her arms out to the side. "Ta-da!"

I gasped. "Wow, that's incredible! Your clothes are hanging off you, though. I'll have to give you some of my stuff."

Her eyes grew wide. "Really? That'd be great!"

"Sure. When we're done here, we'll raid my closet. It'll be fun."

"Gosh, I haven't worn your clothes since after Del Ray was born." She bit her lip. "I don't know if I can wear them, Chance."

"Meh, we'll give it a shot. So, catch me up on the last three months. Obviously you're surviving on saltines and lettuce, but what else?"

She laughed. "Actually, no, I'm eating but I'm working out every day. You remember Alissa bought me that membership, right? Well that was a complete abomination to one young Brandon-san who said I didn't need to spend any more time away from the family than I already did. So,

I started getting up early in the mornings and attending a class. It just went from there, and then I lost my job—"

My mouth flew open. "What? When?"

"About three months ago, I guess."

"Good grief, child, and you never thought to pick up the phone?"

She grimaced. "I was in a . . . dark place, Chance. And I knew if I talked to you or anyone else about it, the checkbooks would come flying out, and I just didn't want to deal with Brandon on any of it."

She had a point. None of us like to see Michelle struggle the way she has, and while it hasn't happened often, we've all taken a turn at giving her money to get her through. Not that she's asked for it—she would never. But giving money when we've got it to spare and wouldn't miss it anyway when one of our own is struggling is what we do. And if she'd called and said she'd just lost her job, you can bet Alissa, Dani, and I would have been racing each other to the wet ink.

Michelle set her coffee cup down and wiped her eyes on her sweatshirt sleeve. I hopped up to grab the box of tissues that had become my best friend over the last few months and placed them in front of her.

"Thanks," she said as she grabbed three out at a time. She took a deep breath. "I tried like hell to find a new job. No one wants to hire a thirty-something whose only real talent lies in a kitchen, and flipping burgers wasn't an option. So, I've been working out every day, and this morning, I was offered a job at the gym."

I grinned. "Michelle, that's great."

She groaned. "*See? You* get it. Why can't he?" She dabbed at her eyes. "Anyway, I made this huge breakfast for the family and Brandon lost his shit when I told him about the job offer. He started in on me, and the next thing I know, Del Ray is standing up for me and yelling at her father, the boys are crying in their scrambled eggs, and Brandon's shoving Del Ray's breakfast plate in my gut. So we left." She blew her nose and reached for my arm. "I just wanted to have one meal with my kids where one of us weren't on the verge of tears. Ya know? Just one meal where we're sitting down like a normal family enjoying each other's company. I didn't really mean to leave-leave, but I don't want to go

202

home." She whispered, "And I don't think they do, either."

I glanced at the kids in the living room and studied their blank expressions. I looked at her. "You know, Michelle, I'm leaving for six months. My apartment is paid up; all of my bills for this place are pre-paid through June . . ."

She held up her hand. "Don't do that . . . just . . . not right now. I can't be tempted with that while I'm trying to make a solid decision for my family. I appreciate it, I really do. But let me just think for a while before you dangle that carrot."

I smiled. "Okay, well the offer is there. Just tuck it back in the back of your mind." I leaned in and whispered, "What about Christmas?"

She shrugged and shook her head as she pursed her lips. Her eyes filled with tears and she shook her head again as they dripped down her face.

I felt my nose tingle with brewing tears and bit my lip. "Will you let me help you? Please? Let me do this for you. I don't have any family to buy for, so let me spoil yours this year."

Her eyes sparkled as she gasped, "Are you serious?"

I nodded. "I promise, I won't miss it as conceited as that must sound, but it's true. I'll give you the money and keep the kids so you can go shopping today. And get yourself some damn clothes while you're at it, okay? Don't make me review your receipts when you get back."

She giggled and slid across the table to hug me. "I would never take you up on this if I wasn't desperate."

"Well that's your own damn fault."

She laughed. "Maybe so. Oh my gosh, I'm so excited! Chance, you don't know what you've just done for me. I feel like the world just lifted off my whole body and I can breathe again."

"Come on, let's run to the bank real quick before they close. It's just up the street, so the kids will be fine here by themselves."

She stood up and pulled on her coat. "Guys, we'll be right back. Don't move, and don't break anything."

I laughed. "And don't flush the dog."

The boys grinned and shook their heads. Del Ray rolled her eyes and came into the dining room. "Where are you going, Mom?"

"We're just going to run up to the . . . store for a minute. Need anything?"

"No, thanks. You're coming back, though, right?"

"Of course. Give me ten, maybe twenty minutes, and we'll be right back."

I made Michelle stay in the car while I went into the lobby and withdrew fifteen hundred dollars from my savings account. While I knew that was complete overkill for Christmas, I hoped to give her a cushion to hide from Brandon in the event she went back to him and got put on lock-down for her erratic behavior. It was really bugging me that three of us were about to be hundreds of miles away from her during this time. Katie was probably closer to her than all of us, but after our phone conversation today, I wasn't sure she was wearing the Team Michelle shirt, and that bothered me.

I got back in the car and handed her the envelope. "Don't bother counting it. Just spend, okay?"

She took the fat envelope. "You've got to be shitting me, Chance."

"Just take it and be quiet," I giggled. "You might need some of that later, so just make sure you get yourself some clothes and give your babies an awesome Christmas. Sounds like they've had a shitty few months, so you can make it up to them. But you cannot tell Brandon you have that money, you hear me? Next thing you know he'll have a new guitar or golf clubs and you won't have beans."

She nodded and stuffed the envelope in her purse. "I don't think I've ever held that much cash at once. I'm all nervous and shit."

I laughed. "Well if you want to leave some of it at the house while you shop, that's up to you."

"Yeah, I probably will. Thanks again, Chance. I can't . . ."

"You are loved. Deal with it."

Chapter Twenty-Five
Say My Name

Alissa

Saturday morning, I stayed in bed rubbing the bump I fell in love with yesterday. Eighteen weeks pregnant, nearly half-way over, and I finally found that feeling that Michelle and Katie had warned me about. The maternal instincts I'd tried my damnedest never to feel again after my sisters turned on me slammed like waves against my shore. I curled into a ball and giggled as the flutters and bumps of an active baby tickled my insides.

"So, you're a morning person, huh baby?" I mumbled. I waited for the Morse code response and envisioned the little person looking around wide-eyed trying to figure out where that voice came from. I didn't even know if the little feller had eyes yet, but the more I thought about it, the funnier it got. I jumped up and raced to my bathroom to pee before I let loose in my bed. I washed my hands and did my daily belly check. Yep, there was no denying that a baby was growing in my belly. To people who don't know me, they'd never notice; to my friends and family who are used to my six-pack abs, it would be evident.

Dani knocked on my door. "Lis? You awake?"

I shouted, "Yeah, I'm in the bathroom."

She came in. "I heard you laughing in here. Well, laughing or crying—I couldn't tell." She looked at me in the mirror as I admired my baby bump and grinned. "Yep, there's definitely a baby in there."

I smiled. "I had flutters when I woke up, and something struck me funny. I think this baby is definitely a morning person."

She pointed to my belly. "May I?"

"Sure."

She placed her hands on my belly and leaned over to speak. "Good morning, beautiful child. I can't wait to meet you and hold you in my arms." She wiped a tear from her eyes and looked at me. "I'm not even going to pretend this isn't awkward."

I laughed. "Well, if you wanted to ruin a beautiful moment, you did a good job." I clenched my teeth to stop the tears swelling in me. I rubbed my belly. "Eighteen weeks, Dani. Just twenty-two more to go, and it will be baby-day."

She sighed and leaned against the wall. "I still can't believe this is real. I keep thinking I'll wake up and my world will still be shattered and vacant." She touched my belly again. "And then I see this, and I'm reminded that dreams come true and prayers get heard."

I smiled and turned on the shower. "I'm, uh . . . I'm going to shower and get this day started."

"Okay. I'll bring you some juice."

"That's fabulous, wifey."

"Oh shut up," she chuckled as she left the bathroom.

The tears I'd choked on rolled down my face as I undressed and stepped into the shower. I needed to talk to Chance. I needed to talk to someone and get all this out of my head so someone could talk some sense into me. I know it must be natural to be pregnant and actually like the little critter, but it shouldn't be like shredding razors going through my heart to think about giving it up when this pregnancy is all said and done.

But, I've never had anyone one-hundred percent on my side, and now I've committed to giving up the one person on this whole earth that would always be my champ, always be in my corner, and would always love me.

Or am I? Look at me and my mother. I couldn't wait to get away from her and leave behind our life of lunacy and neglect. And that right there was why I couldn't take the chance that my offspring would ever feel that way about me. No one but the women coming to dinner tonight had ever been devoted to me. Hell, my own family thinks I'm a nut case. Yes, letting Dani take care of this baby was the best thing for everyone. Even if it meant leaving a permanent vacant hole in my soul for the rest of my life.

I bent down to wash my legs and felt the baby wiggling again. Soft,

206

deliberate, delicate, and consoling. I swear it was trying to soothe me. I choked on a sob as I stood up and whispered, "Thank you, but you just don't understand, baby. This is the only way you'll ever have a chance at something awesome and normal. If my family ever gets wind that you exist, or god forbid your father . . . you're better off with Dani."

A soft knock rapped on the door. "Lis? Here's your juice."

"Okay, thank you."

"You okay?"

I cleared my throat. "Yep. Just finishing up." My heart stopped. Oh God, did she hear me? Did she hear me talking to the baby? How would I ever make her understand what's going on in my thick, selfish head? "What time is it?"

"A little after eight; are you hungry?"

"Yeah, oatmeal sounds fabulous right now."

She chuckled. "I'm on it."

"Do you think people will think we're lesbians? In Florida, I mean." I had to keep her talking to feel out the situation.

She sighed. "Ya know, I wondered that same thing. And I've come to the conclusion that it really doesn't matter, because we won't be there long enough for it to make a difference either way."

Okay, she's good. She didn't hear me. If she'd heard me, her response would have been much shorter and she'd have left. I shut off the shower. "I'll meet you in the kitchen unless you want to see all this."

She giggled. "I'll be seeing more of you than I ever wanted to soon enough. I'll be in the kitchen."

A few hours later, both of our phones chimed with texts from Katie. *Have you heard from Michelle?* We came out of the rooms we were cleaning to stare at each other in confusion.

"Did you get the text from Katie? Have you heard from Michelle?" I asked Dani.

She shook her head. "No, but why is Katie trying to find her?"

"Maybe she needs a recipe." I typed a quick response and waited for Katie to elaborate. She didn't. "Did she reply to you?"

Dani looked at her phone again. "Nope. Oh wait . . . she said if she shows up here to call her." She shrugged.

"Think we should call Michelle?" I asked.

"Nah, if it was serious, someone would have called us and not sent a text. I'm sure it's nothing."

I eyed my phone. "Chance wasn't on the text. So Katie must have already talked to her."

Dani chuckled. "Sheesh, listen to your attorney investigative skills coming through. How can you tell, anyway?"

I winked. "Because I have an iPhone and it tells me who is on the text. Doesn't take a rocket scientist, genius."

"Then Sherlock Holmes, you are not."

I shrugged. "Sometimes it's the obvious that's overlooked. I'd say Michelle's at Chance's apartment but Chance isn't telling Katie. Which means there's trouble with Brandon."

Dani interjected, "So nothing new, then. I'm sure we'll get to hear all about it tonight."

I spent the next few hours finalizing everything for the party and while Dani busied herself making playlists for our trip to Florida. I adjusted the gift bags under the Christmas tree and felt the anticipation of my gifts to Katie and Michelle swelling in my heart. I'd never done anything like this for them, and I couldn't wait to see their faces when they opened them.

Dani said, "I think we should keep the conversation about Florida to an absolutely minimum."

I frowned. "Why? Dammit, I can't get these ornaments to sit right."

She glanced at me. "They look fine just like they are. It's got to be difficult for Michelle and Katie to know we're hightailing it out of life for months at a time. And, they're going to miss so much."

I grinned. "Au contraire."

Dani looked at me sideways. "What's that supposed to mean?"

"Well, I might have gone a little overboard at Christmas. But I got them each something that will help them stay connected to us while we're in Florida."

"This outta be good. What'd you do?"

I grinned. "You'll see. By the way, I didn't get you or Chance anything for Christmas since we're going to be on vacation until May."

Dani laughed. "Girl, if you think I expected gifts this season, you're nuts. You're already giving me the gift of a lifetime." Her eyes glistened before she turned her attention to the laptop in front of her. "Okay so far I have about six hours of music on this playlist."

I chuckled. "You're going to need four times that since it's about a twenty-four hour drive to Naples."

"My goodness, will you give no opportunity for conversation or repeats?" She chuckled.

I shrugged and fiddled with the ornaments again. "Dammit, Dani, will you come fix this?"

She stood. "What's wrong with it, Lis? It looks fine."

"No, it's not hanging right. It's not supposed to lean like that."

She looked at me. "What's the problem? It's completely centered."

I handed it to her. "Just find a place for that one, please. Put it on the back for all I care." I stomped into the kitchen and grabbed a bottle of water. I took a deep breath and tried to shake off the memory attached to the ornament I'd worked over. It was a popsicle stick ornament made by Adriana in kindergarten and was the only gift I got for Christmas that year—I was eleven, and that was the year I quit believing in Santa and my mother. She'd pulled me into her room a week before Christmas and cried as she explained that the girls, then six, four, and two months old were expecting gifts, but that she knew I'd understand that there wasn't enough money for all of us to have something. "Be a big girl, now," she'd said. When Adriana brought me her gift wrapped in toilet paper, I cried. I even kept the paper, because it had her crooked little illegible handwriting on it saying, "To my favrit." I still have it.

Dani came up behind me and draped her arms around my chest. "I love you, Alissa."

I wiped my face and whispered, "I love you, too."

"I fixed the ornament. It's okay now."

I nodded and took a deep breath. "Okay, so that's done." I looked at the clock. "They'll be here in about an hour, if I know those impatient heifers."

Dani nodded. "Yeah, there's no way they're going to wait 'til five o'clock to show up. I'm kind of surprised Chance isn't here already."

"Well, if she's got Michelle like I'm sure she does, then they're busy solving the Morehead problems."

We walked back into the living room, and there was Adriana's ornament hanging perfectly and grinning like she did when she gave it to me. I took a deep breath and let it out slowly. "Dani, if anything ever happens to me, bury me with that ornament in my hand." I looked at her. "Promise me."

Her eyes filled with tears as she nodded and whispered, "I promise."

I clapped my hands. "Okay, what else?"

Chapter Twenty-Six
Since U Been Gone

Michelle

I checked the time for the sixth time in five minutes and groaned as I stood in the long checkout line. That was me—always on the clock. I felt awful for leaving the kids with Chance for the last three hours and knew they'd all be ready for me to get back. I'd made good use of Chance's money and picked out three outfits to update my wardrobe. I'd let her help me decide which one to wear to dinner tonight.

Once I finally made it through the checkout and outside, I tossed the clothes into the trunk with the mountain of Christmas presents for the kids and Brandon. And there may have been a thing or two in those bags for me.

I had to go home. There's no way I can rip my family apart, not to mention Chance's money would soon run out, then I'd be up shit creek without a paddle. There's no way I could expose my children to the life Alissa had growing up, so I made up my mind to return to the house and deal with Brandon as I already knew how to do. I would suck it up and try to focus on the good things. At least now I could provide a good Christmas to our children and buy the groceries for our annual holiday feast. That'd taken a huge weight off my shoulders, and I owed Chance a kidney for her generosity.

By two o'clock, I'd gathered my children, picked out an outfit and hugged the life out of Chance. We piled into my car and headed toward the house.

Del Ray asked, "So did you have fun shopping?"

I grinned. "I did. I got you Christmas gifts."

The mood in the car was borderline hostile. I glanced in the rearview mirror at the boys and asked, "You guys okay?"

Gibson asked, "Are we going home now?"

"Yeah, is that okay?"

Martin said, "Dad's going to be mad that you spent all that money."

I stiffened. "That's between him and me, okay bud?"

He shrugged. "Just sayin'."

Del Ray asked, "Are you still going to Alissa's tonight?"

"Yeah, that's the plan."

Gibson sniffled, "Are you coming home, Mommy?"

My heart flopped as I caught his eye in the rearview mirror. "Oh honey, yes, I'm coming home. Why would you think I wouldn't?"

Del Ray said, "It's a valid question. All your friends are going to Florida after Christmas. Are you going, too?"

"What? No! No, guys, I'm not leaving you. I'd never do that, you hear me?"

Martin nodded. "Good, because I'd go with you."

My sweet little middle child—my loyal son. Gibson whispered, "Me too, Mommy."

Del Ray said, "Me three."

I laughed in spite of myself. "Well, I'm very glad you guys love me so much, but listen, today was . . . I just . . ."

Martin said, "Today was awesome."

I locked eyes with him then glanced at Del Ray. She nodded. "It was awesome."

My mind reeled as I pulled onto our street. Were my children so miserable that they actually *wanted* us to separate? I heard each of them take a deep breath before they took off their seatbelts and open the car doors when we got home. They dreaded this as much as I did.

"Guys, go on inside and go to your rooms. I need to get these gifts in the house and don't want you to see your presents before Christmas morning, okay?"

They grunted out their acknowledgements and walked to the door. Brandon swung open the door and hugged each of the kids as they walked in then leveled his eyes at me. The door slammed as he stepped onto the stoop and folded his arms over his chest.

I swallowed the lump of dread forming in my throat and popped the trunk before I got out of the car. The bitter wind swept through the subdivision and threatened to take whatever oxygen I still had in my lungs. I pulled a few bags out of the trunk and started toward the house.

"Are you fucking kidding me? What is all that?"

"Gifts."

He was unmoved on the stoop. "You've got a lot of explaining to do, Michelle."

I dropped my arms and let the bags dangle off my fingers. "Are we going to do this outside?"

"You think I'm letting you back in our house? You just fucked up big time, Michelle."

I groaned and started toward the door. "Brandon, let me in. It's cold out here."

"Guess you should have thought about that before you ran off this morning with my children and didn't return one text or phone call to tell me where they were."

"What about me, Brandon? What about *me*?" I screamed.

"You can rot for all I care right now."

"Wow, really? Be careful what you say when you're mad, Brandon. Those words might come back to haunt you." I started toward the door again and he moved in front of me.

"No, Michelle, you're not coming in."

I felt my heart quicken as I heard my children in my head saying, *I'd go with you . . . me too . . . me three*. I started up the step again, and he blocked the door with his arm. "Brandon, let me in this house, or let my kids out."

"No. You left. I'll see you in court." He turned and slammed the door in my face.

I dropped the packages and tried to open the locked door. I kicked and pounded on the door while screaming every word I could think. I heard Gibson and Martin shouting for me in the living room before their bedroom doors slammed and their heads poked out the windows. Both of my boys were bawling and pressing their faces to the screens screaming, "Don't leave, Mommy, don't leave!"

I ran to the car and got my keys out of my purse while mentally planning all the ways I was going to kill that motherfucker when I got inside. I raced back up to the door and put my house key in the lock, but it wouldn't budge. I tried a different key thinking I'd pulled up the wrong one in my hysteria, but none of the keys on my ring would move the deadbolt.

Oh God, he's changed the locks. I screamed and pounded on the door and threatened to call the police. Brandon opened the curtain and flipped me off before he threw them back together and walked away.

"You son of a bitch! Give me my children! I'm calling the cops!" I ran to my car to grab my phone and threw it against the seat when I realized it was dead. *This can't be happening, this can't be happening.* They're going to think I'm leaving if I really leave, but I can't get to them. I looked at the height of their windows; if they jump, they'll break their legs. I pounded on the door until my knuckles bloodied and slumped to my knees to weep. "Brandon, let me in! You can't do this!"

He shouted, "You made your bed, psycho! Deal with it."

I ran to the boys' windows. "I'm coming back, okay? I'm coming for you. I have to leave . . ."

"Mommy, no! Please don't go!"

"I have to go get the cops so they'll let me have you, okay? I'm coming back."

Sirens blasted at the end of the road as two patrol cars barreled down the street. I ran to the sidewalk and waved them down. "Please stop!" The cars skidded to a halt when they got in front of my house and four officers approached me with caution and hands on their guns. "Please, help me! My husband's got my kids inside."

"We got a 911 call from this location about a domestic disturbance. Are you okay, ma'am?"

I took a deep breath and sighed. Del Ray must have called the cops. "Oh thank God. He's got my kids."

"Who does?"

"My husband, Brandon."

"Are they his kids, too?"

I nodded. "We got in a fight this morning, and I took off with the

214

kids, but when I got home, he let them in but won't let me in and now won't give me my kids. And he's changed the locks. I just want my kids."

Brandon opened the door. "Oh thank God you're here, officers. She's a nut case and made all kinds of threats toward me and the kids."

I gaped and screamed, "What the fuck are you talking about?"

Brandon pointed at my bleeding knuckles. "Well just look at her hands, man! She's tried to pummel everything she's seen in the last ten minutes."

"Are you out of your mind, you lying piece of shit?"

The officer grabbed my arm. "Ma'am, just calm down."

"He's keeping me from my kids!" I jerked my arm out of his grasp. "Give me my children, and I'm out of here."

"Officer, she's unstable. She's on six different medications to keep her sane, and she's in no condition to be around children. Hell, just look at her."

Everything around me started spinning, and the voices I heard suddenly sounded very far away. Unstable, medications, bloody knuckles, attacked, unfit . . . he planned this whole thing. That evil bastard planned this. I stared at the man I'd spent my whole life loving and had never wanted to rip his heart out and shit on it more than I wanted to in that moment.

The officer looked at me. "Ma'am, do you think it would be best if you went somewhere else tonight to cool off?"

I leveled my eyes at him. "I'll leave this house and everything in it including that bastard in the door if you will just give me my children. Those kids are my *life!*"

"Sir, do you mind if we come in and talk to the kids?"

"Sure, come on in, but she stays outside."

"I'm pretty sure legally I'm allowed to enter my own house and at least retrieve 'all those medications that keep me sane,' right officer? Am I not at least allowed to pack a bag?"

The officer looked at another officer. "Why don't you two sit in the car and stay warm? I'll be back out after I talk to the kids."

The officer guided me to the car and at least let me sit in the front seat instead of the back like a criminal. I stared at the neighbors who'd come out to enjoy my humiliation. "This is the worst day of my life."

The officer nodded. "Yeah, this doesn't look like a good situation at all."

"He's such a douchebag. Even under normal circumstances. The reason I left this morning is because he was such a complete asshole to me and the kids. We just wanted to have a normal day, ya know? Just once. And it was a great day." I looked at him with tears spilling over my face. "It was a great day." He handed me a napkin to wipe my face, and I stared at the door willing my children to come running out. "Will they get a choice, officer?"

"Most likely."

A few minutes later, the officer came out of the house alone and approached the car. I opened it, but he held up his hand and motioned for me to roll down the window. "I talked to the kids, and they want to go with you, but he's insisting we leave them here for the night and you can come back to see them tomorrow."

"See them? Bullshit!" I started to open the door again, but he prevented me from doing it.

"Ma'am, I think it's best for everyone if you find somewhere to go, calm down, and y'all can figure it out tomorrow."

"Officer, I am not leaving this house without my children."

"He's got your journal, Mrs. Morehead. He read me a few things from it, and . . ."

I closed my eyes and put my head against the window. Words I'd written in anger, sentences I'd written instead of saying, paragraph upon paragraph explaining the chaos in my head and dissatisfaction in my life scrolled through my head like a television news ticker. My private thoughts and desire for my ink to give me some guidance had just been used against me. I mumbled, "My children will never understand what's going on. That lunatic will spin this and they'll never forget the day that their mom abandoned them after I just . . . *I just promised them I would never leave them.* Never! You don't know what you're doing! Why do you think I have to take so much fucking medication? It's because of that asshole!"

The officer put his hands up. "And I'm sure that's true, but my job right now is to diffuse the situation. You guys can hash this out in court."

"Court? He will not keep my kids from me until then. I'll pitch a tent on this fucking lawn before that happens."

The officer chuckled. "Ma'am, you can't do that. Now I'm asking you one more time to leave on your own."

"Are you going to arrest me for trying to keep my children, officer? Really?"

He opened my door and reached for my hand. "Please. I'm asking you to go somewhere else and get your head on straight before this gets worse." I got out of the car and started up the yard. "Ma'am, do not go toward the house."

I screamed, "I'm going to get the fucking Christmas presents laying on the ground in front of my house! Jesus, why don't you just shoot me and end this?"

Martin yelled from his window, "Mommy! Don't go!"

I sobbed as I said, "I have to, bud. But I'm coming back tomorrow, okay?"

He screamed, "Can't I go with you?"

I pointed at the window and looked at the officers. "Do you see this? Do you?"

The officers looked at each other then hung their heads as one pointed at my car. Brandon came to the door with a grocery sack. He tossed it on the stoop and folded his arms.

I picked it up and looked at my medication and a ripped piece of paper out of my journal that said, *You should have answered your phone.*

I looked up at him. "I need my charger. My *phone is dead* just like our marriage. I was coming home, Brandon. I was coming home."

A look of shock passed over his face before he stepped into the house and returned with my charger. He waved at the officers and shut the door.

I shuffled toward my car and threw the gifts in the front seat. I climbed in the driver's seat and put the key in the ignition, but I couldn't turn it over. I buried my head in my hands and sobbed while thinking of my children in that miserable house without me. I couldn't turn the key. My hands shook as I reached for it again, but the mother in me couldn't leave my babies. I knew they'd remember the sight of my car pulling out of the driveway; I could hear their hearts breaking from here. The officer knocked on the window. "You have to go, ma'am."

I sobbed, "I can't do it, officer. I can't leave them. I can't turn the key."

He mumbled, "Ma'am, I'll have to arrest you for domestic disturbance if you don't leave, and I know he'll press charges if you don't leave now."

"Will you go tell my children that I'm being forced to leave? Or can you at least bring them out so I can hug them and tell them everything is going to be okay?"

"I'll talk to them. Go on, now."

"I'm begging you. Tell them I said I love them and I'm coming back and that I'd never leave them if you weren't making me."

He sighed and shook his head. "It's time for you to go, ma'am."

I reached for the key and groaned as I turned on the car. My hands shook as I put the car in reverse and willed my foot to let off the brake. *God, please make my children understand I'm not doing this on my own.* I promised them I wouldn't leave them. I promised this wouldn't happen, and now look at me leaving them. I knew if I made them arrest me, I'd make life much worse for myself when pleading my case to get my kids back, and no one would see my gesture as an act of valor; I'd simply be the unstable mother who made the cops arrest her, and my children would have that image emblazoned in their minds.

I backed down the driveway and pulled onto the street. I stared at the kids' windows and saw all three of my children huddled together at Martin's window crying and pressing their hands to the screen. I rolled down the window and yelled, "I love you! Mommy loves you, and I'm coming back for you! Do you hear me?"

They nodded and waved the most pitiful waves I'd ever seen in my life. I put my head on my hands and cried so hard, I couldn't breathe. I sat next to one of the police cars and stared at the officer behind the wheel. He gave me a sympathetic nod and waved me on. How he expected me to safely navigate a vehicle under these conditions was beyond me, but I knew they'd follow me until they were certain I wasn't coming back.

I wound up at Chance's apartment with no memory of how I got there. I knocked on her door and slid to the floor before she answered.

Chapter Twenty-Seven
Roar

Chance

I've never wanted to kill someone so much in my life as I did that miserable excuse of a human married to Michelle. I listened as she melted into a pile of soggy flesh on the couch in front of me. I kicked up the thermostat and wrapped myself in a blanket but still couldn't edge out the frigid ball of hate embedded in my core. We called the police station to plead her case, but they had already heard the officers' stories and determined it was best that Michelle take time to cool off and try to talk to Brandon tomorrow.

Meanwhile, the clock was ticking, because something in me remembered a story where this very situation happened, and the mother was unable to get her children back until after the divorce was finalized— a year later—because technically, she'd left the house and the children, which they considered abandonment. I knew we needed to talk to Alissa and fast, but calming Michelle enough to listen to reason was impossible. She rocked; she sobbed, she paced, she crumpled into the floor, she moved to the couch, she threatened to go back and take care of that bastard herself. She was scaring me.

I went to the kitchen and grabbed my bottle of Xanax and a bottle of water then slipped next to her on the couch. I didn't ask her permission or approval; I handed her a pill and the water and nodded my orders. She swallowed the pill and water then curled back into a ball with her face buried in the same pillow laced with my own recent tears.

Watching someone I love being so completely broken and inconsolable was on my top three list of things I hated in the world. I'd take my own heartache and troubles any day over watching someone like Michelle take the beatings from life.

Michelle was simple—not cognitively or intellectually—but she's always been just a simple person. Things were black and white, good or bad, easy or hard; she had her whole life mapped out by the time we were juniors in high school, and while the rest of us were dreaming of fame on Broadway, Pulitzer Prizes, professional sports, and writing our names in ink across history, Michelle would grin and shrug saying, "I just want to be a mom." We wanted to influence millions, she wanted to raise three. As I stared at her, she was the only one that had her dreams come true and would probably leave a much greater legacy than all four of the rest of us put together. One thing all the greats had in common—they all had mothers.

I watched as the medicine took effect; her breathing evened out and sobs slowed to whimpers. She sat up, wiped her face on her sleeves and reached for the bottle of water I held for her.

I smiled. "Good shit, ain't it?"

She nodded and stared at the coffee table. "I'm stoned."

"Maybe you should have let me slip you one of these when I threatened." Humor was my only ally.

She took a deep breath and let it out slowly as she looked at me, her eyes swollen and her face covered with red spots. If this was any other day, I'd take a stab at her ugly-cry face, but I had no idea if she'd roll off the deep end again. She stared at me with her chin quivering. "Katie helped him, didn't she . . ."

Her statement slapped the air with a new realization I hadn't considered. "Oh God, no, Michelle. There's no way she would have helped him carry out a plan like this."

She looked sideways at me. "You sure? She was awfully interested in where I was."

I shook my head. "No way, girl. I guarantee she was a nervous wreck worried sick about you. There's no telling what line of bullshit Brandon fed her to try to get her to talk."

She returned her gaze to the table in front of us and nodded. "That's true. I'd hate to have to kill two people today."

I chuckled. "You're not going to kill anyone today."

She shrugged. "Well, maybe tomorrow, then. I *am* kind of tired."

I looked at my watch. "Think I should call Alissa and tell her we

221

aren't coming tonight?"

Michelle shook her head. "Is Katie still going?"

"Far as I know."

"Then we're going. I want to see her face when I tell her what she helped Brandon do today."

I swallowed hard and put my hand on hers. "She's been our friend for over twenty years. She didn't help him do anything."

She stood up and mumbled, "Yeah, we'll see."

Helping a drugged-out, weak-from-sorrow woman down three flights of stairs proved to be an interesting adventure. I considered wrapping her in a blanket and rolling her down the stairs, but knowing the luck we'd both been having lately, she'd either break her neck or knock out a wall. She freaked out when she saw her car in the parking lot and insisted we take all of the kids' Christmas presents upstairs and lock them in my apartment before we left. She was certain Brandon would take them and return them. With the story she'd just told me, I could believe it. I left her in my car and loaded the bags in my arms; by the time I got to the car, she was crying all over again telling me about the conversation she and the kids' had on the way home.

I wanted to warn our friends about what was heading their way, but I never got a chance to make a call or send any texts. And the last thing I needed Michelle to think was that I was in any way a questionable ally. As we pulled into Alissa's driveway, I leaned over. "Now, they have no idea what's happened today, okay?"

"I know."

Everything else I wanted to say seemed harsh and insensitive, so I left it to her to decipher what I meant by that. Honestly, I didn't know either.

I held her arm as we walked to the door and was greeted by a glowing, pregnant woman who resembled my friend, Alissa. She squealed, "My friends! Come in, come in!" Her cute sweater dress revealed the secret she'd been desperate to conceal; it was an odd choice for her, but she'd be among friends, and we already knew her story.

I gasped, "Oh my gosh, Alissa, look at you. You look fantastic!"

She beamed. "Thank you. You too!" She looked at Michelle and did a double take. "Holy cow, woman, you've lost weight!"

Michelle offered a weak grin and mumbled, "Thirty-two pounds . . ."

Alissa's eyes widened as she clapped her hands. "Bravo! That gym membership is working out well, I see."

Michelle turned to hang up her coat and hide the tears brewing in her eyes. Dani took her turn at greetings and ushered us into the living room.

Alissa had really outdone herself. The room was filled with meticulously placed Christmas decorations, and one step into the room brought us face-first into a wonderland. It was breathtaking. I reached for Michelle. "Can you believe all this?"

She wrapped her arm around me. "It's beautiful. Alissa, you really did a great job."

Katie appeared in the hallway, and a cloud fell over Michelle. Katie's jaw dropped, and a grin spread over her face. "Look at you!" She started toward Michelle with open arms who sidestepped her and headed to the kitchen.

Katie looked at me in shock. "What the hell was that?"

I waved her off and hugged her. "Good to see you, Katie. Alissa, have you turned this into a dry house now that you're hosting another human?"

Alissa rubbed her belly and giggled. "No, girl, I have plenty of wine for our celebration this evening. Come on into the kitchen, and I'll get you fixed up."

Michelle was tipping back a wine glass while facing the window over the sink. Her fingers tapped to a rhythm only she could hear. Dani, Alissa, and Katie were filling their glasses with their beverages of choice and chattering about Alissa's bulging belly. I stood next to them but watched as Michelle went for her second glass of wine. I'd convinced her to put on one of her new outfits for the party before she and the kids left. She looked like a completely different person than I'd spoken with three months ago. And after today, there was a good chance she was.

I winked at Dani and went to Michelle. I put my arms around her.

"Go easy on that wine, kiddo. You know Alissa doesn't buy the cheap stuff, and I'd rather not dig your face out of the mashed potatoes at dinner." I leaned in to whisper in her ear. "You okay?"

She slammed her hand on the sink and looked at me. "Do you *think* I'm okay, Chance?" She glared over my shoulder at Katie and yelled, "Hey there, Katie! Did you have a good day? Huh? Did you have a great day with your family, there kiddo?"

Katie frowned. "You wanna tell me where the hell you were today?"

"I was eating breakfast with my children, then I went shopping."

Katie sassed, "Was that before or after you stormed out of the house with your children acting like you were leaving your husband?"

I stepped between the two of them and faced Katie. If I could have lit her on fire with my eyes, she'd be charcoal by now. "Katie, need I remind you where your loyalties in this group lie?"

Alissa and Dani looked at each other and then at me. Alissa said, "Okay, what'd we miss?"

Michelle yelled, "Oh let me tell ya!"

Dani interrupted. "Wait . . . let's all go into the family room and talk about this. I'd rather slow this roller coaster down before the claws come out." She pulled on Katie's arm as she and Alissa left the room.

I turned to Michelle. "I brought the pills."

"Give me one. Seriously. I want to rip her face off." She held out a shaking palm and wiped at a tear that rolled down her face.

"She's not the enemy here, Michelle. I guarantee her involvement in today ended with trying to find you—"

She interrupted, "Because Brandon—"

"No, because she loves you and was worried you'd flipped out and was wandering around Columbia with your kids on a cold day. Which was pretty close to true," I winked.

She sighed and shuttered, "If she had anything to do with this . . ."

"If she did, I'll be the first one in line to kick her ass. But she didn't. I just feel it."

"Spidey senses?"

I laughed, "Yes, spidey senses. You know they never lead me

224

astray."

She smiled and grabbed her wine glass. I took it from her hand and replaced it with a Diet Coke from the fridge. "Xanax and wine—not a good mix. You ready?"

She nodded and sighed. "I can't tell this story, Chance. Just let me sit there and cry while you tell it."

I nodded. "I can do that." I rubbed her arm. "You really do look great. You're rocking this sweater and those jeans, sister."

She gave me a half-smile. "It's hard work."

"Yes, it is. But you're doing it one day at a time, right? Tomorrow is a new day."

We walked into the family room and took our places on the couch. Alissa and Dani were in the overstuffed chairs across the coffee table from us, and Katie was curled up on the floor between them. I pointed at the end of the couch beside me and offered Katie a seat, but she waved me off.

I took a deep breath. "Wow, we're all together again. It's hard to believe it's been three months since we've all been in the same room and yet, it seems like a lifetime ago." I grabbed Michelle's hand. "Michelle has asked me to tell you guys what happened today. I'll just hit the highlights for now and say that shit hit the fan this morning at breakfast. As it turns out, our lovely friend has been rocking it so much in the gym that Reggie offered her a paying job this morning."

Dani frowned. "What about the daycare?"

Michelle whispered, "I lost my job three months ago—right after we found out Alissa's pregnancy."

They all gasped and sputtered rounds of "why didn't you call me's" and "how awful's," but Michelle just waved them off and pointed at me.

I continued, "So obviously this was great news, so she came home and fixed a big breakfast for the family and announced her job offer over the meal. Brandon threw a fit, Del Ray took up for Michelle, and Brandon took her meal away from her and shoved the plate into Michelle's stomach. The boys were crying, Del Ray was a mess, and Michelle was livid. So, she and the kids left the house to call time-out and

225

go have a normal, quiet meal without drama."

I watched Katie's face as I told the truth of the story she'd never heard and tears poured down here face. I told them I'd given her money for Christmas and let her go shopping while I kept the kids in an attempt to let everything diffuse and get her head on straight and how I'd tried to get them to stay with me, but that she wanted to go home for the sake of her family. Katie's face screwed into horror as I told about the cops and being forced to leave without her children. I glanced at Michelle's face and cringed when I saw the anguish mixed with hatred as she stared down Katie.

Through a whimper, Katie mumbled, "Michelle, I had no idea that's what he was going to do."

Michelle cocked her head to the side. "Really? I'm just not sure I believe you." Tears poured down her face as she said, "Why would you even help him, Katie? Why even call our friends looking for me?"

"I was *worried* about you! Your meltdowns get pretty serious, Michelle, and this time you had the kids!"

"My kids! *My* kids! I'm a good mother, Katie. Don't you think I would do what I needed to do for my kids? That I've *done* what I needed to do my whole life *because of* those kids? She didn't mention that he told the officers I'm on six different medications and let them read my rants from my journal. My private thoughts! My only outlet where I could write those things that were dancing in my head."

"I'm sorry, Michelle," Katie whimpered. "I was just worried about you. He didn't know if you were coming back."

She leveled her eyes at Katie. "Where was I going to go, Katie?"

"He didn't know! He thought you were seeing someone."

I interrupted before Michelle flew across the table and strangled Katie. "Well, anyway. Alissa, I know this isn't exactly the atmosphere you wanted for your big party, but if you have any legal advice for Michelle, I know she'd be willing to listen to anything you have to say."

Alissa studied her water bottle and shook her head. "There's nothing that can be done tonight." She looked at Michelle. "Family law isn't my specialty; if you'd assaulted him, I could tell you everything you needed to

226

know." She winked at Michelle.

Michelle smirked, "Don't tempt me. I may weigh my options based off worst case scenario."

Katie jumped up and ran to the bathroom. I watched as Dani and Alissa had a mental conversation with each other asking if they should check on her or let her be. Judging by their postures, they seemed just as unsure about how to feel about Katie as I did.

Dani shook her head. "Katie texted us today to see if we'd heard from you, but I figured if it was an emergency, someone would have called us. I'm so sorry this has happened, Michelle, and I wish there was something I could do to fix all of this."

Michelle sighed. "There's nothing to be done. First thing I need to do is get my kids back—whatever that takes."

Alissa asked, "Are you willing to go back to him to do it?"

Michelle winced. "I don't think after what he did today I can ever forgive him or forget. Every time I think about him, I'll think of that smug-ass look on his face as he stared down at me like I was some random stranger worthy of punishment."

I said, "I've already offered my apartment to her while we're gone."

Alissa nodded. "You're all welcome to stay here, too."

Dani said, "I'm not sure it's appropriate to discuss this right now. Depending on how the next few days go, I'm not so sure we should leave next week." She stared at Alissa. "We'll talk about it later, though, okay?"

Alissa nodded and looked at Michelle. "Well, I have gifts for you tonight that might brighten your mood a little. Can I give them now?"

Katie entered the room and slid to the floor. She looked at Alissa. "Oh, are you asking me? That's up to Michelle."

Alissa chuckled. "Well, I didn't get Dani and Chance anything for obvious reasons, but I have gifts for you two." She stood and went to the Christmas tree and returned with two large gift bags. "Merry Christmas to two of my favorite people. I hope it helps while we're gone."

I watched as Michelle and Katie each retrieved three individually wrapped gifts. They tore open their iPads at the same time and gasped in shock. Katie squealed, "Alissa, are you insane?"

Alissa beamed. "Nope, just smart. We can Skype while we're gone, and you won't feel so far away."

Michelle grinned. "This is so great. Thank you."

Alissa said, "But wait . . . there's more. Open the other box next."

The girls got lost in a frenzy of paper and slipped the tops off of the boxes. I grinned when I saw the airline logo in Michelle's hand and nodded at Alissa.

Michelle gasped, "I get to go to Florida?"

Alissa smiled. "That's a gift voucher for a thousand dollars, so you can come down once with the fam or twice by yourself—maybe three times if you watch the ticket prices."

Katie's shocked face was priceless. "I'm so blown away, Alissa! Michelle, we can go down when the baby's born."

Michelle smiled and whispered, "I'm so relieved. I didn't want to miss that." She wiped her face and shook her head. "I'm so relieved."

"Now. Before you open the last one, please understand this is a gesture from me to you, and I want you to know that I love you both and just want to make sure you're good while we're gone. I admit I'm kind of having a little anxiety about us all being so far away from each other for so long."

They slipped the ribbon off the gift box and slid it open as they both gasped in disbelief. I leaned over to see what Michelle held in her shaking hands.

"Holy shit, Alissa! That's a check for ten-thousand dollars!" I gasped.

Katie shook her head. "Lis, I can't accept this! It's too much! I could never take this."

Alissa put her hand up. "Listen, I've done a really good job of not flaunting my money and tried to be just like I've always been before I got it. But I really feel like I'm supposed to give this to you. Katie, I leave it up to you—if you want to tell Landon, fine. Michelle, you absolutely cannot tell Brandon I just gave you that."

Katie asked, "How can I not tell my husband I have ten-thousand dollars? This is a game changer for us."

Alissa grinned. "Well, you could tell him you have five and hide the other five."

Katie shook her head. "This is amazing. I'm still not sure I should even accept this."

Michelle said, "Well I sure the hell am." We all laughed as Michelle stood and went to Alissa. She wrapped her in a huge hug and wept on her shoulder. She mumbled words none of us could understand, but we got her sentiments.

Alissa said, "I'll hook you up with counsel in the morning, okay? We'll get this all figured out." She pulled away from Michelle and wiped a tear off her face. "We'll get this all figured out, okay?"

Michelle nodded and chuckled, "I can't believe you just gave me ten thousand dollars, an airline ticket, and an iPad. I feel so spoiled."

Alissa smiled and waved her off. "It was long overdue. No matter what now, you're in a good place to launch." She clapped her hands. "Who's hungry? I've got a huge feast prepared, and we've got a lot of catching up to do!"

Chapter Twenty-Eight
Stay

Alissa

I should have given them their checks separately so Katie didn't know Michelle had one too. After Chance revealed Michelle's situation, I didn't trust Katie for one minute to hold that in confidence. And if Brandon got wind I'd given her ten grand, half of it would be legally his in court. Dani ushered Michelle and Katie into the dining room, and I grabbed Chance before she could follow.

I waited for the sounds of scooting chairs in the kitchen before I looked at Chance. "Can you believe all that?"

Chance held up her hand. "Girl, you should have seen her today when she showed up at my place—both times! She was a hot mess; she's actually pretty chilled right now, mainly because I'm pouring Xanax down her throat."

I shook my head. "She'll go mad if we can't get her kids back to her soon."

"Legally, can they really keep the kids with their dad? Seems so unlikely."

"If Brandon can prove she's unstable, then yes, they can give him temporary custody until they go to court. And, let's face it; it doesn't look good for her, Chance. She lost her job . . ."

Chance closed her eyes and sighed, "Oh God . . . she lost her job because her boss said she'd gone off the deep end and was snapping at the kids and her co-workers."

I ticked off points on my fingers. "So her boss, her husband, and her best friend will all be called to testify in a custody hearing, and if you put them on the stand, she'll lose those kids, Chance."

"Won't they listen to the rest of us? The kids?"

I shook my head. "I really don't think so. Of course we're going to back her; she's our friend. Of course the kids are going to testify on her behalf; she's their mother. This can't go to court. We have to figure something out fast. Do you think he really wants the kids, or is he just using them to hurt her?"

Chance bit her lip and whispered, "I don't think he has any intentions of raising those kids as a single dad. This is all just to prove a point to Michelle in hopes he can get her to tuck-tail and come home."

I closed my eyes and rolled words through my head to try to gather the correct ones to convey my intentions. "What's the one thing that makes Brandon tick?"

She scoffed. "His precious reputation; gag me." Her eyes widened.

"Yes. This would have to be orchestrated perfectly, but I think we can manipulate this whole situation if we're smart and cunning."

Chance giggled. "Have you been reading again? Your vocabulary is fabulous."

I threw my shoulders back. "I'm an attorney, Chance. I know when to show my intelligence and also when to play dumb. Now. Do you have any interns or newbies on the news desk that could contact one Brandon Morehead for an interview regarding the domestic disturbance at his residence this afternoon?"

Chance clapped her hands. "I know just the person. Eddie. He's on my road crew—well, *was* . . . until I got demoted."

"Demoted? What?"

She blew me off. "One topic at a time, please." I watched her pace in front of the Christmas tree and roll her thoughts across her mental cutting board. "Yes," she said. "Yes, this will work."

I jumped when I heard the shriek from the kitchen. "Jesus, what was that?" I followed Chance into the kitchen and found Michelle bent over the kitchen counter with her phone in her hand.

Katie stood next to her holding her own phone in her shaking hand with her other hand cupping her mouth. Dani draped over Michelle holding her as tears dripped down her face.

I felt every particle in the air as it stood still and sucked the oxygen out of the room. I made eye contact with Dani who stood. "Katie got a text message to relay to Michelle. Brandon has shut off her phone and taken the boys' iPods and Del Ray's cell phone to prevent her from being able to contact them."

Chance mumbled, "What did the text say exactly?" Katie handed her the cell phone, and Chance read aloud, "Please read this to Michelle since she no longer has cell service. I've taken the kids' phone and iPods. See how you like being unable to reach your children. Maybe now you'll know what it was like for me today. I finished reading your journal, too. Very interesting."

I looked at Chance and nodded. "We need to work fast. Tonight would be too soon and he'd get suspicious. Tomorrow morning, though." I walked over to Michelle and wedged myself between Katie and her. "This part is an easy fix. We'll go get you a new cell phone tomorrow on my account. It'll be cheap and easy. Poof, done. He may have them on lock-down right now, but this is temporary. He's trying to strong-arm you because he's angry, but I have a feeling this won't last long."

She looked up at me. "I wish I felt your confidence right now. He's a completely different person. I had no idea he was capable of all of this!"

"What kinds of things did you say in your journal?"

She sighed. "Oh you know, the usual thoughts women have about wanting to peel off their husband's faces and fry them like bologna."

Dani stifled a giggle. "Well, that's not completely unheard of but eloquently phrased."

Michelle cracked a smile. "If Del Ray finds out he read my journal, she'll take full blame for all of this. She's the one who encouraged me to write my thoughts down and said it would help."

"We'll get that journal when we get your kids, Michelle," Chance said.

Her eyes brightened. "Do you really think that's going to happen?"

Chance nodded. "Yes, I absolutely do. I'm saying by noon, he'll have a new tune to sing." She turned to Katie. "And this is the end of your involvement in this, got it? You will not relay any messages, will not tell him anything, and you will not talk to Brandon Morehead ever again. I

232

need you to nod to show you understand what I'm saying, because our friendship is at stake. Katie, I'm not even joking with you right now. You're in way over your head and are too naïve to get the magnitude of how deep you're digging yourself into this mess. I mean it."

Katie tried to defend herself but I cut her off. "Katie, she's right. All you know about family drama is what you've seen on television. Take it from someone who A) lived it, and B) works in the legal system; you need to cut him off completely." I went to Michelle and hugged her while whispering in her ear, "Trust me." I pulled away from her and held out my hand. "I hate to do this, but I need my check back."

Michelle's shocked face shredded my heart, but I knew she'd understand once I explained it to her. "Alissa, please don't—"

"I can't take the risk that Brandon will find out about it, so give it back to me until this whole mess is straightened out."

Katie cried, "Alissa, don't do that. I swear I won't tell anyone about the money. She needs that! You know he's going to cut her off the checking accounts next, so how can you do this?"

I looked at Katie. "The legal system is a tricky process, Katie. I don't have any choice. I can't take the chance that Brandon will find out and drag me into all of this. Which if he drags me in, then he drags Dani in, and that woman has been through enough. It's too risky, so we'll make good on this once the dust settles, okay, Michelle?"

She handed me the check and nodded. "I understand. I don't want to drag any of you aboard my sinking ship." She looked at Katie. "For the life of me, I can't figure out why you're in bed with Brandon, unless you're really in bed with Brandon."

Katie shoved off the counter. "What is with you guys? I was trying to help her! I was trying to find her because I was worried about her!"

I looked at Dani. "Do you have Brandon's cell phone number?"

Dani scoffed. "No way."

I looked at Chance. "Do you?"

"Hell no," she chuckled.

I looked at Katie. "I don't have his cell phone number, either."

Michelle put up her hands. "Okay guys, now wait. I gave her

233

Brandon's number because they've kept the kids before, and my cell phone sucks."

Katie breathed a sigh of relief. "Thanks, Michelle."

Chance looked sideways at Katie. "Did you see what just happened there? She had your back. *That's* what friends do. *That's* how we work. You need to remember that."

Katie said, "You know what? I think I better leave. I . . . I'm going to go." She looked at all of us as though she was expecting us to convince her to stay.

Dani walked toward the door and grabbed Katie's coat. "I'll call you tomorrow. Have a good evening." She helped her into her coat and hugged her before she guided Katie out the door and locked it.

I looked at Chance and bit my lip to keep from laughing. Every now and then, Dani surprises me. And her demure way of handling situations just baffles me. I looked at Michelle and handed her the check. "Under no circumstances does anyone know you have this. Got it? Monday morning, we'll set up a different account for you under a different name or something. I don't know how all that works, but we'll get it figured out. Something tells me Brandon would have known about that check by morning if I didn't do what I did. Eventually, I'm sure I'll feel bad about hurting Katie, but right now, my focus is on you."

Chance chimed in. "And you probably don't want to pick the same bank that Katie works at . . . just sayin'."

Michelle smiled. "Thank you. You scared me to death when you took that check back. For the first time in a long time, I felt like things were going to be okay then whammo . . ."

"It's okay, honey. We're all going to help you get through this, okay?"

She nodded. "I know, and I'm so grateful." She started to cry. "I don't know what I'd do without you guys."

Chance said, "Here, here."

Over dinner, we took turns filling Michelle in on what has been happening in our lives over the last three months. I watched as she morphed into the friend we'd known for over twenty years and shed the horrible events that had transpired over the last twelve hours, even if it was only temporary. She listened as Chance gave an extremely condensed version of her encounter with Tony in St. Louis; I held Chance's confidence and didn't call her out when she blew it off as no big deal. We all knew she'd been crushed all over again, and she knew we knew, but everyone deserves an opportunity to maintain their ego at some point.

I let Dani take the lead on the baby talk and threw in quips here and there about how I was a great hostess for her baby. I know Chance was intentionally not making eye contact with me during this conversation; she has an unnerving ability to read right through me, but I know she'll have her say when we're alone.

Listening to Michelle talk about her experiences at the gym was hilarious as she told stories of being so sore she nearly crawled to the car, but my favorite was the story of the commando queen.

She said, "Oh my word, this woman is unbelievable. She's a six-pack mounted on a popsicle stick with biceps that won't quit. But, apparently, she has a real aversion to panties, because she never wears them to class. Like ever. And somehow, I manage to always be in line behind her. She wears these little shirts and yoga pants that creep halfway down her ass every time we bend over to stretch. I can't help it—every time I see that, I start singing 'Bad Moon Rising' in my head, then I get off count. One day, it was all I could do to stand up and pull that woman's pants up after spanking her ass for being an idiot. So annoying."

We all covered our mouths with our napkins to prevent half-chewed food from spewing across the table. Dani's face turned three shades of red as tears brimmed her eyes. She finally got her food swallowed and gasped, "Oh my gosh, that's the best story I've ever heard in my life."

Chance said, "Oh, I don't know. I'm pretty sure the stories about Alissa's colossal farts rank right up there, no pun intended."

Dani put her hand on the table. "Girl, they were like seven point five on the Richter Scale. If it hadn't been so offensive, I probably would have been proud. I was just concerned she was going to shoot the kid out through her colon if she kept it up."

Michelle howled with laughter and nodded. "I was like that with all

235

three of my pregnancies. I don't know what it is about that first trimester, but I'm pretty sure I altered the foundation of the house a time or two."

Dani said, "You guys should have been there for the first ultrasound. The awkwardness of the whole situation gave Alissa the giggles, because you know, it was an internal exam, so he whips out this long instrument, and out came the one-liners." She gasped for air. "I'm not sure when I've ever laughed so hard in my life, except for maybe tonight."

I shrugged. "I should have asked him for his phone number and told him to come see me in eight months."

Michelle asked, "So how is this whole thing going to work, Alissa? How will you find a decent doctor in Florida?"

I waved her off. "I already did. I made some phone calls and my appointment is all set up. My files have already been sent, so I just have to show up and continue where I leave off here."

"You're the queen of efficiency, my dear," Michelle said. "Have you felt it move, yet?"

"Oh, yes. It's the sweetest thing ever! Definitely a morning person; just like ol' Dani." I smiled at her.

Michelle put her fork down. "Okay, I just have to ask this, because I can't understand this. Maybe it's because I'm a mother, but . . . are you sure you're going to be able to follow through with all of this?" She motioned between Dani and me while tossing stuffing off her fork. "Shit. Sorry about that."

I chuckled. "That's really gross. Um, as for your question—yes, I will be able to follow through with this. I've come to terms with the fact that this baby is mine in some respects, but it's Dani who will be able to give it the best life imaginable." I swallowed hard and took a drink to drown the emotions creeping up my neck.

Dani's voice was barely above a whisper as she spoke. "Please don't think that it's lost on me how difficult this is for Alissa. Or that it will be when that day comes. But, it's not like we're going to be on opposite sides of the country or she'll never see it again."

Michelle interrupted, "But do you think that will help or make it worse?"

You gotta hand it to that girl, she knows how to hit at the core of an issue with sheer curiosity. She had addressed in one sentence hours of thoughts and fears I'd had since I'd felt the baby move. I cleared my throat and glanced at Dani as I said, "I think we both know that tough emotional times are coming. I'm prepared for a grieving period, but guys, you know how I am and how I feel about parenthood. I'm not cut out for this . . ."

"But you don't know that! That's what I can't wrap my brain around. You're basing this decision off the half-cocked way your family has approached parenting, but you might be different. Hell, look at how awesome you were with your sisters."

I scoffed. "Yeah, and look how they turned out. Dani's a way better fit for this, and I'm just glad to be able to give it to her." I shrugged. "I don't expect you to understand, Michelle, because it's not a normal way for a mother to think or feel, but trust me when I say, this isn't a decision I rushed into. I've thought about it and thought about it then thought about it some more. This is something she wants more than anything in the whole world. This was my worst fear come true. Do the math—who's better equipped to be a mother?" I chuckled.

Michelle eyed me but thankfully dropped the subject. "Whose car are you taking to Florida?"

"We're taking Alissa's Navigator. She's got the most room for all of our crap," Chance said.

Dani looked at her. "I'm not taking much, are you?"

Chance shook her head. "No, I'm taking two suitcases of stuff, but that's it. And Chubs, of course."

"My theory is we'll pack light for the trip down, because you know we'll be shopping and buying all kinds of clothes."

Chance chuckled. "I keep thinking I need to pack winter clothes, but it won't be cold down there."

"Well, it gets kind of chilly down there," Dani said.

Chance leveled her eyes at her. "Chilly and freeze-your-face-off-cold are two very different things. Personally, I can't wait to leave this tundra for the winter."

I said, "I just can't wait to see the house in person. The pictures online look amazing. Three bedrooms, beachfront—oh, it will be glorious to sit on the balcony and watch the sun come up over the ocean."

Michelle gaped. "Damn, dude, how much did that set you back?"

I laughed. "Well, it's not cheap, but you know me: go big or go home."

Chance waved her hands. "I don't even want to know. I'm trying not to feel guilty about freeloading off of you for six months."

Dani looked at her. "Are you not going to try to freelance while you're down there?"

She shrugged. "Yeah, I'm still hoping to do something, but it won't be anything like my income from the station."

Michelle asked, "So what happened there? How did you get demoted?"

Chance bit her lip and rolled her eyes. "Oh, I had a small breakdown after seeing Tony and bailed on the road crew. Stuart was less than impressed and pulled me off the anchor position. I should have just quit then, but I wanted to bank more money for the Florida trip, so I stuck it out."

Michelle shook her head. "It's truly amazing how different our lives are and that we're even still friends."

Chapter Twenty-Nine
Criminal

Michelle

Sometimes, rare as they are, the financial differences between all of us come to the forefront. I know Chance and Alissa make a huge effort to keep their financial freedom on the DL, but I had to scoff when Chance decided to work for the last three months to bank money for Florida. I've been scouring sales ads to cut corners just to feed our family, and she's putting everything into a vacation fund. Granted, she doesn't have a family; she doesn't even have parents anymore, so when it all comes out in the wash, I'm extremely blessed in comparison. Still wish I could have gotten a little of the money bug, though.

Life. Family. Blessings. Reality washed over me with the warmth of my fourth glass of wine as I realized I was sitting around the table well on my way to drunk with my best friends while my family was across town imploding. And Brandon was probably stretched out in bed with a smug look on his face thinking I was coming back tomorrow with my tail between my legs to beg his forgiveness. Serves him right to live on his own raising kids for a while—let him see what it's really like and see if he can hang.

The memory of my children standing in the window with their hands pressed against the screen, tears streaming down their faces and mouths begging me not to leave them, settled in front of my mind's eye. My heart cracked with how Martin and Gibson had probably cried themselves to sleep, and Del Ray was probably busy plotting revenge on her father. He sure was doing a good job screwing up any chances he had of having a normal son-in-law.

Chance leaned into me. "Where'd you go, Michelle? Hello?" She waved her hand in front of my face.

I shook my head and lifted my wine glass to my mouth. "Sorry, my mind wandered. What'd you say?"

239

Alissa chuckled. "I asked you about the job at the gym. Do you know your hours yet?"

I shook my head then laughed in spite of myself. "No, Reggie was supposed to call me on the phone that's now shut off. Boy when Brandon wants to fuck my life up, he does a good job."

Alissa sighed. "I'd really love to jeopardize my career just to get him back for all of this."

I loved her big heart. She's always been the first one to run into battle, consequences be damned, when her friends were in a fire fight. She's been maternal her whole life, she just didn't know it. I grinned. "Nah, you can't do that. I'll figure something out. Don't underestimate me. I'm pretty smart sometimes."

I saw Alissa wink at Chance and asked, "What's that all about?"

Chance patted my hand. "Nothing honey. Alissa still has a crush on me, that's all."

Alissa snorted. "You wish."

Dani started clearing dishes off the table, and I pushed back my chair to help when the wine stole my coordination. I stumbled and knocked my chair over before giving up the fight and landing square on my ass in the kitchen floor. Chance was the first one to laugh and extend her hand to me, but I was completely encased in a fit of giggles and had no strength to sit up. I laid on the floor laughing until tears streamed out of my eyes into my hair. Dani's head appeared over me, which only added to the hilarity. I gasped, "I'm under interrogation. The exposed light with the head appearing. I'm innocent! Innocent!"

Chance laughed. "What on earth are you talking about, you drunk bitch?"

I screamed, "I have no idea! It was the first thing I thought of." She pulled me into a sitting position as I gasped for air and steadied myself. "Oh shit, that was funny."

Dani stood over me. "You good? Because I can get a blanket and pillow."

I waved her off. "Nah, I'm good. I'm just drunk and clumsy. I wanted to help you clear the table."

240

"Well, judging by that performance, I'd say that's a big fat no." She extended her hand and offered to help me up.

"No way can you pull all this up, sister. But thanks." I got to my knees and used the table to steady myself as I stood. "See, I'm good."

Chance looked at Alissa. "You know she's a puker, right? Better give her a room close to the bathroom."

"The guest room right across the hall from the bathroom is open," Alissa said.

I frowned and looked at both Chances sitting in front of me. "I'm not going home with you?"

"I've got some errands to run in the morning, and Alissa's going to take you to get a new phone anyway, so you can just crash here, and I'll come get you. Is that okay?"

I shrugged. "Right now, I don't care about anything except getting these jeans off and going to bed."

Alissa chuckled. "I figured that was coming. You're way too predictable, Michelle. Come on. I'll get you set up."

Dani stepped between them. "I've got her, Alissa."

I looked at Dani as she wrapped her arm around me. "You're really pretty, you know that? I mean, you really are."

She grinned. "You're such a great drunk. Off we go. Let's get you to bed."

The morning sun blasted right through the blinds and settled on my forehead trying to burn laser-like holes through my pounding skull. I tried to move, but my stomach resisted, so I pulled a pillow over my face and wondered how long it would take me to suffocate and if I even cared at the moment.

At least my body finally felt like my soul—dry, sick, and torn to shreds. Visions of yesterday rolled through my mind; twenty-four hours ago, I was coming home from the gym excited about a job opportunity, and within the course of eight hours, my whole life was dumped into a pile and set on fire.

Minus a few girl trips, I couldn't remember the last time I woke up without my children being a few closed doors away. I ignored my stomach's encouragement to stay put and rolled onto my side. There was no reason to get out of bed, nowhere to be, nothing to cook, and no sleepy children to wrap in a blanket and cuddle on the couch. The ache in my chest overtook my hangover as I wept with regret for my stand against Brandon. If I'd known twenty-four hours ago what he was truly capable of, I would never have left the house during breakfast.

But, he was being a tyrant to my children and me. Del Ray's look on her face when he grabbed her virtually uneaten breakfast and slammed it into my stomach; Gibson's tears rolling off his face and dripping in his plate; Martin's paling face and quivering chin . . . no, I did the right thing for them. Now I just have to figure out what the next right thing is.

I have ten thousand dollars. I could find us a cheap apartment and pay up the rent for six months, maybe get a used couch and TV—who am I kidding. Without a steady income, I can't support three kids on my own. And Brandon's already indicated he has no intention of letting me have them.

But I give that two weeks at most; he'll never be able to raise those kids like I have.

He'll elevate Del Ray to a maternal position—a modern-day Cinderella in her own house, and she'll be the next Alissa, guaranteed. That thought made my already-weak stomach groan. He's too selfish to assume all the parenting responsibilities, so he'll put her in charge of the house and the boys.

I slipped on my pants and wondered which of the lovely ladies had the pleasure of helping my drunk ass into bed last night. Judging by the room, my bet was on Dani. Alissa or Chance would have left my pants crumpled on the floor, but they'd been neatly folded next to my shoes and socks. I sat on the bed and stared at the closed door in front of me. It seemed symbolic to my life right now—so near yet shut off from everything. My rolling stomach notified me my time in this room was short.

I finished praying to the porcelain god, showered, and when I got out, fresh clothes were laying on the sink with a note from Alissa. *Try*

242

these on. I bet they'll fit, skinny Minnie. I grinned and eyed a pair of Alissa's yoga pants and t-shirt. They looked so tiny when I held them up, and I didn't know if I could take their rejection if they didn't fit, but I didn't have many options at the moment. I slipped into the clothes and stood back from the mirror to see the damage.

Looking back at me was a slender, well-toned woman I didn't recognize. Wearing clothes that actually fit me exposed the drastic change in my body—one I hadn't been willing to see until this morning. I grinned in spite of myself and bit my lip as I ran my hand over my hourglass figure. The T-shirt was a bit tight for my liking, but it didn't look too small. I ran my fingers through my hair and frowned. I should have let Del Ray color my hair; I should have listened when she wanted to talk to me about new cuts. I should have taken advantage of those moments I fear I'll regret shoving to the side because there would always be more time.

I padded down the hall and caught Alissa standing in front of the Christmas tree drinking a glass of orange juice staring at something on the tree. I glanced around for Dani but didn't see her in the room. Alissa giggled and rubbed her baby bump then said something I couldn't understand. I did a double-take and wondered if I was dreaming; she looked . . . happy, maternal. The way she caressed her belly and the glow on her face had nothing to do with the reflection of the tree lights. I knew that look and recognized the feeling that had blanketed her body. I smiled at the sight before realization swept over me. I slowly closed my eyes and shook my head. This was my biggest fear in this whole fucked-up mess; she was getting attached to the baby she'd vowed to give to Dani in roughly five short months.

I felt bad for observing such an intimate moment meant just for her and her baby but didn't know how to move without being busted. I faked tripping like I'd been walking and braced myself against the wall.

Alissa giggled, "Are you all right, Graceful?" She pulled her hand from her belly and walked toward me. "Rough night?"

I grimaced. "Rough year."

She nodded. "Yeah, but it's almost over." She laced her arm through

243

mine and guided me to the kitchen table. "Want some coffee or orange juice?"

I waved her off. "I better start with water." I pointed to her stomach. "You're not going to be able to conceal that much longer, there, sister. You're really starting to show."

She offered a polite smile that didn't last long. "Yeah, I know. We're supposed to leave on the twenty-eighth, but with everything going on with you, I'm not comfortable leaving, now."

My head snapped back like I'd been slapped. "Alissa, you can't be serious. I'll be fine. You can't *not go* to Florida and throw away all your plans just because my life turned upside down." She placed a glass of water and two ibuprofen in front of me and took a seat at the table. "Thank you. Seriously, Lis, don't do that. A lot is at stake if you don't go."

I couldn't believe what I was saying! Here I'd bemoaned my friends leaving me to my boring, dull life, and now I had the opportunity to keep them here, and I was encouraging her to go! I shook my head and sipped the water.

Alissa said, "Dani, Chance, and I have to talk it out. We started last night, but I don't think any of us were in any position to speak rationally after all the drama went down with Katie and the unbelievable bullshit that happened yesterday. We agreed we'd think about it this morning and talk about it more this afternoon."

My throat tightened as I listened to Alissa. This is why they're my life's blood; this is why I run to them when I'm in need or seek them out when I'm not. The level of loyalty my friends showed me in good times and bad was humbling and beautiful. They had five months of sand, sun, and surf planned while waiting for Alissa's baby to arrive, and they're more concerned about me than they are their plans. If Alissa's pregnancy is discovered by any of her colleagues or Mark, she'll be humiliated. Dani's desire to adopt this baby was palpable—anyone in the room could see the longing for that baby to grow and develop so she could hold it in her arms and love it like her own. And Chance? Well Chance just didn't have anything better to do and no reason to stay.

Yet, they're coming together like they always do to stand with me when my life is unraveling knowing full-well the consequences if they stay. While I wouldn't let them do it, I was grateful they even considered staying.

I spoke when I was sure my voice wouldn't betray me. "Let's just see how this week goes. I've got your money and after today, I'll have a phone. I'm going to look around for an apartment on Monday and—"

She cut me off. "About that. If we leave, and that's a big if, my house will be vacant while I'm gone. I've got more than enough room for you and the kids here, and it wouldn't cost you a dime."

I gasped. "Alissa, I can't do that. You've been more than generous."

"Yes, but honey, you ain't got shit! No offense, but Brandon has everything in that house: couches, beds, pots and pans, and if you move into a new place, you'll blow through that ten grand in a week furnishing it."

I laughed. "Well, I don't know about that; you and I shop in very different places." I winked.

She said, "Truly though, think about it. That money won't last you as long as you think. Stay here then nothing is permanent." She flashed a perfect smile at me. "Ta-da!"

I let my eyes wander over her elaborate home and chuckled. "I'd be scared to death to live here, Lis. You'd have to wrap everything in bubble wrap to keep it safe with me and my brood."

She leveled her eyes at me. "I wish you wouldn't do that. I know we have very different lives, but sometimes it's hurtful the way you insinuate that we're in different classes or something."

I sat up. "Okay, well imagine that nice, thick, cream-colored carpet with a big Kool-Aid stain in the middle. Imagine this beautiful solid-whatever-kind-of-wood with a big fat gouge running through the middle of it and handprints all over your walls." I could see the sweat forming on her lip as I spoke and tried not to laugh. "Do you still want to extend that invitation to me and my children?"

She nodded slowly. "I'm not going to pretend that didn't give me anxiety, though."

My laugh escaped that time. "Okay, well I promise we won't drink Kool-Aid in the living room."

Alissa's phone chimed on the kitchen counter. She grinned and tapped my hand. "I bet that's Chance."

"What's she up to this morning?" I choked down another drink of water. "I can't drink this."

She grabbed my glass. "I tried to be nice, but now for the real hangover cure." She pulled the orange juice out of the refrigerator and mixed it with some of the white wine I'd drank the night before. "Here," she said as she handed it to me. "Let 'er rip. Trust me; you'll be better in no time."

I squeezed my eyes shut and downed the concoction then took the ibuprofen. I gagged for a moment then shivered. "Something tells me you know that trick from experience."

She chuckled. "I've overindulged in my fair share of wine. You're about to feel a whole lot better real quick."

"You never answered me about Chance. And where's Dani?"

Alissa looked smug as she rinsed my glass and brought me a cup of coffee. "You should be about ready for this, now." She sat across from me again. "Dani should be back any minute with, drumroll please, your new phone! She was stir crazy and wanted to get an early start, so I told her she could kill two birds with one stone. And Chance is on a secret mission, but trust me, you'll be happy when it's over."

I shook my head and warmed my hands on the coffee cup. "I'm not sure I even want to know at this point. You guys are so good to me, but I swear if she rolls up with a new car for me, I'm outta here."

Alissa laughed. "Oh girl, please. No way. But, trust me . . . things aren't as bad as they seem."

Chapter Thirty
Independence Day

Chance

I looked forward to this more than any revenge mission I'd ever concocted on my own. I had to give it to Alissa—she knows her shit and I'm so glad she's on my side. I didn't even have to set an alarm that morning, because my excitement woke me as the sun was rising.

The plan was all set. I'd called Eddie after Michelle passed out last night and told him the situation. He was more than eager to assist in the plan and agreed to keep it on the down low as Stuart would have my ass and his job if he found out what we'd done. Eddie threw a few interns fifty bucks apiece (which I had to reimburse when I saw him) and swore them to secrecy—it had to look real. And while I couldn't actually participate in the event, I was riding along just for the sheer thrill of watching.

I met them a little before eight near the Highway 63/70 interchange and climbed in the media van. I handed Eddie a fresh Starbucks and greeted the crew before handing Trina her script and telling them the barest of details of why we were doing what we're doing. When everyone was caught up, Trina climbed into the front seat next to Eddie, the driver for the mission. I gave him the street address and waited for the show to begin.

We pulled in front of Brandon and Michelle's house, and the crew went to work gathering the needed equipment: cameras, microphones, a tripod, and their game faces. I faded into the background and slipped a set of earphones over my head so I could hear every word.

Eddie, Trina, and the other cameraman went to the front door of Brandon and Michelle's house and Trina knocked on the door. A visibly frazzled Brandon answered the door in a t-shirt and pajama bottoms. Even from my vantage point, I could see his hair was sticking up in several directions. The last thing he expected to see at his door this morning was a media van with cameras and an eager reporter.

Trina began, "Brandon Morehead? I'm Trina St. Patrick with KJAT news. We received a report that there was a domestic dispute between you and your wife, (she looked at the paper in her hand for good measure) Michelle, and we would like to interview you for the twelve o'clock news. Domestic abuse is something that is extremely heartbreaking, but it's rare for men to be the victims and we'd like to spotlight your situation to encourage more men to come forward if they're in a similar situation as you."

Brandon scratched his head and looked at the camera, but Trina was on her game and wouldn't be interrupted. "Mr. Morehead, I understand you are an insurance agent here in town. Are you at all concerned that this event could impact your career?"

Brandon huffed. "Ma'am, I think you got your wires crossed this morning. I'm not the victim of domestic abuse. My wife and I had an argument last night, but—"

Trina looked at her "notes". "Sir, we have a report that the police were here last night and had to remove your wife from the premises based off of your statement that you felt unsafe—so unsafe, in fact, that you had the locks changed while she was out running errands."

Brandon stood up straight. "Well, yeah, but that's not because I was being abused. Where did you get this information?"

"Mr. Morehead, when you called the police, it went over the police scanners which are monitored by several news agencies. KJAT wanted to be the first to reach out to you to show our support and hear your side of the story. I interviewed one of your neighbors earlier who said your wife was out of control and that you were fearful of what she might do if you let her back in."

He scoffed. "Oh please. Those nosy sons-of-bitches don't know what they're talking about. I'm not a victim of domestic abuse, and you will not report that I was. This is all a misunderstanding, and—"

"Mr. Morehead, is it true you refused to let your wife near your children? Do you fear she's a danger to her own children?"

"What? No! Michelle wouldn't hurt our children."

"Do you fear an impact in your business if word gets out that you're married to a potentially abusive woman or that perhaps you, yourself, may be an abusive spouse?"

Brandon stiffened. "You better get off my property. No, I will not let you interview me, and if any of this makes the news, I will have your jobs. All of you."

"One more question. One of your neighbors said you are holding your children against their will from their mother. Do you have a comment on that?"

"They're my children, too, and my neighbors need to mind their own business just like you." He started to close the door.

"I can't promise we won't run this story at noon. It's a slow time of year for news, and this could really open up a huge untapped problem in our community. Men being victims of domestic abuse and all."

"I'm done talking to you. I had to prove a point to Michelle. She'll be home today just you watch."

"So you won't be filing charges against her?" Trina said with a lilt of disappointment in her voice.

"No, I will not."

"Do you know how to get a hold of Mrs. Morehead? I'd like to interview her for her side of the story."

Brandon's face paled with the thought of what Michelle would tell the press about his behavior. "Her phone's not working," he muttered.

"Do you know where she's staying?"

He shook his head. "I'm serious; let this go. You don't have a story here."

"Would you mind if we talked to your children?"

"No!" Brandon shouted, "Get the hell out of here."

Trina looked at Eddie and shrugged. She turned to Brandon. "Well, thank you for your time. We'll be in touch."

I stifled giggles as they pointed to different houses pretending to argue over which neighbor to interview next. They piled into the van and slammed the doors.

"Bravo! I'm impressed, Trina! You should have considered a career in criminal investigation."

She grinned at me. "CJ was my minor. I want to cover criminal cases and know what the hell I'm talking about."

I smirked. "Well, I'm impressed. Take us back to the station, Eddie. Is your buddy still going to call Brandon?"

Eddie chuckled. "Yeah, he will call in about ten minutes. I'm supposed to text him when we leave. An article in the paper should scare the piss out of him, too."

"Let's hope so. I hope this is a valuable lesson to Mr. Morehead. I just hope we don't get caught."

Eddie waved me off as he turned the van around and headed down the street. "Don't worry about that. Stuart is a prick, but he can't afford to lose his street team."

Eddie dropped me off at my car, and I giggled while I drove as I replayed the visions of Brandon's shocked face and complete disbelief that his actions damn near landed him in the news. That's what happens when you mess with my friends. It was after nine, so I knew Alissa and Dani would be up, but I prayed Michelle was still sleeping off the night before. I sent Alissa a text and told her I was on my way to her house but had a quick pit stop to make—ETA to her house 9:45.

I pulled in front of Brandon and Michelle's house and walked to the door. Brandon answered the door and left it open enough for me to see the complete chaos going on behind him. Gibson and Martin were fighting over something in the kitchen, and Del Ray was folding a load of laundry that was scattered across the couch—most of which was a peculiar faded color of pink. I had to lower my head to keep from laughing at the idea of someone accidentally throwing a red shirt in the load of whites and Brandon wearing pink t-shirts from now on. I just hope Del Ray had done it on purpose.

Brandon sighed. "What do you want, Chance?"

I waved. "Nothing. Guess it's no surprise I have Michelle and she needs some clothes." He looked over my shoulder to the car. "She's not with me. She's scared you'll have her arrested."

Brandon's face fell as he opened the door and let me in. Del Ray's tear-brimmed eyes caught mine as she dropped the shirt she was folding and ran to hug me. I wrapped my arms around her and kissed the top of her head. "Hey, kiddo."

She whispered, "How's Mom?"

I nodded. "She's . . . she's pretty miserable right now, if I'm going to be honest. She misses you guys and hates that she can't get in touch with you." I glared at Brandon but corrected myself when I saw Gibson and Martin wander into the room.

Martin mumbled, "Is Mom with you?"

I shook my head. "No, bud. She's not. She doesn't know I'm here. I just came by to get some clothes for her."

Gibson cried, "Is she coming home?"

I looked at Brandon. "Not right now, Gib."

Brandon ran his fingers through his hair and looked at the ceiling. He looked at his kids. "Boys, why don't you go to your rooms and let me talk to Chance. You too, Del Ray."

She left my arms and wiped her face as she walked down the hall after her brothers. I looked at Brandon who gestured to the couch. "Do you want to sit?"

I smirked at the laundry pile. "I've got to get back, but yeah I could sit for a minute."

He plopped down in his chair and buried his hands in his face. "I really fucked up, Chance."

I eased onto the couch. "I'm not here to talk, Brandon. I just need to get some clothes for her before she wakes up. And yeah, you went too far."

He looked up at me with teary-eyes. "I wanted to shock her back into reality—like an intervention-type thing. She's been a fucking lunatic around here the last several months, and I just wanted to get her attention."

I chuckled. "Well, you certainly did that. What's been so different about her?"

"She's just been so depressed and down about everything. Then she comes up with these hair-brained ideas that make no sense like she's

251

trying to change everything. Like that whole working-out thing and now working for the gym. She lost her job at the daycare and really put us in a financial pinch . . ."

"But, Brandon, you supported the family on your income the whole time she was staying home raising kids."

"Well, yeah, but there wasn't orthodontic bills, band instruments, sports, none of that back then."

"Has she ever tried to talk to you about why she needed to do something for herself?"

"Yeah, but I thought she was just being dramatic. Then I read her journal where she's been writing about what a prick I am and how much she hates her life, so . . . I thought I'd show her how good she has it . . ." His voice trailed off then he continued. "When she left with my kids, I was so pissed."

"Brandon, she told me what you did. She . . ."

He held up his hand. "Just let me finish. She is so pissed off that her life turned out exactly like she wanted—like we'd designed it to be—and she doesn't even know what I've given up in my life to come home to her and these kids every day. I didn't want to be an insurance agent; I wanted to be a rock star. Then when Del Ray came around, that changed it all. My life's dreams shattered in that moment. I had to be a father and a provider. So I don't have much sympathy that she is just finally waking up and realizing her life has passed before her eyes when I *watched mine* slip away day after day." His chin quivered and he put his fist to his mouth to conceal it. "You know in her journal, she's pissed and moaned about your trip to Florida and how angry she is that you guys have these luxurious lives that you can just uproot and go somewhere else, and she can't. Do you know how much that hurts to read in your wife's own handwriting how much she hates her life? The life I worked my balls off to give her? I wanted her to see what it would be like to lose it all."

I listened to Brandon's rant and tried to decide if I believed him or not. I had to admit, his actions were not normal for him; none of us would have ever considered him capable of this level of meanness.

He continued, "And then the cops showed up . . . what a fucking

252

cluster that was. I just figured she'd come home, I'd have changed the locks and show her I meant business that she can't just up and leave with our children and expect to roll back in like it was normal. I figured she'd sleep at your house, come home this morning, and we'd talk it out. But the cops and the reporters and . . ."

"Reporters?" I said faking surprise.

"Yes! Reporters showed up at my house this morning wanting to talk about last night!"

"Wow, must be a slow day for news . . .," I mumbled.

"This whole thing just got out of hand. I wanted her to be cut off for the night and prove a point."

"Well, whatever message you were trying to send, she received it loud and clear. I'm pretty pissed at you, Brandon, because she was a wreck last night. If you'd have let her take the kids . . ."

He cut me off and shouted, "If I'd let her take the kids, I'd never see her again. She'd run off to you guys, you'd set her up in some awesome house and I'd be the dad that gets to see his kids every other weekend and lose his wife. *If* she didn't up and move to Florida with you guys!"

I bit my lip to hide how right he was. We were already planning to move her and the kids into Alissa's house, and her new phone should be activated by now. We'd never considered taking her and the kids to Florida, but that would have been cool, too. "What do you want from me, Brandon?"

He looked at me and mumbled, "I don't want to lose my family, Chance."

I laughed in spite of myself. "You act like I have any pull in that equation."

He raised his eyebrows. "Oh really? You don't have input to this?"

I leveled my eyes. "If I had my way, she'd divorced your ass in a heartbeat and move on with her life after this bullshit. Before, I would have given you a fighting chance, but right now, after all this? It's like you wrapped her hands in barbed wire and dared her to pull away, and when she did, you cut her hands off for being defiant."

He hung his head and sighed. "I know I overreacted, but so did she."

"Oh? You think so? You think it was out of line for a mother to take her children out for breakfast when one had her plate smeared against her mother's stomach and the other two ruined theirs with their own tears? Is that an overreaction to you, Brandon? Because it sounds to me like you were being a raging prick and she had enough of your bullshit."

"Again, I was thrown! She came in happy as a lark to be a fucking belly-dancing aerobics instructor. She had no idea about wages or what her hours were going to be. We don't just make decisions like that without talking it through."

"No, *she* doesn't get to make decisions like that; *you* do. Listen, you wanna make nice with her? Send the kids with me. It will show a good faith effort that you're not a complete douchebag and will calm her down. Then if you want to talk to her, you guys can take it from there."

He spoke but didn't look at me. "Do you think she'll even consider coming home?"

I stood up. "I don't know, Brandon. I really have no idea. Can I take the kids with me?"

He nodded. "If you think it will help, yes."

I shrugged. "It's hard to say. And you can't call or text her because you turned off her phone." I stared hard at him while those words sunk in. "Tell me again how you didn't intend for this to be a permanent punishment, Brandon."

He glared up at me. "I think we're done here, Chance. Have the kids back by seven. He stood and walked down the hallway to tell the kids to get ready then went into his bedroom.

I wandered into the kitchen and stared at Michelle's usually immaculately cleaned counters covered with remnants of last night's attempt at supper and dried, uneaten oatmeal from breakfast in bowls on the counter. If she stepped foot in this house as it was right now, she'd never leave again, because autopilot would kick in. She would "see" how needed she was and find her "place" again.

If he told her the line he'd told me just now, she'd eat it with a fork and digest it as truth. The man is a salesman for crying out loud.

The kids hurried to the door and grabbed their coats. I smiled at their sense of urgency and couldn't wait to see the look on Michelle's face when we showed up at Alissa's. We were nearly out the door when Brandon ran down the hall calling for Del Ray.

"Hey, wait a second. Here. In case you need it." He handed her phone to her. "Be back by seven, got it?"

Del Ray nodded. "Bye, Dad."

I scowled at Brandon and mumbled, "Like I'm going not going to bring them back."

"I'm not worried about *you*, Chance."

I looked hard into his eyes and tried to get a bead on him. If I was this confused, I couldn't imagine how Michelle felt.

It was a quiet ride to Alissa's house. The anticipation in the car was palpable, and it seemed inappropriate to do anything other than drive as fast as I could to reunite the kids with their mother.

As much as I didn't want to, I found myself thinking of Tony and comparing my own unreasonable desire to reach out to him. I tried to blow it off—that I was just feeding off the emotions in the car, or that the Christmas season of love was influencing my need for romance. And, this was no time to rekindle a love affair when I would be moving half a country away in a week. Yes, it's best to let this thing die on the vine and pretend his ballad of affection had never been sung. I had other things to think about and ample distractions to help me pass the time—that which would heal all wounds.

I pulled into Alissa's driveway. "You guys ready to see your mama?"

My car emptied before I finished my question. Martin was first to the door followed by Gibson and Del Ray. Alissa answered the door and the look of shock on her face was worth the surprise. Chairs scraped across the kitchen floor as Michelle squealed and raced to the door to gather her little birdies into the nest. Giggles, sniffles, and chatter filled Alissa's living room as the kids took turns hugging Michelle and telling her how much they missed her. Gibson and Martin gave her a play-by-play action of everything she'd missed: Gibson made it to the final level of his last video game. Martin proudly announced that he'd helped Del

Ray make breakfast and wasn't burned once, and Del Ray looked completely satisfied to just be in the same room with her mother.

Michelle's eyes met mine—all shimmery and filled with gratitude. She shook her head. "How on earth did you pull this off?"

I shrugged. "I just went by the house to get you some clothes, and voilá!"

She looked sideways at me—she wasn't buying it but didn't bust me in front of the kids. I glanced toward Dani and acknowledged her head-nod telling me to join her in the kitchen. She handed me a cup of coffee and leaned against the counter. "Well done, you." She grinned and took a sip of her own coffee. "I come back with a phone; you come back with her kids. Never have been able to one-up you," she chuckled.

I grinned. "It takes a village," I said with a wink.

Alissa entered the kitchen and pretended to march in a parade. "Hail the conquering hero. Or heroine in this case. Tell me everything."

I gave a recap of the morning's events including my conversation with Brandon. The mood in the room changed as we contemplated what he said and exchanged questioning looks.

Dani asked, "What do you think?"

I shrugged. "Honestly, I don't know. He looked sincere, but I wonder if that conversation would have been different if the media van hadn't been there twenty minutes earlier."

Alissa said, "So it worked, then."

I said, "Yeah, but not like I thought. I figured he'd puff up like a bullfrog and it'd be over. I didn't expect the . . . I don't know . . . maybe he *was* trying to get her attention. Maybe it worked, who knows?"

Dani asked, "What do you think she'll do?"

I looked at Alissa and deflected the answer to her. She sighed. "Honestly, I think she'll go back. She's already worried about how she's going to afford living on her own, so if he says all those things to her that he said to you, game over."

I shook my head. "I don't know, Lis. She's pretty pissed off. She might surprise us."

Dani asked, "If she doesn't, where does that leave us?"

I bit my lip and mumbled, "I've been thinking about that." I took a deep breath. "I don't have to go to Florida. I'll stay on at the station and manipulate Stuart into giving me back the co-anchor job and be here for Michelle in case things take a turn for the worse." Alissa started to speak, but I held up my hand. "Listen, you know as well as I do the clock is ticking for you." I pointed at her belly. "You're not going to be able to hide that much longer, sister. And if, God forbid, you run into Mark . . ." I threw up my hands.

Alissa paled with the thought and looked at Dani. "Neither of us feel right about leaving her alone up here. We don't know where Katie's head is, and if Brandon flakes out, she'll have no one to turn to."

I scowled. "That's not one-hundred percent true; her family is still around. But I know what you mean. As I said, I'm totally okay with staying here. If things calm down, I can always come later."

Alissa chewed on her cheek and nodded. "All right. That's the plan, then. Dani and I will go, and you come later. Chance, we can't do this without you."

I smiled. "Sure you can. You just don't want to."

They both laughed and Dani said, "So true, so true."

I couldn't decide if I was disappointed or relieved that the decision had been made. While I would love to spend five months vacationing in Florida with my best friends and forgetting about normal life, I felt my place was here. And just as soon as the decision was made, I thought of Tony.

257

Chapter Thirty-One
Without You

Alissa

I felt my heart crack a little when Chance made her decision to stay behind. Out of the group, Chance is the one who truly gets me. She knows why I do what I do and there is just something calming about her. Now that Michelle ever so eloquently outted my concerns in front of Dani, I had some serious reassurance to give—a reassurance I didn't believe myself.

The truth is I don't know if I can follow through with this. Every time I feel that little twerp flip or wiggle in my belly, I feel this explosion of adoration in my heart and can't wait for the day when I can meet the person I'm already interpersonally connected to in every way. No surprise, I've compiled a list of reasons why I'm moving to Florida and giving away my baby—just saying those words makes me cringe. However, when I review my list, I know I'm doing the right thing.

I admit—watching Michelle devoured in grief while separated from her children made me dread "the day" even more.

We spent the rest of the morning and afternoon playing games with the kids and showing Michelle how to use her new smart phone. Poor girl is going to have a bit of a challenge ahead of her, but I know she'll get it eventually. Gibson had already fallen in love with Michelle's new iPad and took reluctant turns sharing with Martin. We took some practice runs with Skype and tried like hell not to think about the distance that was soon to separate all of us.

I sighed and said to Michelle's kids, "Guys, we're going to go into the family room to talk, but I need you to stay in here, okay? Here's the remote; knock yourselves out." I waved Dani, Chance, and Michelle into the family room and took my seat on the couch.

Chance and Dani chose chairs this time, and Michelle plopped down on the other end of the couch. Chance cleared her throat; Dani smoothed her hair, and Michelle played with the fringe on one of the throw pillows. I took a deep breath and sighed heavily. I looked at Michelle. "Well, the decision has been made. Dani and I are leaving as planned, but Chance is going to stick around for a while. Just in case."

Michelle's eyes shot up to Chance's and she shook her head. "You don't have to do that, Chance. I'll be fine."

Chance shrugged. "Seriously, it's no big deal. They have to go to pull all this off, but I'm just the extra in this stage play. And, the show must go on."

"While that's not entirely true, she does have options that Alissa and I don't have. It pains me to leave you in this situation, but it will make me feel much better about going if Chance stays behind," Dani said.

I added, "And, if things calm down, and once you're set up, she can always fly down later."

Michelle bit her lip and smoothed the fringe across her leg. I watched her face and knew what she was going to say. I saw the resolution wash over her face hours ago as her children draped over her hanging on every word, every smile, every facial expression, as though she was mentally recording each moment. Consequences be damned, she would be back in her marital bed tonight if Brandon would have her, and judging by Chance's conversation with him, Michelle's future was certain once again.

She cleared her throat and sniffled. "I . . . uh . . . I've had a lot of time to think—both sober and drunk," she chuckled bashfully. "And, none of this makes sense. Brandon, I mean. He doesn't want me cut off from my children—he'd never call the cops on me. I want to go home. I want to go talk to him and really listen this time. I feel like I needed this reality check—this absolute knowledge what the other side would feel like, and guys, I'm not going to be happy if I leave him." She looked at each of us in search of approval.

Dani leaned forward. "Michelle, we only want you to be happy. We all know you've been . . . out of sorts for a while now." I loved watching Dani trying to choose her words carefully and half-expected Chance to cut her off. Which she did.

"Sister, you've been bat-shit crazy some days."

Michelle laughed and shook her head. "Way to take it easy on me, Chance."

Chance shrugged and winked at Michelle. "Listen, I don't want you to think you have to look around this room for approval to go back to Brandon. We all know you love that dude, why, it's a continuous mystery to all of us, but you do. And that's okay."

Michelle grinned. "I really do. But more than that, I love those kids."

Michelle

All of the thoughts running through my head over the last twenty-four hours threatened to spill out of my mouth in no certain order. All eyes were on me, and none of them would have any kind of personal experience to understand where I was coming from.

I thought about how to proceed from this moment forward as a single mom and how scared I was to reach for a life I never wanted. I wasn't happy in my life at home, but I sure didn't want this bullshit, either. Every-other-weekend, shuffling kids back and forth, missing special moments while building a life I never wanted to begin with. Entering the work force like a teenager fresh out of high school with no work or real-life experience.

Then I thought about Brandon meeting someone and marrying again. The idea drove a hot knife into the pit of my stomach and nearly made me throw up. Another woman in my house, in my bed—her clothes hanging in my closet, making love to my man, parenting my children. That was the clencher. As mad as I was at Brandon, I still loved him and knew I always would. He was an arrogant, selfish, egotistical prick most of the time. But then again, so was I.

When he told me he'd read my journal, I was humiliated and horrified that my husband read my nasty, awful thoughts about him. I tried to imagine situation reversed and how I would feel. It would make me sick to think Brandon felt that way about me, and now he *knew*. There was no denying, no lying; no covering up . . . he knew what'd been going through my mind. It was as if it was okay to have those thoughts until he read them, then I was instantly flooded with shame and regret for even thinking them, let alone writing them down.

It would be easier to stay in Alissa's house and let the momentum of the divorce overtake me. I'm certain it's coming. I don't know how you come back from something like that. However, I couldn't become Alissa's charity case and appointments to my kids. Always clock watching, alternating holidays. The thought made me cringe.

Being here in Alissa's home on no one's schedule but my own made me lonesome for my home. I had nothing to do, no purpose. I even found myself longing for that dreaded pile of never-ending laundry just to feel some sense of normalcy. And it'd only been one night! The desire to run off with my friends to Florida was killed the moment Brandon stepped onto the front porch and announced I couldn't enter our home. In that moment, there was no other place I wanted to be, even if I was cleaning up his blood after murdering him. I thought again about the things I'd written in my journal and wondered if there was any way that man could ever forgive me for what I'd said in the midst of a mid-life mental breakdown, and if so, would he ever be able to forget?

I played out the scene of me coming home with the kids later and wondered if I was setting myself up for another embarrassing experience at the hand of my husband. I envisioned a replay: me walking up to the house, the kids going inside, and me left cold and homeless on the front stoop. If that was my fate, I'd have to find out the hard way. I couldn't sit here in Alissa's family room crippled by my own fear.

I looked up at my friends and gave my best smile. "I want to go home."

Alissa sighed and slapped her hands on her thighs. "Welp, that's that," She looked at Chance and nodded.

I said, "Alissa, it's more than what you're thinking. I . . . I need to talk to Brandon before I do anything else. He might not let me come home."

Chance smiled. "He'll let you come home. Trust me."

My heart jumped. "Really? Did he say that? What'd he say?"

261

Chance chuckled. "Just trust me, okay, kiddo?"

I was certain I knew how life would play out from this point forward. Brandon and I would find a comfortable routine again and I'd get pissed with how unappreciated I was around the house. I'd pick fights with him and go back to dreaming of life on the other side of the fence, but this time, I would have last night to remind me of how green the grass is in my own yard, even if there are weeds and the occasional pests.

I fought the need to explain myself to my friends and decided my husband was the only person who needed to hear what I was thinking. I said my "see-you-soons" to my best friends, got the kids in their coats, and had Chance take us back to my car.

The butterflies in my stomach threatened to make their appearance alien-style through my abdomen. I put my hand on my belly to calm them, but my shaking hands betrayed me yet again. I pulled into the driveway and killed the engine, took several deep breaths, and tried to conjure the perfect words to win Brandon from "hello". One time, when we were still kids in high school, Brandon and I broke up for a very short time. It was a dumb fight, really, but it seemed pivotal to our future. I'm sure it had something to do with Lottie-the-body. Anyway, we agreed (via notes passed between friends) to meet after school by the bleachers to talk. He got there first and looked both relieved and smug that I'd shown up. We stared at each other waiting for someone to speak first but not wanting to be that person. Finally, he said, "I'm still mad at you." I whispered, "I'm still mad at you, too." He grabbed me and hugged me as if he never wanted to let go . . . or he was trying to kill me. I wasn't sure. I told him I couldn't breathe and his embrace relaxed to a natural effort. We never talked about it again, and a few years later, we were married. From that day on, our apologies came in the form of "I'm still mad at you."

Once again, the kids beat me to the door, and I had a moment of déjà vu when Brandon appeared on the front porch. He was still wearing his pajamas and looked like hell. The kids shuffled past him and once again, I was on the stoop staring at Brandon.

Nearly two decades later, we might as well have been standing outside the high school for the familiarity of it all. Brandon ran his hand through his hair and sighed as he looked at me. My lungs moved, my heart beat, but I wasn't benefiting from their functions. I took a step toward him and he held up a hand. My chin quivered and stomach rolled. Then, he spoke.

"I'm still mad at you."

Tears rolled down my face as I mumbled, "I'm still mad at you, too."

He moved aside, held the door open for me, and I walked back into my life.

Chapter Thirty-Two
Set Adrift on Memory Bliss

Chance

I had a huge decision to make—more like I had to find it in me to follow through with staying in Columbia. Over the last few months, all that kept me going was leaving. We all know Michelle is going to be fine until she isn't. After putting all the details in order, it looked like both parties were equally at fault for the mess at home—even if we all agreed that Brandon's still an asshole.

I threw my car keys on the island in my kitchen and stared at my apartment—all ready for me to high-tail it to Florida, and now I have to tuck tail and beg Stuart to let me stay at the station. On the other hand, I didn't have to go back to the station just because I wasn't leaving the state. I'd paid up my apartment and utilities and still had a nice nest egg to support myself—well, minus the fifteen hundred dollars I'd given Michelle. I gave Chubs his after-potty treat, rubbed my hands over my face and headed into the shower—it's where I do all my best thinking.

One of my favorite things in the world is the feeling I get when I ease my head under the hot water in the shower and feel my hair smooth as the worries roll down the drain. God, I sound like Alissa, now, her and her visualizations. I sighed as my body relaxed, my mind rinsed, and I could see the facts without the cloudy remnants of the last exhausting twenty-four hours. One: Michelle was probably elbow-deep in all the things she loathes and loving every minute of it, so she's fine. Two: I could still leave with Alissa and Dani and spend the next five months with my toes in the sand all day and fruity drinks sweating right along with me at night on the fabulous veranda I'm sure we'll have—at least in my mind the house has a veranda. She better have gotten me a fucking veranda. Three: Alissa needs me to be there. She looks cool and collected from the outside and puts up an awesome front, but just behind her beautiful blue irises is a woman who knows she's in too deep. I'll be honest—I don't know what to do now. Before, it was my job to remind her of how she felt before she got pregnant. However, now it feels wrong and slimy to keep reminding her of all the reasons why she doesn't want to revisit parenthood when she looks so freaking maternal.

Four: Tony—that unsettled open door that creaks in my core. Some days I hide my phone under the couch cushions to keep from texting him. Other days I look at the screen and try to conjure the ability to make him text me first so I can respond ever so nonchalantly that I'm preparing for five months in Florida so he can chew on that. Bastard. Then I think about being in Florida—that feeling of finality that washes over me knowing that I can't just jump in my car, drive ninety miles and throw myself into his arms. Which I would never do anyway, but still.

I can't stay here. There—I said it aloud. Well, kind of. My gut tells me Michelle is going to be just fine. I'd planned to call Katie later to smooth the waters with her—I can't leave with her being so upset, and I know she's at her house devouring herself in misery that her closest friends are angry with her. She probably didn't deserve all that, but it was easier to diffuse Michelle without her there. She's always been one to forgive and forget especially if she feels understood. I'll appeal to her like that. I'll also let her know that Alissa needs me and Michelle needs *her*— so we'll both be right where we need to be.

But more than all that, I need this. I have a feeling that all the answers to my questions are buried in the sand on a beach in Naples, and I intend to take my time sifting through the grains. I think it will help me gain perspective and give me a chance to make the game plan for the next phase in my life.

Whatever that is.

After my shower, I called Alissa to share my breakthrough. She answered on the third ring. "Please tell me you're going to Florida."

I smiled. "I'm going to Florida."

She sighed heavily in the phone and whispered, "Oh thank God."

"Hey there, sister, quit blowing in my ear. You're turning me on."

"You like it. Okay, so the original plan is still intact, then? Same timeline as before?"

265

I said, "Yeah, I don't see why not. I . . . I can't stay here, Lis."

She whispered, "I can't do this without you, Chance."

"Well, then I say we combine out superpowers and do this shit together. You know—all that shit we can't do alone."

She whispered again, "Can I come over for a little bit? I have to get out of this house . . . like alone. Minus one kinda thing."

I grimaced and tried to ignore the drama brewing in her comment. "Sure. I just got out of the shower, so bra is optional. I'm not wearing one. Consider yourself warned."

She giggled. "I'm on my way."

Ten minutes later, she breezed through the doorway shedding her coat, purse, and scarf while never breaking stride. "She's driving me crazy, Chance!"

I shut the door behind her and shook my head. "Well hello to you, too, preggers. What's the dealio?"

She spun around and threw out her arms as she chanted, "'How are you feeling, Lis? Do you need anything, Lis? Is the baby moving, Lis? Are you hungry, Lis? Are you sure you should be lifting that, Lis?' I'm losing my fucking mind!" She plopped down on the sofa and kicked off her shoes. "I feel like a total asshole for even talking about this, but dammit, I just want to be left alone for a minute. Just one minute! Geez!"

I smirked. "I'm sorry, Michelle, I was expecting Alissa. Could you come back some other time?"

"Ha-ha, funny." She threw her head back and groaned. "It's just so frustrating." She sat up straight and pointed at me. "And don't you dare tell her a thing about this."

I threw up my hands. "Oh, hell no. I don't want none of that crazy directed at me. I didn't notice her being overly attentive, but I was more focused on Michelle and trying to keep her from killing Katie."

"Well, she's so stinking sweet and gracious. My gosh, can she just be normal for a minute? I realize this is a big deal for her, but we've got a long time to go before the baby comes."

I sat on the other end of the couch and curled my legs under me. "Permission to ask the tough question, counselor?"

"Granted."

"Are you sure this is about her 'attentiveness' and not a projection about how you're really feeling about everything?"

She blinked twice before the sigh escaped. She slouched. "Maybe."

I shrugged. "Well, it's good you came to me instead of saying something to her. You're going to have to keep this in check, sweets. She's not the reason you're upset. And I don't mean to sound insensitive or cold when I say this, but I really think once the baby is born and Dani takes custody, you're going to realize how spot-on this decision is for you." I sucked in my breath and waited for her to respond. I really put it out there with that one, and I wasn't sure of her reaction.

She sighed heavily and mumbled, "I'm not so sure I feel that way anymore."

"Tell me why you feel that way, Lis." I love the many faces of Alissa. She's such a chameleon, and I blame her mother that—for putting her in such situations of uncertainty that caused Alissa to be able to transform based off setting. Thanks to my fabulous, fine-tuned journalistic spidey senses, I could catch her when she was trying on an emotion for size— how she *should* feel, how she *should* react, how she *should* respond—never really trusting herself. The bad thing is she could read me just as easily. Maybe that's why we're so close. "Lis, I don't want to hear what you think I want to hear. I want to know how you feel."

She chewed on her lip and chose her words carefully. "I don't know how to feel." She looked at me and repeated. "I don't know how to feel."

I chuckled. "Sure you do. You *feel* something right now. What is it?"

She ran her hand across her baby bump. "It's all jumbled up, Chance. My head, I mean. One minute, I think I've made a huge mistake telling Dani she can have my baby, but I can't tell if I'm just hormonal and all sappy because I can feel the little movements. Then I think I might have gotten my one chance to do it right, ya know? Like this was my opportunity to actually be a good mother . . ."

"But Lis, you were never 'a mother.' You were a sister forced to take on a parental role too early in life. And the way your sisters turned out— that's not a reflection of you at all."

"But that's what I'm saying. If this was my chance to prove to myself that I didn't fuck up my sisters."

I sat back and looked at her. "Do you really feel you need a baby to prove that?"

"No, I guess not."

"Okay, let's go at this another way. Midnight feedings, diapers, formula, fevers, teething, colic . . ."

"Giggles, first steps, first words, Santa Claus, cuddles, unconditional love . . ."

I smiled. "You really have been thinking about this."

"I remember when Hilary took her first steps," she grinned. "She was so cute in her little T-shirt onesie and diaper."

"I gotta tell you, kiddo, I don't know how to talk you through this one. I feel like an asshole for pushing you to stay the course, and I also feel like I'm supposed to help keep you focused on what you always wanted—or didn't want—our whole adult life."

She leaned forward and put her face in her hands. "I know. I *know*. God, how did I get myself into this mess? I already know what's going to happen. I just need to know if I can live with it." She looked at me and continued, "Ever have those moments when you wish you could just take one glimpse into the future and see five minutes of your life just to see if you're making the right decision right now?"

Tony.

She smiled and waved a finger at me. "I know what you're thinking, so that answers my question. You tell me what you're going to do about all that right now."

I shrugged. "I'm going to Florida. That's five months and hundreds of miles away from him. I'd say my 'what-am-I-going-to-do' is pretty evident."

"You don't think that's going to eat you alive?"

"Nah, I don't think so. What's done is done, sister. I can't change it."

"But you really didn't give him an opportunity to explain."

I sighed and contemplated hitting her with a pillow, but I can't hit a pregnant lady. "I know, I know. I don't see any reason to let him, okay? Is that better?"

She chuckled. "Not at all. He wanted you back. You heard what you wanted to hear from the Barbie doll so you could slip right back into self-protection mode and not ever have to face the opportunity of rejection again. Isn't it true that you intentionally didn't respond to multiple texts and phone calls?"

"Wow, look at you lawyer-out on me. Okay, I'll be on the witness stand. Yes, that's correct; I did refuse. In my defense, it's easy for someone to say something in private. Who's to say he wasn't going to continue to see her and tease me on the side?"

"Who's to say he was truly with her in the first place, and that she was just being the catty bitch we all assume she is?"

"Objection, your honor. Counselor is entering items into evidence that were not in disclosure."

She laughed. "Oh lord, you've been watching television again. Doesn't matter, Chance. We could what-if this to death. The point is that you had the opportunity to know the answer and chickened out. Why?"

"Because his answer doesn't change anything, Lis! We're still in two different cities with two different lives. He wants me to uproot and move to St. Louis."

"Yet I can ask you to basically quit your job, leave your apartment and life for half a year and you barely blinked before agreeing."

"Ugh, why do you suck so badly?"

"If you hadn't had so many failed relationships prior to meeting Tony, you'd probably be married and living in St. Louis right now. That's all I'm saying."

"I disagree. *Because* I'm not married, I *can* uproot and relocate for half a year and not think twice about it. That's what I like about my life, Lis. That's what I don't want to change—what I don't want to lose."

"You can't have it both ways, Chance. The defense rests."

And that was my predicament. I wanted it both ways. I wanted to have my cake and eat it, too. Tony was so perfect for me in every way, but he wanted me to compromise what wasn't optional. He wanted me to be his wife, his plus one, his (gulp) baby mama—I just wanted to love him. He wanted to wake up to me every morning, and I wanted to sleep in the middle of the bed every night. If we revisit this equation, the answer is still the same, right?

Unless one of us changed our minds.

Chapter Thirty-Three
On Bended Knee

Alissa

It's finally December 28, the morning we leave for Naples, Florida, and forget about life in Missouri for five months. No surprise I didn't sleep last night. I finally gave up the fight a little after five and slipped into the living room to drink some juice and wait for the baby movements to start.

The house looked vacant without the Christmas decorations. When I was a kid, we lived in one place long enough to have a few Christmases there. We had a sad little tree that was maybe four feet tall. After Christmas, Mom just picked it up and took it fully decorated to the garage. I remember slipping out to the garage, plugging in the lights, and staring at the lights all throughout the year. There was something transforming about it. Not that Christmas was ever a big deal to me. I never really benefitted from the holiday. However, I always felt a sense of grief when the tree was gone and Christmas was over. Just another reminder that Santa had once again forgotten me.

A familiar tug of sadness yanked at my heart as I looked at the treeless corner. Eleven months out of the year, it doesn't bother me, but from December 26 through the 31st, it makes me sad. I don't spend much time in this room that week. Then I'm over it.

The next time I sit in this chair, I'll be nearly recovered from childbirth and likely drinking a bottle of wine or three, pretending life goes on. Which it does. Dani will be across town neck-deep in maternal bliss and learning about a completely new level of exhaustion. I may see if Chance will stay with me for a few weeks when we get back. Might put that on my list of things to consider when I'm not pregnant. Many things sound like a good idea right now, but execution may be a problem. Knowing Chance, after spending this much time with people, she'll go into hiding for months when we get back to Missouri. Can't really blame her since she's not used to it. The older she gets, the more introverted she becomes.

The plan was to leave by eight. Dani, being the good little husband, took the Navigator to the gas station to fill up last night so we don't have to stop before we ever get started. We packed the Navigator last night and left room for Chubs's crate in the back and Dani in the back seat. Chance called shotgun the night we concocted this plan. The playlists were loaded on our phones, snacks were readily accessible, and all we had to do was pile in the car and hit the road. I had the address programmed into my phone, Dani had printed directions (just in case), and Chance wanted us to wake her up when we got past St. Louis.

I went through each room unplugging everything and triple checked the locked windows. We bagged up all of the leftovers and took them to the soup kitchen last night, so the fridge was in good shape.

The next two hours will be torture.

I texted Chance: *you awake?*

She responded immediately: *I'm awake but not up. Couldn't sleep for shit.*

I grinned and texted back: *Wanna leave early?*

She said: *I'm hitting the shower now. I'll be ready in thirty minutes.*

I squealed, ran to Dani's room and jumped on her bed. "Are you awake? Are you awake? Huh? Huh?"

She mumbled, "I'm awake, Lis."

"Good! So is Chance. Let's leave in thirty minutes."

She threw back the covers. "Are you serious?"

"Sure, why not?"

"It's not even six yet. If we leave now, we're going to hit St. Louis traffic which was the whole point in leaving at eight."

"Who cares? We have five months to get there. Come on! Get up! Let's get this trip started."

Dani sighed and stretched. "All right, I'm up."

I bounced on the bed, "Yay! We're going to Florida!"

She shook her head. "This is going to change the itinerary, though."

"Oh, who cares, Dani? Live a little. We're tossing out the Daytimers, remember? Flying by the seat of our pants. It's going to be so much fun."

272

She slid out of bed. "I assume Chance is on board with your last minute change of plans?" She grabbed her perfectly folded outfit for the day from her dresser.

"Yep. Already talked to her."

"Okay, well let's get ready to go."

Thirty minutes later, we closed my house and set the alarm. I stood at the front door and imagined how it would feel coming back with an empty womb and empty arms. I shuddered and joined Dani in the Navigator. "Just think, Dani. No twenty-degree Missouri mornings for months." I backed out of the garage and headed toward Chance's apartment.

She hummed and grinned. "No scraping ice off the windshield at the office."

"No tiptoeing across icy sidewalks."

She pointed at me. "An excellent thing for a woman in your delicate condition."

I laughed. "You sound so debutante sometimes, you know that?"

She shrugged and flipped through her phone. "Looks like the weather in the south is going to hold out for the trip. I programmed key cities on the route into my weather app and it looks clear through Atlanta." She closed her phone. "Good. I was worried about driving through Tennessee. I hear they get some intense storms sometimes."

I nudged her. "You worry too much."

"It's genetic." She frowned when she heard my blinker clicking. "Where are you going now?"

"If you think I'm going to show up at Chance's house before eight o'clock without Starbucks in my hand, you're out of your mind."

"Chicken."

"Nope—smart."

We pulled into Chance's apartment complex, and my instructions were clear. I was to wait in the car while Dani went upstairs to help Chance bring down her things. So annoying. I guess a pregnant woman plus three flights of stairs multiplied by carrying a bag was too risky to our sweet, worrywart, Dani. God, I'm glad Chance is going with us. I sent Michelle and Katie a text telling them we'd decided to leave early and to keep their iPads handy. Michelle responded with a frownie face: *I was going to come see you off at eight.*

I replied: *I'm too antsy. Can't stand it anymore. Love you!*

Dani returned with Chance closely behind. A gust of cold wind blew through the Navigator as the back hatch opened and Chance put Chubs's kennel and the rest of her luggage in their designated places. I'm surprised Dani didn't have them labeled.

Chance jumped in the front seat and slammed the door. "Good God I think I lost my nipples out there." She shivered and rubbed her hands together.

I handed over her Starbucks. "Let me know when it's safe to make eye contact."

"I hope to be asleep in less than thirty minutes."

Dani asked, "Then why should I sit in the back? Lis needs someone up front to help her stay alert."

I said quickly, "I'm fine, Dani. Chance is going to be a good little navigator and stay awake. Right, Chance?" I knew Chance would get it.

She turned to look at Dani. "I got this, okay little mama? Just relax. We're going to have fun."

Dani sighed. "I'll just be glad when we get to Florida. I'm worried this trip will be stressful on Alissa."

Chance pointed at me. "You stressed?"

"Nope," I said.

Chance pointed at Dani. "You stressed? I'm not stressed; she's not stressed. Chubs, are you stressed, little buddy?" She shouted back to the trunk. "Yeah, okay he's probably stressed, but he's got good reason to be." She slammed her hand on the dash. "Onward, Dasher and Dancer. Let's get this party started."

I grinned in spite of myself and thanked God for the umpteenth million time that Chance was on this trip, and we hadn't even left her apartment complex yet. I was about to change that.

Two hours later, we slid through St. Louis without much traffic at all. It hadn't dawned on any of us that we were leaving on Sunday. I glanced at Chance and teased, "Want me to take the next exit?" I wagged my eyebrows and winked.

She slapped my leg. "Nice. Keep on rolling, sister."

"Just thought I'd ask." Chance is making a big mistake with Tony. Or not with Tony, however you want to say it. I know she's just trying to get through St. Louis, and once we're on the other side, her proverbial ideology that there's literally no turning back will come to pass. I sighed.

She mumbled, "Noted."

"I can still take the next exit. We can drop by for a second, you can tell him you're moving to Florida and just see what he does."

"Stay the course, Lis."

"You're making a mistake, Chance."

"Probably."

"Well, I have to pee, anyway." I flipped on my blinker and took the exit. "I'm ready for a refill, too. You need more coffee?" I met her blazing eyes and stifled the holy-shit-she's-pissed grin that tried to surface.

"I swear if we see him, I'm tattooing 'I suck 'em good' on your forehead in your sleep tonight."

"Oh Chance, it's St. Louis on a Sunday morning. What are the odds we'll run into Tony at Starbucks?"

Chance

The baby must be sucking her intelligence to an all-time low. What the fuck kind of human takes an exit that leads to my ex-boyfriend's apartment while I'm trying like hell to be the chicken getting to the other side of this blasted city? It's straight-up horse shit,— that's what it is. And, I've been holding my pee for thirty-six minutes pretending I don't have to go so we can *get* to the other side. Totally insensitive.

Dani stirred in the back seat. She asked through a yawn, "Are we stopping already?"

I answered, "Alissa-the-magnificent has to pee."

She replied, "Oh, good. I need to go, too, and I need more coffee."

Alissa was smart enough not to speak. She pulled into Starbucks, threw the Navigator in park, and headed into the building. I scoped the parking lot and didn't see anything that resembled Tony's car. Inside, I did a quick scan of the customers, found the coast clear, and decided I could like Alissa again. But I still hope she gets pee on her hand.

Maybe I'll meet some handsome, young, tanned hottie with an extreme passion for life and an insatiable hunger for sex while I'm in Florida. Maybe he'll be there with two of his buddies hiding out because one of them knocked up a successful attorney who's on the manhunt for his balls. Wouldn't that be ironic? Meeting someone intriguing would be the sure-fire way to get Tony off my mind—if I can get out of my own head long enough *to actually see* people in front of me. That'd be a nice change.

After we used the bathroom and replenished our beverages of choice, we headed to the parking lot in a better mood than when we left it. As Alissa was pulling out of the parking lot, Dani asked, "Okay, can I be the superfluous bitch, here and point out that between the three of us, we spent over fifteen dollars on drinks just then? That is outrageous."

Alissa said, "I can't even begin to imagine how much money Starbucks makes in a year. Chance, write that down. I want to look that up when we get to Florida."

I looked at her. "Are you being serious?"

She chuckled, "Well, yeah I'm being serious. They sell coffee. For five dollars a cup."

I mumbled, "Yeah, but it's more than just coffee. It's a little liquid heaven in your flavor of choice. It's worth every dime to me."

Dani said, "I don't see how people can afford that, and you know there are people who go there every day. Every day! That'd be what . . . an average of three hundred dollars a month spent on coffee?"

I said, "I highly doubt most people go there every day, Dani. But yes, we can look it up when we get to Florida. Sure." I made a note on my invisible note pad. "Research the Starbucks scam."

Alissa said, "Okay, okay, maybe we've enlisted the help of the enemy, here, Dani. I'm on your side, though."

276

Dani said, "Thank God for that."

I had to laugh. "I find it so humorous that the two of you are concerned about a five dollar coffee—especially since we've all just left our careers, boarded up our houses, and are going to spend several months living in an oceanfront house. Wanna talk about extravagant spending, there, bitches?"

They were both silent until we all laughed. Alissa said, "Touché."

I did a fist pump. "Now that's worth writing down. I actually won an argument with Alissa *and* Dani at the same time. This trip is worth it already."

It slipped out. Thankfully, Dani didn't catch it, and Alissa let it go. "How about we drown out this gloating with a little trip music? Maestro, will you do the honors?" She handed me her phone. "You can pick the first playlist. The Breakup Mix might be your best option right now. Just sayin'" She winked at me and returned her eyes to the road.

And that's how we spent three days in the car. If Alissa wasn't pregnant, we could have made it in two, but Dani thought it would be best to spread it out over three days and we didn't argue. By the time we made it to Naples, I was ready to grab Chubs, walk the full length of the Gulf of Mexico and be alone. Not that I don't like my friends—I love them. They're the sugar and creamer that make my life's coffee worth drinking. But I need to be alone—I'm used to being alone, so constant chatter and being restricted to plans makes me want to randomly punch people. Yet another reason why Tony and me weren't a good match.

On our last stop, I let Dani have the front seat so she could help Alissa find the house. I was tired and Dani was nervous, so it was a good swap for both of us. After a few wrong turns and a trip down a one-way street, Alissa fired Dani from the navigation and turned on the GPS. I was content to gasp and point from the back seat at the houses that dripped money.

Dani snapped, "Well we can't be too far from it. There's the damn ocean right there."

"Begging your pardon, Miss Dani, but there are a helluva lot of houses on said ocean, and I'd rather not unpack at the wrong one," Alissa barked.

Two minutes later, Alissa slowed near the driveway of a house. "I think that's it. I recognize it from the pictures." She looked at her phone. "Aren't you going to tell me—"

The phone chirped, "You have arrived at your destination. It is on the left."

Alissa tossed the phone on the dashboard and muttered as she turned into the driveway. "Looks smaller than I'd imagined."

Smaller? The house looked to be at least two stories with a two-car garage underneath. My heart pounded in my chest as a grin spread across my face. I opened the car door and tilted my face to the afternoon sun. "Hello, lover."

Alissa grinned. "Tada! What do you think?"

We got out of the car and stared at the perfectly manicured lawn, palm trees, and the house that would be ours for the next five months. I didn't even want to think about how much this cost, and I'd only seen the back. I grabbed Chubs, attached his leash, and nearly sprinted to the front of the house to see the view.

Once again, Alissa did it up right.

The front of the house was more immaculate than I could ever have pictured on my own. The two-story yellow house with white trim stood proudly with opened arms that curled slightly and ended with glass rooms. Above the front door was a white wooden deck that sat like a crown. Mentally, I called dibs on whatever room those double doors enclosed—even if it was a laundry room, it was mine. An elevated deck surrounded the front of the house with palm trees, sea grass, and a perfect view of the Gulf of Mexico to complete the scene. The evening tide was whipping and rolling, providing just enough surf sounds to make tears flow down my cheeks. It was perfect. While the house didn't have a veranda, there was a gazebo, and that was good enough for me. I didn't care if I ever stepped foot in the house at this point—I was content with the yard.

"Chance, can you believe this place?" Dani gaped as she circled the sidewalk. "Every detail is so intricate and meticulous."

Alissa slid next to me and linked her arm with mine. "Well? What do you think?"

I swallowed hard and whispered, "It's perfect, Lis."

She giggled and squealed, "Yay! Welcome home, Chance Bradley."

I shook my head and laughed. "I cannot believe this is happening. We made it." I wiped my face. "Can you believe this view?"

She beamed. "Go big or go home, right?"

"I've never known you to be any other way, kiddo."

Dani scampered down the wooden steps that led to the beach. "Chance! Come on!"

I slipped off my shoes and socks, rolled my jeans and ran to catch up with her. I can't remember a time when I've ever felt freer in my life. My long hair whipped in the breeze, the ocean applauded with our arrival as though it had been waiting for us. I giggled then squealed in spite of myself. I sped past Dani who'd stopped to take off her shoes and ran the width of the shore until I was ankle-deep in the ocean water. Alissa was hot on my heels splashing and stomping as she threw back her head and laughed just for the joy of it.

"Is this really happening?" Dani gasped as she tested the water. She stepped into the ocean with us. "It's colder than I'd imagined."

"Well, it is nearly January, silly."

If I'd brought any cares with me to this place, the sea greeted me and took them to its depths. The ocean commanded our attention—the trance of its melody wrapped around me like a grandmother's hug.

I glanced down the beach and saw Alissa scampering in and out of the waves with her arms out like an airplane. I nudged Dani. "Will you look at her?"

Dani chuckled. "She's a mess."

I followed her eyes down the coast and whistled. "Get a load of those houses, man."

"Oh, I'm looking. This is over the top." She turned to look at our house and shook her head. "Shall we check out the house?"

I grinned. "Oh, absolutely." I turned toward Alissa and yelled,

"Come on, girl! Let's go see the house!"

She tilted her arms and circled the plane our way as she screamed, "Isn't this amazing?"

Thousands of stories from Alissa's childhood invaded my mind. I envisioned her pretending to be a ten-year-old kid on vacation with her parents—the way it should have been. She was breathless and giddy when she got to us. She let her arms flop to her sides and looked at the house. "I did good," she said.

"You did good, kid. Race ya! Loser has to cook supper." We took off running and squealing for the house. Of course, Dani was the sore loser, but I was sucking wind when we reached the boardwalk.

"But wait, there's more," Alissa grinned as she stepped up to the outdoor shower and pushed a button. Water sprayed across her feet rinsing away the sand. "Holy shit, that's cold. Agh! Okay, Dani, your turn."

Dani slid her feet under the water and gasped. "Holy shit, that's cold!" She flipped her feet trying to hurry the process. "Chance?"

I took my turn, and suddenly that water wasn't nearly as funny as it had been when the other two were under it. "Good god, that's freezing." They took their turn laughing at me as I danced and shook my fists. "Okay, good enough. Let's go inside." I picked up Chubs and wiped the sand off his feet as he licked my hands.

Our wet feet slapped against the boardwalk and wooden steps. Alissa slid the key in the lock and asked, "Are you ready for this?"

I laughed. "I feel like I should be carrying you across the threshold or something."

Alissa laughed too. "Dani, you go first. In case there are burglars. You can use your mad punching skills."

"Great, we're all dead, then," Dani said.

Alissa swung open the door and we stepped into what would be considered a mud room in the Midwest. Benches lined three walls and towel hooks were spaced evenly around the room. A shelf next to the door held a dozen white towels all rolled to perfection, and a plush rug covered most of the hardwood floors. I pointed at the rug. "Smart."

Dani looked down. "Can you imagine the scuffs sandy feet would leave on these floors?"

I set Chubs down and shortened his leash. I smirked. "I can't wait until your baby draws a Crayola masterpiece on your walls."

She smacked my hand. "Stop that."

Straight ahead, the sunroom opened into the largest kitchen I've ever seen. Off to the right was a little sitting room. "What's that for, morning coffee?" I stuck my head in and saw one of the all-window rooms I'd seen from the beach.

"I'd say that's exactly what this is. A coffee room/breakfast nook," Alissa said.

I whispered, "It's fabulous. God, look at that view."

"Chance, come look at this!" Dani called from deeper in the house.

Alissa and I fought to be the first one out of the breakfast nook and laughed as we crossed the kitchen, which led into the living room. I gasped and didn't know where to look first. The high ceilings, the white couches with brown pillows that matched the furniture and floors. "Oh god, Chubs." I looked down at my dog. "You will not get on those couches, you understand?"

Alissa nudged me. "We'll put some blankets over them. You know how clumsy I am and how wine affects Dani. Chances are we'll have to have those professionally cleaned before we leave, anyway." She winked. "If we ever leave."

I nodded. "Right? I'm thinking Mama's home. As much as I love my apartment, I could be persuaded to stay here forever."

Alissa laughed. "Oh girl, even I can't afford this place for life. But it's something to consider."

Dani was still on the prowl and gasping every thirty seconds at her latest find. She found the library, a study, and an indoor pool which was the surprise behind the other all-glass walls. She grinned and asked, "What's upstairs?"

We took off for the stairs—I won that time and got to see my room first. I threw open the door to the room that had a balcony which overlooked the ocean. "Dibs! Dibs, dibs, dibs, *mine*!" I threw myself on the king-sized bed and rolled around. "Mine, mine!" I threw out my arms and legs and wiggled like a pig in fresh mud. "Oh my god, I'm in heaven."

Alissa called down the hallway, "I found my room!"

I sat up and frowned. "You didn't even see this room, sister!" I jumped off the bed to see what treasure she'd found and gaped at the room she'd claimed. It was twice the size of mine and had a Jacuzzi tub in the corner surrounded by tropical plants and a window that overlooked the ocean. I mumbled, "Well shit the bed. She outdid me again."

Alissa crawled into the tub and pretended to hold a wine glass. "Oh servant, I need more, please. And could you wash my back?"

I grabbed one of the towels beside the tub and threw it in her face. "Oh you got served, all right."

Dani yelled, "I don't know, ladies, I may have both of you beat."

We stared at each other for a split second then started for the door at the same time as Alissa squealed, "Dammit, Chance, you had a head start!"

I stuck my tongue out. "You shouldn't have bellied up to the tub, *ma chérie!*"

Dani's room was pure elegance, just like its occupant. She had a window that overlooked the ocean as well, but the room seemed to be custom made for her. One wall was floor-to-ceiling bookshelves with a reading nook on one side of the room. The bed would have taken up a normal room in any of our houses, but it seemed small in the expanse of a room. She grinned. "Check out the closet."

I stuck my head into the closet that seemed never-ending. "Damn, that's the size of my room back home!"

She giggled. "I didn't bring enough clothes to fill a tenth of those hangers."

I wagged my eyebrows at her. "We need to go shopping."

Alissa came around the corner and asked, "Did someone say shopping?"

Chapter Thirty-Four
A Thousand Years

Michelle

New Year's Eve. A time to reflect on the past year and make wishes for a new one. For most people, it's a time to make a list of things you're going to change in rapid succession then feel bad about never following through. My changes started four months ago. My wake-up call came a week ago, and my resolutions started the morning I woke up hung-over in Alissa's house missing my family thinking I'd never have my horrible wasted life back.

I think I'll remember the night I came home for the rest of my life. Brandon and I walked around the elephant in the room as I picked up my normal routine, scoured my filthy kitchen only to dirty it again with the same boring meal I'd cooked just a week earlier. The mood at the table was lighter than it'd been in a long time, but there seemed to be guillotines hung over everyone's heads. No one made sudden movements, stupid comments, smart-ass retorts, or brought up touchy subjects. I guess you could say it was fake.

After dinner, clean-up, showers, laundry, and good-night routines, Brandon and I found ourselves in our bedroom standing in opposite corners with the elephant on our bed. I fidgeted and stole glances at him; he stood with his hands in his pockets staring at the bedspread.

He whispered, his voice husky and shaking, "Yellow, sunflowers, Kelly Clarkson, Hawaii, Riverboat Red Wine, cats, reading, have sex." His eyes never left the bedspread.

I swallowed hard and asked, "What's all that?"

His gaze cut to meet mine. "Your favorite color, flower, musician, dream trip, beverage of choice, favorite animal, favorite hobby, and favorite thing to do on a rainy day." He sighed. "How'd I do?"

I bit my cheek to ease the ache in my throat and heart. "Very good."

He nodded. "Thought so."

"Why'd you do that?"

He shrugged. "You said in your journal I didn't know the answers to any of those things. But I do, Michelle."

"Brandon," I whispered. Tears poured down my face. "I'm so sorry."

"I also know that I'm an asshole, okay? I know that. I have to say I didn't think I was *that* bad—"

I sobbed, "I was mad—"

He cut me off. "No, a lot of what you said is probably true. But, Chelle, not all of it. Okay? Not all of it." His voice cracked as his chin quivered.

I went to him and knelt. "Brandon, I'm begging you on my knees to forgive me for what I wrote. I didn't . . . I don't . . . you're not . . . Fuck, I can't even talk."

He knelt in front of me and put his forehead to mine. "Look at me, baby. I knew you were bat-shit crazy years ago. It's part of the fun of being married to fifteen different women wrapped up in one body."

I buried myself in his chest and cried out the memories of all his wrongdoing. With each swipe of my hand, I felt the resentment and bitterness I'd held as my ally wave the white flag of surrender. My husband was not my enemy; I was.

I'd love to say we had fabulous make-up sex all night long and woke up like newly-weds the next day, but we all know that's not how it works in real life. We held each other 'til the crying was over then went to bed completely exhausted—him on his side, me on mine. But we held hands. It was a start.

And now, it's the night of December 31, a day of ending and the dawn of a new beginning. I feel optimistic about the new year, but not because I expect many things to change, but because I know they won't, and that I have. And I'm okay with that. I've got my family, my home, and my new job at the gym. I've got the best friends in the world, and while I long to be with them right now eating up the gulf sun and drinking mimosas 'til noon and fruity drinks 'til midnight, I know I'd miss my chaotic, hormonal, scream-filled house and all the crazy occupants.

It was Del-Ray who called the cops that night. That's why Brandon ended up taking her phone and the boys' iPods. He never intended for "the incident" to go that far. Turns out she panicked when she heard us fighting and thought we were *really* fighting. Brandon told me about it; she blames herself for the whole mess. As much as I've tried to tell her that was probably the best thing that could have ever happened to me, she still thinks the whole thing is her fault. It still doesn't explain why he turned off my phone, but I'm letting that little detail die in the embers of the past. Plus, I love my new smart phone. I think.

I didn't tell Brandon about the money Alissa gave me. I'm willing to forgive and move forward, but I'm not going to forget that helpless feeling for a while. Brandon's an insurance salesman, so certainly he of all people can understand the importance of having a private insurance policy . . . just in case. I opened an account in Martin's name at a bank in Centralia about thirty minutes northeast of Columbia and deposited nine thousand dollars. I kept a thousand for a little "me" money. When I know for sure Brandon's sincere about our new start and there's no threat of him cutting me off from my life again, I'll tell him about it. Just not right now. I opened my journal one more time and began to write.

It's nearly midnight. The house is quiet since Del Ray is at a friend's house and the boys are face-down in their new video games from Santa. Brandon fell asleep on the couch watching television an hour ago, and this is my last entry in this journal. I've got a special way I want to ring in the new year, and it's fitting that I do it by myself.

I grabbed my wine glass, my journal, and the grill lighter before I slipped out the back door and into the yard. I stood in front of our makeshift fire pit filled with dead branches and old newspapers I'd collected earlier in the day. I lit the fire and took a sip of wine as the flames danced in the cold night air.

Houses all down the block erupted in cheers as the new year rolled in. I envisioned confetti, kisses, laughter, and awkward drunken hugs. I thought of my friends sitting on the beach watching fireworks explode; each of them wondering exactly how much their life was going to change in the coming year. I thought of Katie curled up in bed still filled with

285

guilt and regret. She's on my list of things to make right in the coming year, I just can't do it yet. Being hurt by your husband is something you almost expect from time to time, being betrayed by a best friend is unspeakable.

The fiery dead wood and old news created a nice bed for my journal. I took another drink of wine and gently nudged my journal into the epicenter of the fire. The flames seemed to pause and look at me, giving me one last chance to reach in and grab my sacrifice. I nodded and watched the flames nibble at the edges of my pain until it decided it was delicious and ravaged every word, every memory, every tear-stained page. The fire moaned in delight, or maybe it was the last anguished cry of my misery being consumed by something much more powerful. Forgiveness. Acceptance. Wisdom. Courage. It was easy to be a victim. Too easy. It was easy to blame Brandon for my unhappiness. It was easy to feel trapped and unappreciated. It was easy to be mad. I was tired of easy.

I watched the fire until every last sheet of paper was transformed to ashes, and when it was over, I poured the last part of my wine over the fire to confirm the sacrifice. I slipped back into the house, put my glass in the sink, and went to bed after I kissed Brandon's sleeping face and whispered, "Happy new year, baby." He looked so comfortable on the couch, I didn't have the heart to wake him.

I woke up to the smell of frying bacon and fresh coffee. I reached for Brandon but found cold sheets and an empty pillow. Either he didn't come to bed last night, or he's in the kitchen cooking. I looked at the clock and gasped. *9:15! What the hell?* I flew out of bed, threw on my yoga pants and practiced my apologies all the way down the hall.

Martin sat on the couch plunking at the guitar he got for Christmas while Gibson played Xbox. I kissed them on the head and slipped into the kitchen to see the damage. Del Ray and Brandon fluttered through the kitchen, each of them taking their respective breakfast mission very seriously. The look of concentration on their faces, the identical profile and synchronized way they moved while she cooked scrambled eggs and he fried bacon—I had to giggle. They turned to look at me and grinned.

"What's all this?" I asked.

Brandon stabbed at the bacon a few more times then returned the lid to the frying pan and turned toward me. "Good morning! Happy new year!" He greeted me with a cup of coffee and a kiss. Del Ray hugged me. "Hi, Mom."

I kissed the top of her head. "You're cooking breakfast? When did you get home?"

She grinned. "Around nine. Dad's teaching me to make scrambled eggs. You know. In case there's a zombie apocalypse."

I chuckled. "Well, I hear scrambled eggs are kryptonite for zombies, so good on ya, Dad."

Del Ray tossed me a sarcastic glance then returned to the skillet. She said to Brandon, "I'm almost done. You close?"

Brandon switched off the burners. "Yep, I'm done. Did you start the toast?"

She nodded. "I've got eight pieces right now. Is that enough?"

He said, "Oh yeah, that's plenty. If not, we can make more." He pointed at me. "More coffee?"

I glanced at my cup. "Sure, I'll take a warm-up." He took my cup and pointed to the table. "Have a seat. We're serving *you* this morning," he said with a wink.

I looked sideways at him and smiled. "Maybe you should sleep on the couch more often. It does something to you."

He grinned. "I came to bed right after you. Not that you noticed since your wine put you out cold."

I giggled. "It's always done that."

His gaze met mine, his eyes burning with a life I hadn't seen in a while. He placed my coffee in front of me and leaned down. "I know, Chelle."

I felt parts of my body light up with an intensity I hadn't felt since I was a teenager. I wanted that man naked in my bed immediately—bacon be damned. I stared at my husband and saw my high-school sweetheart, the boy who took my virginity, my heart, and my hand for life staring back at me. In that moment, he wasn't the father of my children or the

287

paycheck for bills, he was the boy I'd loved my whole life. And he wasn't looking at me like the mother of his children, the cook, the roommate; he was looking at me like he did from the stage years ago—like, "If there weren't fifty people on the dance floor between us, I'd have you naked in thirty seconds flat." My face flushed as it remembered how to flirt. I flipped my hair and slid my hand through it—our signal to each other over the years to meet me in the bedroom in ten minutes. He winked, looked at the clock. "Make it fifteen."

I grinned. "Deal."

Breakfast was amazing. Simply amazing. Martin and Brandon talked guitar chords, Gibson chimed in with questions, and Del Ray and I talked about cutting and coloring my hair . . . again. She's obsessed with making me over.

She said, "Well, look at you. You've lost all that weight, and your hair still looks like you just stepped out of 1999. You need a new 'do to go with your new body."

I sat back and stared at her. A slow grin slipped across my face as I asked, "New body?"

She chewed her food and mumbled around it, "Yeah, Mom, look at you. You're hot! But that hair . . . that hair has to change."

I glanced at Brandon and shrugged. "What do you think?"

"She's right. You look amazing. Just don't shave it and dye it purple."

I chuckled. "No worries there. If it's okay with you, I'll make appointments for Del Ray and me tomorrow."

She sighed. "I don't want to wait, Mom! Let's do something today. I've been studying haircuts. I think I could do it."

"No offense, honey, but I'm not going to let you cut my hair."

Martin asked Brandon, "Dad, is it G, C, and D for that song we played this morning?"

Brandon nodded. "Sounds like the guitar bug has bitten you, bud. It's all you can talk about."

"Welcome to my world, Brandon," I said and winked.

He smiled. "I've been waiting for this moment my whole adult life."

288

He stood and took his plate to the sink, washed his hands, and went to the living room. He grabbed Martin's guitar and slung the strap over his neck. He tuned a few strings then strummed a few chords. I smiled and started clearing the breakfast table as the sound of acoustic music hummed through the air. I ran a hundred songs through my mind trying to place the tune he was playing but couldn't nail it down.

Then he started singing.

She's given me all she ever had.
Sometimes, she makes me mad.
Little things, they turn real bad.
But she loves me, and I'm so glad.

Spellbound, I slowly walked into the living room where Brandon was perched against the back of the couch.

Didn't get what we wanted out of life.
Expected a sword but got a knife.
A lot of laughter, a lot of strife.
But I'm so glad she's my wife.

He fingered the strings and built to the chorus.

I've made mistakes, more than a few.
You'd ask for ten, I'd offer two.
I'm no fool, and I'm still mad at you.

He stared at me with pleading, apologetic eyes and repeated, "I'm still so mad at you." Tears poured down my cheeks as he set down the guitar and mumbled, "It's still a work in progress."

I took a staggered breath and wiped my face. "That was awesome," I whispered.

He drew me into his arms. "I really love you, Michelle. I can't imagine not having you in my life." He paused then said slowly, "And I'm so sorry."

289

My heart flopped as I heard the words I'd never heard from him—ever. I whispered, "Could you repeat that?"

He chuckled and hugged me tighter. "Nope. First and only."

I laughed and snuggled into his neck. "You smell good."

He made a show of throwing his shoulders back and puffing out his chest. "I've got a woman to win over. I pulled out all the stops."

I grinned. "Guess that means I need to start shaving my legs."

He winked. "Let's go see how bad it is, then we'll make that call."

I glanced over my shoulder and saw Del Ray busy cleaning the kitchen. Martin was already engrossed in his guitar, and Gibson was back to his video games. "Gibson, please take the trash out before you get started playing again. Martin, make sure Del Ray doesn't need help." I looked at Brandon and whispered in his ear, "I think we're late for an appointment." I took his hand and led him to the bedroom.

Chapter Thirty-Five
Blaze of Glory

Alissa

I sat on the deck watching the sunrise as I'd done every day for the last two weeks. Chance has yet to wake up in time to watch, and that's okay with me. She prefers sunsets anyway. After watching the sunrise the first time, though, I never wanted to miss another one. Being on an extended vacation, I expected to sleep until I was ready to wake up, but the baby movements came mostly in the morning. Another thing I didn't want to miss.

I only had a few more minutes to enjoy the world waking up before I had to jump in the shower and get ready for my eight o'clock appointment with the new OB doctor. I had my script rehearsed and knew the routine questions from my previous appointments in Missouri. Dani had been counting down the days to the appointment and couldn't wait to hear the heartbeat and see how the baby was progressing. She'd devoured the book I'd given her and even read ahead a little. She should have been a boy scout with how prepared she always was. Ten bucks she wants to leave thirty minutes early to make a twenty-minute drive.

I've heard pregnant women become annoyed with their spouses a lot during pregnancy. Men at the office joked about having their scrotums tied to a whipping post for nine months. I guess my punching bag is Dani. I don't know if it's because she's all up in my shit all the time trying to be loving and supportive or a repressed resentment I won't acknowledge. It's not her fault, I know that, but some days playing house with the person who is taking my baby four months from now is more than I know how to handle. And there's no getting away from it. From her.

But I didn't have time to sit around thinking about it. I got up, downed the rest of my orange juice and headed into the house. The aroma of coffee enveloped me as I stepped into the kitchen. Dani leaned against the counter sipping her coffee and grinned when she saw me. "Today's the big day."

I smiled. "Yep. What time do you want to leave?" I already knew the answer to this question, but I wanted to seem like I cared.

She slid a piece of paper across the counter. "I printed directions to the office. It says it takes twenty-three minutes to get there from here, but with morning traffic, I say we leave no later than seven-thirty."

Ding ding ding! Called it. I grinned. "I figured you'd say that. I'll jump in the shower."

Dani set her coffee cup on the counter and softly said, "Lis, I feel your hostility toward me. I've tried to pretend it's all in my head, but I see it in your eyes now. If . . . if you're changing your mind about giving up the baby, then please just tell me. Don't make me your enemy over this."

Guilt slammed into my chest. I rinsed my juice glass and set it in the sink. "I don't know what's going on with me, Dani. I'm chalking it up to hormones and getting fat." I turned. "I'm going to tell them I'm your surrogate and that you're the baby's mother." I swallowed hard and sighed. "You're just going to have to give me some room to process this. I never . . . I didn't . . . I wasn't expecting . . . I didn't know." I leveled my eyes at her. "I didn't know it would be like this." I offered her my best smile while gritting my teeth. "I'm going to jump in the shower." I slipped up the stairs and left her staring at her coffee mug. I hated myself already for the look that settled over her.

I knew that look.

I knew that feeling.

I knew how it felt to be the pregnant woman's confidante, then enemy. Good god, I am turning into my mother.

I slid into Chance's room and closed the door. I tiptoed to her bed and stood over her.

"Are you going to speak or just stand there like a creepy stalker?" she mumbled.

"I'm turning into my mother," I said.

She rolled over and looked at me. "Not even close, Lis."

"No, I am. I just treated Dani like Mom treated me when she was

292

pregnant. I said the same words. I said, 'I didn't know it would be like this.' That's her catch phrase for everything, Chance."

She sat up and rubbed her eyes. "Listen to me, girlfriend. You're not turning into your mother. You're a little jacked up, right? Today's the appointment, and you're probably just a little hormonal. Maybe a lot."

I sighed and stared out the window. "You really should get up and watch the sunrise with me sometime."

"The only way I'm seeing a sunrise is if I stay up all night waiting for it."

I chuckled and looked at her. "Promise me I'm not turning out like her."

She grabbed my hand and squeezed. "I'll kill you myself if I see it."

I took a deep breath and let it out. "Good." I nodded and repeated, "Good."

She asked, "Do you want me to go with you guys today?"

I shook my head. "Nah, go back to sleep. I'm find. I need to make nice with Dani, anyway. I'm not sure how, but I'll think of something."

"Okay, now get out. I was having an awesome dream." She snuggled into her blankets and buried her face in the pillow.

At 7:58, Dani and I pulled into the OB parking lot. I slid the keys out of the ignition and grinned. "See? We're right on time."

Dani collected her purse and sighed. "Thank God you were driving. We'd be halfway to Miami now if you'd listened to me."

I smirked then refreshed my face to offer a genuine grin. "Let's go see what they have to say." We got out of the car and I linked my arm with hers to try to be more like the Alissa I was five months ago before I was knocked up with the child of a man who hates my guts. "I'm thinking after we're done here, we need to go grab some ridiculously expensive Starbucks drinks and do a little baby shopping. What do you think?"

Dani grinned. "Music to my ears."

We stepped through the sliding doors and sighed as the blast of air conditioning swept over us. I whispered to Dani, "Sheesh, is this a doctor's office or five-star hotel?" We admired the modern décor and posh furniture. "Wonder how many ladies' water has broken in those chairs?"

Dani elbowed me. "Shush, that's disgusting," but a smile cracked her mouth.

I pointed. "Oh, go on, have a seat, my lady."

She shook her head. "Not on your life. I'll wait for you."

We stepped up to the receptionist. "Good morning, may I help you?"

I smiled. "Yes, I'm Alissa Franklin, and I have an eight o'clock appointment with Dr. DeMario."

The receptionist's fingers clicked on the keyboard. I've never seen nails that long ever. I glanced at Dani who intentionally avoided my gaze and concentrated on the counter in front of us. The corner of her lips twitched, so I knew she knew what I was thinking.

"Okay, Mrs. Franklin, here's the new patient packet to fill out." She pushed the clipboard toward me.

I pushed it right back and smiled. "I've already filled all of this out prior to the appointment."

She frowned. "Okay, let me check on that. May I have your insurance card, please?"

"I'll pay cash for services."

She cocked an eyebrow. "You don't have insurance?"

I bit my lip and smiled. "Yes, I have insurance."

"May I have your card, please?"

"No, I will pay cash for Dr. DeMario's services."

The receptionist leaned on the counter. "Miss, do you know how much it costs to have a baby?"

I leaned in but Dani interjected. "Excuse me, hi, I'm Dani Miscato. Pleased to meet you." She extended her hand and shook the receptionist's hand. "This is an exceptional circumstance as Ms. Franklin is my surrogate. I'm paying for her doctor bills, so this will not be going through insurance."

The receptionist sat back in her chair. "I see. Go ahead and have a seat, and I'll have the business manager come talk to you."

294

I gritted my teeth and followed Dani to a set of chairs under a piece of abstract art that looked like the color orange had vomited into a silver platter. "If that drips on me, you're paying the dry cleaning bill," I muttered.

She giggled. "You know she thinks we're lesbians, right?"

"I don't give a shit what she thinks. Did you see how she looked at me? 'You don't have insurance?' Bitch, please."

Dani shushed me and put her hand over her mouth. "She can probably hear you, Lis."

I rolled my eyes and whispered, "I could pay for the whole damn thing right now. Why would she—"

A pretty woman with long, curly hair walked toward us with a file in her hand. My file. The one I'd spent hours filling out to avoid this stupid interrogation. She extended her hand. "Ms. Franklin, I'm Janice; we've exchanged phone calls and emails."

I stood and shook her hand. "Janice, it's nice to meet you. This is Dani, the baby's mother." I swallowed around the knot formed in my throat as they shook hands.

"Come on back to my office so we can finalize a few things. It's more comfy there." She shrugged and wrinkled her nose before she turned to guide us toward her office.

I looked at Dani and mimicked Janice's actions before following her. Dani giggled, grabbed my arm, and whispered, "Alissa Franklin, you need to calm down."

I whispered back, "I freaking hate OB offices. Like a lot."

She nodded and asked, "Do you think we should hold hands when we walk past the reception desk?"

I chuckled. "Kiss me, and I'm outta here."

We entered Janice's office and admired the spacious yet efficient setting. We took our seats in front of her desk and waited for her to begin the spiel. She didn't waste a moment before placing a stack of documents in front of me to begin the "initial here/sign here" regimen. The last document was authorization allowing the doctor to discuss concerns with me or the baby with Dani. I frowned. "Why do you need this? I'm right here. I mean, I'll be here the whole time."

Janice chose her words carefully. "This would be in the event that you're not okay. Or, if you have questions or issues and Dani wants to call the doctor for you."

I signed the paper and let it go. Janice flipped through my papers. "Who is Chance Bradley?" She looked at me.

"My best friend," I replied. "Why?"

"You've got her listed as your emergency contact." She pointed her pen at Dani and asked, "Shouldn't we include Dani on there as well?"

"Yes, of course. Habit." I smiled. "Chance has been my emergency contact for some time." I glanced at Dani who smiled and winked.

Janice said, "Okay, the last thing we need to discuss is payment." She looked up and smiled. "We understand you are choosing not to use your insurance and wish to pay cash."

I smiled a little too widely for the nature of this conversation. "Yes, that's right. I believe you and I have already done a preliminary explanation of expenses. I'd like to go ahead and pay that estimate now, and we'll settle up the balance after the baby is born." I grabbed my checkbook out of my purse and locked eyes with Janice. "Is that satisfactory?"

Janice blinked twice and nodded. "Yes, I think that would be fine."

"Good," I said as I wrote out the check. I snapped the pen down on the desk. "I presume this is the last time we'll have the awkward moments with the receptionist regarding payment, correct? Should I take a picture of this check and post it next to her computer monitor?"

Dani mumbled, "Lis . . ."

I sat back and watched Janice grab the check before the ink was even dry. She said, "We'll have to do preauthorization for a check this large."

I waved her off. "Want me to tell you the balance on that account, Janice? You'd be impressed."

Dani squeezed my leg. "Lis!"

I folded my arms over my chest and tapped my foot as I looked at the clock. "It's 8:30, Dani."

Janice glanced at the clock and made a phone call. "I have Ms. Franklin in my office. We've just finished up, so if you're ready for her . . . very good, I'll tell her." She hung up. "They're ready for you." She stood and reached for my hand. "I'm glad to finally meet you, Ms. Franklin. I think it's very noble what you're doing for your friend and want this to be as rewarding for you as it is for her. Please don't be angry for the procedures. It's just policy we all have to follow."

I nodded. "I understand. Thank you."

They led Dani and me to an examination room complete with ultrasound equipment and a shelf full of pregnancy magazines. Dani was in literary heaven, and I was drowning in my anger. "I have to pee. I'll be right back." She nodded but didn't speak. This was becoming her go-to move. Don't speak around the dragon; you might get an ass full of flames. I stepped into the hallway and right into the chest of the best smelling man I'd ever had the pleasure of sniffing. I rolled my eyes up to see a strong chin and green eyes staring down at me.

He said, "Excuse me," in a deep voice that rumbled in my belly. "Are you all right?"

I stuttered, "Good heavens, thank you *Jesus*. Yes, I'm fine. I'm sorry. I'm headed to the bathroom."

His eyes cut to the left as he pointed. "Right around the corner."

I took a few steps back still looking at this fantastic display of manhood and prayed like hell that he wasn't my obstetrician. While I wouldn't mind getting naked for him, I sure didn't want it to be so he could size up my cervix. I grinned and turned to walk to the bathroom but nearly walked into a wall. I didn't bother looking back at him; in my mind, he hadn't seen my mishap.

I finished my business and washed my hands. I smoothed my hair and patted at my eyeliner hoping I'd see Mr. HotBod in the hallway again. I glanced down at my bulging belly and snickered at the absurdity of it all. I whispered in the mirror, "Hi, I'm Alissa. I'm carrying the baby of a failed relationship, but would you like to go out sometime?" I rolled my eyes and walked back to the room with my eyes trained on the floor.

As my hand reached the doorknob, another man approached me. "Ms. Franklin?"

"Yes?"

He extended his hand. "I'm Dr. DeMario."

I smiled and sighed with relief. "Oh thank God. Would you like to step into my office?"

He laughed. "You're stealing my lines already. After you." He held the door open for me and greeted Dani. "Mrs. Miscato, it's nice to meet you."

Dani corrected him, "It's Ms., now. I'm recently divorced."

He nodded. "Sorry to hear that. Been there. It's tough." He clapped his hands. "Okay, Ms. Franklin, let's get down to business." He flipped through my chart. "I don't see that you had a morphology prior to leaving Missouri." He looked up at my blank face and smiled. "The big ultrasound looking at all of the body structures in the baby."

"Oh, no, I haven't had an ultrasound since the very first one when I found out I was pregnant."

He grinned. "Well, today is your lucky day. Would you like to see your baby?"

I glanced up at him and smiled, but he was looking at Dani. Of course. I asked, "Do I need to remove my clothes?"

He smiled. "If you're wearing elastic waistbands, we might be okay."

I laughed. "Oh honey, I don't wear elastic waistband anything. Except yoga pants."

He smiled. "Well, your life is about to change." He held my gaze longer than I'd expected. He was boyishly cute with cavernous dimples on each cheek and didn't look a day over forty.

A day over forty.

When did I start judging men's ages at forty? Probably when I turned thirty-four and forbade anyone handsome to be younger than me.

I snapped out of it and looked at him. "I'm sorry, could you repeat that?"

He looked sideways at me and repeated, "You're in excellent shape, and obviously take care of yourself, so you may not experience the same discomfort in pregnancy that others do."

I looked at Dani who raised an eyebrow and smirked but left it at that.

He said, "Go ahead and lean back and get comfortable. I'm going to listen to the baby's heartbeat, and then we'll do an ultrasound."

I stared at the tiles in the ceiling and asked, "Why don't doctors put fun pictures on the ceilings in examination rooms?"

He slipped a stethoscope from his pocket. "Probably because we never think about it. We're always looking at patients not ceilings."

"Well someone should think about it."

"I'll be sure to pass the word." He slipped the stethoscope in his ears and slid it around my belly. "How far along are you?"

"Twenty-three weeks, I think."

Dani said, "Twenty-four, Lis."

I looked at the doctor. "Twenty-*four* weeks, Dr. DeMario."

He chuckled. "Moms are good about keeping track of that." He gave Dani thumbs up.

Ouch. Damn.

He finished his examination and turned to the ultrasound machine. "Let's see if the baby will show us something."

He rolled the instrument over my stomach, and the image of a growing baby appeared on screen. Dani slid next to me and grabbed my hand. "Look, Lis, there's the baby." Perfectly rounded little head, little hands, little fingers . . . precious.

The doctor said, "Everything looks good. Do you want to know what you're having?"

Dani and I looked at each other in shock. We'd never discussed if we wanted to find out the gender. Her eyes grew as wide as her smile. "What do you think?"

I breathed, "Hell yes, I want to know!"

She looked at the doctor. "What is it?"

He moved the instrument a few more times and pointed to the screen. "That is a very proud little boy."

Relief poured out of me in waves of laughter. A boy. It's a boy. The curse has been broken. Fuck you, Mom. It's a boy, and he's going to be fine and normal and perfect and unburdened by the female curse in our family. I buried my face in my hands as my laughter turned to tears and sobs replaced my guffaw. Dani rubbed my hand. "Shhh, it's okay, Lis."

Dr. DeMario quizzically looked from Dani to me and back. "Is there something I'm missing?"

I pointed to Dani and let her take the lead on the lie. "We had a bet . . . nothing, never mind."

"A boy," I whispered. Thank You, God. Thank You, Thank You.

"A boy," Dani repeated.

The rest of the appointment was a blur to me. They gave Dani instructions for my glucose screening, made my follow-up appointment, and I followed behind like a lost-but-found puppy. The mid-morning Florida sun matched the glow I felt inside. A boy. I grinned and looked at Dani. "It's a boy, Dani."

She smiled and handed me my purse. "Yes it is, Lis."

I dug for my keys. "Holy shit, we need to celebrate. Call Chance and tell her to get ready."

Chapter Thirty-Six
Against the Wind

Chance

Two weeks. Two weeks of sleeping 'til I'm ready to wake up—uninhibited by schedules, alarm clocks, appointments, interviews, or responsibility. I could get used to this. As much as I wanted this lap of luxury, it was a little lumpy at first. I'm definitely the flexible one in the bunch, but even I was having trouble peeling off the layers of "be-here-go-there-now" life. Alissa had a head start on us, though, since she quit her job well before Dani and me.

I spent my mornings walking the beach with Chubs, drinking coffee in my favorite spot and staring at the waves of the ocean. Dani and Alissa respected my need for alone time in the mornings and let me be. We all had our "Saturday morning" routine back home, and each of us slipped into that then came back together after ten o'clock every day. When I was alone on the beach, I thought of Tony. It's funny—this is where I was intending to forget him, yet he was everywhere I looked. His chuckle lapped with the waves, his sighs mixed with the wind, and his eyelashes blinked with the feathery clouds. I accepted this on day three and welcomed his presence in my morning routine. He really would love it here—he's always wanted to vacation in Florida.

Correction: he wanted a honeymoon in Florida. The first time he mentioned it, I laughed 'til I cried. We'd been lying in my bedroom. It was a bitter cold day, so we stayed under my down-filled comforter naked all day and only got up to pee and eat. You can't eat in my bed. Just . . . no. Or pee for that matter.

It was like a scene out of a perfect romance movie. My grey walls created a soft background lit up by the snowstorm outside. His head was buried in my pillow—the blankets pulled up to his chin, and all I could see was the right side of his face. I stared at the day-old stubble on his cheek, the contour of his cheekbone and jaw line. He was pure perfection wrapped in human skin. Every time he opened his eye to look at me, my stomach flopped and I grinned. It became a game.

He opened his eye again. "How many times are you going to do that?"

I smiled. "What?"

"Smile just because I look at you."

I made a mad face. "Is this better?"

He laughed. "No, but I think I just wet myself."

I smiled. "What were you thinking about?"

He looked at me. "Want me to tell you the truth?"

I leaned up and put my head on my hand. "Of course. This oughta be good."

He sighed and rolled onto his back. "I was thinking about our honeymoon."

My heart paused then slammed against my chest. "Our what?"

He glanced at me and grinned. "You heard me."

I chuckled. "Okay, I'll play along. Where are we?" I rolled onto my back and closed my eyes. "Set the scene."

He took a deep breath and curled up next to me. He slid his head onto my pillow, his arm across my stomach, and whispered, "It's eighty-two degrees outside. You're stunning in a white bikini that barely covers your tan breasts. . ."

I mumbled, "Ain't no way in hell I'm ever wearing a white bikini . . ."

"Hush. It's my fantasy."

I bit my lips and waved him on. He continued to rub circles on my stomach. The blood in my veins matched his rhythm as my chest swelled with anticipation. I curled my toes and took a deep breath to calm the hell down. His hand slid down my hip and across my thigh. I gritted my teeth to keep from pouncing. He whispered, "The palm trees swoon in the ocean's breath." He pulled the comforter from my chest and huffed his hot breath between my breasts—his chin stubble grazed my nipple and a whimper escaped my throat.

302

"Not nice," I breathed.

He chuckled. "You're lying on a beach chair slicked with the tanning oil I've rubbed all over your body." His hands moved over my skin, up my body, and across my cheek. "God, you're beautiful."

I swallowed hard and asked, "Where is this magical place?"

He leaned into my ear and slowly whispered, "Florida."

A hundred tropical majesties had appeared in my mind—Tahiti, Jamaica, but Florida was unexpected. I burst into laughter and the harder I tried to quit, the harder I laughed. I glanced at his face then laughed harder at his confusion. I tried to speak, but words wouldn't form. He chuckled and asked, "Why is that funny?"

I wiped my eyes and waved him off. "I . . . I don't know." I wrapped my arms around his neck and curled against his chest as the laughter poured out. He laughed with me and from that day forward, we had a one-word inside joke that instantly sent both of us into hysterics— "Florida."

I sat on the sand and ran my hand through the grains just like I used to run my hand through his patch of chest hair. I wrote "Florida" in the sand with my finger and sighed. Now I see why he wanted to vacation here. Well, one of us made it at least. I squinted against the wind and pinched back the tingle in my nose. No more tears. I grabbed my coffee cup and whistled for Chubs. He abandoned his post just this side of the wet sand and ran to me. I picked him up, shook the sand off his feet, and kissed his head. "My sweet boy." I rinsed my feet and padded into the house to shower and wait for Alissa and Dani to return.

I really thought when I came to Florida, I'd have so many distractions and fun things to do I'd have no time to think about Tony. Or our failed relationship. Or my part in that. But mostly Tony. I decided today was the last day I would allow myself to think about him at all. I could practice Alissa's tried-and-true methods of avoidance and eventually reprogram my mind to consider thoughts of Tony to be added calories. For every minute I thought of him, I'd convince myself I'd gain a pound. Yes, that will work. Today I'll binge on thoughts of him, but tomorrow he'll be cut from my mental diet. No tears though. No more tears.

I was ten minutes deep into The Breakup Mix playlist and covered in body wash when Dani's ringtone cut the music and interrupted my Tony memory buffet. Dread took the place of annoyance. This must be bad. I slipped out of the shower, suds and all, and grabbed the phone. "Dani?"

She giggled. "Don't sound so worried. We're ten minutes out. Alissa wants you to be ready to roll when we get there."

I took a deep breath. "Sure, is she okay?"

"Oh yes, she's fine. See you in a bit."

I sat the phone down and finished my shower in record time. Dani sounded way too happy, so there must be good news in there somewhere. Maybe it's twins. I shuddered with the thought and looked at Chubs. "What do you think, Chubs? Think they've been drinking without me?" I dressed and dried my hair enough to make it look like I didn't just jump out of the shower before twisting it up in a loose bun. Two soft curls fell and framed my face. Tony loved it when I wore my hair up—he liked to twirl his fingers in those very curls that bounced beside my face. God, that man adored me, and I blew it. I finished my makeup and headed downstairs to wait on the deck for whatever that carload of crazy was bringing my way.

Exactly ten minutes later, Alissa and Dani walked up all grins and chattering like squirrels. I studied Alissa's eyes—the telltale window to her soul and found euphoria. I raised my eyebrows and grinned. "Good news today?"

Alissa climbed the stairs and threw her arms around me. "It's a boy, Chance. He's a boy. Like, not a girl."

I hugged her and laughed. "Well yeah, that's usually what a boy means. Oh, thank God." I hugged her tighter and whispered, "That's great, Alissa."

She nodded but didn't speak as she pulled away from me. "Let's celebrate!"

I waved my hands across my body. "I'm ready for anything. Where to?"

She grabbed my hand and handed me the keys. "Everywhere. We've got shopping to do."

A boy. She's having a boy. The curse is broken, and before me stood my friend. She reappeared before me as though God Himself had draped an Alissa cloth over her and stripped away the anxious woman she'd become. We drove through Naples singing at the top of our lungs and laughing when someone flubbed the words. We Googled every baby shop in Naples and didn't give two shits when I turned on the wrong road and ended up on a one-way street. Even Dani was laughing and seemed to be her old self again. If these two could do it, so could I. The countdown to being Tony-free was on.

We walked through charming boutiques and oogled over extremely overpriced clothing while loading our arms with the must-have items for a child that we wouldn't even meet for at least fourteen more weeks.

I tossed Alissa's bags in the trunk of the Navigator. "Um, this trunk was pretty packed on the way down here. How are we going to fit all this in here and a baby?"

"We're going to strap you to the luggage rack," Alissa said. "We already talked about it."

"Oh nice. I'll be the figurehead of the highway."

Dani laughed. "Yes, but you'll be so pretty with your flowing hair."

I pointed at her. "I'll look much prettier on a flight."

Alissa laughed. "I figured I'd ship a bunch of stuff home a few weeks before we leave so it will be there when we get back." She looked at me. "Chubs won't mind FedEx, right?"

"Ha-ha, very funny. I'm starving. Anyone else hungry?"

Dani faked a faint. "Dear God, feed me before I implode."

Alissa raised her hand. "Count me in for two for lunch."

We decided on Olive Garden—hardly Florida ethnic, but we all wanted soup, salad, and breadsticks. When Dani excused herself to the bathroom, I swooped in on Alissa. "Okay, we have four minutes. Spill it."

She smiled. "It's a boy, Chance. I feel like I could fly to the moon and back shouting to the heavens how grateful I am that this baby isn't a girl."

"I know that part, but what about the rest?"

Alissa patted my hand. "We'll talk about all that later. Right now, we celebrate the breaking of my family's curse."

I've always admired Alissa's ability to turn her emotions on and off like a light switch. One little flip and she just quits feeling. She's the queen of being able to enjoy a moment and not allow anything else to interfere with that little sliver of time when she's happy. I could learn a lot from her. But not today. Tomorrow. We'll work on that tomorrow when I start my Tony detox. I looked at her. "Today is the last day I'm going to think about Tony."

She sipped her water. "Think you'll be able to pull that off?"

I shrugged. "Sure. You can do it, so I can too." I smiled and picked up my glass. "Cheers. Here's to new starts all around."

Dani returned to the table and asked, "Did I just miss a toast?"

I smiled and lifted my glass. "I'm toasting to new starts. Tomorrow, I'm done thinking about Tony."

She arched an eyebrow. "But not today?"

I smirked. "Well, I just mentioned his name, so technically I can't start 'til tomorrow, right?"

She sipped her water. "Or you could just call him." She peered over her glass and winked.

I sat my glass on the table. "No, that's not how this works. In this chess game of love, I'm black, and he's white. Which means one of us loses in the end."

Alissa pointed at me. "But you hate to lose."

I offered my best change-the-subject grin. "Indeed I do."

Dani asked, "What if he's changed his mind and that's why he keeps trying to contact you?"

I swiveled in my chair and mumbled, "Where *is* that waiter?" I looked at Dani and slumped in my chair. "I don't know, Dani. Can we please change the subject? Let's talk baby names."

I ignored Dani's searching eyes and eventual glance at Alissa who nodded and gave me reprieve. Dani took the cue. "Baby names? Gosh, I have no idea. I can give you a list of names it won't be, would that help?"

I winked. "Crossing off all the names of the douchebags we've dated or married over the years would be a nice place to start."

Alissa chuckled. "That ain't no lie."

"I've always liked traditional names," Dani said.

"Like George, Albert, or Ralph?" I winked at Alissa who laughed into her napkin.

"Oh, God, please not anything like that, Dani," she gasped. "Otto." She laughed again.

Dani laughed. "No, nothing like that. Names like Jacob, Edward . . ."

I interrupted, "Or Carlisle or. . . Alissa, what was that other vampire's name in Twilight?"

She whimpered through a giggle, "Jasper."

I slammed my hand on the table. "Jasper! Yes!"

Dani waved at the waiter. "Excuse me, I'm going to need some wine to put up with these two today." She pointed at me. "Are you in?"

"Hell yes, I'm in. Bring a bottle." I bit my lips and gave Dani my best puppy dog eyes. "I'm just kidding."

She waved her napkin at me. "Oh, stop with the big eyes. You creep me out when you do that. I'll have to think about the name. Alissa, what do you think about using your last name somewhere?"

"Franklin? Oh, hell no. I don't want to punish the little guy like that." She turned to me. "I have an idea."

I frowned. "The last time you said that, I had to change careers and zip codes."

She laughed. "No nothing like that. The best way to get over one guy is to. . ." She extended her hand to me to finish.

"Buy fabulous shoes and eat ice cream for supper?"

She slouched. "No. You need to find another guy. One down here. A hot Floridian would take your mind off he-who-shan't-be-named."

My stomach dropped, but I played along. "Should I stand next to a construction site and fake a broken ankle?"

"Be serious, will ya? Think about it. You meet a new guy; he sweeps you off your feet, and whammo. You'll be saying 'Tony who' in no time."

Like that would ever happen. "So I'm going to find someone else to play with and potentially break his heart to get over *my* broken heart? Need I remind you I'm only going to be here for few more months then we're going back to Missouri?" Sure. Fall for a guy that lives far away. No, that doesn't sound familiar at all.

"You don't have to go back to Missouri," Dani said.

Alissa gaped at her. "Um, yes she does. If she stays, I stay. And if I stay, you stay. So . . . oh! I got it. What about online dating?"

"What? Ew, gross! No way."

Dani leaned across the table. "Chance, listen to me. You are stunningly beautiful, smart, and sharp as a tack. It won't take long for you to find someone if you put yourself out there. But I'm begging you to forget she ever mentioned online dating."

I laughed. "Already forgotten. How the hell did we make this turn back to me? I thought we were picking out baby names." The waiter showed with the wine. "Oh thank god. Pour it up, bartender."

Alissa said, "I'll stick with water, but thank you."

He grinned at her. "No celebrating for you?"

She offered a sly smile. "Not today."

He stared a little longer than normal and nearly overfilled my glass. I said, "I hate to interrupt, but that whole bottle won't fit in my glass."

He pulled back the bottle and moved to Dani's side with a blush creeping up his neck. After he filled Dani's glass to an appropriate height, he took our order and scurried to the kitchen to retrieve our salads and his ego.

I shook my head. "Alissa, he could be your boy-toy while you're in Florida."

She laughed. "Yeah, because single guys are super hot to bang a pregnant lady."

I smirked. "You never know. At least he knows he can't knock you up."

She turned to Dani. "What about you? Think you'll start dating anytime soon?"

She waved us off while sipping her wine. "I have no interest in going back down that road. Besides, I'm about to meet the perfect male. And if *he* pees on the floor, I can spank his ass."

I glanced at Alissa to see her reaction, but she took it in stride. Maybe she really is doing okay with all this. I looked at Dani. "I get where you're coming from. There's a lot of appeal to being single."

Dani nodded. "When Barry left, I felt like I was staring at this vacant black hole of a future. Same day, day after day, only to wake up the next morning and realize it was going to be the same day all over again." Her eyes misted. "But when Alissa . . . now it feels like that last perfect piece has completed my puzzle."

Alissa smiled at Dani and asked, "You're not nervous at all?"

Dani chuckled. "Nervous? I'm scared to death! What if I can't make him stop crying? What if I get sick? What if *he* gets sick? This is all so foreign to me, but I know mothers do it every day, and I want this so badly."

I said, "And, we'll all be around to help you, too. It's not like you're going to be alone in this. Katie and Michelle have years of experience and itchy palms for babies."

Alissa said, "And, I'll still be in the picture. Not a leading character. More like a best supporting actress." She grinned. "It will be fun to buy boy stuff for a change."

An awkward silence drifted across the table. Dani and I sipped our wine while Alissa stared longingly at my glass. I threw off wine etiquette, drank a little faster, then refilled the glass.

Alissa grinned. "Someone's on a mission."

"What? It's good wine."

Alissa mumbled, "Mmhmm. Okay, I'll break the ice. Dani, we probably need to talk about the boundaries when the baby is born."

I peered over the rim of my glass and took another drink. I alternated watching the two mothers' faces and waited to see how this showdown would go. Dani glanced at Alissa and cleared her throat. "I don't know what boundaries are appropriate, Lis. I've spent a lot of time thinking about this, probably more than you'd give me credit for." She smiled. "I've wondered if joint custody would be better than a total adoption." She held her breath and waited for Alissa's reaction. I held my breath, too.

Alissa frowned. "No, I don't think that's an option, and here's why. I think a child needs a mother—one mother. I can be the cool aunt who swoops in and makes you look like the overbearing jackass."

Dani's relief poured out in her giggle. "Would you like to hear something that plagues me?"

Alissa sat back. "What?"

"What if he looks just like you? There'll be no denying anything if that happens."

Alissa's face blanched. "I hadn't thought of that."

I fanned my face and wiped my lip. "Damn, wine always makes me so hot." I refilled my wine glass. "Look. Alissa, no offense, but I think your ego is inflated a little bit. You may be one of the wealthiest women in Columbia, but no one really knows that. The only people who may put two and two together already know your big secret. And besides, there's no shame in admitting that you surrogated Dani's baby if people start asking questions. No one has to know that you got knocked up by Señor Fucknut."

Dani chuckled. "You're so eloquent when you're drunk."

I gasped and spat, "I am not drunk. It's midday. I don't get drunk during daylight hours."

Alissa pointed at the bottle of wine. "You've downed half that bottle in less than ten minutes. You might rethink your last statement."

I looked for the waiter. "I just need to eat. What the hell takes so long to get fucking salads on a plate?"

Alissa shushed me. "Chance, it's the lunch rush. We're not in a hurry, but if you keep that pace, you'll be passed out and miss the sunset."

I scowled at her. "I'll be fine after lunch." I reached for my water. "I'm not drinking this because you suggested I slow down. I'm thirsty."

Alissa laughed. "Okay, Chance. It's your reality. Live it how you like." She winked at Dani. "Ten bucks says she's passed out by seven."

"You're on."

After lunch and another bottle of wine at the house, I was toast by suppertime. I participated in the walk of shame to my room and threw myself on the bed to end my misery. I made a mental note to either quit drinking altogether or start drinking more to build up a tolerance—at that moment, I was voting for never drinking again. Damn that wine.

Chapter Thirty-Seven
The Song Remembers When

Michelle

Three Months Later

I gave Brandon's T-shirt a few hard flips then smoothed it against my stomach. The evidence of my failure to fold laundry for a week rippled across the shirt. I sighed and tossed it in the re-tumble basket that was already overflowing. This pile of laundry was the last thing to tick off the to-do-before-my-flight list. My bags were packed, four days of food were prepared in the fridge, and Katie had already texted me four times today counting down the hours. The plan was for her to pick me up right after work, head to the airport and be in Naples by nine-thirty tonight.

My thirty-fifth birthday was last Saturday, March 14. It was a moderately uneventful day, but the cake was good. Brandon gave me money for clothes and the green light to go visit my friends in Florida. I made a plan with Katie before he could change his mind. We could have gotten cheaper tickets if we'd waited, but since we both still had our gift certificates from Alissa, we jumped on the phone and online to book our tickets at the same time. We used to do that exact thing when the new *Teen* magazine came out. We had a strict rule we wouldn't open or read it until we were both on the phone.

A few weeks after the new year, I called Katie and asked her to meet me for coffee. After five minutes of apologies, we slipped into our old routine and made a vow to meet weekly while our friends were gone, and we've stuck to it. With them being gone, it would be even easier for me to slip into isolation mode, but after my breakdown in December, I was adamant to follow through with taking care of myself. Brandon was a little huffy the first time he had to take Gibson to a Saturday morning basketball game so I could keep my appointment with Katie, but even he had realized the importance of my need to see her.

Gradually, Brandon and I slipped back into the same old routine. We tried to be more flirtatious and affectionate for a few weeks after "the incident," but when it became forced, we both silently agreed to go back to normal. Conversations revolve mostly around the kids and kitchen, but at least I don't feel like peeling his face with the cheese grater anymore.

My last attempt to catch his attention was a huge fail. I snuck off to a lingerie store on Valentine's Day and bought a teddy to surprise him at bedtime. We exchanged valentines, shipped the kids off to my parent's house for the night, and went out to a nice dinner. I dressed to kill wearing a low-cut black sweater, new jeans, black boots, and my first matching bra and panty set. I was rocking my new haircut that framed my face and made me look youthful again. I was on a mission to dazzle my man.

I'm sure it would have worked if he'd actually looked at me.

Dinner was nice, but conversation involved three-word questions and simple answers. Trying to find something new to talk about with someone you've known since high school was tougher than I thought. He knew better than to shoptalk with me since I'd bit his head off one too many times, and there's only so many times you can describe a workout before it bores even the instructor. I felt my evening crashing and burning but couldn't wait to get home and model my teddy. I had a few new tricks up my sleeve. I've been reading.

My palms started sweating on the way home as I tried to recall my plan. I watched Brandon out of the corner of my eye and felt my face flush. I almost talked myself out of it, but I recited the order of events as I had them listed in my head and waited for the headlights to hit the garage.

Brandon turned off the car. "Ah, home, sweet home."

I smiled. "Even better, we're alone."

He smirked. "That we are."

We went inside, took off our coats, and Brandon headed to the bathroom mumbling about the stupid beer. I took my opportunity and scurried into our bedroom. I stripped off my clothes and retrieved my

313

ornamentation hoping I could remember how to put this garment of strings and patches on my body. The red thong rested on my hips and attached to the bra with two thin ribbons meant to provide some semblance of a garment. The red lace left little to the imagination, but my tits looked fabulous. I stood back from the mirror and admired my body wrapped in pure sex appeal. I fluffed my hair, applied lipstick (which was part of my plan. Lipstick stains on underwear, prints on the stomach— oh yeah, he was about to be rocked.). I smoothed the blankets on the bed and practiced my sexy pose. I repositioned the mirror so it would be visible from the bed (yet another trick I learned this week) and slid back into the bed. I stared at the cobwebs on the curtains, looked at the ceiling fan, studied the basket of clothes sitting on top of the dresser, checked Facebook, and fluffed the pillows—still no Brandon.

I threw on my robe and snuck into the hallway. The bathroom was empty and the television in the living room was blasting a commercial about erectile dysfunction. I smirked at the irony and peeked at Brandon's chair. He tipped back a bottle of beer and sighed with delight. I raised my eyebrows and thought the plan could easily begin in the living room and might even be hotter in execution. I sashayed into the living room and took my place on the couch. I let my robe fall apart revealing my freshly-shaved legs and painted toenails, which was such a rarity for me, I nearly turned *myself* on just by looking at them. I tilted my head so I could see Brandon's face with a stolen glance. He stared at the television and took another pull on the bottle.

I tried my sexy voice. "What are you watching?"

He pointed at the screen. "I don't know, some reality show."

I adjusted my position and allowed my robe to fall open a little more. "Is it good?"

He shrugged. "Nothing special."

That was my cue to make my move. I stood and slinked across the room to stand between him and the television. I looked into his eyes. "I may have something special for you." I loosened the robe belt and let it fall open revealing a very different body than he was accustomed to seeing.

He grinned. "Wow, that's . . . quite a get-up."

I swallowed around the lump in my throat and let the robe fall to the ground. My heart pounded against my breastbone no doubt making my boobs jump. I assumed it would be an added bonus for a little breast jiggle under these circumstances. I turned to the television revealing my thong and sexily turned my head to look over my shoulder. He stared at my ass then met my eyes. I asked, "Are you sure you want to watch this show? I may have something better in mind."

He said, "Sure, I'll be in in a minute."

I swear I heard the record scratch as the music of my sexcapade stopped. I blinked and turned to look at him. "I'm sorry?"

He looked at the television and looked at me. "That looks great on you. You've really toned up a lot. Looking good, babe." He smiled and looked at the television again.

I stared at him and felt humiliation brewing in my gut. I wouldn't be swayed, though, so I altered my plan and went for phase two. I slid between the coffee table and his chair and leaned over him. I donned my best seductive look and whispered, "I'm certain what I'd like to do to you is much more enjoyable." I slid my hand down his chest and played with the button on his pants. I met his surprised eyes and grinned. "Should I stop?"

He waved. "Be my guest."

I repositioned myself and prepared to pleasure my husband in a way I rarely performed. I never have been much of a fan of giving oral sex. I always felt like a one-year-old with its first Snickers bar. I just never quite got the hang of it, so I never did it. But, I'd been studying, and I wanted to show off my newly acquired skills.

My new methods were effective—highly effective. Too effective. Two minutes later, Brandon sprawled out breathless with his fingertips embedded in the chair arms. And since Brandon had always been a one-shot wonder, I knew my chances of getting laid on Valentine's Day had just ended in my mouth. He never even touched my new teddy or any other part of my body for that matter. He stared at me with glassy eyes and a goofy grin spread across his face as I stood. "All three of you are beautiful."

I smirked and offered my final surprise for the night. I said, "Would you like to return the favor?" I slipped my foot on the chair arm revealing my crotchless panties and everything they weren't supposed to cover.

He chuckled. "I can't even move right now. Give me a minute."

I lowered my leg and hopes and headed to retrieve my robe and a glass of wine from the kitchen. I guzzled the first glass trying to cleanse my bruised ego and console my disappointment. I poured my second glass and heard the gurgle of his first snore. This game was officially over.

He tried to make up for it the next morning, but I was too embarrassed to let him touch me. I pretended to be asleep then hung over. Okay, that part wasn't exactly a lie, but I wasn't that bad. I was in punishment mode. It wasn't supposed to go down like that, pardon the pun. It ended up being one of the most memorable nights in our marriage—each for two very different reasons. Within a week, though, we were right back to normal life around the house.

Only this time I wasn't planning his slow death with a steak knife.

At three-thirty, I hugged my kids for the sixteenth time, kissed Brandon on the cheek, and wheeled my luggage to Katie's car. We were only going to be gone four days, but we both packed like we were never coming back. She squealed when we pulled out of the driveway. "I can't believe we're doing this."

"I so need this right now."

She sighed. "Girl, me too. Part of me knows I'll be green with envy when I see the house."

I nodded. "You know it's going to be immaculate. I can't wait to see Lis's pregnant belly in person. When I see her on Skype, it's so foreign she looks Photoshopped."

Katie laughed. "I know, right? It just doesn't seem like it's real. Good lord I need this break."

I mumbled, "You and me both. Did you talk to Landon about playing softball again?"

316

She winced. "No, it hasn't really come up yet. It hasn't been a good time. He's been really busy—"

I interrupted, "So you pussied out."

She sighed. "Yes, I totally pussied out."

I shrugged. "Well, if you want to play, you're going to have to tell him quick-like."

"I know, I know. I just hate arguing with him."

"Look, Katie, take it from the pro of mental breakdowns. This is how it starts. You need to assert yourself and tell him what you need."

"I also believe compromise is important, and I totally see where he's coming from, Michelle."

I figured it best to change the subject. Bottom line: she won't play softball again this year because she's too scared to inconvenience Mr. Pampered Pants. If I hadn't been guilty of spending years doing the same thing, I'd probably be supportive of her submission. But I know what it did to me, and I would rather not watch her go through it. I said, "I intend to drink mimosas every morning til noon and margaritas til sunset."

She hummed. "Mimosas. God I haven't had mimosas in forever."

"I figure I'll sleep with Chance and you'll sleep with Dani. I think it's only a three bedroom."

"Fine with me. Chance snores."

"She can't be any worse than either of our husbands." I laughed.

"True, but if I'm on vacation, I'd rather not wake up wanting to suffocate someone like I do every other night of my life."

"Ah, finally some of that frost is thawing and my old friend Katie is showing up."

She giggled. "It takes me a minute, but I come back around."

I got a text from Alissa and said to Katie, "Alissa says she has a surprise for us at the airport."

"Wanna take bets on what it is?"

I rolled a few ideas through my head. "Well, it's pretty obvious she probably hasn't met anyone, so it can't be a dude."

She pointed at me. "Stranger things have happened. I'm saying it's a limo."

"Dammit, I bet you're right. It'll be late when we get to Fort Myers, and they probably don't want to drive.

"Or maybe Chance has met someone." Katie gasped. "Or Dani!"

I laughed. "Oh hell no. I would have heard about it by now."

She frowned. "Why would you hear about it and I wouldn't?"

I tried to figure out how to dodge the obvious and not confirm that Chance confides in me much more than she does Katie. Chance is a forgiving person, but she hadn't fully gotten over Katie's virtual betrayal during "the incident." I had to let it go, because I needed my friend. Chance didn't have to do shit and said so. I pushed the sleeves up on my arms. "I wish I'd tanned more before the trip."

Katie groaned. "I wish I'd tanned at all. I'm liable to burn the first day and spend the rest of our time slathered in aloe hiding under shade trees."

"Nah, you'll be fine. Just ease into it."

Six hours later, we slipped off the plane in Fort Myers and scanned the crowd for the faces of our dearest friends. I felt the wiggles of anticipation sliding through my stomach and took a deep breath. "Oh my gosh, Katie, I think I'm going to pee from excitement."

"I don't see them, do you?"

We walked through security and entered the waiting area. A man dressed in a dark suit held a sign that read, "Welcome to Florida, Katie and Michelle."

I grinned at Katie. "You were right."

She smiled. "Called it."

We approached the man and introduced ourselves. He showed us to the limo, took our luggage, and opened the door to the back seat. Inside, Chance, Dani, and Alissa screamed, "Surprise!" They crawled out of the limo and buried us in group hugs. I choked back my tears as Chance embraced me. "How ya doing, kiddo?"

I nodded and whispered, "I'm so glad to see you."

She pulled away from me and looked me up and down. She whistled. "Ladies, get a load of our Michelle Hot-Mama!"

"Oh I love your hair!" Alissa said. "And look at this body. Wow, Michelle, well done."

Dani took my hand. "You look lovely. It's so great to see you."

We crawled into the limo and twittered like birds in a nest. Katie and I marveled over Alissa's perfect basketball belly and listened as they told the same story from three different perspectives. It was just like old times and the fastest forty-five-minute drive I'd ever experienced.

The house. Wow. I didn't get to fully appreciate the outside since it was dark, but when I heard the ocean, I dropped my bags. I looked at Katie and grinned. We peeled out of our shoes and took off running down the boardwalk. We didn't stop until our feet were sinking into the Gulf of Mexico. I stared at the dancing waves illuminated by the moonlight and was spellbound by the soft sounds of surf. I couldn't wait to see the ocean in daylight. I turned to Chance and whispered, "This is the first time I've seen the ocean."

She linked her arm with mine. "Then I'm so glad I got to be here when you saw it, sister. Isn't it amazing? Wait till you see it from our balcony."

I looked at her. "Why the hell do we live in Missouri?"

She laughed. "I've asked myself that same question daily since we arrived, honey."

I turned to look at the house and whistled. "Damn, she did it up right."

"As usual," she said. "The inside is beautiful. But I spend most of my time out here." She looked at the ocean again and sighed. "It's just so peaceful."

I read that look on her face and felt my stomach drop. Tony's ghost had followed her here. I watched Katie, Dani, and Alissa on the porch waiting like soldiers on post for us to come up. I yelled, "Katie, are you already done out here?"

She gestured to the house. "Do you see this thing? I sure want to see what's inside. Come on!"

I grinned at Chance who said, "Come on. We've got time for all of it."

We were a little parade of Missourians admiring the incredible house chosen by Alissa. The three of them had acclimated well to the extravagant house and were comfortable—as well they should be. Katie and I kept locking eyes, and I knew she was thinking the same thing I was. There's no way I'd ever be comfortable living in a house this luxurious. I carried my suitcase to Chance's room and whistled. "Damn, girl. This is amazing."

She admired the room with me. "You get used to it. It took a few days to stop tiptoeing everywhere and washing my hands fifty thousand times a day."

I chuckled and took a deep breath. "I don't know how you'd ever get used to this."

She shrugged. "It's overwhelming at first, for real."

I looked over my shoulder when I heard Katie gasping down the hall. "They've found more rooms."

Chance smiled. "The other rooms are both impressive in their own ways. But that's what hooked me." She pointed to the double doors that led to the balcony. "Come on." She grabbed my hand and led me through them. Once again, I was spellbound by the view of the ocean through the palm trees. Solar lights illuminated the boardwalk and reminded me of the fairy garden I'd always wanted. Chance said, "You're going to love this at sunset."

"I still can't believe this morning I woke up in frigid Columbia and will go to bed in warm Naples."

"Gotta love modern transportation. How are things, honey? You good?"

I shrugged and smiled. "I'm great right now."

She tugged at my arm. "Now is good enough for me. Come on, let's go see what the others are doing."

We settled into our seats in the living room and took turns giving the five-minute overview of the last three months of our lives. Thanks to texting, Facebook, and Skype, we'd really never had much of a break in communication. But it was fun to hear the details often missed during quick chats. Once we'd covered the basics, the Q/A began.

I started. "Alissa, how've you been feeling?"

She smiled and rubbed her belly. "Like I'm pregnant with a street fighter."

I laughed. "Gibson was like that. I swore that kid was leaving bruises inside."

Dani chimed in, "He kicks hard! When he's really active, we wad up a tissue and see how far he can kick it off her stomach."

Alissa beamed, "He's done a pretty good job. Might have a future in the NFL."

Dani faked a shiver. "Oh goodness, I hope not. I really hope he's a book worm and plays piano."

We all laughed, and Katie said, "You'll be surprised when he starts playing sports. Some kind of internal killer mode kicks into place, and the next thing you know, you're rooting for your kid to draw blood."

I hitched a thumb at Katie. "True story. She went to one of Gibson's football games and yelled, 'Kill that kid, Gibson.'"

Katie buried her head in her hands. "That's not what I meant at all. It just slipped out."

I said, "Yeah, you've spent too much time watching games with Landon."

Alissa changed the subject and asked, "How's things at home with Brandon, now?"

I nodded. "Things are good. We still have some rocky days, but overall, I think things are good. I think he's going to live." I winked.

Chance asked, "Did you guys do anything special for your birthday last week?"

I shrugged. "No, not really. The kids were super cute and made me a cake, and I got gift cards, so that was a plus."

Dani asked, "Are you still liking the instructor gig?"

"I absolutely love it. I teach three classes a day. I'm definitely getting my workouts."

Alissa grinned. "I'm so glad your membership worked out like this. I can't get over how awesome you look."

I blushed. "It's been fun to feel the transformation."

We stayed up way too late and by the time I hit the sheets, I could barely keep my eyes open. I fell asleep listening to Chance talking about things we could do tomorrow and have no idea what she said.

Chapter Thirty-Eight
No Surprise

Alissa

I snuck out of bed and drew the curtains so Katie could sleep later. I slipped past Dani's room and hightailed it to the downstairs bathroom before I peed down both legs. If Dani heard the toilet flush upstairs, she'd be out of bed in no time to make sure I was okay. And she's never been one to go back to bed.

I grabbed a glass of orange juice and headed out to the beach to begin my morning routine of watching the world and feeling my baby wake up. In six short weeks, this would all be over, and my heart would be forever broken. At the recommendation of my therapist (who I called a few months ago in the midst of a full-blown meltdown), I've designated one part of my day to sit with my feelings, embrace them, and then move on with my day. I picked early morning. I tossed my blanket on the beach and began my routine.

I rubbed my belly and whispered, "You are so loved, little guy. More than anything, I want you to know I made this decision to save you. I just don't have good luck, and I don't want to drag you into my insanity. Chances are I'll fall in love again shortly after you're born, then he'll bolt. And it will happen again a few years later, and he'll figure out something he doesn't like about me, or worse, you, and I can't put you through that.

"Dani is so full of love for you already. She can't wait to meet you, hold you in her arms, kiss your sweet face, and give you a stability that I'm unable to provide. She'll be such a good mother to you, little guy. Just know that the day I hand you over, I'll die a little inside."

I wiped my face and watched the first peep of the sun as it illuminated the watery horizon. I started my chant, "Out with the sadness, in with peace. Out with sadness, in with peace." I patterned my breathing to match the words and smiled at my progress. The first several weeks, I couldn't say the words, "out with sadness," through my sobs.

Maybe my therapist is worth a damn after all. To say she didn't support my decision to give up my baby is an understatement. She could see my point just didn't agree with my logic. Seemed like semantics to me. I finished my catharsis and started my walk down the beach, the best part of my day. The first morning on the beach, I found a perfect seashell and put it in a glass bowl on the dresser in my room. Every morning, I search for one perfect seashell to add to the collection, which will go in the baby's room in Missouri. Dani's already promised me she'll keep it. I say a special prayer of blessing over my baby's life and wish for something different every day. Sometimes I tell a story of my pregnancy and envision the story attaching itself to the shell to be whispered to him in his sleep. It makes me feel better—less forgotten.

By the time I found the shell of the day, the full sun was smiling its good morning to me, the baby was kicking, and it was time to go in the house and let Dani feel him punch and wiggle. Watching her face is bittersweet, especially since she cries nearly every time he moves. I often tease her and ask which one of us is experiencing the pregnancy hormones most. I still think it's me. Totally me. I'm just a better actress.

Katie stood on the beach near my blanket with a cup of coffee and look of awe. "Pretty amazing, huh?"

She gasped. "It's breathtaking, Lis. My God, will you look at that?"

I walked up to her and shared the view. "I get to do this every morning, and it never looks the same or gets old."

"How will you ever be satisfied living in Columbia after this?"

I sighed. "I've thought the same thing a million times."

She looked at me. "You *are* coming back, right?"

I smiled. "Yes, I'm coming back."

She studied my face longer than I wanted. "Lis . . ."

I cut her off. "Don't, Katie. Don't say it. It's the right thing to do. For everyone involved."

She sighed. "Okay. I still . . . well, anyway. What are we going to do today?"

I gestured to the ocean and asked, "What more could you want?"

She giggled. "That's perfectly fine with me. I could be a beach bunny and be perfectly content. It's just unusual for you not to have a full itinerary in place."

I shrugged. "Sometimes slowing down and enjoying the moment has its perks."

"Florida looks good on you, Lis. I mean that."

I grinned. "And I make Florida look fabulous. Even with this big ol' belly."

"Oh it's such a cute belly, too," she laughed.

"I have to go in. Stay out here as long as you want. We're not going anywhere unless you guys decide to."

"Okay, I'll be in shortly. I want to sit out there and drink my coffee."

"I totally understand."

I walked up the boardwalk, washed my feet, and headed into the house to find Dani. She wiped the counters then moved to stir something on the stove. "Smells good, wifey."

She turned and grinned. "Thanks. It's a new recipe, an egg scramble something something. I thought we'd use the breakfast nook this morning and let Katie enjoy the view. What do you think?"

"I think that sounds great, but don't count on Michelle or Chance. You know they're probably up there spooning."

Dani laughed. "I highly doubt that."

Michelle walked down the stairs. "I heard that, bitch. And we weren't spooning, we were trying on each other's clothes and putting on makeup."

I said, "Okay, now I know you're lying. Chance hasn't worn makeup before eight since we got here."

Michelle padded to the coffee pot and inhaled. "Hello, my sweet, Colombian lover."

Dani pulled a cup out of the cabinet and handed her the sugar bowl. Michelle waved it off. "No sugar for me, thanks."

Dani blinked. "You've always put sugar in your coffee."

Michelle smiled. "Yeah, and I carried those sweet little calories around in fat rolls like the caffeinated trophies they were. I still use creamer though. Can't lose all the luxuries in life."

Dani pointed to the refrigerator. "Take your pick. We have a whole collection thanks to Chance."

Michelle asked, "What are you cooking? That smells fantastic."

I answered. "It's an egg scramble something something Dani found online." Dani turned and pointed the wooden spoon at me. I laughed. "Hey, I was just quoting you. I'm sure that's the technical name for it."

Dani shook her head. "We're going to call it the Dani Surprise. How's that?" She winked at Michelle and spooned the meal into four dishes. She left some in the skillet in case Chance made an appearance. I said, "If she isn't down by the time we're done eating, it's mine."

Dani waved. "At that point it will be fair game. I'm going to go ask Katie if she wants to join us."

Michelle and I grabbed our bowls and drinks then headed into the breakfast nook. Michelle whistled. "Man, this place just gets better and better." She chose a seat facing the windows and bounced up and down in the chair. "Comfy. Love this big, round table, too. Nice touch."

"I'm telling ya, they thought of everything."

She shoveled a bite into her mouth. "I don't even want to know how much this cost a month."

I chuckled. "Your table manners are phenomenal."

She flipped me the bird and wiped her mouth. "Does it have a workout room?"

I frowned and sat back in my chair. "No, actually, I don't think it does. Wait, does the indoor pool count?"

Michelle laughed. "Yes, I suppose I'll have to make do with that." She rolled her eyes.

"It doesn't get much use, honestly. We spend so much time on the beach, it seems silly to swim inside."

"You'll have to give me the grand tour outside after breakfast."

Katie squealed when she and Dani walked into the nook. "Isn't this the coolest room ever? I think I'd spend most of my time in here. This is so amazing." She touched the tropical plants that lined the glass walls and stared at the waves. "I don't know how you'd ever be satisfied living anywhere else after this."

Dani hummed. "It's going to be a huge adjustment, that's for sure. I spend a lot of time in here. It's funny; we all have our little places. Alissa likes a blanket on the beach, Chance likes her balcony, and I like this room. But, we all know I've never been fond of sweating."

We laughed as they took their seats and started eating. Katie asked, "So how's Chance doing with the whole Tony thing?"

I cleared my throat. "Well? She has good days and better days. She's going to be fine, though."

"Has she heard from him?" Katie asked.

I shrugged. "I don't think so. And she'd tell me if she did, so I'm going to say a confident no."

Michelle asked, "So is the plan still for you guys to come home May thirtieth?"

Dani took the reins on this one. The eternal planner. And I thought I was bad. "That's all going to depend on Alissa's recovery. But if she goes early, we could always leave early."

"What if she's late?" Katie asked.

"Oh she's not going to be late," Dani said. "If we don't have any action by the fourth, we're looking at induction."

Michelle laughed. "That doesn't surprise me at all."

"We have a schedule to keep, ya know." I smiled and tapped my wrist.

Dani winced. "Ouch."

I rubbed her hand. "Oh, now, I didn't mean that to be mean. We've always teased you."

She smiled, but I knew I'd pricked a wound. She looked at Michelle. "She can't go too much past the fourth because we have to be out of the house by the thirtieth. It's already rented for the rest of the summer." She glanced at me then focused on her breakfast.

Katie saw the tension and went into smooth-it-over mode. "Well, I think you are both handling this very well. I know Alissa's fully aware of the move-out date, and I know Dani is sympathetic to the situation, and the doctors will make the best decision based off Alissa's progress at the time. We just need to make sure the little fellow is fully cooked before he comes out of the oven."

Michelle asked, "Any progress on the name?"

I groaned. "No, we can't find one we agree on. I like modern; she likes traditional."

Michelle shrugged. "Okay, split the difference. One of you pick the first name and the other pick the middle name."

I stared at Michelle and wondered marveled at her intermittent genius streak. I grinned at Dani. "I can't believe we never thought of that."

Dani laughed. "Me neither."

I arched an eyebrow. "Okay, but who picks what?"

She gave me an evil grin. "Either way, I win, because I can always call him what I want."

I yelled, "Doh! I'll never best you."

She giggled and did a fist pump. "Yes!"

Katie gaped at Dani. "Did you just do a fist pump? I've never seen that from you ever."

"These two are wearing off on me."

"Okay, traditional names," Michelle said. "Well obviously, Daniel is out. That's just too weird having two people in the house with the same name."

Katie cut her off, "Because you know people will call him Danny."

I said, "Yes, but that could be handy. Call out one name and two people come running."

Dani shook her head. "No, Daniel was eliminated in round one. I'll grab my journal and tell you what I've considered." She stood and took her and Katie's plate to the kitchen. Michelle and I were nearing a serious game of rock/paper/scissors to see who got Chance's portion if she didn't make it down in time. She had ten minutes to appear. Dani reappeared with her journal and a pen and flipped to the back. "Dang, I'm almost out of paper in this thing."

Katie asked, "Damn, girl, have you written a play-by-play action while you're here?"

Dani smiled. "No, I just wanted to make sure to document our vacation and the baby's progress." She shrugged. "It's been fun. Okay, so the names that have made it to the final round are—"

Michelle pounded on the table. "Drumroll, please."

Dani read her list: "Jacob, Isaac, Nathan, Leland, Joel, and Elliot."

Michelle mimicked her best E.T. voice. "Elliot . . ."

I laughed. "Right? Every time I hear that name, I think of that little alien and Drew Barrymore."

Katie said, "Isaac's a little too . . .symbolic. Let's scratch that one."

I frowned and asked, "Why?" I saw Michelle and Katie exchange glances and bite their lips. "What's the story with Isaac?"

Michelle pointed to Katie, "You're better at the bible stuff than me. I'll probably mess the whole thing up and tell her Isaac was the dude in the lion's den."

Katie laughed. "You're safe. That was Daniel, and that name's been scratched already." She cleared her throat and looked at me. "Isaac was the first son—a miracle child born to Abraham and Sarah. They were like, old. One hundred, nineties, something like that."

"In their nineties? Go Abraham."

Katie put her face in her hands. "Oh lord, no, you can't make sexual jokes about Abraham. That's just . . . wow." She chuckled. "Okay, so when Isaac was still a boy, I always pictured him being like twelve, I don't know why. Anyway, God tells Abraham to take Isaac up the mountain and sacrifice him." I felt my stomach drop. I closed my eyes and took a deep breath. Katie continued, "Don't worry, he doesn't kill him. God grabs Abraham's hand before he can kill him and praises him for his willingness to be faithful."

I whispered, "You're right. Little too close to home. Scratch Isaac."

Dani lined through Isaac and bit her lip. The atmosphere in the room changed with that story; I know it wasn't just me. Reality is a straight-up bitch even when it parallels a story in the bible. Dani said, "Okay that leaves Jacob, Nathan, Leland, Joel, and Elliot."

Katie said, "For a similar reason, let's scratch Jacob, too."

Dani made another scratch on the paper. "Were Nathan, Leland,

Joel, or Elliot involved in anything scandalous in the bible?" She leveled her eyes at Katie then glanced at Michelle. They both shook their heads and looked at me. "Alissa, why don't you share the names you've come up with so we can start pairing them with these four I've got?"

I squirmed in my chair. "I feel like if I answer this wrong, I'm going to lose my recess."

Dani slammed her chair backward and snapped the journal closed. "Perhaps we should revisit this later."

I jumped up. "Whoa, Dani, what's the problem?"

"You are all looking at me like I'm this evil, awful person for following through with this horrible plan to steal away with your baby the day it's born. Let's just out the elephant standing in every room in this house, shall we? *You* are the one who got knocked up with a baby you didn't want. *I'm the one* who has been robbed of the privilege of having a baby of my own. *This* was supposed to be the perfect solution to an impossible situation. Yet I'm constantly walking on these glass shards of your decision, and I am tired of it."

She took a breath before continuing. "I'm not the bad guy, here. There *is no* bad guy in this situation. There are two women eager to love the same little miracle, so personally, I think Isaac would be the perfect name! And Katie and Michelle? I realize you're both mothers and think Alissa is making a huge mistake. And I also know that Alissa, herself, wonders if she's making a huge mistake. However, no one has ever once considered if I've wondered that myself."

A single tear ran down Dani's cheek. "You see me as this greedy, salivating baby snatcher with no care outside of getting what I want. Do you not know how much this is going to shred her the day she hands the baby to me? Because I do. The happiest day of my life is also going to break my heart, because my best friend's heart is going to break. I haven't spent my life in a career where I have to read people because I like the desk. So I would appreciate it if you would *all* quit with this bullshit of holding your breath when I speak about the baby and stop treating me like I'm too stupid to know what you're thinking." She picked up the chair and her journal and stormed past a wide-eyed Chance.

Chance turned to watch Dani run up the stairs then turned to look at me. "Did Dani just say bullshit?"

I shook my head and tried not to laugh at Chance's well-timed icebreaker. I took a deep breath. "She said a lot of things. Holy shit."

Chance took a sip of her coffee. "Yeah, I heard. Which one of you gets their ass kicked first?"

Katie and Michelle looked at each other and sighed. Michelle said, "Katie, you go first and wear her out."

Katie put her head in her hands. "This is bad. This is really bad."

Chance frowned. "No, it's not. I've been waiting for her to blow for a while. I'm kinda surprised it happened with you two here, but then again I'm not. You two make life normal again. Like we're all sitting in someone's living room back home." She took a drink of her coffee. "Not a soul at this table can be pissed about what she said. Take your ass chewing and be done with it. I've been guilty of it, too, so I take my part as well."

I nodded. "I know."

"What can we do to make up to her?" Katie asked.

I felt my eyes widen with the idea that blasted to the front of my brain. "Oh! What if we throw her a baby shower?"

Chance said, "Lis, we're trying not to buy a bunch of stuff here. The Navigator was packed tight on the way down. We won't have much room for anything else."

Michelle said, "We could still do cake and punch."

Katie said, "If the baby is going to be born around the first and you're not leaving until the thirtieth, you're going to need all kinds of stuff in that time."

I looked at Chance. "We could get a crib and changing table then donate it before we leave."

Katie said, "You're going to need a bathtub, diapers, wipes, bottles, formula, lotion, soap, clothes, a car seat, pacifiers . . ."

I looked at Chance and squealed. "Can we? Can we? Can we?"

She looked at Katie. "You're in charge of refreshments. Cake, punch, those cute little mints that no one ever eats, and cake pops. I have

331

to have cake pops today. Michelle, you need to make a list of everything Katie just said plus whatever food she wants and keep it in your hand until we get in the car. Alissa, you clean up the kitchen from breakfast and go get ready. I'm going to go lie to Dani and tell her you guys are all upset so I'm taking you out for a bit. We leave in thirty minutes. Go!"

Chairs scooted away from the table as everyone went about their missions. I cleared the table and thanked God over and over for something to do to stay in motion and not let Dani's words sink into my guilt-ridden soul.

Chapter Thirty-Nine
Bridge Over Troubled Water

Chance

I knocked on Dani's door and didn't wait for her to answer. I opened the door. "Hey, sister. You okay?"

Dani sat in the rocking chair by the window and sniffled. "Yes."

I closed the door. "You're not the bad guy, Dani, so you need to get that out of your head. I know looks can be deceiving and that this situation is uncomfortable at best, but I think you're handling it very well. I'm surprised it took you this long to blow up, sister."

Dani shook her head. "I should go apologize."

I put my hand up. "No, just let them all think about what you said and take time to cool off. I'm going to throw on some clothes and take them out for a bit. Then we'll all congregate back here for a big group hug."

She smiled. "If you think that's necessary."

"I do. Want me to bring you a Starbucks?"

"No, I'm fine. Thank you, though."

"Alissa's cleaning the kitchen, so why don't you just relax up here for a while, and I'll text you when we're on our way back."

She nodded. "All right. Thanks Chance."

I tipped my nearly cold coffee at her. "It's what we do. I'll see you after while." I slipped out of her room and sped through the fastest get-ready routine I've ever busted out. It was impressive, really. Exactly thirty minutes later, we were loaded in the Navigator on a mission to make Dani feel like the mother she was about to become.

We were like the folks you see on television with four thousand dollars to spend in thirty minutes or less, or whatever that show was. Michelle and I grabbed one cart, Katie and Alissa grabbed another. I said, "Okay, chickadees, we divide and conquer. Lis, show Katie around the food section, and Michelle and I are going to head to baby stuff. When you're done, come look for us in the car seats. I'm sure that's where we'll get stuck."

Katie yelled, "Ready? Break!" And we were off.

The only time I'd ever spent in a diaper aisle, I was checking Facebook while listening to Katie or Michelle bitch about buying something a baby would violate once then be thrown away. Michelle said, "Okay, you want these, not these. That kind leaks something awful. Never buy them, got it?"

I said, "Got it."

She continued down the aisle. "These kinds of wipes? They're a no-no. They have too much perfume for newborn bottoms. Always use these kinds until you see how sensitive his little ass is."

"Sensitive ass. Got it. Go."

We rounded the corner and stopped in front of row after row of baby toiletries. Michelle said, "This is the best one for—"

I cut her off. "Michelle, I don't give a shit. It's not my baby. Just load up the cart and save the advice for the mother."

She looked at me. "You're a douchebag."

"Massengil, baby. I will never need this information and we're on the clock. Alissa's going to have the baby by the time I develop a give-a-damn. Seriously. Let's roll."

Michelle mumbled, "I should have shopped with Lis."

"Yeah, but you're stuck with me, sister."

"You're totally the man in this relationship, you know that?"

I laughed. "I know. I've been around way too much estrogen lately. I feel like I should buy some golf clubs just so I can go outside and clean them while Dani and Alissa cry over chick flicks."

Michelle laughed and shook her head. "You're a mess. I forgot how pleasant Morning Chance is. I'm looking forward to my real friend."

I looked at the clock on my phone. "You have another hour before she actually wakes up. And, to make matters worse, I've only had one cup of coffee that was cold before I got to finish it. I'm a little pissy."

"I can see that."

I watched as Michelle-the-parenting-expert navigated the baby aisles and tried to nod, smile, and croon when the moment called for it. The cart was nearly full by the time we made it to the car seats and cribs and met up with Katie and Alissa. Their cart wasn't much better than ours, but I grinned when I saw champagne and orange juice. I pointed to it. "Who's my best friend, today?"

Alissa said, "Always me, baby. Always me."

"I think I love you."

She said, "I know. They all do."

We found a reluctantly helpful store associate, asked her opinion about the car seat and crib, made our selection, and had her wheel them to the front of the store so we could check out. In an hour and ten minutes, we'd managed to get everything on the lists and a few dozen outfits the mother twins insisted we needed. Katie made a fast trip back down to the laundry soap aisle and came back with a huge jug of Dreft, then we all left the check-out lane to get sheets and mattress pads for the crib. Good lord, babies are expensive.

I made Katie and Michelle go pull the Navigator to the front of the store. I didn't want them to faint when the cashier announced the total of our shopping spree. It's a good thing, too, because I nearly shit my pants as I swiped my card. Alissa offered to pay, but that just seemed inappropriate. Plus, my balls were bulging as the only "man" in this group, so I felt it was my duty to pay.

When the lady handed me the receipt, I said, "Shouldn't I get a free year's supply of coffee or something for that ring-up?"

She smiled as Alissa pushed me in my back. "Move."

We loaded up the Navigator and headed toward the house. I made a fast detour through Starbucks and instantly found my good mood in the bottom of the cup. By the time we got back to the house, I was ready to throw a party. Plus, I knew mimosas were on the menu. I was a happy girl.

I handed my phone to Alissa. "Will you text Dani and ask her to take Chubs for a walk down the beach? That'll get her out of the house while we're unloading."

"Where are we going to take all this stuff?" Katie asked.

"What about the pool room?" Alissa suggested.

I shook my head. "Glass walls. She'll see everything."

"What if we take it all to her room?" Michelle said.

"No, I think we should do it downstairs," Alissa answered. "We could throw all this stuff on the other side of the big couch. We can stuff the gift bags over there."

I looked at Michelle in the rearview mirror and bit my lip. "Did we get gift bags?"

"Got 'em." Michelle smiled.

"Shew. I'm such a dude. I think we should send Alissa down the beach to go make nice with Dani, which will buy us more time. You two probably need to talk, anyway."

Alissa sighed. "Probably so."

"Okay, that's settled. Katie, you'll be the look-out from the porch while Michelle and I lug all this stuff inside."

Michelle flexed her arms. "Beef cake."

I laughed. "Hot mess."

Everything went according to plan. Dani was a dot on the beach when we got there, so we sent Alissa to stall her while Katie kept watch. Michelle and I hauled everything into the house and dropped it in the middle of the floor. We both broke a sweat while stuffing bags and ripping off price tags. Michelle took Katie's place so she could come in and set up the cake, punch, and all that shit I know nothing about. Except mimosas. I know mimosas. And I had two before Alissa and Dani made their way back to the house.

Michelle stuck her head inside the door. "You've got about one minute before party time."

Katie clapped her hands. "Done!"

I flipped the last gift bag into place. "Done!"

Michelle came in and grinned. "Aw, it's so pretty. She'll love it."

I said, "Katie, you got the camera ready?"

"What? No way! You're on camera duty."

"Shit. Okay." I pulled my phone out of my pocket and flipped it to camera mode. "Video or pictures?"

336

Katie said, "Video. Totally video."

"On it."

Alissa and Dani walked in with the conversation lingering over their heads. Chubs bounded in and left a little trail of sand where Dani forgot to wipe his feet. Oh well, I'll clean it up later. As long as my OCD doesn't make me stop everything and do it now. We'll see.

Dani lifted her eyes and gasped. Her hand flew to her neck as her eyes bugged and chin quivered. "What is this?"

"Surprise!" We all yelled. Alissa joined the party-thrower's side and clapped.

Dani buried her face in her hands. "Oh my gosh, I can't believe it. Thank you so much. A baby shower. A real baby shower." She looked at the cake and pointed at the blue booties. "Oh that's so sweet." She wiped her face. "This is amazing."

Katie handed her a glass of punch and guided her to the guest-of-honor chair. We should have gotten balloons. Every picture I've ever seen of a baby shower, there's a helium foil balloon in every shot bobbing just over the head of the mother-to-be. I watched Dani take her place and look with disbelief at the massive display of gift bags on the floor in front of her. It looked like the carpet had puked rainbow sherbet. I downed the rest of my mimosa and went for round three. This was challenging my good mood.

I'd probably have more interest in the gift exchange if I hadn't just participated in the dash-and-stash shopping spree. Nah, I wouldn't have been interested either way. I stood next to the kitchen island thinking it would be more appropriate for me to have a cigar. I smiled and alternated between pictures and video footage of the baby shower. I was careful not to get any pictures of Alissa's belly even though we already had the plan of telling people she was Dani's surrogate if we got careless and uploaded a picture to Facebook that revealed Alissa's condition.

Watching women's faces at a baby shower is priceless. They keep a silly grin on their faces in anticipation for the full-face smile which precedes the gasp and, "Awww. . ." Michelle and Katie were at Dani's feet schooling her on every product. Michelle turned to me and stuck her tongue out. "See? Someone appreciates my experience."

I tilted my mimosa toward her. "Do your thang, sister."

Today was day one all over again. I've had sixty-seven of them in the last three months. Operation Phase-Out-Tony wasn't going as well as I'd hoped. Even standing in the midst of one of the happiest days of Dani's life, his freaking face pops into my head. I researched hypnotism around day fifty of "day one" but couldn't bring myself to do it. You just never know what they're going to do when you're under hypnosis. The last thing I needed was to bark like a dog every time I see a flashing yellow light or some shit like that.

Alissa sauntered over and leaned against the counter. "Penny for your thoughts," she whispered.

I smiled. "I'm trying to imagine Dani changing a poopy diaper."

She grinned. "Liar."

I sighed. "Nope. Honest truth. Scout's honor."

She nodded and gave Dani a grin over her latest treasure. "I can read you like a book, Chance."

"Really? What am I thinking now?"

She stared at my face and scowled. "No, you don't want to go to prison for killing me."

I smirked. "I do look awful in orange."

"But, you'd make a great play toy for some six-foot-nine triple homicide lady."

I nudged her. "That's nasty." I took a few more pictures of Dani and looked at Alissa. "Look at the little hens just clucking away."

"Do you remember Michelle's first baby shower? God, we were so hung over."

I put up my hand. "Don't say another word. I remember it very well, and I still can't eat fried chicken."

"That's the last time I ever drank Jaeger, too."

"You're going to make me gag if you keep it up." I shivered. "How'd it go on the beach?"

Alissa shrugged. "I told her I had a lot of that coming and that I was sorry for making her feel like my enemy. The same conversation we've

338

had a few times already."

"Think it held this time?" I glanced at Alissa then took another picture of Dani holding one of the outfits Katie had picked out. "That's super cute, Dani." She flashed me a perfect grin and sipped her punch.

Alissa said, "Yeah, I think this time she believes it."

"I'm glad she had that blow-up. I think it was good for her. And I think this shower probably settles a lot of mixed emotions she's been having."

"How so?"

I took a deep breath. "If I were Dani, I'd live in complete torment wondering if you're going to change your mind at the last minute. Now, before you interrupt me and explain for the four hundredth time why that can't happen, hear me out. It happens all the time in the adoption world. I think legally the birth mother has something like three days to change her mind. If she does, whammo. Done and done. I realize this situation is unique in that you're friends but still, shit happens, and I don't think she's going to breathe that sigh of relief until she has that baby in her arms. So this shower is symbolic in that she's opening the gifts and getting schooled by the mama hens. I think you'll see a big difference in her."

Alissa sighed. "I hope so. Come on. Let's get the crib and car seat."

I followed Alissa to the other side of the living room and giggled. "Alissa, you've got that pregnant waddle going on. Haha, that's awesome."

She flipped me the bird over her shoulder and motioned to Katie to come help me. Alissa said, "Just like on the television shows, I'd like to announce that, Ms. Dani Miscato, we're not done yet. What's behind couch number one?"

Katie and I took our cue, slid the crib box around the couch and leaned it against the wall. I performed my best Vanna White while Katie curtsied. Dani squealed, "Oh my goodness, that's a crib! The baby has a real bed."

"A *real* bed for a *real* boy," I said with a big smile.

"Way to go, Jiminy Cricket." Michelle laughed.

Katie's eyes widened. "Oh, oh! I know! When we get home, we'll throw another shower for Dani's friends and family with a Disney movie theme!"

Michelle clapped. "Oh Katie, that's perfect!"

I put my thumb on my nose. "Not it!" Alissa followed suit, then Katie, so that left Michelle with the nomination to host. I said, "Haha, you lose again, Chelle."

She said, "I don't mind planning a party at all. It will be so much fun. Oh I can't wait to hold that baby, smell him, see his sweet little hands and feet. Gibson had the cutest little cheeks."

I pointed at her. "You need to quit that, now. You've got that look in your eye."

She laughed. "First of all, one must actually have sex before they can conceive."

Dani said, "Oh, is that how it works? I bet that's where I went wrong."

We all laughed and shook our heads. I said, "Point, Dani. Alissa, what else do we have for the lovely mother-to-be?"

Alissa grinned. "Glad you asked, my friend! What does every prince need to ride in a chariot fit for a king?" Katie rounded the corner and picked up the car seat. "His very own car seat! Blonde bombshell model sold separately."

"Don't make me laugh while I'm holding a prize," Katie said.

Dani stood and took the car seat from Katie. "You guys should not have done all of this. Thank you so much. It's . . . I'm . . ." She wiped the fresh tears from her eyes. "I'm so grateful. This feels real, now, like this is really going to happen."

I pointed at Alissa's belly. "Was there ever any doubt? Look at that thing."

Alissa slapped my hand. "You're a jerk."

"You love it."

"Come on, Katie." Michelle pointed to the pile of presents. "Let's help Dani take all this stuff upstairs and see if we can put the crib together."

I looked at Dani and cringed. "Maybe we should see if there's a handyman around here. Have you ever seen the things those two have put together?"

Michelle put her hands on her hips. "Hey, they were cheap shelves to begin with."

I chuckled. "Yeah but the bookcase still took a side lunge and poor Freddie the fish perished."

She huffed. "You never forget anything."

I pointed to my temple. "Steel trap, baby."

Katie, Michelle, and Dani took armloads of gifts up the stairs, and Alissa and I started gathering up gift bags and tissue paper. I said, "I'm pretty sure this is about forty dollars worth of gift bags we'll never use again."

Alissa shrugged. "I'm paying for an indoor pool you've never stepped into. Deal with it." I rolled the idea in my head then decided she had trumped me. She said, "Go ahead and think for a comeback. I'll wait."

I stuffed the last bit of tissue paper in the trashcan and cinched the bag. I grunted as I hauled it out of the can. "I don't have to think of something clever. I'm just trying to decide if I'm going to cut your hair in your sleep or sell your Coach bags on eBay."

"Go for the hair. It grows back," she said.

"Not if I keep cutting night after night." I swung open the door with the trash in my hand and felt the air in the room explode past me and right into Tony's face. I dropped the bag and stumbled backward. This was no vision; this was no flashback or memory. The man I had tried to erase stood in the door in front of me looking scared to death. I saw the little black swirlies trying to cloud my vision and took a deep breath. "Jesus," I whispered.

He said, "No, Tony, but I get that a lot." He looked at my stomach and met my eyes with a puzzled gaze.

"What are you doing here?" My voice resembled a terrible vibrato in a pubescent boy.

"I . . . I tried to see you. I went to the station, but they said you'd

341

taken an extended leave. No one knew why." He looked at my stomach again and swallowed hard. "I thought . . . I figured . . . I was afraid you . . ."

Alissa entered the mudroom. "Damn, Chance, were you born in a barn? Shut the damn . . ." She saw Tony and stopped. His eyes dropped to her bulging belly and softened. He closed his eyes, took a deep breath, and sighed as he put all the pieces together. Alissa stood unmoving but said, "Surprise."

Tony shook his head and stuttered over his words. "I . . . I'm so sorry to barge in, Alissa. I didn't know. About you. I didn't even think . . ." He pointed at me. "She disappeared. I . . . ."

She smiled. "Stop it before you make me seasick with all that wavering.

He sighed. "Thank you."

I couldn't take my eyes off him. "Are you really here?" I whispered.

He locked eyes with me. "I'll prove it." He stepped into the door and wrapped me in his arms. My chest swelled as my soul sighed. He rubbed his hands over my back and buried his face in my neck as he whispered, "God, I missed you."

I swallowed hard and tried to speak, but all I could muster was a nod. I nearly broke my jaw as I clenched my teeth to stop the sobs of joy, relief, confusion, and shock from rolling out of my body.

Michelle called my name as she wandered down the stairs. "Chance, do you have any . . . holy shitballs! Is that Tony?"

He pulled away from me and grinned. "It is, indeed, Michelle."

She squealed as she ran past Alissa and threw her arms around his neck. "I can't believe this shit! This is such a shock. God, you look great!"

"Me? Look at you, skinny mini!"

She grinned. "Thanks. What are you doing here?" As if reality stomped on Michelle's toe, she jumped and looked at Alissa. "Oh, shit. Tony's here." She pointed at Alissa's belly then pointed at Tony.

Tony raised his hand. "I can assure you it's not mine."

Leave it to Tony to save an awkward situation. We laughed as

Michelle pulled him through the mudroom toward the living room. "Come on in, come see this place."

He stopped. "Actually, I left my car running. I wasn't sure if I was in the right house." He looked at me and grinned.

I found my voice. "How many have you stopped at?"

That perfect, sly half-grin that was panty-melting hot appeared on his face as he said, "Twelve—give or take a few."

Twelve houses. Eighteen hundred miles and twelve houses. He was determined to find me. The knot I'd just cleared from my throat reappeared with two more friends. I took a deep breath. "Damn. I'll walk with you to turn off your car." I pushed him toward the door and reminded myself to keep breathing. Tony was six inches away from me and still too far. I wanted to bury my face in his chest and sob every apology I've longed to say for all the ways I'd fucked up. He turned off the car and grabbed a bag from the back seat.

"Mind if I bring this inside? I've got my laptop and a bunch of stuff that might explode in the car."

I nodded. "Yes, that's fine." I pointed to the car and asked, "Rental?"

He sighed. "Yes, and that little piece of shit is governed. Can't drive over seventy miles an hour. I intend to complain."

I smiled. "You shouldn't be speeding anyway."

His eyes buried into mine as he stood inches from my face. "I had somewhere I needed to be. I didn't want to dick around."

I alternated between not breathing and panting like a dog. "Why are you here, Tony?"

He sighed and looked over my shoulder toward the ocean. "Wanna go for a walk? I've always wanted to come here."

I grinned and whispered, "*Florida.*"

He tossed his head back and laughed. "Right. Florida. Shall we take advantage of my dream?"

I smiled. "Might as well. I've been living it for three and a half months. I guess I could share."

He smiled and touched my face. "God, it's good to see you,

Chance."

I closed my eyes and took a step through the unknown. "I've longed for you every day." I looked into his eyes and felt my chin quiver as tears pricked his eyes.

He grinned. "I *knew* it. I *knew* it." He shouted, "I *knew* it!" He grabbed my face in his hands and put his forehead to mine. "I knew it," he whispered. He kissed my lips so lightly, I barely felt anything but his breath. He kissed me again with the sweetest, most tender expression of love I've ever felt. My knees felt weak as he pulled away and sniffled. "I don't want to quit holding or kissing you." He chuckled then kissed me again.

I touched his face. "Let's take your bag inside and go on that walk. I have so much to show you."

"Do you mind if I change first? I'm dressed for Missouri not balmy *Florida*."

I giggled. "Yes, that's fine." We couldn't quit looking at each other. Even as we walked the short path to the deck, we kept staring at each other and laughing when the other tripped. "The sand will be easier on us."

"Any chance you have a white bikini?" He grinned.

"Maybe." I winked.

"You really are undeniably beautiful." He faked a shiver.

"You're still thinking of the white bikini." I smiled.

"Well, yeah. I'm not dumb."

I showed him through the house to the bathroom, and the minute the door closed, my friends surrounded me jumping up and down and squealing under their breaths. I put my hand over my heart and leaned against the kitchen island. "Someone tell me this is really happening."

"I think this is the most romantic thing I've ever seen in my life," Katie gushed.

"Why is he here?" Michelle asked. "How did he find you?"

"I don't know! I swear I'm disconnected from myself right now and can't even think."

Alissa handed me a fresh mimosa. "Here. Down this. You'll center right back up."

I followed orders and sighed. "Again." I handed her the empty glass and watched her prepare another one.

Dani grinned and asked, "Do you want me to mix a bottle of that for you to take on the beach?"

"Yes, and I might be back for more before he gets out of the bathroom."

Michelle put her hands on my shoulders. "This is not the time for you to think. Right now, you feel. You need to listen to him and listen to your heart. No thinking. Thinking has kept you heartbroken for over a year now. You love him more than I've ever seen anyone love another human being. Well, maybe minus me and my kids. But seriously, Chance. I'm begging you."

I nodded. "I will." I looked at Alissa. "Did you have anything to do with this?"

She raised her eyebrows. "Why the hell would I bring him down here to bust me? Nope. Wasn't me."

I pointed at Katie, Michelle, and Dani. "Anyone want to fess up before he busts you?"

They all denied involvement and scattered like autumn leaves when he opened the bathroom door. I grabbed my glass, the bottle, and an extra glass for him. "Ready?" I asked.

He nodded. "Yes, Princess Jasmine. Show me your new world."

I shook my head. "You're way too hetero to reference Disney movies as much as you do."

He shrugged. "I'm secure in my manhood."

We stepped onto the deck where I ditched my shoes and grabbed my trusty blanket. Never in a million years did I believe I would actually get to share my Tony blanket with its namesake. I slipped my flip-flops back on. "The sand is probably hot this time of day, so we better keep these on until we get to the wet sand."

He admired the house and whistled. "Damn, I don't even want to know how much this cost."

"Me neither."

345

"You don't know?"

"It's a long story."

"Good thing I have all the time it will take." He followed me down the boardwalk and stared at the ocean. "Wow."

"It's breathtaking, isn't it?"

"Understatement."

I tossed the blanket on the sand and poured a mimosa for Tony. I lifted my glass. "Cheers. To crossing something off your bucket list."

He raised his glass. "I kind of wish it was under different circumstances and you were wearing a white bikini."

I shook my head and laughed. "Okay, spill it. Tell me everything. Why did you come?"

He swallowed and took another drink. "Man, that's the shit."

"Right? Want more?"

"Yes." He held his glass out. "Why am I here? Well I think that's pretty obvious. I came to find you. I went to your station yesterday to beg you to talk to me, and they told me you left late December and wouldn't be back until June or July."

I muttered, "If I still have a job there."

"Yeah, well, Stuart isn't very happy with you." He smirked. "So I found your boy-toy, Eddie, and asked him a few questions. He was extremely vague at first, but when I appealed to his softer side, he sang like a bird."

Eddie. I didn't know if I wanted to hug him till he suffocated or push him in front of a bus. I would have a solid answer after this visit. "So Eddie told you I was going to Naples, but he didn't know why."

"No, but there was a lot of speculation and rumors. No one could figure out why you'd up and leave your job, your life . . . none of it made sense until I started doing the math." He bit his lip and mumbled, "I thought you were pregnant."

My eyes widened as I said, "Pregnant? Tony, we haven't slept together in well over a year."

His eyes dropped as he whispered, "I know."

The panicked look on his face, the desperation to know the truth,

346

the look of relief when he saw Alissa—it all made sense now. "Tony, there hasn't been anyone since you."

He took a deep breath. "All I could think was you were pregnant and maybe had come down here to get married like . . . like we'd talked . . . and I thought you were gone. Like forever gone."

My nose tingled and eyes misted as I watched his pain exposed. "Nothing like that, Tony."

He looked at me. "Then what? Well, I guess I know a big part of the situation, now that I've seen Alissa. And holy shit that was a shock, but such a relief."

Don't think, just feel.

I had never lied to this man outside of telling him I didn't want to spend my life with him. I wasn't about to start now. "Alissa found out she was pregnant after Mark broke up with her. About the same time, Dani found out she's barren. Alissa has never wanted children and would never consider abortion, so adoption was the only option. The problem is that Mark knew she was pregnant. She went to him to do the right thing and have him sign off his parental rights, but he flew off the handle and said a lot of awful things to her. He told her to get rid of it, so she let him assume she was having an abortion."

"So she had to leave town."

I nodded. "She had to leave town, yes. She offered to give the baby to Dani, legally of course, and begged me to come with her. I didn't have any reason to say no and thought maybe the . . . distance from St. Louis would help me gain perspective."

"And did it?"

I took a deep breath. "Yes and no. More yes than no. Actually, all yes."

"So what's the verdict?"

My heart pounded and hands began to shake. "Why did you come here, Tony?"

"I already told you."

"What were you going to do if you found me with someone else? Found me pregnant?"

He ran his fingers through his hair. "I was going to tell you I love you then ask you to help me bury the bastard's dead body."

I laughed. "Oh, that's great. Have a pregnant lady help you bury a body."

"I'm kidding. I don't know. I didn't know what I was going to do. I guess I just needed to know. I knew you weren't going to answer my calls or texts, so that left one option. I hopped the first flight I could catch out of St. Louis and here I am."

"But how did you find the street?"

He smiled slyly. "I'm a journalist, Chance. I know how to get the scoop."

"Fair enough, but you'll tell me someday."

He grinned. "Maybe. Now, tell me; what's the verdict?"

I slipped my hand into his. "The verdict is that no matter where I go, no matter how much I try to chase you out of my mind and heart, I love you and only you, and I'll love you the rest of my life if you'll let me." I held my breath and thought, *Holy shit, I can't believe I just said that.*

He stared at my face until I met his eyes. "I was hoping you'd say that." He pulled a package from his pocket and popped the lid on the blue velvet box. "Marry me, Chance. This weekend. On this beach at sunset."

I stared at the diamond standing proudly in the box shining and eager. I wondered how long it had been cooped up in that little box waiting for this moment. I thought about all the reasons I'd said no before then remembered the pain and regret I'd lived with afterward. I closed my eyes, took a deep breath, and whispered, "Deal."

He flopped back on the blanket spread eagle and yelled, "Holy shit, she said yes!" He kicked his legs and pumped his arms in a full-out giddy-fit as my grandmother used to say and laughed his perfect belly laugh before flipping onto all fours and crawling onto me.

I squealed, "Tony! Shit!" as he pinned me under his body and looked at my face.

"Say it again," he panted.

I bit my lip then kissed his nose. "Yes, I will marry you on this beach

348

this weekend at sunset. On one condition, though."

His eyes darkened and his eyebrows kissed with worry. I could tell he was holding his breath. "And that is?"

I whispered, "I have to stay here until Alissa gives birth."

A slow grin spread across his face. "A thousand things ran through my mind, and I was ready to agree to any of them. You never cease to surprise me. Chance." He sighed and whispered, "I've been so lost without you. When I saw you in St. Louis, I knew you felt the same way. She wasn't my girlfriend. Ever. She wanted to be, but how could I ever downgrade when I had the top of the line?"

"True. So true," I smiled.

He pulled me to my feet and wrapped his arms around me. "If I stay on top of you much longer, we're going to get an early start on the honeymoon."

I whispered, "'Florida' . . ."

He smiled. "You're going to marry me."

I nodded and bit my lip to stop the tears from falling. I whispered, "You're really here." I touched his face and slid my hands down his chest. "I longed for you."

He tilted his head. "All you had to do was call."

"All you had to do was come."

He curled his arms around my body and pressed against the small of my back—that magical place that ignites every nerve ending in my body. He knows that. I groaned. "That's playing dirty."

He cocked an eyebrow. "Let the games begin, my beloved. We have approximately thirty-six hours of toying to do before we say our vows. I intend to create a smoldering inferno in you until then."

I smirked. "I know you'll find me a worthy opponent. Game on, brother."

"I almost forgot something," he said as he pulled away from me. He bent over, grabbed the blue box holding the engagement ring, and dropped to one knee. He reached for my hand, slid the ring on my finger,. "Now, it's official."

Chapter Forty
From This Moment On

Michelle

I pressed my face against the window. "They're looking pretty comfy out there."

Alissa waddled up behind me and craned her neck to see Chance and Tony on the beach. "What do you think he's saying? He looks pretty intense."

"How can you see all that?"

She outlined his body with her finger. "See how he's leaning toward her? Oh, they're really talking about some shit."

"Well, she's not throwing sand in his face, so I'd say it's going well."

Dani called to us, "You guys, get away from the window and give them some privacy."

I gasped. "Holy shit! Is he proposing?"

Dani and Katie raced to the window and squeezed between Alissa and me. Katie gasped, "Oh my gosh, I think he is."

I sucked in my breath. "Let the sand fly in three . . . two . . . one."

We watched as Tony flung himself on the blanket then kicked like a kid having a tantrum. "I'm guessing she said no?"

Alissa mumbled, "She's the dumbest bitch I've ever met if she does."

Katie pointed. "No look! Guys, I think she said yes."

Dani whispered, "I think she did too."

I gasped again. "Oh she totally said yes."

We all jumped up and down squealing and hugging each other. Katie said, "This is the best thing ever. Like getting a front-row seat to a real romantic comedy."

My eyes were glued to the two figures on the beach. "I want to see him put it on her finger."

"I bet the poor bastard lost the ring when he threw himself on the blanket," Alissa said.

Dani nudged her with her elbow. "You're a mess."

"Lis, do you have binoculars?" Katie asked. "I want to see this shit!"

Alissa laughed. "Absolutely not. We're prying enough as it is."

"He's doing it! He's dropping to one knee," Katie squealed.

I laughed. "Well, his nuts aren't in his throat yet, so I'd say that's a good sign."

"Oh shit, they're coming to the house." Alissa turned from the window. "Quick. Disperse. Act like we don't know."

We flew into various parts of the living room and took seats in random places. Dani picked up a baby magazine, Alissa grabbed her iPad, Katie redirected her path to the kitchen island and I curled up on the couch with the smart phone I still didn't quite know how to operate. Five seconds later, we burst into laughter at how ridiculously posed we all looked and knew Chance would give us one look and know we'd spied.

Chance barely had the door open before Katie flew into her arms squealing, "Lemme see, lemme see, lemme see."

I shook my head and mumbled, "Way to act cool, Katie." We lit on them like kids on birthday cake and all took turns hugging both of them and admiring the rock on Chance's hand.

Alissa grinned and hugged Tony. "Well done, well done."

He faked a hat tip. "Thank you, thank you."

"Well ladies, I have some news," Chance said.

I laughed. "I think it's a little too late for your big news, Chance."

She grinned. "But wait, there's more." She pointed to Alissa and asked, "Want a new project?"

Alissa waved her off. "Oh Chance, I don't have patience to train Tony for you."

Chance giggled. "No, but perhaps you'd like to put your excitement to good use and help me find a minister and a place to get a marriage license. We're getting married this weekend on that beach out there."

I'm pretty sure some glass shattered and dogs five miles away heard the shrieks that erupted from the teenage girls still deep inside each of us. Alissa paced and ticked the list of things to do on her fingers. "Okay, it's

Friday, so everything is open. You just want someone ordained, right? Not like a specific denomination? Good. We need to go to the courthouse and get the marriage license. I'll make a few phone calls . . ." her voice trailed off as she got lost in planning mode and engrossed in her iPad.

Chance shook her head. "That's when she's at her best. Look at her go."

"I didn't bring anything suitable for marrying the woman of my dreams, so I need to find a place to get slicked up," Tony said with a grimace on his face.

From across the house Alissa shouted, "Hot damn, there's no waiting period for out-of-state residents! Tony, I'll text you the address so you can get the marriage license while you're out."

"Thank you!" Tony said, "I'm all over it."

"We need to go dress shopping." Katie smiled at me before throwing herself on the couch and sighing. "Best vacation ever."

I looked at Dani. "What do we do?"

Dani shrugged. "You can be the flower girl."

I leaned against the island and laughed. "All we really need for a wedding like this is the bride, groom, minister, and wine. Lots and lots of wine."

"Yes, wine." Dani said. "You and I will work on the area where they get married. We'll do something to make it pretty."

The bride-to-be had something to say about that. "No, I just want it to be us on the beach with the sunset in the background." She blushed. She actually blushed.

I nodded. "I love it."

Tony excused himself from the house and went to start his whirlwind expedition. I bellied up to the mimosa bar and helped myself to the remainder of Chance and Tony's bottle. I stared at my friends all bustling around giggling and wondered which one of us was getting ready to win the lottery. It seemed like a natural progression to this dream-filled day. I just hoped it would be me.

Chance is getting married tomorrow at sunset. Chance, my Chance,

352

our Chance, the eternal bachelorette, the woman scared shitless of permanent commitment is tying the knot. While I'd always hoped to see the day, I never thought I'd actually *see* the day. Everything in the universe seemed to be righting itself just as it should be. Dani and the baby, Chance and Tony, my marriage to Brandon . . . well, let's not get too carried away. He's still a troublesome little peckerhead, but I love him anyway.

Alissa stood. "Okay, we've got some shopping to do. Load up, ladies."

I linked arms with Katie. "Didn't we just do this?"

She smiled at me. "Leave it to us to go from baby shopping to wedding dress shopping within four hours."

"I know I'll sleep well tonight."

We walked into the first dress shop we saw and were greeted by a gaunt though elegant woman who seemed to float in her three-inch heels and pencil skirt. She had teeth big enough to write a week's worth of groceries on and eyes that disappeared when she smiled. I had to stifle the giggle bubbling in my throat. Every time I looked at her, I envisioned an awkward county fair caricature. The harder I tried to stop it, the bigger the giggle grew. I locked eyes with Alissa who widened her eyes and bit her lip as she shared my thoughts. The woman reached for Dani's hand. "You must be Alissa. I'm Beatrice. We spoke on the phone."

Dani shook her hand and pointed at Alissa. "Actually, she's Alissa. I'm Dani Miscato. It's a pleasure to meet you."

Beatrice glanced at Alissa's pregnant belly and blinked forty times in a row. "Oh, well, Alissa, it's nice to meet you."

Alissa smiled and shook her head. "Relax, Beatrice. Allow me to introduce you to Chance Bradley, the bride-to-be."

Beatrice exhaled and smiled at Chance. "Congratulations, Ms. Bradley. You've come to the right place. Let's see, you're about a size eight, right?"

Chance's head snapped back. "Wow, you're good."

Beatrice smiled. "It's my job to know women's bodies. What kind of dress would you like for your special day?"

Alissa leaned in my ear and whispered, "Did she just sound like a pimp, or was it just me?"

The giggle I'd tried to stifle erupted in a hearty guffaw that echoed through the elegant showroom. Beatrice eyed me then guided Chance to an area of dresses on display. I looked at Alissa. "You got me in trouble."

Alissa grinned. "I wish I had popcorn and a soda right now. Watching Chance get fondled by the dress drill sergeant is going to be epic."

I pointed at Katie who was two steps behind Beatrice hanging on her every word. "I'm pretty sure Katie was a cat in a former life."

Alissa considered it then said, "Nah, I'd always figured her for a Labrador retriever."

"Want me to throw my phone and see if she fetches?"

Alissa laughed into her hands to soften the sound and shook her head. "No, but I think we should stir up Beatrice a little." She sauntered toward them and asked, "Do you have anything backless, strapless, and perhaps cut above the knee?"

Beatrice did the fast blink thing and offered the thinnest line of a smile. "Alissa, if that's the kind of dress you desire, I'd recommend a bath towel. It would offer much more class than that style of wedding dress."

Alissa winked. "See Michelle? That's what I said, too, but I wanted to hear it from the best."

Beatrice turned her attention to Chance. "Why don't I bring you a few dresses that sound like what you're looking for, and you can try them on."

Chance nodded. "Yes, that's fine."

Beatrice excused herself, and Alissa took her turn on the showroom floor. She walked, or should I say waddled, and imitated Beatrice's deep, slow speech when she said, "Now, Ms. Bradley, would you like to wear something that makes you look elegant or fuckable?"

Chance threw her shoulders back and responded, "Oh, Ms. Franklin, I'd like to try on the bath towel, please."

354

Chance was summoned to the dressing room, but we were instructed to stay in the half-circle sitting area in front of a string of mirrors. Alissa stood on the platform and admired her figure from all angles. She looked at Katie. "What do you think, Katie? Does this belly make me look pregnant?"

Katie said, "Oh, not at all. In fact, I think you've lost weight since I saw you last."

Alissa spun around and whispered, "How pissed off do you think Beatrice would be if I tried on dresses?"

Dani laughed and shook her head. "Will you stop it?"

"Well, damn, did you see the scathing look she gave me when I dared bring my eight-month-pregnant belly up in her store looking for a wedding dress?"

Dani shrugged. "I doubt it has anything to do with your condition."

"It's cool," I said. "I told her you two were married already, so you weren't living in sin."

Dani rolled her eyes. "You would say that."

I giggled. "Not really, but I wish I had, now." I looked around. "Think she's got drinks here? I wish I'd brought my mimosa."

Katie set down the bride magazine she'd flipped through. "Yeah, we should be drinking right now. So like, technically, this is the night for the bachelorette party, right?"

Dani wagged a finger. "Am I the only one that remembers you nearly having to stop halfway down the aisle to vomit in your cousin's purse?"

"Oh god, that was completely awful." Katie sat back and sighed. "At least Chance is getting married in the evening."

"Am I the only one having a hard time wrapping my brain around that sentence?" I giggled.

They all raised their hands.

"While I always figured one day she'd get married," Alissa said, "I just never thought she'd ever really get married. It's weird."

Chance appeared in a floor-length white flowing gown with exaggerated, loose sleeves and the saddest looking bustle I'd ever seen.

355

The boatneck style slid just below her collarbones making them look like completely stunned protruding, hairless eyebrows. She said, "I look ridiculous."

Alissa's hand flew to her mouth then she bit her lips. She gestured for Chance to take her place on the platform so we could get the full affect. Alissa said, "This is an . . . interesting choice."

Chance scowled. "I look like fucking Princess Leah."

We laughed and agreed.

"Go take that thing off. I can't let you do this. Run." Alissa pointed in the direction of the dressing room.

The next dress was even better. It was a sleeveless white dress that hugged her hourglass figure and had elaborate, puffy stuff around her breasts and ankles.

"Are you going as a Q-tip for Halloween?" Alissa said between giggles.

Chance laughed until tears shown in her eyes. "Um, I don't think we're going to find anything here that matches my taste. You should see what else is in the dressing room. It's awful."

Beatrice appeared and clapped her hands together. "Oh, that's exquisite. Like that dress was tailored just for you." She beamed. "I think that's a keeper."

Chance offered a tight smile. "No, ma'am, I disagree. While I'm grateful for your time, I believe we're late for another appointment." She looked at Alissa. "Unzip me. Get me out of this thing."

The next two dress shops were more of the same and I was half-expecting Chance to ask for a new bath towel. And that's when she saw it in the window of the fourth boutique. She pressed her face against the glass and whispered, "That's it. That one right there."

I smiled and nodded. "It's beautiful, Chance. Let's go try it on."

The boutique was more relaxed and less expensive than the three we'd visited. The showroom attendant was more than happy to assist but didn't try to wrap herself around Chance's legs while purring. We were chatting about lunch options when Chance appeared wearing the most beautiful smile and elegant dress I'd ever seen on her. She sashayed to the platform and admired herself while the rest of us sat in awe. The pearl-white dress had two-inch straps that draped across her tanned shoulders and led to a draped neckline that provided plenty of coverage but accented her cleavage. The rest of the dress fell to the top of her feet. Nothing ornate, nothing extravagant, but on Chance, it looked like a masterpiece.

Chance turned to face us. "What do you think, ladies?" No one spoke. We stared at her and took turns wiping the trickling tears that snuck out of the corners of our eyes. A satisfied grin spread across her face. "That's enough for me. That was exactly the reaction I wanted." She looked at the attendant. "I'll take it."

The woman asked, "Would you like to see a few jewelry options that accentuate this dress and really make it pop?"

Alissa shook her head. "No. I have the perfect earrings, and a necklace isn't necessary. She is perfect just in the dress."

"Thanks, sister." Chance beamed.

"I'd marry you." Alissa winked at her.

I looked at Dani and Katie, mesmerized by the vision in front of them. I tried to imagine the look on Tony's face when he saw her and made a split decision. I said, "We need a photographer."

Alissa's jaw dropped and she gasped. "God, you're right. There's no way any of us will remember to take one picture."

The attendant shyly said, "When is the wedding? I, uh . . . I have a photography business on the side. Nothing big. Just something I like to do."

Alissa grinned. "Do you have a tripod and a friend? We need pictures and video. No pictures of me, though."

"Absolutely there will be pictures of you." Chance put her hands on her hips.

"No, Chance." Alissa pointed to her stomach and shook her head.

"It will just be for me, anyway." Chance frowned.

"No, Chance." Alissa shook her head sadly.

"Fine. We'll do headshots only, but I will have pictures of us together on my wedding day." Her face flinched and eyes widened. All of the color drained from her face as her eyes dropped to the floor.

I jumped to my feet and grabbed her hands. "Chance, look at me." Her eyes slid to mine as her chin quivered. "It's Tony. It's your Tony. He flew halfway across the United States to search twelve different houses just to find you and make damn sure he never loses you again. You love him more than I've ever seen anyone love a man and you're going to be happier than you've ever imagined. Marriage can be tough, but it doesn't *have* to be, Chance. It doesn't *have* to be. It doesn't label you like you think it does. Just remember that you and Tony will be together forever. You won't ever have to wonder again if he's thinking of you, longing for you, missing you, wanting you. You will know. The mind fuck is over, Chance. You win."

"I win." Her face softened and a smile spread across her face.

"Yeah." I blinked back the tears brimming my eyes. "No more misery, no more day-ones, no more pretending. Just happy with Tony. Just be happy with Tony forever, okay?"

She nodded. "Don't think, just feel, right?"

"For now, yes. As for this dress, I can't wait for Tony to hit his knees in disbelief when you walk down that boardwalk."

Alissa whispered to the attendant, "You're hired. I'll give you the address. Can you be there tomorrow around three?"

"Tomorrow?" she gasped. "You're getting married tomorrow?"

"It was a spur of the moment decision."

The attendant laughed. "I'll say. Do you need shoes?"

"No, we're all barefoot tomorrow. The ceremony is on the beach in front of our house."

She sighed. "I've always wanted to shoot a wedding on the beach."

Alissa pointed at Chance. "Well here's your chance. No pun intended."

While we waited for Chance to change, Alissa came up to me and threw her arm around my shoulders. "Great speech. I admit I felt that 'holy shit, what do I say' moment when her face fell, but you scooted right on up there and took care of business. Good job."

I smiled and shrugged. "She was about to crash and burn."

"You might have just saved the day. I owe you one."

I laughed. "I think we've got a long way to go before you ever start owing me anything."

"Still . . ." She smiled.

Katie walked up with her nose crinkled and her bottom lip pinched between her teeth. "Um, I hate to state the disgusting obvious, but . . . do you think they're going to stay with us the night of their wedding? Like . . . you know. Do you think . . ."

I cut her off. "Do you mean are they going to go at it like wild monkeys? Well, I'd say that's likely."

"I was afraid of that. Like seriously thinking about getting a hotel room somewhere."

Dani shook her head. "Do you honestly think Tony's going to travel all this way to have a sleepover with us on his wedding night? I guarantee he's making arrangements for their honeymoon while he's out."

"I bet you're right." Alissa nodded. "If I was a good friend, I'd offer to vacate the premises so they can have some privacy, but I'm paying through the nose for that house. He can go get his own."

"Plus, he's loaded," Katie pointed out. "It's not like he can't afford a freaking hotel room. He's so romantic. I can't wait to see what he comes up with next. Like, I bet it's a glass house on a private island. Something crazy extravagant like that."

"He'd have to make arrangements months in advance for something like that. But who knows. He's surprised the shit out of me today." Alissa chuckled.

"It's definitely been a day of surprises." Dani grinned.

I nudged her with my elbow. "First you blow up at breakfast, then the baby shower, then an oceanfront proposal, a wedding tomorrow."

Katie pointed at Alissa. "Do not go into labor tonight, got it? I've had all the excitement I can handle."

"Nope. No premature birthing this weekend." Alissa laughed and rubbed her belly. "We've still got six weeks 'til baby day."

"Are you doing birthing classes?" I asked her.

But Dani answered. "Well, we thought about it, but um . . ."

"But it doesn't matter, because at the first sign of discomfort, I'm getting the epidural. I'm not trying to be a hero."

Dani gestured to Alissa. "And there you have it."

"Don't be a hero. Get the good drugs," I laughed.

Chance rounded the corner with her gown bag draped across her arm. "Ladies, I'm starving, and my buzz is wearing off. Let's go wine and dine." We followed her out of the store and walked toward the car.

"We may have one more stop to make." I couldn't believe we'd almost forgotten this.

"For what?" She frowned.

"Um, a ring for Tony?" I laughed.

"Shit! Yes, one more stop. But, I don't have any idea what size ring he wears."

"That could be a problem," Alissa said. "Text him and ask."

"Oh that's romantic." Chance smirked.

Alissa punched her on the shoulder. "It's not like you're asking condom sizes. Just text and ask."

"They come in sizes?" My eyebrows shot to the sky.

"Are you serious?" Alissa blinked twice.

I put my hands on my hips. "What do I know about condoms? I've been with the same man since I was seventeen. Why would I need to know about condom sizes?"

"Well, you have a good point, but yes, condom sizes are important." Alissa grinned. "It's not like you can wrap chapstick in a sausage casing and expect it to work."

Chance turned to me. "Ever tried to put on panty hose two sizes too small? What happens?"

"They rip."

"There ya go. Now you know the importance of condom sizes and that I've also been much more fortunate with my sexual experiences than Alissa, here." Chance patted Alissa on the shoulder.

"Do you remember that guy I dated before Dirk? That was the craziest thing I've ever seen in my life." Alissa reached in her purse, pulled out a tube of chapstick, and held it up. "See this? I'm not even kidding."

Chance giggled then doubled over with laughter. "She . . . she called me all pissed off."

"Well, damn. We were making out, or so I thought, then he starts groaning and saying, 'doesn't that feel good, baby?' I was still waiting for the moment, ya know? I was like, 'oh god, he's in, he's in,' and I had no idea." Alissa rolled her eyes.

"She said . . . she said he was like a wind-up toy gone mad then thirty seconds later, he was completely passed out." Chance wiped her eyes and sighed. "That's one of my favorite Lis stories ever."

Alissa chuckled. "I'm so glad you enjoyed it. At least one of us did. Will you please text Tony so we can get this done?"

Chance pulled out her phone and grinned that cute little grin that people get when they're in love. I remember when Brandon and I started dating in high school—long before cell phones or the Internet erupted on the scene. We had a few classes together, but most of the time we saw each other in passing in the hallway. He made it a point to leave a note in my locker in between every class to make sure I knew he was thinking of me. The first few years of marriage, I'd find post-it notes or random cards left in the refrigerator on the milk carton or tucked in my panty drawer. Sometimes they were poetic, sometimes they were just smiley faces. When we got cell phones, he sent sweet texts or inside jokes that always made me smile. Then the texts turned into reminders, and then they slowly faded into questions from the grocery store. After D-Day, the sweet texts returned for a while, but then the slow fade hit again.

Listening to my friends talk about their vast sexual experiences left me grateful for my one-hit wonder. I'm glad I never had to deal with all that. Brandon still swears I was his first, but he's a lying little shit, so I don't know if I believe him.

I had an idea and whipped out my cell phone. *Walking through Naples talking about condom sizes. So glad I know nothing about this. Love you.* I hit send and waited for the three little magical dots to appear telling me he was responding. When they appeared, a familiar tug pulled at my heart. I missed my husband. He responded, *Me and you both, beautiful. Miss you.*

361

Love you too. For the first time in months, I, too, had that cute little grin on my face.

Chapter Forty-One
Fallin'

Alissa

Chance is getting married tomorrow. "Holy shit!" doesn't even begin to cover the whirling going through my mind.

On one hand, I feel it's my responsibility to grab her, shake her, and remind her of all the reasons she never wanted to get married and not let her get wrapped up in the heightened emotions and romance. The eternal wingman, that's me. It's like diving in between your drunk friend who's about to go home with someone from the bar who will have her gnawing at her own arm to get free the next morning.

I do admit Chance has been a much better wingman to me over the years, since even when she's drunk, she's sensible. She's come up with some awesome lines, that's for sure. I think my favorite was when she told this guy we were Navy SEALs and had just been paged to a secret mission. One that wasn't so funny was when she told a guy I had a spastic colon and had to wear diapers to bed. She asked where his car was parked so she could leave my "special bag" on his side mirror. It took a few days to get over that one. I still remember him being smoking hot, but Chance remembers him as a dead ringer for an extra in Miami Vice. So yeah, I guess she's been a better wingman than I have, even if she's an ass.

But this was different. It's Tony, for Pete's sake. I glanced at her then looked over my shoulder to see where the other three had stopped. "Okay, we've got a minute. You know I wouldn't be a good best friend if I didn't ask."

Chance smiled. "I've been waiting for this. Go ahead, sister. Let it fly."

"Are you absolutely sure this is what you want to do?" I held my breath and hoped Michelle wouldn't rip off my tits for this.

Chance exhaled loudly. "Living without Tony . . . I've sat on the beach every night thinking the next day I'll make an effort to meet a man's eyes, smile, maybe strike up a conversation, and see where it goes. I thought about taking off to the bar after you two went to bed to find a one-night-stand so I could do *something* to break the tie to Tony. But Lis, when he showed up in that doorway, I've never wanted anything more in my life than to wipe away all this grief—to sit on the beach tonight knowing yesterday was the last day I'll ever have to try to talk myself out of loving him. If this is the one thing that will make that happen, game on, sister."

I stared at her face and looked for the telltale signs she was lying, but they weren't there. I tilted my head. "Okay. Just doing my part. You know most married people live together."

She sighed. "We've got time to work all that out. I told him I'd accept this on the condition that I stay in Florida until you leave."

Relief washed over me. "I'm so glad to hear you say that."

She frowned. "You didn't think I was going back to St. Louis with him when he leaves, did you?"

I shrugged. "I didn't know what you were going to do. If you'd asked me this morning if you were getting married tomorrow, I would have put all my money on no."

"If you'd asked me that same question, we'd both be broke and hungry."

"Things have a funny way of working out like they're supposed to. Look at Dani."

She nodded. "I guess."

I looked over my shoulder and saw Katie, Dani, and Michelle chattering and trying to catch up to us. No doubt they were pumping her full of mothering tips and trading stories about first baths, midnight feedings, and colic. I looked at Chance and asked, "Do you think I'm doing the right thing?"

Chance whispered, "I don't know, honey."

I unlocked the doors to the Navigator and mumbled, "Me neither."

One thing I won't miss about being pregnant is how exhausted I am all the time. Our afternoon outing left me completely spent, and by the time we got back to the house, my feet were swollen, my back hurt, and my mood was touchy at best. I sat on the couch with my feet up eating ice cream while the rest of the crew went about the business of preparing for a wedding ceremony. I giggled as the baby kicked at the cold bowl sitting on my stomach and moved it back in place. I considered calling Dani to come watch, but I decided this moment would be just for me. The days of that happening were dwindling as it was.

Around nine, Chance came in from the beach. "Tony left. He said to tell all of you not to get me drunk unless I start getting cold feet then start pouring drinks down my throat."

"Did you tell him that's why we kept you drunk all day?" Michelle laughed.

She put a finger up to her mouth. "Shhh, he doesn't have to know that, sister."

Michelle held up two fingers. "Scouts honor."

"You won't get cold feet," Katie said. "I think you're over all that now. Are you going to let your apartment go?"

I sat up to break up the convo. "Well that's enough of that. Chance, come help me up."

"Having trouble navigating, there, honey?"

"You put a basketball on your bladder and tell me if you'd trust your own muscles to get the job done. Plus I'm tired. We put on a lot of miles today."

She pulled me off the couch and whispered, "Thank you."

"It's what we do." I winked.

Dani yawned. "I'm headed to bed. Sleep well."

"Oh I don't know how you can go to sleep right now," Katie said. "I'm so excited about tomorrow. Like Christmas for a six-year-old. Sunset is at six thirty, so I figure if we start this show a little after six, the sun should be stunning by the time Tony kisses his bride." She beamed at Chance and clapped her hands like a little girl. "This is so exciting. I've never seen anything like it."

"It's pretty surreal, honey. I put down some conditions tonight that Tony wasn't overly fond of." Chance smiled.

Oh god, here we go. "What kind of conditions?" I asked.

She waved. "Nothing huge. No deal breakers, if that's what your tone of dread suggested, Lis. I told him I want to keep my last name— for my career. Chance Bradley has a certain ring to it. Chance Agustin sounds . . . I don't know . . . foreign."

"Try Morehead on for size," Michelle said. "See if that doesn't make you cringe."

"Lots of people keep their maiden names these days. What else?" I silently prayed, *Please don't let her move to St. Louis, God. Please don't let that happen.*

She said, "Well, the living arrangements are going to be a problem. His job is in St. Louis, and my life is in Columbia." She glanced at me and shrugged. "I need more time to decide about that."

Michelle frowned. "Chance, you move to St. Louis. End of story."

"It's not that simple."

"It is that simple, Chance," Katie said. "You just do it."

She shook her head. "Not for me, ladies. I've got 'til the end of May to make up my mind, so . . ."

I studied her face and saw her ears turning red. She was getting pissed. I announced, "Subject change. We need to make our game plan for tomorrow."

I felt my excitement of the end of Chance's heartbreak fading as reality swept over me. While I was happy for her, I was sad for me. This was a game-changer all the way around. Chance had been one of the only constants I had in my life. And now I'd be sharing her with someone who by rights should come first in her life. As much as I wanted Tony to take his rightful place in her life, I didn't want him to take mine. I left Katie and Michelle to finalize the timeline for the big celebration and went upstairs to nurse my aching feet and heart.

Chance knocked softly on the door and poked her head inside. "Lis?"

I waved her in. "You all right?"

She closed the door. "I was about to ask you the same thing."

"Just like when we were kids." I patted the bed. "Only usually it was

366

me sneaking out and coming to talk to you."

She grinned and climbed onto the bed. "That seems like a lifetime ago and yesterday all at the same time."

"You're going to be fine, Chance. You're doing the right thing, ya know."

"Let's hope so, honey."

"Well, if you need a good divorce attorney, I know one." I chuckled.

"Let's hope it's not *that* big of a mistake, kiddo."

I tilted my head and looked at her. "You think this is a mistake?"

She sighed and looked out the window. She shook her head and whispered, "No, I really don't. Doesn't mean I'm not scared to death now that everything is in action. It's just so fast."

"Chance, this is exactly how it should be for you. You've never been the kind of girl to plan anything for too long. You ponder and ponder, think a little too much then plow in headfirst. When you came in announcing you're getting married this weekend, I knew how perfect it was. No agonizing over dresses and cakes, no arguing over churches and invitations. It's perfect for you, Chance, just like Tony."

"He is pretty perfect." She smiled.

"You're going to be so happy, you won't know what to do with yourself."

She swallowed hard and whispered, "I want you to think about something."

"You're asking me to think?" I chuckled.

She gave me that sly side grin that's broken a thousand hearts in bars across the Midwest. "It doesn't hurt, I promise, honey." She took my hand but couldn't look at me. "I want you to think about relocating to St. Louis when we get back."

I raised my eyebrows and cleared my throat. "That's . . . yeah . . . that's a lot to think about," I mumbled.

"I know I'm asking a lot, Lis, but I don't think I can live in a different city from you." She swatted at a tear trickling down her face. "I need you. When you showed up in St. Louis the night of the media ball, I felt like Richard Gere had showed up in the white limo. I just kind of expected that it would always be me and you, ya know? I knew you'd get married at *least* once more before we shared a nursing home room, but . . ."

I laughed and smacked her leg. "Thanks for the vote of confidence. At least once, huh?"

"Just calling it as I see it, sister." She winked.

I shrugged. "Yeah, well if it was good enough for Liz Taylor, it's good enough for me." I sighed and wrinkled my nose. "St. Louis?"

"It'll be great! Please, please just think about it, okay?"

"What about . . . what about . . ." I pointed to my bulging belly.

She laughed. "I doubt he can make out what you're saying, Lis. Well, of course I'd never ask you to leave if, you know, if it's easier for you than I expect."

I nodded slowly and smiled. This offer was more of a two-way street than I'd initially considered. She's still acting like my wingman and preparing to give me a way out of an uncomfortable situation. God, I love that woman. I shook my head. "You're amazing, Chance Bradley."

She waved me off. "Oh, girl. I know. I'm so awesome, I'm in love with myself. But I'm glad you recognize it."

"Yes, I'll think about it." I laughed. "So does that mean you're moving to St. Louis when we get back?"

She threw herself back on the bed and groaned. "I don't know. I've got six weeks to make up my mind." She rolled onto her side and blinked several times. "Damn, I'm still pretty drunk."

"I'm scared, Chance," I whispered.

She sighed. "I know, babe."

"I wish we could stay here forever. Stop time."

"You could always buy this house." She grinned.

"This place is too rich for my blood." I huffed.

"You are coming back to Missouri, right?"

I looked at her and grinned. "Do you really think I wouldn't?"

"In the delivery room, they're going to hand the baby to Dani, Lis. You know that, right?"

I swallowed around the lump in my throat and nodded. "Yeah, I know. One of many moments I'm dreading in the next six weeks."

She hesitated, started to speak, then hesitated again. "Remember I love you. I think"—she sighed and looked at me.—"I think you should let Dani name the baby."

"Wow, you're full of surprises tonight. Didn't see that one coming."

She held up her hand. "Listen, Lis, I think this is going to be way harder on you than you think—"

"You think I think this is going to be *easy*? Jesus, Chance, you *must* be drunk."

"Honey, I'm not trying to be a douche. I think it would mean a lot to Dani if . . ."

I leveled my eyes at her. "Dani and I have already agreed we're each going to pick a name."

She stared at me and nodded. "Okay." She slid across the bed and hugged me. "I'm taking my drunk ass to bed. Did you hear the rumor I'm getting married tomorrow?"

"Yeah, I heard hearts all across Missouri crack wide open."

She grinned. "At least this time it wasn't mine." She shuffled toward the door and mumbled, "Man, I'm drunk."

I yelled, 'Ibuprofen and water."

She held up a thumb and closed the door.

The next morning, I headed down the beach with my juice and blanket and found Chance sitting by the water. I tossed my blanket on the sand next to her. "The last time you were up this early, you hadn't gone to bed."

She wiped the tears off her face and chuckled. "Nah, I slept. Not much, but I slept. How you doing, honey?"

"Uh uh, spill it."

She shrugged and looked at the water. "Just . . . reality. Been thinking about my parents a lot."

That took me by surprise. Chance never talked about her parents. "I suppose that's normal. Today is a big day."

She sniffled and played with a stick in the sand. "They've been gone longer than they were in my life at this point. This year is twenty years."

369

I remember when Chance's parents died. We were at her house working on algebra homework and talking about boys when her grandmother and two police officers showed up at the door. At fourteen years old, she was an orphan thanks to an impatient driver who ran a red light. That driver walked away with scratches but the Bradleys were pronounced dead at the scene. Her grandmother sold her house and moved in with Chance to lessen the loss. "No sense in uprooting the poor girl and making her change schools," she'd said.

Chance flipped more sand with the stick. "Dad won't walk me down the aisle. Or boardwalk, in this case." She offered a weak grin.

I said, "I can walk you down the aisle. If that's what you want."

She looked at me and whispered, "Really?"

I nodded. "Sure, I'd be honored."

"Lis, I need you today. I'm freaking out, and I don't know if I can do this."

I smiled. "You can do anything. You're Chance-Fucking-Bradley. Stop being a pussy. This is Tony. *To-ny.* Do you want to live the rest of your life living in regret?"

She shook her head. "God, no."

"Okay. So then just keep your eyes on the prize. How freaking romantic is it that he came all this way to find you? That in and of itself is a crotch-buster. But then the proposal and oceanfront ceremony? Holy shit, I can see why you're thrown. That stuff only happens in the movies."

"Yeah, but what happens after the credits roll, honey? What happens when it's all said and done, and I'm . . . married?"

I smiled and grabbed the stick from her hand. "You live happily ever after. Give me that damn stick. You're driving me crazy. You can sit out here and try to talk yourself out of marrying Tony or freak yourself out about the what-ifs, but you're going to rob yourself of your peace and excitement for today. You broke that man's heart in a million pieces and he still came back for you. Just . . . just be grateful for it, okay? I'd hate to punch you on your wedding day. Sheesh."

She chuckled. "I'd hate to hit a pregnant lady."

I pointed to the sunrise. "You have from this moment right now until that sun is fully up to get out all those bullshit thoughts running through your mind. But when that sun comes up, you have a fresh new start. You know I wear the Team Chance shirt twenty-four/seven, but Tony deserves for you to start this day madly in love with him and excited about your life with him. Don't rob him of that."

She stared at the sand and nodded. "You're right."

"I'm sorry, could you repeat that? I don't think I heard you."

She smacked my knee. "One time shot, there, honey."

I grinned. "You're running out of freak-out time. The sun is almost up."

She smirked. "Nah, I'm good. That last part got me. Tony doesn't deserve this. Time to put on my big girl panties and quit being a pansy, sister."

"Atta girl, Chance."

Chapter Forty-Two
Love Will Lead You Back

Chance

Alissa and I spent the morning laughing and making fun of the other three as they twittered about like birds on the first day of spring. Ironically enough, it was the second day. Alissa shaped and painted my nails and chattered on about whatever random thought crossed her mind. There was a silent agreement amongst all of them that Lis's job that day was to keep me out of freak-out mode. She accepted and completed the mission.

It was killing me knowing Tony was in the same town just miles from me, and I couldn't see him. I sent him a text after my seaside revelation and told him how much I loved him and wanted to be his wife. He responded with: *I need to change your name from Do Not Call to My Beautiful Wife. I love you too.*

I took it as good ju-ju that his statement didn't send me running to the toilet to puke my guts out. I actually smiled and got butterflies in my stomach. Me. I got butterflies. God, I'm such a puss.

I only had one rule for myself for the day. Well, two, actually. I wasn't allowed to think about after the wedding and I had to show up on the beach at sunset. Talk about a leap of faith. But, I trusted Tony. Me? Not so much. I've managed to make soup sandwiches of everything I've done in relationships up to this point and shred my own heart in the process. Tony's been good to me. Which one of us is more trustworthy, here? Not me.

At five o'clock, the transformation of Chance-the-eternal-bachelorette into Chance-the-bride began. Alissa lost her patience watching Michelle try to fix my hair and scooted her to the side. Thirty minutes later, my long locks were loosely pinned in the back with an up-do that would make the best hair professional envious. The rest of my hair laid in loose curls down my back. She added a few snips of baby's breath (which is the creepiest name for a flower and the topic of a lively discussion amongst friends) and stood back to admire her handiwork.

She smiled. "I think that's a keeper."

"It better be. My scalp can't take much more abuse, honey."

"Want me to thump you on the head with this?" She waved the hairbrush at me.

I patted my hair and grinned. "It's perfect, Lis."

"Want me to do your makeup?" Katie asked.

I waved her off. "No, I've got lots of practice with this. Being 'the face of the station' has its privileges. I pay attention to the makeup artists."

Michelle and Dani stuck their heads in the bathroom.

"Everything is ready downstairs," Dani said. "We even have a groom."

Michelle smiled. "You look beautiful, Chance."

I blotted my lipstick. "Ah, thank you, dahling. How much longer till sunset?"

I'd been forbidden to even look toward the balcony that overlooked where the ceremony was to be held. Basically I was being held like a princess in a tower and wasn't allowed downstairs until I was making the walk to Tony. I had a little fun with Katie earlier making her run up and down the stairs to retrieve three things right in a row. She caught on, but it took a minute.

Alissa moved the curtain on the door. "It's time to put on your dress, Chance."

Tingles raced from my heart to my palms, and I took a deep breath as I slipped out of my robe and stepped into the dress Dani held. I steadied myself against the bed and grabbed her shoulder. "Shit. Balance was never my forté."

"Good thing you don't have to wear heels tonight." She smiled.

I turned as she pulled the dress up my body, and I slid my arms through the holes. One long pull of the zipper, and I was officially a bride. I turned to examine myself in the full-length mirror and my breath caught in my chest. I met Alissa's teary eyes in the mirror and shook my head. "Oh no, sister. You can't do that."

She bit her lip and chuckled. "You are absolutely stunning, Chance."

I smoothed the dress over my stomach and half-turned to see the back. "It's a great dress, huh?"

Michelle and Katie stepped toward me and offered shy smiles. Katie said, "We, uh, we have something for you. Nothing special or anything, but uh. . . well it's tradition. Something old, something new, something borrowed, something blue." She held out her hand. "It's not much, but this was an anniversary present from Landon, and you can borrow it for the ceremony." She offered me a pair of diamond earrings with silver teardrop shapes dangling from the setting.

"I love these!" I grinned. "Thank you, honey. I'll get them right back to you."

"Mine isn't personal to me," Michelle said, "but it is to you. I dug through your jewelry box earlier, and I found this. I think it's perfect for today, and I didn't think you'd remember it with everything going on. It will satisfy the something old and something blue."

My throat constricted as she opened her hand and revealed my mother's silver sapphire ring. I gasped and took the ring from her. "You're right, I totally forgot about this." I slipped it on my right hand and held it up to get a better view. "I should have had it cleaned." I thought about the argument my grandmother and I had about the ring. I wanted Mom buried with the ring, but she insisted we remove it after the funeral and that I keep it. I lost her four years ago, but I could feel her smiling at me and whispering, *See? Aren't you glad you listened to your grandmother?* I blinked several times to hold back the tears and clenched my jaw as I held up my hand toward Alissa.

She smiled and nodded. "It's perfect, Chance. Let's take a few more pictures then head on down."

Michelle, Dani, and Katie each took their turns hugging me then went downstairs to the beach. Alissa turned to me. "You ready for this?"

I smiled and shook my head as I said, "Yes."

She laughed. "Every bride feels that way right before the doors open. Don't think, just feel. Isn't that what Michelle said to you?"

I took a deep breath. "God, can we just go? I can't wait to see Tony's teeth fall out when I walk down the boardwalk."

She slipped her hand in mine. "Don't forget to take off your flip-flops. They totally don't go with the dress."

I laughed. "I'll ditch them on the deck, I promise."

We walked down the stairs, and everything went into slow motion. All I could hear was my heart pounding in my head, and my mouth went dry. I squeezed Alissa's hand and she squeezed right back. I took a deep breath and nodded as she opened the door to the rest of my life. The sky was illuminated with the most brilliant display of orange and gold I'd ever seen. It was like God Himself had offered His blessing and taken all afternoon to mix a perfect collection of bright, happy colors to celebrate the end of my dark days.

The ocean clapped and sighed when I appeared on the deck. I followed Alissa down the boardwalk and trained my eyes on the spot where Tony should appear. We made the last turn and I saw him standing thirty feet away. He was here. He was really here. He was talking to the minister when I appeared at the foot of the boardwalk; the minister cut him off and pointed at me.

Tony turned and put his hand over his heart as he took a step back. He slipped his hand up to his mouth and shook his head. I took Alissa's hand and stepped into the sand. She whispered, "Take off those fucking flip-flops right now."

I obeyed and tried not to laugh. Tony stared at me with his hands in his pockets. He looked completely edible in his black pants and white button-up shirt with the sleeves rolled to his elbows. I glanced at his feet and saw Chubs sitting beside him on my blanket wearing the black tie from Tony's tuxedo. I nudged Alissa. "Check out the best man."

She giggled. "You know he's hating that thing right now."

I smiled at Dani whose eyes were misting, but she was doing all right. Michelle and Katie, on the other hand, were blubbering messes. I bit my lips to keep from laughing and crying right along with them. I knew if I looked at Alissa, it'd all be over. Her occasional sniffle and eye swipes had already given her away. I was close enough to make eye contact with Tony and that's when it happened.

I've read a lot of sappy novels, watched a shit-ton of romantic comedy movies, and done my fair share of making fun of the leading ladies when they described 'the moment the world fell away.'

But when my eyes locked with his, there was nothing else in the world but the man I loved with tear-rimmed, love-filled eyes staring at me like I was an ethereal goddess. I felt Alissa slip my hand into his and step away, but I couldn't look at anything but Tony. Gone were the nerves, the questions, the doubt. I would be his wife, and he would be my husband to have, hold, kiss, cuddle, and love with every fiber in my soul.

He looked at the minister and held up his hands. "I know this is out of turn, but I have to hold her." He wrapped me in his arms and sighed as he whispered, "You're here."

My chest swelled as I whispered, "So are you."

He released me and stepped back in place. I took a deep breath, nodded to the minister, and stared into Tony's eyes. I listened as Tony repeated his vows, and then it was my turn. I slipped the ring on his finger and whispered, "You're mine forever, Tony."

He grinned that panty-dropping half-smile and whispered, "Dreams do come true. *Florida*." He slid his hands up my arms and grabbed my face. "I can't wait any longer." When his lips pressed against mine, he sighed. "God, I love you." He kissed me again then wrapped his arms around me. He lifted me off my feet and twirled around in the sand. I squealed and laughed as I hung on for dear life and kissed him again. He set me down. "I love you, Chance. My wife, my heart, the air in my lungs." He touched my face and whispered, "I'm dead without you."

"Forever, baby. Then you'll live forever."

After the ceremony, pictures, cake, and lots of champagne, Tony slid his arm around me and announced, "Ladies, thank you for the happiest day of my life. With your permission, I'd like to whisk my wife away on our honeymoon getaway." He looked at me and whispered, "I can't wait to get you out of that dress."

If looks could melt, my panties would have puddled at my ankles. I didn't even want to go upstairs for my bag—I just wanted him to get me out of that dress immediately. Alissa nodded at Michelle who slid one of my suitcases from behind the couch and brought it to me. Alissa said, "I just packed a few outfits and your makeup. Even though I highly doubt clothing will be required."

Tony took the suitcase. "You're a good woman, Alissa."

I laughed and shook my head. "Come on before she falls in love with you."

Alissa hugged me. "Have fun. See you soon."

When we got in the car, Tony leaned over to kiss me. "I couldn't get much on short notice, but I promise I'll give you a proper honeymoon soon."

I smiled. "We're married, Tony. Like husband-and-wife shit."

"Like joint-taxes shit."

"Like emergency-contact shit."

"Like changing-your-name shit."

I stared out the window and bit my lip. "Like never-having-to-wake-up-missing-you shit."

He whispered, "Like never-having-to-talk-myself-out-of-calling-you shit."

I sniffled and wrapped my fingers in his. "Tony, I'll do anything to keep from losing you again."

He kissed my fingers. "You just did everything I'd ever hoped for."

Twenty minutes later, we pulled into the parking lot of the hotel and made out like high-school kids in the elevator. I panted, "If you keep this up, we're not going to make it to the room."

He grinned. "Fine with me. Bucket list item—check!"

"Doing it in an elevator? Good to know." I kissed him again and straightened myself when the elevator door opened.

He chased me down the hallway. "Man, I can't wait to get that dress off you. This is us." He slid the card into the reader and set down my suitcase. "May I?" He wrapped one arm around my waist and swept me into his arms. "Gotta carry the bride across the threshold, right?" He swung open the door and carried me to the bed. "Stay right there. Don't move."

I flopped my arms and legs around. "Oops. I moved."

He shook his head and took a deep breath. "I'll be right back." He kissed my nose and went to get my suitcase from the hallway. I shivered with anticipation of being with Tony again. By far the best sex of my life has been with him. Sweet and tender, hot and rough, always satisfactory—multiple times.

I walked to the foot of the bed and kicked off my flip-flops. Tony returned. "You moved."

I turned my back to him and looked over my shoulder. "I thought you wanted to take this dress off me."

He groaned and ran his hands over my shoulders. "You have no idea how much." He ran his fingers down my back and kissed my neck.

Six Weeks Later

Chance

Alissa lay in bed drenched in sweat and gasping for air. "I can't do it, Chance. I can't! I got nothing left."

"Yes, you can. You're doing great, honey. Just a few more pushes and you're done." I looked at the monitor. "Okay, you're getting close." I wiped her face with a cold washcloth.

Dr. DeMario's face appeared between her knees. "You're doing great, Alissa."

"He's crowning, Lis. He's almost here." Dani stood over his shoulder and wiped tears from her face.

"Do you want to see the head? I can hold up a mirror—" The doctor asked.

"No, I don't want to see my shit right now!"

"Okay, okay. We're ready when you are." The doctor chuckled.

I positioned myself behind her for the next round of pushing. She gritted her teeth and bore down as she screamed, "God, please! Give me something for the pain!"

"Breathe, Alissa. Big, big push," the doctor yelled.

"You got this, honey. You got this." It was killing me to watch her in so much pain. Her labor had come on quickly, so there was no time for epidurals or spinal blocks. She was flying solo, and every time she screamed I felt my heart break all over again right along with my right hand.

"The head is out, Alissa. Another big push. That's it. Keep breathing."

She moaned and panted then collapsed onto me. "Oh, he's out. He's out. Oh God, he's out."

I wiped her face and smiled. "You did it. You're my hero, honey. It's all over."

Her face contorted with the realization of what came next. She shook her head and bit her lip as tears rolled down the sides of her face. I

379

held her hand and cried with her as Dani cut the cord and cooed, "Oh my goodness, hi, baby."

I wanted to look at Dani and see the baby, but I couldn't take my eyes off Alissa's. She squeezed my hand and shook her head. I nodded and whispered, "I know, honey. I know." I leaned over her and held her head to my chest as she cried while the doctor continued to work on cleaning her up.

The baby's squeaky little cry pierced through the delivery room causing Alissa to cry harder. She mumbled, "Is he okay? Is he okay?"

I smoothed her hair. "He's supposed to cry, Lis. He's probably pretty pissed off that he's gone from being snug as a bug to cold and manhandled. He's fine, and so are you, honey."

"I want a drink."

"That makes two of us. I'll bring back a bottle of wine later."

"Don't leave me, Chance." She squeezed my hand.

I choked on the sob in my throat. "I'm not going anywhere, Lis. I'm right here with you."

I looked at Dani, the other side of the coin, and I've never seen her glow like she did in that moment. The nurse announced, "Ten fingers, ten toes, and a great set of lungs, Mom." She looked at Dani. "Congratulations."

Dani came to the bed and grabbed Alissa's other hand. She wiped her tears on her shoulder. "Alissa, he's perfect. He's healthy and he's perfect."

They took the baby to the nursery to do whatever it is they do to newborns. Dani followed and I stayed with Alissa. Dr. DeMario walked to the side of Lis's bed and shook her hand. "You did great, Lis. Just a few stitches and no other damage. You were a real trouper. We'll get you some good drugs and let you rest." He waved at me and left the room.

When we were finally alone, Alissa looked at me. "That was brutal."

I grinned. "For you and me both, honey. I'm pretty sure my hand is broken."

She rolled her eyes. "My junk is shredded. I win." She looked at the ceiling and sighed. "What do I do now, Chance?" Her chin quivered as she repeated, "What do I do now?"

I pressed my hand to my nose to stop the tingles and bit my lips. "I don't know, honey," I whispered.

"I haven't even seen him."

"You will. They're just getting him all cleaned up and they'll bring him in. Dani will make sure of it."

She nodded. "She'll be a good mother."

"Yes, she will."

"Katie and Michelle are going to be so pissed they missed the birth."

"Well, if he'd come any faster, *you* may have missed it."

She huffed, "True dat. Little impatient bastard."

"Sounds like someone I know." I winked and patted her hand.

"I wonder who he looks like."

"Want me to go see?"

She gripped my hand. "Please don't leave me."

I said, "Okay. But I do have to pee. I'll use your bathroom, so I'll be right here, okay?"

She nodded and released my hand. "Might shoot a text to Katie and Michelle and tell them what happened."

"While I'm peeing?"

"Bitch, please don't act like you don't text and poo. I know you do."

"Keep sassing and I'll smack you in the uterus."

"Oh, you're such a bitch," she laughed.

"I'll be right back."

I stared at myself in the mirror while washing my hands. So this is what I look like at four in the morning. How Tony could ever love this face, I'll never know. Alissa had waddled into my room a little after midnight panting and panicking. I walked her downstairs and gathered up the bags then went to wake up Dani. That one can roll out of bed, smooth her hair, brush her teeth, and look like a million bucks. I, on the other hand, don't work that way.

I let the warm water run over my hands and wondered what I would say to Alissa in the days to come. The next few hours, the next minute. I stared at my reflection and tried to find the courage to face this

381

impossible situation with Alissa while not alienating Dani. For someone with a gift of always saying the right thing, my words were failing me.

Chapter Forty-Three
Not Gon' Cry

Alissa

I woke up to the sun shining and mild cramping. They said this might happen. I glanced at Chance who was asleep in the chair and would be really pissed by the crick she's definitely going to have after that position. I ran my hand over my belly to confirm the absence of the little guest. Elvis has left the building. I tried to move, but the delivery left me feeling like I'd gone eight hours in the gym, so I gave up.

It's over. He's officially Dani's son and my part is done. I shoved aside the ache in my heart and thought of the positive things surrounding this day. I could drink heavily when I get home. No more heartburn. I can sleep on my stomach. I can sleep through the night. (*Haha, Dani, eat that. Those days are over for you.*) No more peeing eighty-seven times a day. No more prenatal horse pills or weekly doctor's visits. I can get back in the gym and start running again. No more food aversions and weird cravings of shit I don't even like.

A soft knock at the door roused Chance. She looked at me with glassy eyes. "Who the fuck is that?"

I shushed her. "Come in."

The nurse came in pushing a basinet with Dani close behind. "Good morning," the nurse said. "You have a visitor."

I fingerwaved at Dani and smiled. She smiled back and shook her head. "Alissa, you're the toughest woman I know."

I grinned. "Takes more than natural childbirth to beat me. Although, I do feel like I've gone ten rounds with Tyson." The nurse checked my vital signs and asked about my comfort level. I said, "A little cramping but nothing major."

"I'll bring you something. Are you ready to use the bathroom? Maybe shower?"

Chance frowned and asked, "She just gave birth four hours ago. Do you think that's a good idea?"

The nurse smiled. "The female body is a miraculous thing. She'll be fine."

I removed the blankets from my legs and tried to sit up. "Good god, I'm whipped." I sucked air between my teeth as the pressure of sitting grabbed my attention. "How long is that going to last? Damn."

"You have a few stitches, and you're going to be sore for a week or two. I've got a list of instructions for you when you get home."

I heard the baby grunt and looked at Dani. She smiled. "Would you like to see him?"

I nodded and looked at the nurse. "I've carried the little guy for the last forty weeks, certainly I can see him before we do all this."

"Of course. I'll go get the meds and fresh water." She grabbed the pitcher and left the room.

Dani reached into the basinet and retrieved the tiny grunting bundle. She kissed his forehead and placed him in my arms. I stared down at his little red face, his sweet little nose, and tiny little lips. Dani lifted his hat. "Look at all that hair." Black hair, just like Mark.

I smiled. "Let's just hope that's all he got from his father."

"He's perfect, Lis." Dani whispered.

"Yes, he is. Hi, buddy." He cracked his eyes and looked at me. "Oh goodness, do you recognize my voice? Hi, there. You've been a pain in my ass for the last nine months. Yes, you have."

Chance chuckled. "Way to cuss in front of the baby, Lis."

I lifted the corner of the papoose roll and inspected his hands. "Nice big hands. You gonna be a ball player? Huh?" I kissed his cheek and tightened the blanket back around him. "There." He stared at my face and into my soul. I felt the questions boring into my mind. *Why didn't you want me? How could you give me away?*

The ache in my heart threatened to surface, and I couldn't break down in front of Dani. I handed him to her. "I, uh . . . I'm cramping pretty bad. Here. Take him, please."

She scooped him up. "It's about time for his bottle, anyway. Lis, there's something we didn't talk about. I didn't even think about it, but they asked me, so I'm asking you. Are you interested in pumping breast milk for him?"

Chance's voice split the air. "No, she is not."

Dani was taken aback and frowned. "Is that an inappropriate question?"

Chance said, "No, but the answer is no."

I met Dani's questioning gaze and shook my head. "I don't think so, Dani. That's a big commitment, and I don't think it's a good idea."

"Fair enough," she said as she put him in the basinet. "Are we still good with the name we picked out? I have to fill out the birth certificate information."

I nodded and asked, "Are you still good with it?"

"I think it fits. Tristan Joel it is."

"You know I'm going to call him T.J., right?"

Dani shook her head and chuckled. "If that's as bad as it gets, I'll be happy."

The nurse returned. "Here you go. Take these, and here's some fresh water. Are you ready for your shower?"

I nodded and slid my legs to the side of the bed. Gotta keep moving, right?

Early the next morning, Dr. DeMario made rounds and deemed me fine for discharge. He smiled. "We'll get you scheduled for a follow-up appointment, and if you need anything in the meantime, please feel free to call." He shook my hand and waved at Chance.

She hadn't left my side outside of the occasional coffee run since she'd driven like a bat out of hell when I was in labor. I blame her for the quick progression, because she scared the baby out of me. But we'll address that later. I looked at her and smiled. "I'm busting out of here today."

She rolled her head and groaned, "Thank God. I need a shower and a real cup of coffee. And my bed. And my dog. And my pillow."

"So what you're saying is you'd like to leave?"

She sipped her coffee and flipped her middle finger at me. "Yes. I need to find out what the plan is for Tristan. When they're discharging

385

him, all that." She stood. "Be right back. Need anything?"

"Nope. I just want to get out of here."

She gave me thumbs up and left the room. I stared at the clock and ignored the vacant hole in my chest. Round and round the little second hand ticked. No matter what was going on in the world that little hand would still be ticking away. The happiest moments of my life? Tick, tick, tick. The miserable? Tick, tick, tick. You can beg and beg for more time or for time to fly, but it's its own master and watchers beware.

Chance returned. "They're discharging Tristan, too, so we can all leave at the same time." I nodded and slid my legs to the side of the bed. She held out her hand. "You got it?"

I grunted, "Yeah, I'm good. Will you hand me my pants, please?"

"These yoga pants are probably going to be a little stretched out."

"I'm just going home. As long as they stay up 'til I get to the car, I'm solid." She hesitated then handed them over along with my bra and t-shirt. Her face held fifty emotions in place as she avoided my eyes and slid my flip-flops to me. "Thank you," I said. "I know you're exhausted, but thank you so much for staying with me."

"It's what we do, sister. Not going to lie, I'm really worried about you, but I figure we'll get drunk tonight, have a good cry, and start trying to figure all this out from there."

"Oh yes. I want lots of wine tonight."

"You shall have it. Look, Lis . . . I don't . . . I don't know what it's going to be like at home.

I leveled my eyes at her. "It will be fine. I did my job, all right? I was the good little organ donor, and now it's up to Dani to be the mother."

Chance's eyes widened and she sucked in her breath. "Is that how you feel?"

I slid my shirt over my head. "Yep." I slid back into bed and stared at the clock waiting for the second hand to motivate the rest of the hands to move and get me the hell out of there.

An hour later the nurse wheeled me to the front of the hospital where Chance was waiting with the Navigator. Dani and Tristan were close behind. Once the big, happy family was all loaded in the car,

Chance eased into traffic and headed toward the house. I stared out the window and watched the scenery pass by. People in cars, people on foot, people working, people laughing, people staring back at me. Hollow. They're the ones I nodded to.

Tristan fussed in the back seat, and my boobs instantly responded to his cry. They said it would go away in a few days when my body figured out I wasn't going to breast feed. Meanwhile, the need to feed him was primal. I took a deep breath and let it out slowly.

Out with the hatred, in with peace. Out with hatred, in with peace.

I thought of my sisters, their babies, and my mother. I thought of midnight feedings, colic, diaper rash, high fevers, potty training, and all the other things I learned to do before I ever got my first period. I thought of that cold bedroom and how it felt to be discarded by my own mother to satisfy another douchebag who wasn't fond of kids. I thought of the blood that ran through my veins—my mother's blood. I thought of cocktail parties and spur-of-the-moment weekend getaways, things I couldn't do if I had a baby.

Chance reached for my hand and gave it a squeeze. I squeezed back then slipped my hand to my lap. We pulled into the driveway at the house and started the procession into the house. I half expected Michelle and Katie to come squealing into our arms and help divert the attention off me so I could hide in my room, but I knew they weren't there. According to Chance, they both were ass-deep in kid functions and domestic hell and couldn't get flights to work. Yeah, those airline gift cards were a waste of money. Yet another reason why motherhood isn't for me.

I headed upstairs and left Chance to help Dani get Tristan's stuff in the house and all put away. She didn't have an opportunity to aunt-out on the little guy in the hospital since she was on sentry duty with me, but I had needed her more. I dropped my purse and slid into bed while listening to Dani and Chance coo over Tristan in the next room. He must have had one nasty diaper judging by Chance's expletive and simultaneous gag.

She slid into my room and took a deep breath. "Holy hell, that's

387

awful."

I mumbled, "Wait til he gets a little older. It gets much worse."

"Need me to get you anything?"

I shook my head. "Nah, I'm good. I'm just tired."

She stared at me a little too long then nodded. "Well, let me know if you want something. I'm your servant at your beck and call." She bowed.

"Actually, I would really like a glass of wine."

"Just a glass?" she winked.

"Better put on your tennis shoes, because I'm going to run your ass up and down the stairs."

She glanced over her shoulder. "Why don't you come sit on the balcony with me? I'll bring up a bottle in ice and we can enjoy the view while we get tore down."

I said, "I just shoved a seven pound kid through my vagina. The idea of sitting isn't appealing yet."

She laughed and faked a shiver. "God, don't say such things. Okay, you lay here, and I'll sit. How's that?"

"You don't have to babysit me, Chance. You better keep an eye on Dani, though."

She huffed, "I'm not *babysitting* you. I'm just—"

"Babysitting."

She threw up her hands. "Want me to leave you alone? I can do that, sister."

I nodded. "Yeah, close the door behind you, please."

She blinked a few times, sighed, and walked to the door. "Do you still want the wine?"

"Yes."

She mumbled, "I should push you down the stairs and make you get it yourself."

"Love you too."

She shook her head and left the room. I sighed and buried my face in the pillow. I did what I said I was going to do. I followed the plan, executed it to perfection, and Tristan is a healthy baby boy. I signed him over to Dani, and she's legally his mother. In a few days, after the shock of childbirth wears off and the giant rip in my soul starts to heal, things will look better. I hope.

One Week Later

Chance came in the room and threw open the curtains. "Come on, Lis. Up and at 'em."

I groaned and shielded my face from the light. "What the hell, Chance?"

She pulled the blankets off me and clapped her hands. "You're getting up today."

I rolled over. "In a little bit."

She said, "Alissa, it's been a week and you've only been out of this bed to pee." I heard the wine bottles clink together as she gathered them in her arms. "Come on. I need your help today."

"Chance Bradley doesn't need help with anything."

She stood over me. "Do I have to pick you up?"

I chuckled, "If you think you can." She put one arm under my neck and the other under my legs and lifted me off the bed. "Chance, put me down!"

She huffed, "You gonna do it on your own? Jesus, you smell."

I mumbled, "If you weren't up my ass right now, you wouldn't smell me."

She faked dropping me. "Can't hold on much longer. You gonna move?"

"Yes, put me down, dammit."

She sat me on the bed and stretched her back. "You're heavier than you look."

I scratched my greasy head. "I would have bet a thousand dollars you couldn't lift me."

She flexed her arms. "I work out."

"Liar," I chuckled. "What do you need help with?"

"You'll see." She held out her hand. "Come on."

I took her hand and let her lead me to the shower. She turned it on.

"Get naked, sister."

I gaped, "Are you going to monitor me?"

"You wanna act like a crazy person? Hell yes, I'm going to monitor you." She adjusted the water and asked, "Is that too hot?"

I put my hand in the water and sucked air through my teeth. "Geez, are you trying to boil me?"

"Nope, just trying to knock the funk off. There. Step on in."

I slipped out of my t-shirt and pajama pants. "Will you at least turn around so I can tend to my maxi pad alone?"

She spun around. "Yeah, 'cause I've never seen a bloody pad ever."

I rolled my eyes, finished my business, and stepped into the shower. I sighed in spite of myself and groaned, "Mmm shower."

Chance said, "I'm going to change your sheets. I'll be right back."

I stood under the water and let it roll over my head and face. Out of habit, I ran my hand over my now shrunken belly, and reality slapped me in the face. The baby was out in the world, and I was alone again. I adjusted the water to chase away the chill trying to settle on my skin and moved further under the showerhead.

Out with the sadness, in with peace. Out with sadness, in with peace.

The baby wasn't mine. I was a surrogate for Dani, and I did a good deed for a friend in need.

Out with the sadness, in with peace.

I sighed and thought about the house in Columbia. I never got the living room repainted. I should probably do that before I put it on the market.

My heart slammed in my chest. Dani and the baby live in that house, too. Dani planned on buying a house when we got back from Florida but hasn't done it yet. Fuck. My pulse quickened as my breath halted in my lungs. I bent over and put my hands on my knees to keep from falling over. I squeaked, "Chance?"

She appeared in the door and pulled open the shower stall door. "Jesus, what's wrong?"

I panted, "They live with me."

"Yeah, honey, they do, but just for a few more weeks."

I shook my head and spit out the water running over my mouth. "No. In Columbia. They live with me, Chance."

"Wait right here, Lis. Take a few deep breaths, and I'll be right back."

I inhaled slowly and exhaled as I braced myself against the cool ceramic tile. Electric shocks coursed through my veins and exploded out my palms. I waved them around and took another deep breath as Chance reappeared.

"Here. Take this." She put a pill in my hand. "Use the shower water to rinse it down."

I popped the pill in my mouth and filled my mouth with hot shower water. I swallowed the pill and took another deep breath. "What the hell is wrong with me?"

"Panic attack, Lis. I used to have them all the time. Listen, okay? Just focus on one thing right now. You focus on breathing and listen to my instructions. Have you washed your hair yet?" I shook my head. "Okay, grab the shampoo bottle and squeeze shampoo into your hair."

I took a deep breath and grabbed the bottle. "Geez, my hands are shaking."

"I know, but they'll stop soon, honey. Just focus on doing the next thing and don't think. Right now, you're just taking a shower. You're not in Columbia, you're not living with anyone, you're just naked as a jaybird in front of your best friend who's a little pissed that you gave birth a week ago and still have a better figure than she does."

A half-laugh escaped my lips as I glanced at her. "You're so full of shit."

She shrugged. "My reality. Hair. Now."

I rubbed the shampoo into my hair and took another deep breath.

Out with the panic, in with peace. Out with panic, in with peace.

I rinsed my hair and fell into my shower routine without Chance having to give instructions. I felt the pill take effect as my scalp tingled and all panic washed down the drain. I looked at her. "Oh, damn. I want a whole prescription of this shit right away."

She laughed. "We'll see what Dr. DeMario says. Maybe he can give you something to knock off the edge for a while. If not, I've still got my stash."

"That's highly illegal, you know."

She raised her eyebrows and hands. "Just trying to help a sister out. You all done?"

I killed the water and took the towel from her hands. "Man, I love these towels. I need to get some of these for my new place."

She tilted her head. "And where might that be?"

I said, "Oh, I don't know. Maybe some city that has a huge arch. That would be cool. Think one of those exist?"

She smiled. "I know of a city like that. You sure about this?"

I shook my head. "No, but that's heavy on my mind." I clenched my teeth to stop the prickling in my nose and eyes. I whispered, "I can't stay there, Chance."

She nodded. "I know, babe. I'd hug you, but it would be extremely awkward since you're naked and wet. Rain check." She stepped toward the door. "Do your thing with your junk and get dressed for a casual outing."

"Where are Dani and the baby?"

She stared at me and frowned. "They're either in Dani's room or downstairs."

I nodded and waved her on. "I got this."

Chapter Forty-Four
Ready to Run

Chance

The baby. She called him the baby—she didn't use his name. I don't know if that's a good sign or bad sign. I stepped into the hallway and peeked into Dani's room before heading to my bedroom. They must be downstairs. Watching Alissa swirling down the drain broke my heart. Every attempt I made to get her to talk, get up, move, or go somewhere in the last week failed, so I knew I needed to do something drastic. Unfortunately, I'm probably going to be nursing a sore back for the next week. If she snaps out of it, I'll consider it worthwhile.

I slipped into my room and saw Dani sitting on my bed. "Holy shit, you scared me half to death."

She stared at the baby monitor in her hand. "Have you ever felt like you've gained and lost everything at the same time?"

I exhaled slowly and inched toward the bed. "Only every day of my life, sister."

She glanced up and half smiled. "How is she?"

"She's . . . uh . . . she's up and moving. I made her get up. She wasn't happy about that."

"No, I imagine not."

I sat next to her on the bed and patted her leg. "Out with it."

She shook her head. "What's done can't be undone and I hate myself for it."

And there it is. "Dani . . ."

"I've gained my life's dream, and I've lost my best friend. Not only have I lost her, *she's* lost herself. I should have known, Chance. I should have known when she offered to let me adopt Tristan that she hadn't thought it through. All the snap decisions, the bad outcomes, and regrets that came later. I should have known. This guilt is consuming me, Chance. I already love him in a way I've never felt and I will devote every breath to him for the rest of my life."

"Then you know why she went through with it, honey."

"But at what expense to her? Look at her. Have you ever seen her so destroyed? She hasn't left that room since we got home. I'm right down the hall from my best friend and I can't even talk to her."

"Why not?"

She leveled her eyes at me. "I've been walking on broken glass around her since we moved to Florida. She tolerates me at best. I know how she feels about me, about this situation, and it's tearing me apart."

"What do you suggest, Dani?"

"It's not like I can return him like a borrowed pair of shoes, Chance. I'm in a no-win situation. We all are. She made a snap decision based off years of feelings she can't face, and I let her. I *let* her follow through with this. Any minute, I could have backed out and been the doting aunt, but I really thought this was what she wanted. I'm ready to be a mother. I craved the opportunity to be a mother, and when the chance presented itself, I took it. She *never* wanted to be a mother, Chance, she was repulsed by the idea. It seemed like such a logical solution, but as time passed and I saw her struggling—going out to the ocean every morning, coming back looking like she'd been crying, avoiding eye contact—and I didn't do a damn thing about it, Chance."

"Dani, I don't know what to say. About *any* of it. I think in time all of this is going to work out."

She whispered, "I miss my friend. I want to show her my baby and take pictures and oogle over him like normal friends do. I want to share this amazing experience with her, but then reality slams into place as I think of how razor sharp that will feel to her, watching me fawn over the baby she just gave up. I feel like I'm grieving. Like she's died, and I can't even talk to her anymore, but she's in the very next room."

"Give her some time, honey. Everything she's been through and tried to avoid just slammed into her like a freight train. Please try not to take it personally, because she loves you very much. If she didn't, there's no way she would have gone through with it."

"I think that's what kills me the most. Alissa is loyal to a fault and would rather break her own heart than hurt someone she loves."

"I think when Lis made this decision, she knew it was going to suck for a while, then she'd get over it. When she weighed that against the drastic change her life would have, she made the best decision she could."

"But, Chance, she would be a great mother."

I nodded. "Yes, she would. But so will you. You'll be the mom that organizes and attends every school party, sits in stifling heat during little league, makes hot cocoa on snowy afternoons and waits up till curfew to kiss him good night. You've already said it, Dani. You'll devote every minute of your life to him and Alissa's not wired like that, and she knows it. We were talking about this one day. She said she's the kind of person who would be making time in her schedule to be home with him, and you'd be the mom that scheduled your life around him. She said she was afraid she'd grow to resent him, but you would savor every minute.

She smiled and nodded. "I *am* going to rock this."

"Yes, you will, honey. Just give her time to come around, okay? In the meantime, maybe you could reach out more to the mother twins in Missouri and let them be your outlet for Tristan. And of course, I'm always here."

"I know. But I also know that you're in mama-bear mode with Alissa, so—"

"Hey, I'm still your friend, too. She's got me worried sick but I'm still here for you."

Tristan fussed through the monitor and Dani stood. "I'm on duty, again. Thanks, Chance, I really mean that."

"I know you do. Hopefully after today, she'll start morphing back into her old self again."

Dani left the room and I threw myself on the bed. I stared at the ceiling and wondered if anything I just said to Dani was true. Alissa would have been a great mom if she'd given herself a chance, but it was too late now to prevent the milk from spilling.

I unplugged my phone and checked my texts. Michelle and Katie had been rapid-firing texts all week asking about Alissa. I asked them not to come to Florida right now, and they didn't take it well to say the least.

Especially since they both had free tickets burning holes in their pockets. But, I know if they show up oogling over Tristan, Alissa will flip a script. I lied to Lis and told her they couldn't make it work with their families. We're in preservation mode right now, and I can't take the risk of Alissa going off the deep end. One Michelle in the group is enough. I updated them and said she was finally getting out of bed and going out with me today.

Alissa appeared in my doorway. "Okay, I'm ready for our big outing."

Oh, god, did she hear any of that? I turned and smiled. "Wow, you look great! You look so normal."

"Weird, isn't it?" She rubbed her stomach and said, "I still look pregnant."

"Not nearly as pregnant as you were, though."

We walked downstairs and headed for the coffee pot. Dani walked around the corner with Tristan in her arms. "Chance, will you— Alissa. You're up."

Alissa shrugged. "Chance threatened me."

"It's good to see you." Dani smiled.

I studied Alissa's face and waited for my moment to intervene, but she did fine. She smiled and said, "We're heading out for the day. Need anything?"

"No, I think we're good." She patted Tristan's back and stared at the counter.

"Text if you change your mind." Alissa looked at me and said, "Ready?"

I nodded and waved at Dani. "We'll be back later."

Over the next two weeks, Alissa found reason after reason to leave the house—shopping at the same boutiques we'd visited three times in one week just to see if they had new merchandise, running to the grocery store for one thing at a time, going to lunch on the coast to try new drinks and watch the ocean. It was hard to watch her virtually snub Dani and Tristan as she snuck into her own reality pretending it was just her and me on a fabulous vacation in Florida. And, I couldn't keep up with her drinking, though I gave it the old college try.

I played moderator between Dani and Alissa and reassured Dani that Lis was just in a funk and would come around, but Dani's own guilt was eating her alive. Not only did she feel like she'd stolen Alissa's baby, she felt she'd lost her best friend. And what do you say to that? We had ten days until we left Naples and started our cross-country journey back to the Midwest, and yes, I was counting down. While I would miss my oceanfront sunsets and the freedom of having no schedule, I missed Tony, and I wanted to start my life with him. As much as that scared the shit out of me. I guess it goes without saying I'm giving up my third floor apartment and life in Columbia to join Tony in St. Louis. I guess Miss Miriam O'Bannon shit kittens when she heard Tony married me and turned tyrant on the set. The clock's ticking on the old girl, and her services will no longer be required when I make it back to Missouri. I can't say that doesn't make me giggle—a lot.

So, it looks like I'm going to get my happy ending after all.

One Week Later

Alissa

I woke up just before sunrise and slipped down the stairs, through the door, and out to watch the sunrise again. I'm going to miss this beach for the rest of my life even though I never want to see it again. A new sunrise offers a new beginning, and that's what I'm counting on today. Dr. DeMario said yesterday during my four-week checkup I'm good to go, so that's what I'm doing. Time to put all this behind me and start moving again.

I inhaled the morning air and exhaled the mistakes, regrets, and sorrow of yesterday as I wiped the tears from my face. I nodded at the sun and smiled at my faithful friend as it warmed me with its sunbeam hug. I slid my feet deep into the sand and wiggled my toes. No. No more standing still. No more sitting around feeling sorry for myself. I kicked my feet free and headed back to the house.

I thought I was strong enough to do this. I planned it to perfection, prepared myself for every possible scenario and like always, it backfired. I never expected to love the baby as much as I did. Someone I'd never met and held only once. When Dani put him in my arms in the hospital, every cell in my body longed to keep him right there forever. I had to shut it down—had to shut them out. It was the only way to keep from dropping to my knees and begging Dani to reconsider our agreement. And, I couldn't break her heart. This was her once-in-a-lifetime opportunity. Maybe someday I'll think about having another baby. I always have that option. Dani doesn't.

Maybe Mom was right to move as much as she did. Maybe the excitement of a new beginning will be a good distraction, and I can put this whole mess behind me. I always thought she was a coward for running from her problems, but now I think I get it. I see how strong she was, how empowering it is to reclaim yourself after being devastated when life doesn't go as planned. At least I'm not dragging a litter of children along behind me. At least this time, it's just my heart that's broken.

I retrieved the suitcases I'd hidden in the downstairs closet last night, pulled my overnight bag over my shoulder and headed to the driveway where my cab was waiting.

Chance

I buried my face in the pillow and regretted not closing the drapes before bed last night. That morning sun was brutal. I reached for my phone to check the time and found a note draped across it.

My dearest friend,

Pretty sure you're going to be pissed when you wake up, not like you aren't always pissed when you wake up. Ha-ha. I think we both know I'm not doing so hot with all this, so I'm taking off for a while. I can't go back to Columbia—we both know that. Tell Dani she can stay in the house as long as she wants and to let me know if there's anything she needs. Ship home anything of the baby's she wants to keep and let me know how much it costs. I'm sorry to bail on you and the trip home, but I'm sure you get it.

Not really sure where I'm going at the moment. I thought of going out to see my mom and sisters. Or maybe I'll see what Southern hospitality is like. Maybe I'll meet some dashing Southern boy who will teach me to shoot from the tailgate of his pick-up truck. Ha ha, can you imagine? You and Tony deserve time to get the rest of your life started, and you don't need to babysit me any longer. Don't worry. I'm leaving breadcrumbs and will be in St. Louis before you know it.

I'll call you later for my ass chewing. Don't be mad at me, Chance. Gotta keep moving, right?

I love you,

Lis

I threw back the covers and scrambled down the hallway to Alissa's room. It looked just as it had the day we squealed our way through the house with jaws dropped and laid claim to our space. She was gone. I wandered down the hall with the letter in my hand and peered into Dani's cracked door. She sat in the rocking chair feeding Tristan a bottle and looking at the little guy with complete adoration. A lump formed in my throat as I shared this intimate moment with them and felt my heart break as I wondered how many times Alissa had done this same thing over the last four weeks.

I slipped back to my room and threw open the doors to my balcony hoping to see Alissa down on the beach. If she wasn't gone yet, maybe I could talk her out of it. Maybe I could convince her to hang on just a little longer.

Or maybe she'd finally broke and had to run.

She was always good at that. But she always finds her way back.

I turned to head back downstairs when something caught my eye. A fat envelope was propped against an empty wine bottle on my bedside table. There was a short message scrawled on the front:

No more sad songs. I'll see you soon.

Inside were four CDs, Alissa's unmistakable handwriting on the front: *The Sunrise Mix.*

Now that sounds like a plan.

****

Acknowledgements

A huge thank-you to Joey Houston and Cynthia Moyer for your hard work and dedication to making sure The Breakup Mix shines like a new penny. Without you, this book never would have made it to publication. Thank you to the folks at Sprinkles on Top Studios for the fantastic cover. Thanks to my awesome street team (shout out to #CarterCrew!) for your loyalty and support, and to my sweet children for being my biggest cheerleaders. Thank you, Lindsay Stoneking and Kate Long, for answering technical questions about pregnancy and timeframes. (It's been a while since I've been through that. Ha!) Props to Casey for being so patient while her BFF finishes her latest novel. We can go play now- ha! To my awesome stylist, Mikey Salisbury, thank you for making sure I look fabulous during book signing events and photo shoots. Last but not least, thank you, Liz Schulte, for being an awesome mentor and talking me off the ledge when I wanted to jump. Love you, lady!

Thank you to my writing group, 80,000 Words, for being in the trenches with me and encouraging me to stop whining and write. For the late night writing jags, input and feedback, and your friendship – I salute you!

A huge thank you to God for giving me the talent and boldness to pursue my dreams and to my fans for loving my work. I love you!

About the Author

TK Carter is a Southern born-and-bred middle child with all the complexes that accompany this birth order. She loves the color red, anything shiny, and has an unnatural love for peanut butter Snickers and Diet Coke.

In response to her chaotic, single life as a divorced mother and head of household, she started a blog called My Ms. Adventures where she holds nothing back as she tells exactly what it's like to be her.

Tami, as she is casually known, was raised in mid-Missouri and now lives in Centralia. She has two children, two dogs, a mortgage, and a dream. She is the author of women's fiction novels: Independence, An Afternoon with Aunt Viv, and the Dystopian Suspense series: Collapse and Three Meals to Anarchy. Book Three of The Yellow Flag Series is due out Summer 2015.

Follow TK Carter's career at:

tkcarter-author.com
www.facebook.com/mstkcarter
Goodreads- TK Carter
My Ms. Adventures (http://mymsadventures-tami.blogspot.com/)
Twitter: @TamiCarter2
Instagram: tk_carter